SMALL TOWN GIRL

Center Point
Large Print

Also by Ann H. Gabhart and available from
Center Point Large Print:

The Seeker
The Blessed
The Gifted
Words Spoken True

**This Large Print Book carries the
Seal of Approval of N.A.V.H.**

SMALL TOWN GIRL

Ann H. Gabhart

CENTER POINT LARGE PRINT
THORNDIKE, MAINE

This Center Point Large Print edition is published
in the year 2013 by arrangement with Revell,
a division of Baker Publishing Group.

Scripture used in this book, whether quoted or
paraphrased by the characters, is taken from the
King James Version of the Bible.

This is a work of historical reconstruction; the
appearances of certain historical figures is therefore
inevitable. All other characters, however, are products
of the author's imagination, and any resemblance
to actual persons, living or dead, is coincidental.

The text of this Large Print edition is unabridged.
In other aspects, this book may
vary from the original edition.
Printed in the United States of America
on permanent paper.
Set in 16-point Times New Roman type.

ISBN: 978-1-61173-788-2

Library of Congress Cataloging-in-Publication Data

Gabhart, Ann H., 1947–
Small town girl / Ann H. Gabhart. — Center Point Large print edition.
pages ; cm.
ISBN 978-1-61173-788-2 (library binding : alk. paper)
1. Large type books. I. Title.
PS3607.A23S63 2013b
813′.6—dc23

2013014229

To my mother,
Olga,
and her sisters,
Evelyn, Margaret, and Bill

It wasn't a good thing to be in love with the man your sister was going to marry. Kate Merritt had no doubts about that. Especially when you were helping that sister button up her wedding dress and adjust her veil. Still the truth was what it was. The trick was making sure nobody ever guessed it.

"Wow!" Kate stood back and gave Evie a big smile. "You look like you just stepped off a magazine cover."

Evie made a face as if she didn't believe Kate and turned back to peer into the oval mirror attached to their mother's old dresser. A wavy spot in the old mirror bent her reflection out of shape.

Evie stuck out her lower lip and blew air up to lift her red curls off her forehead. Leaning closer to the mirror, she carefully patted them back into place. "The first thing I'm going to buy for our apartment is a new mirror. Not something passed down, but a new one right out of the store."

"Wouldn't you rather have a radio? Something both you and Mike could enjoy." Kate grabbed a folded newspaper off the dresser to fan Evie.

It was extra hot for September. Another reason Evie was cross. Evie had planned everything out to the last detail for a perfect wedding day. She'd picked the last Sunday in September, because it never rained much in September and it wouldn't be too hot inside the Rosey Corner Baptist Church no matter how many people packed the pews to see their young preacher get married. And now the weather on September 28, 1941, the day she'd picked to be perfect, had betrayed her. That morning she'd sat in the middle of the bed and cried for a half hour while thunder rumbled in the sky outside. Finally Kate warned her how people might talk if she showed up at the altar with bloodshot eyes.

Evie leaned closer to the mirror and rubbed her finger across her nose, then touched a flecked spot on the mirror. "Mike has to look in a mirror to comb his hair, doesn't he? And if we had a radio, he'd be listening to war news all the time. President Roosevelt telling us how bad things are. One minute the president is promising to keep us out of the war and the next he's talking about drafting more boys. That's just too depressing."

"But true. You know the Germans have surrounded Leningrad now. They're cutting off the supply lines to starve the Russians out."

Kate didn't like thinking about the war either, but that was all the talk at Merritt's Dry Goods Store these days. Hitler's blitzkrieg. The Nazis occupying France and Poland. The Red Army holding against Hitler's forces. Ships going down.

It was always a relief when Graham Lindell came in the store talking about how many hits Joe DiMaggio was up to now, just so they could think about something besides the war news.

Evie didn't care about baseball either. For weeks, she hadn't thought about anything except having a perfect wedding day and being a perfect bride.

"For heaven's sake, Kate, don't ruin my day with war talk. We can't do a thing about what's going on in Russia. And don't they have millions of soldiers in that Red Army they're always talking about? All I'm asking for is a nice little wedding." She raised her arms and lifted her veil to cool her neck. "How can a piece of material with a thousand holes in it be so hot?"

"You don't have to wear the veil. Your hair looks great. As always." Kate pulled the veil out away from Evie to fan her neck.

She really was beautiful. She'd always been the pretty sister with her wavy red hair and clear blue eyes. Kate had plain brown hair that didn't curl unless she pin curled it, and her eyes jumped from green to blue to gray according to what color she was wearing.

And according to her mood, or so Carl Noland was always telling her. Everybody, including Carl, thought they were a couple. Everybody except Kate, that is. She should have told him months ago there was no chance of that ever being true, but it was easier to let him hang around and hope he'd lose interest. He was a nice enough guy, and she'd known him forever. Some of her friends thought she and Evie should have had a double wedding. Carl had a good job with the post office. Kate was already nineteen. So why wait? Except Kate was never going to say yes to Carl Noland. Never.

The only man she'd ever wanted to say yes to was less than an hour away from marrying her sister, just as soon as Evie quit finding things to complain about and headed for the church. Kate had been in love with Mike Champion since the first Sunday he'd come to fill in at the church after Grandfather Reece had a stroke. That was five years ago now.

Way long enough to know the whole idea was hopeless. And she did know it. Had known it since she was sixteen. By then, Mike and Evie had been dating for a year. By then, she'd cornered Mike leaving the church on a Sunday night before he drove back to Louisville and told him straight out that she loved him. He hadn't exactly laughed, but she had the feeling he wanted to.

"Ah, Kate. How sweet." He put his arm around her shoulders. "But trust me, it's just a crush. Nothing serious. You'll forget all about me when you get a little older and meet the man the Lord has in mind for you."

Kate had been glad it was past twilight so Mike

couldn't see how her face was flaming. Or how her heart was breaking. "You won't tell Evie, will you?" she managed to whisper.

"Tell her what?" He had tightened his arm around her shoulders for a few seconds. "You're my sister in Christ, Kate. The Bible says it's good to have brotherly love in your heart."

Even now after so many years, Kate flushed when she thought about that conversation. She flapped the paper at herself to cool her face. At least the heat trapped in the house from all the baking for the wedding reception would keep Evie from guessing the real reason for Kate's red cheeks. Evie stepped away from Kate so that the veil settled back in a soft cloud over her hair and neck. "No, no. A girl has to have a veil to be a real bride." She swished her skirt back and forth. The whispery sound of silk on silk didn't bring the smile it usually brought to her face. Instead she looked near tears again as she appealed to Kate. "Do I really look pretty?"

"No, Evie, you don't look pretty." Kate threw her hands out wide. "You look gorgeous. Absolutely, completely gorgeous. Mike is going to melt when he sees you coming down the aisle."

Evie hugged Kate. Carefully, so as not to wrinkle either of their dresses. "Thank you, Kate. I know you wouldn't tell me that if you didn't think it was true." Evie moved back to give Kate the once-over. "You're looking pretty gorgeous yourself. I'm glad we decided on the aqua-green material. It makes your eyes look very mysterious."

"That's me. Mysterious Kate." Kate smoothed down the chiffon skirt of her dress. She doubted she'd ever find an occasion to wear it again. It was way too fancy even for church. A few years ago there would have been no way she would have ever gotten a dress to wear one time only, but Evie wanted a wedding like the ones she read about in the magazines. She'd refused to set a date until she got a job and saved enough money to buy a ready-made wedding dress.

At least she'd agreed to let their mother make Kate's dress. Mama had been sewing for months to have new dresses for all of them. The ones for Tori and Lorena were much more practical than Kate's. While they didn't have to worry about every penny the way they had during the Depression years, that didn't mean they had money to throw away on dresses that would never be worn again.

Even Kate's. Her mother had looked at the flowing skirt and poufy sleeves and said maybe Kate could wear it to a dance sometime. Kate had never been to a dance, but to make her mother laugh, she'd grabbed her and waltzed across the room. She thought about doing the same thing with Evie now, but Evie wouldn't laugh.

She was smiling as she raised her eyebrows at Kate. "Mike's buddy, Jay, certainly seemed to think so when he was here last night. Carl better watch out."

"Yeah, yeah," Kate said. "But if anybody's mysterious, it's Jay Tanner."

"He's not much like our Rosey Corner boys. That's for sure." Evie looked back at the mirror to adjust a curl peeking out of her veil. "But you have to admit he's cute."

"Cute?" Kate made a face at Evie in the mirror. "Kittens are cute."

"Okay. Handsome then. In a devil-may-care way. I'll bet he has a girlfriend for every day of the week."

"I wouldn't be surprised," Kate agreed.

Jay Tanner was good-looking with his wavy black hair and deep brown eyes. He'd breezed into the house with Mike the night before as if he'd known them forever instead of just meeting them for the first time. No doubt he was a charmer. In no time flat, he had Tori laughing so hard she was holding her sides, Lorena singing with him, and Kate's mother talking poetry. He tried flashing his eyes at Kate too, but she didn't see any need borrowing trouble by flashing her eyes back. One thing about Kate. She had always been sensible. Except when it came to being in love with her sister's soon-to-be husband.

Kate dipped a washcloth in the pan of ice water on the dresser and dabbed Evie's arms with it. She lifted up the veil and let the rag rest on the back of

Evie's neck for a few seconds. "Maybe that will keep you cool until you say 'I do.' Speaking of which, we'd better be moving on to the church."

"You do think you can start Mike's car, don't you?" Evie gave her a look as she slipped on her white shoes. "Maybe we should have made Daddy stay here with us until we were ready."

"A lot of good that would have done." Kate rolled her eyes. "Dad knows practically nil about cars. He'd rather walk any day. You know that. But don't worry. Mike has shown me how to start it plenty of times, and if the battery won't turn it over, I'll just give it a crank or two. Easy as pie."

"Some pies aren't all that easy. I don't want to be late for my own wedding." Evie looked at the clock on the dresser. "In less than an hour I'm going to be Mrs. Mike Champion."

"The preacher's wife."

"You don't have to say it like you don't think I'll be good at it. I can be nice to people." Evie stuck her bottom lip out in a little pout. "I *am* nice to people. Every day."

"I didn't say you weren't."

"Yeah, but I heard what you were thinking. You can't hide anything from me. We're sisters, remember? But you're wrong. I'll make a good preacher's wife as long as that preacher is Mike. You're just jealous because you're not getting married."

Kate turned to drop the washrag back in the pan of water so Evie couldn't see her eyes and guess how close she'd come to the truth. Kate kept her voice light. "I'm not in the marrying market."

"Every girl is in the marrying market. And Carl is a nice boy. You could do worse."

"So everybody tells me." She picked up the rose bouquet their aunt Gertie had fashioned for Evie by picking every last rose off her bushes and those of several neighbors. "Here. Your turn first. Let's go get you married."

Out at the car, Kate helped Evie arrange her skirts before she carefully shut the door. As she hurried around to the driver's side, a familiar thrill shot through Kate. She loved to drive, to feel the tires turning under her, getting her somewhere. Anywhere.

She hit the starter button and the engine made a weak attempt at turning over. The second attempt was even weaker. "Guess I'd better give it a couple of cranks." Kate pushed open the door and climbed back out.

"Don't you dare get grease on your dress," Evie called as Kate went around to the front of the car.

"I'll be careful." Kate turned the crank a couple of times, but the engine still wouldn't turn over. She dabbed at the sweat on her forehead and got out to try again. This time after she turned the crank, she told Evie to hit the starter and pull the choke. That was a mistake. The engine did start up, but then it sputtered out as the smell of gasoline filled the air.

Kate ran to push in the choke. "You can't leave the choke pulled out."

"You didn't tell me that." Evie glared at Kate as if she'd caused the car to die.

"I guess I should've. Anyway it's flooded now. We'll have to let it sit for a few minutes before we try again."

"We can't just sit here." Evie sounded near tears. "I've got to get to the church. I knew we should have made someone stay here to help us start the car."

Kate hated it when Evie was right. Especially about something like this. "We can walk. It's not that far."

"Walk?" Evie was getting unhappier by the second. "In my new shoes?"

"Okay. Then we'll just wait. They can't start the wedding without the bride. Somebody will come get us." Kate climbed back into the seat. She didn't bother shutting the door. "At least the car's in the shade."

"Listen to you. Little Miss Sunshine." Evie went on in a singsong voice. "And the two Merritt sisters had a nice little chat under the big oak tree while everybody else in Rosey Corner sat packed in the church, waving their fans and wondering what was holding up the wedding."

"I'm glad you're mad at me." Kate peeked over at Evie.

"Why would you be glad of that?" Evie frowned.

"First off, if you're mad, you won't be crying and messing up your face for the wedding. Second off, it's natural. Feels just the way it's supposed to between you and me. One or the other of us has been mad at the other one half our lives."

Evie twisted her lips, but she couldn't keep from smiling. She gave up and laughed out loud. "You're right about that."

Kate reached over and touched Evie's hand. "I'm going to miss you so much."

"I'm not moving to California. I'm just getting married." Evie turned her hand over and squeezed Kate's hand.

"I know. But it'll be different. It's already been different with you away at school and now working in Frankfort." Kate swallowed hard. Here she was worried about Evie tearing up and instead she was.

"Don't you dare cry, Kate Merritt. You have to be happy for me." Evie shook Kate's hand a little. "You have to."

"I am." Kate managed a smile. She was happy for Evie. Her heart seemed to be divided right down the middle. Happy on one side for her sister. Crying on the other side for what could never be.

❧ 2 ❧

Jay Tanner watched his friend Mike Champion pace back and forth under the big oak tree beside the white clapboard church.

Mike pulled a watch out of the pocket of his black suit and frowned down at it a few seconds before he said, "They should be here by now."

Sweat was beading up on Mike's forehead that Jay didn't think was entirely due to the heat, although the sun was beating down more like July than September. Certainly not suit weather.

No weather was suit weather for Jay, but here he was in a suit he'd spent next month's rent money to buy. He didn't worry about that. He'd been ready to move on anyway. He hadn't stayed anywhere for more than six months since he'd gotten out of high school, and he'd been down in Tennessee five months now. He could always live out of his car for a while until he found another job. Besides, he'd sleep on the ground before he let Mike down.

Mike had been twelve, a year older than Jay, when Jay showed up at his new school after he'd moved in with his aunt and uncle. It wasn't a big school—all eight grades in two rooms—and it had been easy to see that Mike was the boy every-body listened to. Even the teachers. So that's who Jay picked to beat up at recess.

They had rolled around on the schoolyard with first one of them and then the other landing a punch. Finally Mike pinned Jay in the dirt. Jay expected Mike to pummel him into the ground, but instead he said, "You're tough for such a scrawny kid. What did you say your name was?"

"Tanner. Jay Tanner." Jay's swollen lip gave him a lisp. He stared up at Mike without blinking. So what if he got punched in the face. It wouldn't be the first black eye Jay ever had.

Mike turned loose of Jay's shoulders and sat back. "I like you, Tanner." He stuck out his hand. "Friends?"

Jay had taken his hand. Let him pull him up. Accepted the friendship. Found a brother. So if Mike wanted Jay to dress up in a suit to stand up with him while he married his girl, then that was what Jay would do. As soon as the girl showed up.

Jay kept his smile hidden as he said, "Maybe she got cold feet. Or came to her senses. A girl has to be half crazy to marry a preacher."

Mike was too distracted to notice Jay was goading him. Instead he answered seriously, "No, not Evangeline. Even if she did decide to throw me over, she wouldn't do it until after the ceremony. She's been working too hard for this show."

"Show?" Jay frowned at Mike. "You sure you want to marry a girl who's more worried about the show than the groom?"

Mike put his watch back in his pocket and pulled out a handkerchief to run across his face. "She's already got the groom. She knows I would do anything for her."

"Anything?" Jay raised his eyebrows at Mike.

"You'll understand someday when you meet the right girl." Mike poked Jay's upper arm. "Then not only will you be standing sweating in a black suit, you'll have talked your best friend into doing the same thing just to make that girl happy."

"If that girl ever comes along, I'll talk her into eloping."

"Not an option with Evangeline. She had her heart set on having a real church wedding with everybody watching. Her mother wanted to get married in the church and it didn't work out for her, so Evangeline is sort of trying to make up for that. Give them both a chance to enjoy."

"What about you?" Jay asked. "You enjoying?"

"Well, not the suit. Who'd have thought we'd have a heat wave the end of September?" Mike peered around the corner of the church to see if a car might be coming up the road. "Poor girl. She's probably down there crying because the Lord didn't bless us with better weather."

"Could be worse. Could be storming the way it was this morning."

"Don't say that." Mike scowled up at a few clouds gathering in the west before he shut his eyes.

"You praying? About the weather?" Jay couldn't keep the laughter out of his voice. While Mike was his best friend on earth—sometimes he thought his only friend—Jay hadn't gotten used to him being a preacher. It didn't matter that he'd been preaching now for five years. Jay had only seen him a few times since they'd gone their separate ways after high school—Mike to follow the Lord and Jay to drift wherever the winds of chance blew him.

"Don't laugh. The Lord answers all kinds of prayers. You're here, aren't you?"

"The Lord works in mysterious ways his wonders to perform. At least that's what my uncle used to say. I can't remember if that was before he belted me one or after." Jay laughed. "Uncle Henry had a special fondness for Scripture. Especially that one about being sure not to spoil the child by sparing the rod."

"Henry was poorly the last time I was back home. They didn't expect him to make it." Mike had on his preacher's voice.

"You think I should care, Mike, but I don't."

"He and Sadie took you in and put a roof over your head after your mother died."

"It was a roof. That was all. I more than earned any food I ate. Your mother showed me more kindness than either one of them ever did. Letting me bunk in on the daybed on your back porch that last year of school."

"She was afraid you might kill your uncle Henry."

Mike smiled to take the edge off the words, but they both knew the truth of what he said. At sixteen Jay was as big as his uncle. The last time Henry tried to whip him with his belt, Jay had grabbed the belt away from him, wrapped it around his fist, and punched the man in the face. He'd wanted to keep punching him even after he fell down, but his aunt Sadie was screaming. Jay had dropped the belt and gone out the door. He walked the five miles to Mike's house. Mike's father hadn't wanted to let him stay, but Mike's mother looked into Jay's eyes, held her arms out to him, and overruled Mr. Champion. Jay had leaned his head on her shoulder and cried like a baby.

"Your mother is a saint. I just showed up at the wedding because I thought she might be here."

"That's probably the truest thing you've said since you got here. But it's a long way from Gaffney up here to Rosey Corner. Way too far for something as common as a wedding."

"Your folks were always sensible," Jay said.

"They are that. Evangeline and I will drive down sometime next month to let everybody meet the new Mrs. Champion." Mike pulled his watch out again and stared at it. "Something must be wrong. I'd better go see."

"You can't go. Then we might lose the bride *and* the groom. I'll go check on her. That's what a best man is supposed to do, isn't it? Make sure both parties make it to the altar?" Jay clapped Mike on the shoulder and started toward his car in front of the church.

"Make sure you come back too," Mike called after him.

"Don't worry. The sooner we get this over with and I get out of this suit, the better."

The littlest sister, the one Mike said wasn't really a sister, came running down the church steps when she saw Jay. Last night when he was at the bride's house for dinner, the kid had followed Jay around like a puppy dog. She told him all about the book she was reading, the new kittens in the barn, and that she'd turned ten last June. That was how kids were. Ready to tell everything, but she was cute.

He slowed down to let her catch up with him before he got to his car. She could have been Jay's sister, with her curly black hair and brown eyes, but more than that, he felt a kinship with her because of how Mike said she'd been dropped on the church steps and abandoned by her parents. He knew how that felt. Not that his mother had wanted to abandon him. She couldn't help getting sick, but his father had been ready enough to be rid of him when he got remarried. At least this kid had found a loving family to take her in and looked to be happy enough.

"Where are you going, Mr. Tanner? We haven't had the wedding yet."

"And we aren't going to if we don't get the bride up here." He smiled down at her. "I thought you were going to call me Jay."

The kid ducked her head. "Kate said maybe I should get to know you better first." She drew a line in the grass with the toe of her shiny black shoe and peeked back up at him.

"Well, you can't call me mister. Nobody calls me mister. And if you can't call me Jay, then I guess you'll just have to call me Tanner. At least until you get to know me better."

"Okay." She giggled before she said, "Tanner."

"That's more like it. Now I've got to go bride hunting."

"Mama said Evie should be here by now." The kid looked around the churchyard.

"E.V.?" Jay looked around too. "That your dog or something?"

The girl put her hand over her mouth to smother another giggle. "No, that's Evangeline. Nobody calls her Evie but Kate and me. She lets us because we're her sisters."

"How about you? What do they call you?"

The little girl looked at him as if he'd asked the

stupid question of the day. "Lorena. My name is Lorena Birdsong."

"Right. So Birdie it is. You want to go bride hunting with me, Birdie?" He got in his car and pointed to the other door.

"You're funny." The kid opened the passenger-side door and climbed in.

"Tell your sister that." Jay backed the car out onto the road.

"Who? Evie?"

"No, your other sister. Kate."

"Do you think Kate's pretty? Kate says most boys don't, but I think she's pretty. The first time I saw her I thought she was an angel."

"An angel, huh?" Jay glanced over at her.

"You probably think that's crazy, but I don't care." She crossed her arms over her chest and stared straight ahead with her lips together in a stubborn line.

"I thought angels had wings and wore white and floated around in the clouds." Jay grinned at the kid, then looked back out at the road.

"She's not that kind of angel." Every hint of laughter in her voice disappeared as she went on. "But she's still an angel. When I came here, my mama—my real mama—told me to pray and an angel would come take care of me. I did and Kate found me."

"Did she take care of you?"

"She loved me. Right then. As soon as she saw

25

me. She's my angel sister." The kid stared over at him as if daring him to say it wasn't so.

"An angel sister. Sounds like a good thing to have." Jay kept his eyes on the road. "Does this angel sister of yours have a boyfriend?"

"You do think she's pretty. I knew you did." She sounded extra pleased. "She has a boyfriend, but Carl likes her better than she likes him. They're not about to get married or anything. Now Tori— that's my other sister, Victoria—she and her boyfriend, Sammy, are already talking about when they can get married. Mama says they're both way too young and they'll have to wait until Tori gets out of school. But we all like Sammy."

"And do you like this, who did you say? Carl?"

"Sure. He's okay. He lets me go to the movies with them, but Kate says it doesn't matter who everybody else likes. It's who she likes that matters."

"Sounds reasonable to me. But does she like anybody?"

"She likes lots of people. Me and Evie and Tori and Mike. She might even like you, Tanner. When she gets to know you better." The kid smiled over at him. "Since you're so funny."

"I keep them laughing, Birdie." They both laughed then.

Birdie pointed out through the windshield. "Uh-oh. Looks like Mike's car won't start. Kate's giving it a crank."

"A girl shouldn't try that. You don't do it right, a crank can fly back and break your arm." Jay turned off the road into the yard. There wasn't a driveway, just a dirt spot where Mike's car was sitting.

"Not Kate's arm. Kate can do anything," Birdie said.

As if to prove the kid right, the engine rattled to a start. Kate gave Jay a cool look as she climbed back behind the wheel.

Jay pulled up beside her, window to window. "Looks like I'm too late to be of help."

Before Kate could answer, Evangeline leaned over. "The car wouldn't start and then the engine flooded. We've been sitting here forever. Is Mike in a panic?"

"Not our Mike. He's waiting at the altar. Patiently. Said you wouldn't miss your own wedding. He didn't have any way of knowing the bridesmaid was doing mechanic's work." Jay turned his eyes back to Kate and blasted her with his best smile. The one no girl could resist. Her lips barely turned up at the corners in response.

"It was kind of you to come check on us, but now the bride is a bit anxious to get to the church." Kate put the car in gear and, without another look his way, bounced out of the yard.

"Guess we'd better follow them back to the church, don't you think?" Jay shot a grin at the kid as he wheeled the car in a circle through the yard. "And you know what, Birdie? You're right. I do think your sister is pretty. All your sisters."

"Me too?" Birdie asked.

"You too. Especially you. The four of you are by far the prettiest bunch of sisters I've ever met."

Every pew at the Rosey Corner Baptist Church was packed. Cardboard fans were waving all over the church as the people tried to keep cool in the unseasonable heat. Even Evie appeared to be wilting as she stood at the altar beside Mike while Reverend Haskell from the Christian church across the road read the Scripture about a man cleaving to his wife.

For way longer than Kate could remember, Rosey Corner's two churches had always joined forces to celebrate special occasions. So it was fitting that Rosey Corner's other preacher was performing the ceremony for Mike and Evie. Somehow kept it all in the family. At least that was what Mike said. No need to bring in somebody from Edgeville or Louisville. But Reverend Haskell did have a way of droning on and on.

Kate had been to church with Aunt Gertie when she thought he might never get to the amen on his prayers.

He was giving them the full service today. He had to have covered everything the Bible said about getting married. Maybe twice. As if Mike didn't know all that already. Kate let her eyes touch on Mike's face. He looked happy. In spite of the heat. In spite of the other preacher's long-winded droning. It was easy to see how much he adored Evie as he held her hand and waited for Reverend Haskell to pronounce them man and wife.

A naked feeling of longing stabbed through Kate. If only Mike were looking at her that way. If only she were the one standing beside him at the altar. Kate jerked her eyes away from Mike's face. She was surely lower than the lowest worm to be thinking such thoughts on the happiest day of her sister's life. Mike had chosen Evie. Kate had never even been in the running. She was just the younger sister.

Her eyes landed on Mike's friend standing at the altar with him. Jay Tanner smiled at her, and she had the uncomfortable feeling the man had caught her unguarded look at Mike. That he was guessing things about her she had kept hidden from everybody in Rosey Corner. If so, he'd just have to guess again. She gave him a chilly look that didn't dim his smile at all. Instead he looked like he might be biting his lip to keep from laughing. At her.

Let him laugh. She didn't care. She lifted her chin and turned her eyes away from him back toward Reverend Haskell, who seemed to finally be winding down toward the end of the ceremony at last. She had the prickly feeling Jay Tanner was still watching her, but she wasn't about to give him the satisfaction of looking back toward him.

She'd met men like Jay Tanner. Men who thought they could charm any girl they met just because the Lord had blessed them with good looks. Definitely not her type. She liked men who were sincere and loyal, true to their beliefs, strong and capable. A man like the man marrying her sister.

"I now pronounce you man and wife. You may kiss your bride." Reverend Haskell looked up from his Bible to smile at Mike.

Mike didn't smile back. He looked as serious as Kate had ever seen him when he turned toward Evie. Beads of sweat were leaking down from his forehead and sliding around his eyebrows, but he paid no attention. He lifted up the veil from in front of Evie's face and carefully draped it back over her hair. Then he stared at her for a long moment before he leaned down to whisper in her ear. "I will love you forever, my beautiful Evangeline."

Kate, standing so close beside Evie, heard his every word before he covered Evie's lips with his. Kate couldn't see Evie's face, but she had to believe she was exploding with happiness. What girl wouldn't be?

Mrs. Taylor started pounding out the recessional Evie had insisted she learn. The woman's fingers stumbled over some of the notes, but nobody gave much notice. They were all watching their preacher tuck his new bride's hand up under his arm to escort her out of the church toward their new life together. Every face was smiling. Sharing in the joy of the moment.

As Kate took Jay Tanner's arm to follow the newlyweds down the aisle, she saw so many people she loved in the pews. Kate's father had his arm tight around her mother as she dabbed away a few tears. Tori and Sammy were looking at each other as though wishing they were the ones saying "I do." Lorena had jumped to her feet and clasped her hands together. Kate winked at her and Lorena's smile got even bigger. She was practically sparkling.

A few seats behind them, she spotted Graham Lindell, who turned his smile from Evie to raise his eyebrows at Kate as though asking if she was going to be next. Kate gave her head a tiny shake, and his shoulders shook with a silent laugh. She searched on through the faces in the church until her eyes landed on Aunt Hattie in the back pew.

The little black woman's hands were lifted up toward the ceiling and her face was an explosion of happy wrinkles. Graham's sister, Fern, was right beside her with her hair combed and wearing what looked to be a new dress. Even Fern was smiling as much as Fern ever smiled.

The whole church was practically pulsing with happiness. Kate could feel it hopping from person to person. She wasn't a bit surprised when one of the men in the back corner laughed right out loud. Everybody was happy for Evie. Happy for Mike. Kate was smiling too. Inside and out. How could she not on this day when her sister had to be the happiest girl in the world? And the luckiest.

Kate's smile didn't even dim when Jay Tanner gave her another amused grin as they reached the door of the church. What did she care what Jay Tanner thought? He'd driven in from who knew where. He'd be driving back out to the same place as soon as the festivities were over.

He wasn't the kind of guy to let much grass grow under his feet. Mike told them Jay drove up from Nashville. And before that he'd been in Memphis. Not a man who would see anything of interest in a little one-store, wide-spot-in-the-road place like Rosey Corner.

They formed a line outside on the walkway. Evie claimed a receiving line after the wedding ceremony was every bit as important as the proces-

32

sional up to the altar. It was simply unfortunate the church faced toward the west. The sun was hitting them full force, and Kate hadn't talked to three people before sweat rivulets began to slide down her sides. The fancy dress was going to be ruined. But at least she wasn't wearing a black suit like the man beside her. He had to be melting, even if he did appear totally unbothered by the heat as he kept smiling at the people grabbing his hand and welcoming him to Rosey Corner.

Kate kept smiling too as they all squeezed her hand in turn, while giving her that knowing look and telling her she'd be next. She wanted to ask them, next to do what—faint from the heat? But she remembered her manners. It was Evie's day, and Kate had promised her mother to be nice no matter how many people asked her when she and Carl Noland were going to follow her sister and Pastor Mike down the aisle into wedded bliss.

She even managed to keep her smile from flagging when Carl came out the door, his high cheekbones stained red. No doubt he'd been getting the same kind of remarks inside the church that she was hearing outside. If so, Carl's ears were readier to hear them. He was looking at her like a little boy staring at a plate full of his favorite cookies after he'd just been told he could eat them all.

She liked Carl. She really did. After all, they'd grown up together in Rosey Corner. Had heard each other recite lessons in school. Had waded in creeks catching frogs. Had climbed trees and played hide-and-seek in her yard. But she'd never given the first thought to falling in love with Carl. It wasn't going to happen.

She tried to keep the dismay from showing on her face as he grabbed both of her hands and gave her a bashful smile. He wasn't a bad-looking guy. Ordinary with light blue eyes and brown hair that even with pomade never seemed to lay right on his head. He'd shot up five inches his senior year in school, and even though that had been a couple of years ago, he hadn't quite figured out what to do with his longer arms and legs.

But none of that was why she couldn't fall in love with him. It didn't have anything to do with how he looked. It was everything else. How he didn't like books. How he couldn't imagine going anywhere farther than Edgeville. How he had to ponder every decision until the cows came home. Even something as unimportant as which piece of pie he wanted at a church dinner. He had no imagination at all. Kate needed imagination the way a rainbow needed color.

She tried to gently free her hands, but he grasped her fingers tighter. His hands were damp with sweat, and when he swallowed hard, his Adam's apple bobbed a bit.

"Kate, you look beautiful," he said, then stuttered a little as he went on. "I–I . . ."

"You look nice too, Carl." Kate spoke up fast to cut him off. She had the horrible feeling that all the jibes from the church people were giving him the courage to pop the question right there in front of everybody. No way could she let that happen. Not now. Not here. She smiled her best smile and managed to tug her hands loose at last. "We can talk later. You need to go give Pastor Mike your congratulations."

He kept his hands reached out toward her for a few seconds before he awkwardly dropped them to his side. "Right," he said. "Later."

She didn't let her sigh come out. She kept smiling as Mrs. Jamison stepped up to take Carl's place and tell her what a nice wedding it was and wasn't love a beautiful thing.

When at last Mrs. Jamison turned toward Evie to tell her the exact same thing, Jay Tanner leaned closer to Kate and kept his voice low as he said, "Later, eh? Carl is one lucky fellow."

Kate pretended not to understand him as she smiled at the next person in line. By the time every person had come out of the church and wrung her hand and talked about how pretty everything was, her cheeks were frozen in a smile and her dress was sticking to her back. Evie didn't appear to be faring any better. Her cheeks were bright pink, the curls she'd worked so hard to straighten were going kinky again, and her lipstick was gone, along with her smile. But Mike looked happy enough for all of them as he put his arm around Evie and started to pull her close to him.

Evie pushed him back. "Watch out, Mike. You'll mess up my dress. I have to look nice for the reception."

She sounded almost cross. Newly married to the most wonderful man in the world and already forgetting to be happy. It was more than Kate could imagine and she had to force herself not to reach over and give Evie a shake.

"You look nice. You look better than nice." Mike reached for Evie again and captured her this time, holding her gently as though she were a priceless treasure.

"They're all waiting for us." Evie put a hand against his chest to hold him away.

"They don't need us to enjoy your mother's pies and cakes. Everybody there will have a full plate." Mike's smile got bigger. "In fact, why don't we let Kate make our excuses and just get in the car and head for the hotel in Louisville?"

"We can't do that," Evie protested. "Whatever would we tell everybody?"

"We wouldn't tell them anything. We'd be in the car on the way to our honeymoon. But Kate could tell them we were overcome by the heat. It wouldn't be a lie. I'm warming up to the idea of being a married man for sure."

"Why, Mike Champion! What a thing to say!"

Evie flushed beet red. That was the thing about being a redhead and so fair skinned. Every emotion bloomed bright on her face.

Kate knew exactly what was going through Evie's mind, and Kate's own cheeks warmed a little too. Evie would be thinking about the awkward conversation their mother had with them both a few nights earlier. About honeymoons and what to expect.

None of it was new to Kate. She'd found out how babies came to be when she was twelve. She hadn't bothered asking her mother. She'd gone straight to Aunt Hattie, who helped women birth babies all the time and who told answers straight out if she knew them.

"It sounds some strange when a body talks it out," Aunt Hattie had told her after explaining the way things worked. "But it ain't nothin' for you to worry your head over. When you meet the right feller and get married, it'll be natural as breathing." Aunt Hattie narrowed her eyes on Kate then as she went on. "But you make sure you do wait for the right feller and let the good Lord bless your union before you step down that path. Ain't much worse for a woman than being led astray by a fast-talkin' man with no thought of settling down. Babies can come on quick."

Evie had found the right man and had stood before the Lord and her friends and family and promised to love, honor, and obey till death do them part. So even though her face was burning red, her eyes were soft, yielding, ready.

Mike's face had a different look too—one Kate had never seen—as he said, "I'm your husband now, Mrs. Champion." With eyes tight on Evie's face, he laughed softly, a low throaty sound.

Kate turned her eyes away from them. The look they were sharing was too private. Something Jay Tanner must have noted too. He took hold of Kate's arm and whispered loudly, "I think you'd better show me where those cakes and pies are, sister Kate. The loving couple seem to be in need of a little time alone. Or maybe a lot of time alone."

Kate started away with him, but then looked back at Evie. "It won't be right if you don't come. Everybody expects you to be there." She didn't look at Mike. She couldn't very well tell him what to do, but she could Evie.

"Oh hush, Kate." Evie flashed a look toward Kate. "You wouldn't go if you didn't want to. You'd probably just elope to begin with."

"Maybe so," Kate agreed. "But I wouldn't have had everybody baking for days for a party I claimed I had to have and then not show up."

"Girls, girls! No fighting on my wedding day." Mike laughed and took his eyes off Evie long enough to glance toward Kate. "Go on ahead and let them know we'll be there soon as I pray over the car and get it started. Nobody will expect the bride to walk." He smiled back down at Evie. "That way we can make a quick getaway."

"After we cut the cake. We have to cut the cake." Evie was smiling again too. "Kate, make sure Uncle Wyatt has his camera ready so he can take pictures of us getting there. I told him to get extra film."

Kate bit her lip to keep from saying anything as she turned away from the happy couple. She reminded herself yet again that it was Evie's day. Next week would be soon enough to tell her sister she wasn't boss of the world. Or even of Rosey Corner. She hiked up her skirt a little and started off up the road as though she were the one who was late.

She'd almost forgotten Jay Tanner until he hurried after her. "Wait up. You want me to get my car?"

"No need. It's not far." She didn't slow down and she didn't look over her shoulder to see if Evie and Mike had headed toward his car. If they didn't show up, they didn't show up.

Jay fell in beside her, matching her stride. "So you and lucky Carl are planning to elope. Not tonight, I hope."

"Whatever are you talking about?" Kate slowed a little to stare over at him. He was nice looking. She couldn't deny that.

"You and Carl. Eloping."

Kate let out a sigh. "I'm not eloping with anybody. And especially not Carl."

"That's probably good. He didn't look like the eloping type." He was pretending to be serious, but his eyes were full of teasing.

"Oh?" She raised her eyebrows at him. He was acting like he'd known her for years. There was something that easy about him. Something that was making her like him in spite of herself. "What or who is the eloping type?"

"You." His smile came back full. "Me." Now he was the one raising his eyebrows at her. Not just raising them, but waggling them. "What do you say? I've got a nearly full tank of gas."

She couldn't keep from laughing. "You're out of your mind."

"No doubt about that," he agreed. "But we might have some fun."

She shook her head at him. "The only place I'm going with you is to Grandfather Merritt's house to eat wedding cake. Evie's wedding cake."

"Oh well." He let out an exaggerated sigh. "You can't fault a guy for trying when he meets an angel."

"You've been talking to Lorena." Kate laughed again. "She's a sweetheart, but I can assure you that she's the only one who has ever imagined me anything like an angel. Just ask Evie."

"Or Mike?"

She heard the underlying tone of his question,

but she ignored it. "Or Mike. He's been preaching at me since I was fourteen."

"Fourteen, huh? He's been preaching at me since I was eleven. So see, we have something in common already." He grinned over at her. "We've both heard plenty of Mike's sermons and we love him anyway. You do love him, don't you?"

"Of course. He's my brother-in-law."

"Right, he is. And just think. After we elope, he'll be my brother-in-law too."

"You're dreaming, Mr. Tanner. Completely dreaming."

"But what a dream." His grin turned into a laugh. "Eloping with an angel."

His laugh was infectious and Kate couldn't keep from smiling back at him. "Everybody needs a dream. But dreams don't always come true."

"I can't argue with that." His smile faded as he studied her. "Then again, sometimes if a man finds the rhythm that speaks to his heart and if he can dance the right steps, if he can find a way to pull hope out of thin air and not let doubt steal his dream or cause him to whittle it down too small, maybe he can grab hold of that dream and hang on for dear life. That kind of dream can make the sunrise brighter every morning."

Kate stopped walking and stared over at him. "That sounds like something out of a book."

"Could be. It's hard to separate the words you

41

read from the ones you think up all on your own sometimes. Either way, it's no less true." The corners of Jay's lips twitched up. "How about you, Kate Merritt? What makes you welcome the sunrise in the morning? What's your dream?"

"Kate!"

The little sister running down the road toward them saved the girl beside Jay from having to give him an answer. She was a dreamer. He was sure of that. Someone like him who was forever reaching for the biggest apple on the tree no matter how impossibly out of reach it was. He'd seen her looking at Mike, but that apple wasn't even on the tree anymore.

A girl like Kate would be wasted on Mike anyway. He needed a woman who would lean on him and be the good little pastor's wife. Someone who would wear the right clothes and say the right words whether she meant them or not. A girl like the one he fell in love with. Unless Jay missed his guess, Evangeline was the kind of girl who would have no trouble putting on her hat and painting on a lipstick smile every Sunday morning to play the role. The old gray-haired ladies, the backbone of every church Jay had ever spent any time in, would love her.

The sister beside him, well, Jay figured she'd be better at improving the old ladies' prayer lives. He didn't really know her, but he'd learned to read people fast a long time ago. Helped him know when to throw the first punch or when to duck his head. He didn't know which he was doing with Kate—punching or ducking—when he threw out that crazy eloping idea. Sometimes he opened his mouth and let words fly out without thinking. For sure, he would have had to do some serious backpedaling if she'd called his bluff. He had zero plans to elope or stand at an altar with any girl. Even one as appealing as the girl beside him.

She wasn't pretty-pretty like her sister who had just tied the knot with Mike. He studied her face as she turned her attention to the little sister, the one he'd called Birdie. She was telling her to slow down before she fell and messed up her new dress. It did look like a crash waiting to happen. The little sister was all legs and arms at that age when a kid could trip over air from growing so fast. The kid was cute, with all the earmarks of growing up to break the heart of every boy in the neighborhood someday with those big brown eyes. Eyes more the color of his than any of her sisters. But then she wasn't really a sister. Not in the kinfolk, look-alike way.

Actually he'd noted that none of the three

sisters looked that much alike. Mike's new bride was a blue-eyed redhead with fair skin that pinked up easy. Very pretty, and Mike was certainly entranced. The teenage sister, Victoria, had hair almost as dark as the curly-headed little sister in front of him, but her eyes were a green that made a person look twice. By the time she got all the way grown up, that one was going to hit the mark a good ways above merely pretty. She was already there in the eyes of the gangly boy hanging around her. O beautiful is love. More words out of a book.

Nothing wrong with borrowing words from a book. Jay liked books. Books took him to other worlds when the real world was closing in on him. The girl beside him liked books too, if what he saw at her house last night was any indication. Books had been everywhere. Shelves of them behind the father's chair in the sitting room, and more place-marked with torn bits of newspaper on the tables around the room. Jay had talked poetry with the mother. That along with her brown sugar pie and all the pretty daughters had him wondering if he'd stepped up into heaven.

Kate had been the only one not to take to him friendly. Except for the bride, who'd been in such a dither about the wedding that friendly was the farthest thing from her mind. She'd given him the once-over and asked if he had a suit. When he assured her he did, she'd nodded slightly as if he'd passed the best-man test and she could mark him off her worry list. One that appeared to be long as she began fretting over the wedding cake, her mother's dress, the flowers, whatever came to mind about the big event. Jay hadn't paid much attention.

He had paid Kate plenty of attention. Something about her grabbed him. She had brown hair that fell straight down around her shoulders. Her eyes flashed between green and the blue of water with the sun hitting it. Nothing really remarkable about her looks, but at the same time she was remarkable. Very remarkable. So very remarkable that he wasn't absolutely positive he would have backpedaled if she'd taken him up on that eloping idea. Even now he might be in the car headed out toward Louisville or wherever to find an accommodating Justice of the Peace.

He'd never been one to turn down an adventure, and he had a feeling he was looking at a girl anxious to chase after a little adventure of her own. They might have both been saved from their own foolishness by the kid sister who was leaning against Kate, catching her breath.

"Mama sent me to see what was taking you so long. Everybody's waiting."

"Not for us. For Evie and Mike." Kate took the kid's hand. "But come on. We'll go sample Mama's applesauce cake while we're waiting for the slowpoke newlyweds."

The little sister peered around Kate. "Is Mike having trouble getting the car started? They could have walked like you."

"Not Evie. She aims to arrive in style," Kate said.

Jay laughed. "Not much chance of that in Mike's old heap."

The kid slipped her eyes over toward Jay and smiled shyly. "Hello, Tanner."

"Hi there, Birdie. Tell me that your mama made some lemonade to go with that cake and I'll be one happy man." Jay shrugged off his coat, hooked his finger in the collar, and pitched it over his left shoulder. Black coats should be outlawed for everybody but undertakers.

"Birdie?" Kate looked at Jay and then back at the little sister. "Tanner? Don't you mean Mr. Tanner?"

"He told me nobody calls him mister." The child hunched her shoulders and peeked up at her sister. "And you ought to call people what they want to be called, oughtn't you?"

"So you want to be called Birdie?" Kate said.

"Not by everybody. Just by Tanner." She shot a grin over toward Jay.

"Give the kid a break, Miss Merritt. Tell you what. You can call me Tanner too. And how about we call you Katie?"

"Ooh, that won't work." The kid's eyes popped open wide as she looked from Jay to her sister. "Nobody calls Kate Katie."

"Nobody?" Kate was giving him such a cool stare that he couldn't keep from poking her a little more. "Not even lucky Carl?"

"What my friends do or do not call me is none of your concern, Mr. Tanner." She emphasized the mister.

"But I want to be one of those friends, Katie." She shot him another look and he backed up a step. "Excuse me, I meant to say Miss Merritt. It's just that if I say Miss Merritt, I could have four girls looking my way. Which wouldn't be too bad. Lovely misses, every one."

"Only three now," Kate said. "Actually only two." She looked like she might be biting the inside of her lip to keep from grinning. That was good. He wouldn't want to be thinking about eloping with a girl who stayed in a snit all the time.

"But aren't there three sisters still unmarried?" he said. "Three Miss Merritts."

"Just Kate and Tori," the little sister spoke up. "Remember, I told you my name."

"That's right. It was Bird something," Jay said. "Birdwhistle or Birdbrain. Birdhopper maybe."

The little sister giggled, and the big sister couldn't keep her smile hidden any longer as she said, "Tell him your name, Lorena."

"My name is Lorena Birdsong." Her voice had a lilt as she almost sang her name.

"And my name is Katherine Reece Merritt."

Kate grabbed the kid's hands and danced a little circle with her.

It was obviously some kind of game they played. They both looked at him, almost laughing, as Birdie pulled a hand loose from Kate's and reached for his. "You have to say your name too, Tanner."

The two of them seemed to be holding their breath to see if he would join in. So, like a kid on a playground, he grabbed the little sister's hand and, not one to pass up a great opportunity, captured the big sister's hand too. She didn't try to pull away but just kept looking at him with a kind of assessing smile to see if he was going to pass this playground test.

"My name is Mr. Jay Tanner." He squeezed Kate's hand a tiny bit as he said the mister. She laughed out loud. The sound touched something inside him, and he had to keep himself from holding on tighter when she began easing her hand free.

With a quick look over her shoulder back down the road toward the church, she said, "Well, Mr. Tanner and Miss Birdsong, now that we've got all the names straight, we'd better get moving or we'll let the new Mrs. Champion beat us to Grandfather Merritt's house. That wouldn't do."

The sound of a car starting up back at the church seemed to prove her words. The little sister kept hold of both of their hands and started back the way she'd come, tugging them after her. "Hurry."

Jay let the little girl pull him along. He liked the family feeling radiating off the two of them, reaching out welcoming fingers toward him. Of course, he was on the outside and couldn't really step into it. He was always on the outside. Ever since his mother died. Even those months he'd lived with Mike and his family, he'd not belonged. Not really. But it was better that way. No sense wanting to belong somewhere he didn't. It was better to stay a little apart where a man could keep a cool eye on what was going on around him and be ready to run if he needed to.

They did run the last few feet to the big white house beside the road to beat the bride and groom there. The two sisters laughed every step, and when the kid stumbled, he and Kate grabbed her up into the air without even exchanging a look and swung her back to her feet. Like a dance they both already knew, even though no one had ever shown them any steps.

They slipped through the picket fence gate and joined the people waiting in the yard to welcome the newlyweds. He let go of the kid's hand and stepped back to lean against the fence and watch Mike help his bride out of the car. Mike had his preacher face on again. A good thing too. These people probably didn't think a preacher ought to be in a hurry to get to his honeymoon night.

Jay let his eyes flash from the flushed pink face of the bride back to Kate. She was surrounded by friends vying for her attention. It had been crazy for him to think she was anything like him. She belonged. She was part of these people. A few more months and she'd probably be the bride on the arm of that lucky Carl. He was right there in the crowd beside her. The two of them would eat their wedding cake, drink their lemonade punch, and settle down in a house here in Rosey Corner. Five years from now, Kate would be chasing after a couple of kids and Jay would still be chasing a dream of belonging somewhere.

"She's pretty, isn't she?"

The man who moved up beside Jay wasn't young, but it was hard to say his age. His face had deep lines that spoke of hours outside. A farmer, no doubt. The same as a good number of the other men scattered around the yard with their hair slicked down and wearing their Sunday best. But if this man had made any attempts to slick down his hair, it hadn't worked. He didn't appear to be a man worried all that much about outward appearances. At the same time, there was something piercing about his gaze, as though he intended to see past a person's slicked-down hair and smooth veneer to whatever might be making him tick.

Jay smiled over at him, wondering what the

man might be thinking about him. "Most brides are pretty on their wedding day."

"It can bring out the best in a woman, right enough." One corner of the man's mouth turned up and a smile filled his eyes as if Jay had said something funny. "But I wasn't talking about Evangeline. I was talking about our Kate over there." Now his eyes were practically laughing. "It appeared your eyes were turned more her direction than the bride's."

"Could be they were," Jay admitted. "I haven't seen this many good-looking girls all in the same place since I don't know when."

"Enough to give a young feller like you wedding fever."

"Not likely." Jay laughed. "I just sweated through a wedding. I'm not planning on doing a repeat of wearing this suit anytime soon." He swung his jacket down off his shoulder and draped it over a picket on the fence.

"There's some here that are a mite more eager than you." The man's eyes went back to the group around Kate. "Poor Carl, for one."

"Poor Carl?" Jay looked at the man beside him. "I'd think you'd be calling him lucky Carl with a girl like Kate."

"If he had a girl like Kate, maybe so, but Carl ain't got nothing but a wish that ain't coming true." The man turned and stuck out his hand toward Jay. "By the way, I'm Graham Lindell.

Not right of me to keep you talking, knowing who you are and you with no idea what Rosey Corner yokel is bending your ear."

The man's fingers were long, a little bony, but his grip was strong. "Glad to meet you, Mr. Lindell."

"Ain't no need being so formal and all. Graham will do," the man said.

"All right, Graham. You related to the bride?"

"Nope. Got no blood kin left living in this whole world 'cepting my sister, Fern, over there." He gestured toward a woman sitting on the edge of the porch looking off toward the fields without seeming to pay any mind to the commotion in the yard. "But we been neighbors so long I feel the same as kin. Ain't nothing I wouldn't do for those girls. We been through some times together. The Merritts and me. Some good like today. Some hard like them that may be coming at us."

"Things bad here in Rosey Corner?" Jay asked. "It's looking like all happiness to me right now."

"Things is rosy here for a fact, but if I don't miss my guess, the world is likely to come calling with all its troubles."

Jay's smile disappeared. "You're talking about the war over in Europe. But that's over there. We're over here."

"For now," Graham said. "For now. We were over here last time too and ended up over there."

"Did you serve in the World War?"

52

"Nope. I was studying to be a doctor and hoping to go over soon as I got out of school, but the war ended first."

"So I should call you Dr. Graham." Jay looked at him a little closer. He'd have never guessed him for a doctor.

The man shook his head. "Didn't get that done either. Things happened. Some of those bad things, and I started down a different path. Made some good turns though and live with more freedom than most I know." Graham's smile came back. "But no need dampening the day with past worries. You're looking like you got enough of them your own self anyhow."

"Not at all. I live that free life too. Go where I want. Do what I want."

"Ain't got no family then."

The man's words skewered Jay, but he pretended not to be bothered by that truth as he said, "None that matter."

"Family always matters. You can see that plain as day right here before your eyes." Graham motioned toward the people in the yard. "We got family all over in Rosey Corner. Family families. Church families. Neighborhood families. Nobody goes wanting for family around here."

Jay looked back at the people who had let Mike and his bride pass through them into the house. It would be cake cutting time soon. He didn't see Kate anywhere, and he was sorry he'd let the man distract him so much that he didn't know where she'd gone. "Yeah, I can see that. Same kind of place Mike grew up in."

"I thought you grew up in the same town."

"His growing up and my growing up were some different," Jay said. "Guess I was free of that kind of family ties back then too."

"A loner, huh?" The man didn't wait for him to admit it. "Not a bad thing." He narrowed his eyes on Jay before he went on. "If that's what a man hankers after."

"A free man does what he wants." Jay kept his voice light.

"That he does," Graham agreed. "Where you going from here?"

"Hard to say for sure." Jay shrugged a little. "I may go north awhile. I hear Chicago is a busy town. A man should be able to find work there."

"Why don't you spend some time here in Rosey Corner? That is, if you don't have nothing pulling at you. Victor, that's the daddy of the bride, he lets me sleep up over his smithy. It can be kind of warm at times with the forge running, but it's bearable with all the windows and doors flung open. I got an extra cot if you can keep Poe off it. Poe, that's my dog. And truth be told, the poor old boy has a struggle climbing up on the cot these days anyhow. He might be glad for the chance to sleep on the floor."

"He have fleas?"

"It's likely, seeing as how he's a dog. But he generally keeps them all to hisself." Graham clapped Jay on the shoulder. "You look like a man who needs to take a pause in his traveling, and I could use fresh ears for my stories."

"But a man has to work." Jay didn't know why the offer was tempting him. He'd left country living behind as soon as he got out of school. Cities were where life was happening. That was where he intended to be now. As far from the cow barns and cornfields as his car would take him.

Graham gave him another considering look. "Fact is, I do some odd jobs around Rosey Corner now and again. Just to keep from getting too lazy, but then folks find out you're willing to paint a house, they all start wanting their houses painted. I could use a fellow like you. Somebody who wouldn't have no trouble climbing around on a ladder to do the tall painting. I'll split the profits even with you."

"That might be too generous of you," Jay said.

"Worth every penny if it keeps me from breaking my neck. So what do you say? A couple of weeks wielding a paintbrush outside in the fresh air. Then you can be on your way to some big town where they'll shut you up in a factory and make you screw bits and pieces together. I'd take the sunshine and rain every time."

"I've never done much painting."

"Don't take no genius."

55

Jay was smiling, getting ready to shake his head and thank the man for the offer, when Kate came out the door of the house and down off the porch straight toward him. Suddenly he was thinking a few weeks in a place called Rosey Corner might not be so bad. Give him a little change in his pocket before he moved on. October could be a beautiful month. He looked over at Graham. "Well, I'm no genius for sure. So maybe I'll just take you up on that offer."

"You know. I just thought you might." Graham laughed. He looked from Jay to Kate and repeated, "I just thought you might."

When Kate saw Jay Tanner laughing with Graham out by the yard fence and then grinning her way like maybe Graham was telling him some embarrassing story about her, a little finger of irritation poked her. She thought about turning around and going back in the house. Let Mike come out himself and make sure his friend wasn't left out.

They'd been all set to cut the cake when Mike noticed Jay hadn't followed them into the house. Mike claimed the best man had to be there watching. Why, Kate had no idea. Jay Tanner didn't look like a man who cared about wedding cakes, but Mike asked Kate to go find him. Evie wasn't pleased. She didn't stop smiling. Oh no. People were watching, but Kate knew Evie. She saw the twitch at the corner of her eye and knew a flood of tears might not be too far behind. Evie did like things to go smoothly, and she was already holding the special knife she'd festooned with blue and white ribbons exactly the same as the one she'd seen in a magazine. She was showing Mike how to put his hand overtop of hers to make the first cut in the cake when he had looked around for his best man.

Kate was ready to get on with it too. So many people were crowded into Grandfather Merritt's front parlor that the place was as hot as her father's blacksmith shop. Several of the men had out handkerchiefs, wiping off their faces, and a few of the more amply blessed ladies looked near to fainting. Worse, the icing roses and fluted edges on the cake Kate's mother and Aunt Hattie had spent the better part of two days decorating were beginning to melt.

That morning Kate had declared the cake too pretty to eat, but Aunt Hattie had waved that off as nonsense. "Cakes is supposed to be eaten. 'Course it's good this one will get some looking at first. It was a mite of trouble." She'd licked a smear of frosting off her finger. "But nows we're practiced. We can get yours done in half the time, Katherine Reece."

"No cake for me," Kate told her, picking up the icing spoon to scrape a taste of the sweet concoction out of the bowl. "I'm eloping."

The word echoed in Kate's head now as Jay Tanner kept staring her way. She should have scared the socks off him by grabbing his hand and pretending to say yes when he asked her to elope. Then the joke would have been on him.

He was a charmer. Had even charmed Lorena. Calling her Birdie. Kate would have to have a talk with her. She might only be ten, but a girl was never too young to learn to be careful around some guys. Guys like Jay Tanner. Kate had been reminding herself of that very thing since the first smile he'd sent her way last night had sent a strange little tickle up her spine. A tickle that had turned to a delicious little shiver while they were laughing and running down the road with Lorena between them. A dangerous man. She was surprised Graham wasn't picking up on that instead of smiling like he'd just found a best buddy.

That made Kate want to frown even more. She was Graham's best buddy. It didn't matter that Graham was several years older than her father. Age disappeared between real friends. But she had a feeling now he was plotting something. Something to do with her and Mike's best man.

Something he shouldn't be plotting if the grin on his face was any indication.

Kate stopped halfway across the yard to call to them. "Hey, you two. Get on in here. They're waiting on you before they cut the cake."

"Aww, Kate." Graham's grin slid off his face. "You know as much as I love your sister I can't be smothered in amongst all those people."

"You can stand by the door, but you've got to come on. It's so hot in there the icing is threatening to slide off the cake. That happens, Evie will be a puddle of tears." Kate's eyes touched on Jay. "Mike says his best man has to be in attendance and not lollygagging out here in the shade."

Graham pretended a wounded look. "We weren't lollygagging. We were talking business."

"Business?" Kate gave Graham another suspicious look. "What business is that?"

His smile came back. "Men's business."

"Then it's nothing I want to know about." Kate waved her hand in dismissal. "But I've never known you to pass up a piece of cake."

"If it's anywhere near as good as your mother's brown sugar pie, then I'm not wanting to miss out on it either." Jay grabbed his coat off the fence, put his arm around the older man's shoulders, and started him toward the house. "Let's go, partner. We can finish our men's business later."

"Perhaps I'd best warn you, Mr. Tanner, that this man cannot always be trusted. Or believed."

"Now, Kate," Graham said. "Ain't no need you talking like that about me. You know I never lie to you." He winked at her. "Fabricate some fine stories now and again, but merely for your entertainment."

"We'll all have to be fabricating some good excuses if we make Evie wait much longer." Kate turned away from them toward the house. She didn't want either of them to see the smile sneaking out on her face.

The cake eventually got cut, and the couple sampled the first cups of punch just the way Evie read in her magazines that it was supposed to be done. Then Evie and Mike slipped out the door, right behind Graham, who had stood half in, half out of the screen door. At least a dozen flies had taken advantage of the open door.

Kate kept waving them away while she helped Mrs. Patterson slice and hand out the cake. Things would have gone a lot faster if the woman hadn't had to exclaim over every icing curlicue as she sliced through it. It took all Kate's self-control not to grab the knife out of the woman's hand so she could get the job done.

People were standing around all over the house, talking and forking in the cake. Aunt Hattie would be cleaning up the crumbs for a week. If she didn't have to worry about being rude, Kate would have shooed them all out of Grandfather Merritt's house the way Aunt Hattie was trying to shoo out the flies with her tea towel. Let them spill their crumbs and drinks out in the yard. For certain, her grandfather would have been having five kinds of heart attacks if he'd been there to see the people tromping in and out, slamming doors, poking around in the corners to see if there was anything of the man left there.

Few of them had ever been in the house while Grandfather Merritt lived there. They knew him. They did business with him. He owned the store and practically ran Rosey Corner. But he'd been a hard man who didn't encourage company, not even that of his family. The few times Kate had carried him a pie or a jar of jam from her mother, the big house seemed full of brooding shadows ready to swallow her.

That had all changed when Aunt Hattie threw open the doors and started living in the house where she'd once been a servant. Grandfather Merritt had told her to in the note he left when he took off for Oregon. He'd found a wife out there and hadn't mentioned the first word about ever coming home in the two postcards he'd sent back to Rosey Corner. He was living a new life in the West where the past didn't matter.

In Rosey Corner, the past would always matter. It made up the fabric of life, whether that cloth was newly woven or ripped and torn with spots worn bare. Her grandfather appeared to have shrugged off his Rosey Corner past, but it still lurked in the corners of this house. His chair and footstool in the parlor with a couple of account books on the table next to it. A cap hanging on a peg of the hall tree. His things waiting for him.

Kate's father didn't think he'd ever come home, but Aunt Hattie said people could surprise you sometimes. She wasn't about to change things around except for the kitchen. "Mr. Preston never spent no time in the kitchen. He won't notice I put up new curtains. It's plumb amazing what some red checked curtains will do for a room."

Some Rosey Corner people thought it wasn't exactly proper, Aunt Hattie living in one of the biggest houses in the little town. They thought she ought to have given it over to Kate's family, who were squeezed up in a house half its size. All four sisters had to sleep in the same bedroom with barely enough room to get around the two beds to pull the covers straight. But Kate was relieved that Grandfather Merritt hadn't told them to live in the house. She couldn't imagine getting up in the morning here and singing Lorena's name song. Or reading romantic stories or writing poems about the sunshine streaking down through the trees in Lindell Woods. Sometimes the Lord blessed a person by letting her keep what she had.

That didn't mean a person always got what she wanted. She heard Mike laughing out on the porch. She loved his laugh. She loved the way he was always saying the Lord meant for his children to have a good time. That the Bible advised Christians to have a merry heart. She liked the way he listened to old Mr. Johnson with fresh attention, even though he'd heard his stories a hundred times. She loved the way he didn't condemn her father or Graham when they didn't show up at church every Sunday but simply said a man could worship on the outside of a church the same as the inside. She admired the way he was so close to the Lord that sometimes when she was reading about King David in the Bible she was seeing Mike's face. He was a man after the Lord's own heart. He'd already won hers.

And Evie's. From the first Sunday he preached at Rosey Corner Baptist Church. Naturally, Evie had won out. Evie always won out. She had the looks. Kate had the backbone, but guys went for looks, not backbone. Even guys like Mike. Maybe especially guys like Mike who deserved the best.

She certainly didn't deserve the best. Somebody who would yearn after her sister's beau. Kate tightened her mouth and bent down to wipe a glob of icing up off the floor. She was going to block all thoughts like that of Mike out of her mind. Forever. He was Evie's husband now. Her brother by marriage and by Christian love. That was how she would think of him from this moment on—as a brother. That was all. She had the backbone. She could do whatever she set her mind to do. And she was going to set her mind to be very happy for Evie and for Mike.

"I think everybody has cake now, Kate," Mrs. Patterson said after Kate stood back up from cleaning the floor. "You go on out and join the young people. Us old ladies will clean up in here." She smiled and gave Kate a knowing look. "That Carl has peered in the door a dozen times and we know who he's looking for, don't we?" She picked up the remains of the cake and laughed as she started toward the kitchen. "No need in letting a few dirty dishes stand in the way of romance. No need at all."

Kate wanted to tell her she'd rather wash a cabinet full of dishes than entertain romantic thoughts about Carl, but she bit back the words. Carl was Mrs. Patterson's great-nephew. In her eyes, he was a prize catch. She thought Kate was lucky to have a boy like Carl making goggle eyes at her. Maybe she was. Kate sighed as she grabbed a napkin to wipe off her hands. Maybe Carl was the best she could hope for here in Rosey Corner.

She turned toward the door and spotted Grand-father Merritt's hat again and thought of him way out in Oregon. Miles and miles from Rosey Corner. A little thrill went through Kate as she imagined the world beyond Rosey Corner. She could be like her grandfather and go somewhere, explore places she'd only read about in books.

She could go on to school. Not some business school that taught shorthand and typing like the one Evie had gone to. But to college where the doors to learning would be thrown wide open. Where she could figure out her place in that world outside Rosey Corner.

Kate held in a little sigh. She couldn't even figure out her place in Rosey Corner. Oh, she knew what she did. She took care of her sisters. She helped her mother at the store. She read every book she could get her hands on. She made up stories for Lorena and even wrote some of them down. She had a dozen notebooks full of words stuck under her bed. Dreams on paper. But that's all they were. Dreams.

Dreams she wasn't even sure she wanted to chase after. She loved Rosey Corner. She belonged in Rosey Corner. And there was Lorena. It made her stomach hurt to think about not being there if Lorena needed her.

As if summoned by her thoughts, Lorena popped through the door and grabbed Kate's hand. "Come on, Kate. You have to help me sing Mike's song."

"Mike's song? What song is that?" Kate asked as Lorena pulled her outside. A welcome breeze touched her face. It was good to be out of the stuffy house, away from the church ladies with their pointed remarks about Kate being the next bride.

"Oh, you know. That sweetheart one with the love light burning. I won't remember all the words if you don't help me."

Kate peered down at Lorena. "What are you talking about? You know the words to every song you've ever heard." Lorena collected songs the way some of the church ladies collected recipes.

Lorena ducked her head before peeking up at Kate. "Okay, I do know the words, but everybody will be watching."

"So?" Kate said. "You sing at church all the time."

"That's church people. They have to be nice while they're at church. But these are wedding people. They might laugh." She tugged on Kate's hand. When Kate didn't move off the porch, she went on. "Please. For Evie. Please."

"I'm sure Evie would rather Mike sang that to her." The last thing in the world she wanted to do was sing a love song where Carl could hear her and decide she was singing to him. Even now he was coming across the yard toward her. To claim her.

"He wanted to, but you know he can't even sing hymns. Not without making people hold their ears. He said Evie didn't want any sour notes at her wedding and that included his. Besides—"

Kate didn't let her finish. "Besides you want to sing. You always want to sing."

"If you'll sing with me." Lorena's face lit up with excitement.

"You don't need me." Kate was sorry for her words even before that worried look slipped into Lorena's eyes. Ever since Kate had graduated from high school last spring, Lorena had been nervous about Kate moving away. She never said anything, but Kate knew. Lorena did need her. Another reason Kate couldn't very well leave Rosey Corner no matter how suffocating it felt at times.

Lorena squeezed Kate's hand tighter and her lip trembled as she said, "Please."

"Okay." Kate gave in with a little sigh. "Let's go sing a love song to Evie."

Lorena squealed and jumped up and down. "Evie won't be the only one listening."

"I know." Kate blew out a long breath. "That's what I'm worried about. Carl's already thinking things he shouldn't think." As she followed Lorena toward the shady side yard where people were clustered around Evie and Mike, she sneaked a look toward Carl. He'd been waylaid by a couple of men who were laughing and clapping him on the back. It appeared the whole town had turned into marriage brokers.

Lorena looked back over her shoulder at Kate. "I wasn't talking about Carl. I was talking about Tanner."

"Don't you be falling in love on me, Lorena,"

Kate said with a laugh. "Not with the likes of Jay Tanner."

"He's cute." Lorena grinned. "But you don't call somebody you're sweet on Birdie."

"Oh really. What do you call them?"

"Katie." Lorena giggled. "He thinks you're pretty. He told me."

Kate groaned. "We need to have a talk, young lady. And soon."

❧ 6 ❧

The little sister had a great voice for a kid. The song seemed to almost flow out of her without effort. Kate sang along with her, harmonizing but letting the kid have the spotlight. Mike was smiling at his bride, mouthing the words along with the kid. Enjoying himself.

Jay didn't think the bride was all that tickled with the whole production. She had a smile, but not an easy one. Unless Jay missed his guess, Mike was in for some rough sledding in the years ahead. This one didn't look to be an easy one to please. Irritated even by her sisters singing her a song. One Mike had requested of Birdie. Jay heard him.

Oh well, he'd learn. Or maybe she would. Mike

could be pretty determined in his own way about some things. Jay had been on the receiving end of some of that determination at times. Back when they were in school, Mike was always after him to figure out what he believed. "A man has to know what's true. What matters. He can't just drift. Not without being in danger of some rocky landings."

Jay couldn't argue the truth of Mike's words. He'd known a few of those rocky landings, while Mike's landings had all been clean and easy. Now he was a married man. A preacher. Loved by one and all in this little Rosey Corner. Jay was beginning to feel like he'd fallen into a happily-ever-after fairy tale, and he was one of those faceless movie extras in the background, dancing to the music.

His mouth twisted up into an amused smile. A happy extra wasn't bad. He might as well enjoy the song like everybody else. At least listening to it. It took more than fruit punch to loosen his tongue enough to try belting out a song. Others around him weren't so hesitant as a few of the boys began picking up the sweetheart chorus line. Here and there, a girl was blushing while a guy pushed the words straight toward her.

The other sister, the one between Kate and Birdie, was getting a good dose of sweetheart singing from her pimply-faced boyfriend. Those two were so awkwardly in love it almost hurt to look at them. Too innocent. Too trusting. Something Jay didn't remember ever being. Not that he wanted to visit those feelings. Innocent and trusting opened a man up to getting blindsided by trouble. Better to peer on down the road with a jaded eye and be ready for whatever was barreling toward him.

Across from Jay, that tall, skinny farm boy, Carl something, had an idiot grin as his buddies pushed him forward. The man must have found something to spike his punch, because he started practically shouting out the sweetheart words toward Kate. She didn't give him the first glance, but she heard him plain enough. The color was rising in her cheeks. Not because she was pleased, if Jay knew anything about girls.

He'd seen plenty of both kinds of blushes—the pleased ones and the better-get-out-of-the-way ones. That older guy, Graham, appeared to be right about poor old Carl. The man was speeding his love train down a track with the bridge out. Nothing but unhappiness in store for him.

Thinking that didn't make Jay a bit unhappy. Maybe he would hang around Rosey Corner. Get his bearings. Stay ahead of the draft notices for a month or two if he was lucky. Graham and his old flea-bitten dog might make interesting companions for a few weeks. Till winter moved in anyway. A little honest outdoor labor. He could slap paint on a house. Help the man out and put a jingle of coin in his own pocket and gas in his car. All good things.

His eyes drifted back to Kate. Another good thing. A girl on the rebound was sometimes ready for a good time. He wasn't Mike, but he wasn't that hayseed Carl either.

She and the little sister got to the end of the song amidst cheers and laughter. Mike put his arm around his bride and brushed her cheek with his lips before he turned to the friends around them. "We've said the vows. We've eaten the cake and sung the song. Done all we need to do except for the honeymoon."

The guys let out a few whistles, and the bride and a good number of the girls colored up and ducked their heads. Not Kate. She was looking at Mike like she just now was noticing that he was a guy the same as the rest of them instead of whatever unreal fantasy she'd been carrying around in her head. Girls, they always wanted men to be heroes instead of regular guys.

The bride gave Mike a playful shove. "Give me a minute to change into my traveling clothes. I can't ride to Louisville in this." She held up the lacy skirt of her wedding dress.

Her sisters surrounded her at once and separated her from Mike to escort her toward the house.

"Don't take too long, darling," Mike called after her. "I'll be waiting."

More whistles and catcalls. Pastor Mike was going to have to do some preaching on lustful thinking to calm these boys down. Jay had never heard Mike actually preach behind a pulpit. That might be an experience if he was still here next Sunday. His buddy preaching the Word, solemn like, and officially trying to save Jay's soul. Mike had a way of believing anything was possible. He'd told Jay that once. That with the good Lord's help, all things were possible.

Jay didn't doubt it. What he doubted was the good Lord sending any help his way. That was all right. Jay had made it on his own so far. He'd keep making it on his own.

The bride must have been readier to head out to her honeymoon than Jay had thought. He figured it would take her an hour to change and say her goodbyes, but she was back out the door in half that time with the sisters trailing after her. Guess a girl could be eager to start married life the same as a guy. Her parents came out to watch from the porch.

The mother brushed away a few tears and the father put his arm around her to pull her close to his side. Old, steady love. New, fresh love. Kisses and hugs all around. Slaps on the back for Mike. Shouts of good wishes as Mike handed his new wife up into his car like she was some kind of fragile treasure.

Maybe she was. For Mike. Each man had to find

his own treasure. When he was ready. Jay wasn't ready. Not by a long shot.

Mike shut the car door, but then instead of crawling in the other side, he came over to Jay. "You can't know how much I appreciate you coming to stand up with me, Jay."

"You didn't think I would?" Jay said.

"I knew you would." Mike didn't let any doubt show, but Jay figured he'd not been all that sure. He'd probably had a backup plan to ask that Carl or maybe the bride's father to stand in if Jay didn't show up. Mike grinned now. "Not as sure about the suit."

"Only for you, buddy." Jay grinned as he pushed Mike away from him toward the car. "Your bride awaits." He peered past Mike toward the woman in the car. "A tad impatiently or I miss my guess."

Mike glanced over his shoulder and laughed. "Patience is not her strong suit. But loving me is." He grabbed Jay's shoulder and gave it a squeeze. "Don't be such a stranger. Let me know where you are when you get settled again."

Jay could have told him that he might be settled right here in Rosey Corner when Mike came back after his honeymoon, but he didn't. Let him find out for himself. That way Jay wouldn't be tied to any words if he decided to move on down the road. Free and loose was the way to be. He was sure of that, even if his gut did twist with a bit of lonesome longing when he watched Mike climbing into the car and calling out to his friends. His family. Laughing. Happy.

Jay ignored the feeling. He had the offer of a bed with an old hound dog. Things could be worse. He'd go hunt up Graham Lindell. If he couldn't find the old guy, he could find the blacksmith shop. That would be easy enough. But first he'd tell Kate goodbye. Or Birdie, if Kate turned an unfriendly eye his way. She wouldn't stay unfriendly forever. He'd heard that promise in her laugh while they were running down the road with the kid.

The party was breaking up. Once the couple of note was gone, the farmers started remembering the cows waiting to be milked. Mothers were gathering up their kids. Even the young people seemed to have lost the sparkle that had been shooting between them all earlier. Jay didn't have to search for Kate. She drew his eye. He saw her when she slipped away from her friends to disappear around the side of the house.

He pushed away from the tree he'd been leaning against and followed her. He found her staring at the pump on top of a well in the backyard. Like she needed water but didn't know how the thing worked.

"Hey there," he said softly. "Everything all right?"

She looked up at him and pushed a smile out on her face. "Everything's great. I just came out to get some water."

Jay looked around. "Be hard to carry it in without a bucket."

She clucked her tongue and gave her head a little shake. "I knew I was forgetting something." Then she grinned a little sheepishly.

He went over and sat down on the concrete base around the pump. "You want to talk about it?"

"About what? Forgetting the bucket?" She raised her eyebrows at him.

"About what's on your mind that made you forget the bucket." Jay patted the rock beside him. "Nice comfy seat here. Not much give to it, but I think it'll hold us up."

She sat down beside him. "I can see why Lorena likes you."

"Why's that? Because I call her Birdie?"

"No, I'm amazed she lets you get away with that. Her given name is very important to her." Kate looked over at him. "No, because you know how to make people smile."

"It's a learned art," Jay said.

"Did you learn it from Mike?" She turned her eyes away from him and looked sorry she'd asked that as soon as the words were out of her mouth. "I mean, Mike had people here smiling in church from his first sermon. Our preacher before that—actually my own grandfather—he didn't believe much in smiling anywhere. Especially in God's house. Church was serious business with him."

"I've learned a lot from Mike. He's been better than a brother to me, but his smiles and mine are probably some different. Especially his preacher smiles. Me, I just try to level out some bumpy roads with a smile now and then."

"You on a bumpy road right now?" She held up her hand before he could say anything. "You don't have to answer that. I shouldn't be so nosy."

Jay let out a short laugh. "Don't worry about it. Fact is, I'm most always on a bumpy road. How about you? Your roads all smooth and straight?"

"Everybody thinks so."

"What do you think?"

She sighed and didn't answer. Instead she scooted a little to the side and stared at the pump. The handle looked well oiled from many hands pumping it to bring the water up from the deep. Spots of rust were proof the pump had been there a long time. Jay was getting ready to fish around for something else to say when she finally spoke, but she didn't answer his question.

"My grandfather Merritt used to take a bath here every morning. Right here at this pump. No matter the weather, winter or summer. Said a man shouldn't give in to the elements." She reached up and ran her fingers down the pump handle.

"So what happened to him? Did he take pneumonia and kick the bucket?" Then thinking about what he'd said, he rushed on. "I didn't mean to sound disrespectful to the dead." There were some things a man shouldn't joke about. Especially to a girl.

She reached over and touched his arm lightly. "It's okay. He's not dead. Still going strong as far as we know. Maybe taking cold-water baths same as always. Just not at this pump any longer. He left Rosey Corner about five years ago." She looked back at the pump.

"Left here?"

"Yeah, surprised us too. Just up and drove away one day without saying boo to any of us. Well, he left a note. Told Mama to run the store and Aunt Hattie to live here in his house. Giving orders even as he put Rosey Corner in his rear-view mirror."

"Where'd he go?"

"Oregon."

Jay whistled softly. "Must have got a real case of the wanderlust."

"Have you ever been to Oregon?" She looked back at him.

"Haven't wandered that far yet. Been to Tennessee. South Carolina. Ohio. Thinking about Illinois next. They say the Great Lakes are something to see. I'll get out to the West sooner or later though. A lot to see out that way too."

"How does it feel to just pick up and leave home?"

"You gotta have a home before you can leave

one." He ran his hand over the concrete beside him as if he needed to smooth it down. "So that's not something I've had to worry about. I've been pretty much on my own a long time."

"No family?"

"None that give me any thought." He had family. A sister and three half brothers, last he'd heard, but it had been years since he'd seen his sister and he'd never seen the brothers.

"But family's important." Her shoulders slumped and she stared down at her hands.

"You missing your grandfather? Were the two of you close?"

"I wouldn't say that. Nobody was really close to Grandfather Merritt. At least not here. I don't know about out there. He got married again, so maybe."

"Then what's making you so blue, Miss Merritt? You wishing you were the bride instead of your sister?"

"Oh no. I wouldn't steal Evie's happiness. Not for anything." She glanced up at him with a genuine look of denial, but then she let her eyes drop back down to her lap. "It's just that nothing will ever be the same again with her married. I guess I'm missing her already. She's irritating and bossy and drives me crazy, but she's my sister. And now she won't be living at home anymore."

Jay wanted to put his arm around her, but thought better of it. Instead he reached over and gave her hand a sympathetic squeeze. Then he kept hold of her hand and scooted a little closer to let his shoulder touch hers. He wondered if she'd slap him if he tried for a kiss. His own lips tingled with the thought, but she kept her head bent, looking down at his hand on hers. She didn't pull away.

He leaned over to peek up into her face. "She's not going to Oregon. She'll be right here in Rosey Corner every weekend, driving you crazy like always. Being the preacher's wife will give her the chance to be double bossy."

A corner of her mouth twitched up in a smile.

"You're right," she said without looking up. "She'll be unbearable."

"Completely," he agreed. He took a chance and reached with his other hand to tip her face toward his. That put her lips enticingly close, and he had to moisten his own lips before he could continue talking. "If you ask me, Mike picked the wrong sister. But I'm kind of glad he did."

Her eyes popped open a little wider at that. Beautiful eyes sparkling with life. Her breath was coming faster, mingling with his.

"Can I kiss the sister of the bride?" he whispered.

She tilted her face up toward him, a truer yes than one spoken. But he wasn't quick enough. There was a shout behind him. A rough hand on his shoulder jerked him back.

"What do you think you're doing with my girl?" The farm boy balled up his fists and glared at Jay.

Jay scrambled to his feet and gave the farm boy what he hoped was a calming look. He didn't want to ruin his new suit in a fight with the hayseed. Besides, it was his best friend's wedding day. Not a good time to punch out one of his church members. Too bad Mike wasn't around to soothe the guy's ruffled feathers.

"Whoa, buddy." Jay held up his hands in a gesture of surrender. "Take it easy. Nothing's going on here that you need to get all worked up over. We were just having a little talk."

"Looked like more than talking to me." The farm boy put up his fists.

"Carl, for heaven's sake, stop acting like an idiot." Kate was on her feet glaring at the boy.

"Stay out of the way, Kate. This is between us men." The farm boy's face looked ready to burst into flames any second. His buddies, who had followed him around the house, were hanging back, waiting to see what was going to happen next.

"I'm not fighting you." Jay searched through his mind for the guy's name. "Carl. Why don't you take a deep breath and we can talk this out?"

Jay thought he was sounding just like Mike. Peace loving. The stray thought popped into his mind then to ball up his fist and deck the guy before he knew what hit him. That was the way to do it when a man kept talking about fighting. Get it over with. But Kate was watching. He wasn't going to make any points with the girl by smacking down the farm boy, and he wanted to tally up a few points with her.

"There's nothing to talk out. Kate's my girl, and I'm not about to let no fly-by-night slick talker mess with her." The farm boy took a menacing step toward Jay. He wasn't wanting to be talked down.

"Carl Noland, you leave him alone." Kate grabbed for the hayseed's arm, but her words only made the guy's blood run that much hotter.

"Look, buddy, I'll just back away and you and Kate can work things out." Jay took a peek over at Kate and knew that wasn't going to happen. He didn't want it to happen, but the words sounded peacemaking. Again what he thought Mike might say.

When in Rome do as the Romans do and all that. Rosey Corner people probably didn't engage in fisticuffs at wedding parties. At least not usually. However, this Carl fellow did seem determined to punch somebody. Well, not just somebody. Him. That wasn't something Jay intended to let happen, but the top of the well was blocking his easy retreat.

"What's the matter, pretty boy? You chicken to fight?"

Some of the farm boy's friends started doing a little crowing behind him. Jay took a long, slow breath to keep from making fists. Instead he tried to step sideways away from the guy, but the guy moved over in front of him. Jay took another peek at Kate. She looked about as ready to explode as the poor, deluded farm boy who believed she was his girl. From the look on Kate's face, the guy was going to have his illusions shattered, and soon.

Jay should have pushed past him and left the whole mess behind. Let Kate straighten the farm boy out. But ever since he was a kid, Jay had a way of poking at whatever sore place he could see on whomever he was up against.

"I don't fight boys," he said, and then he smiled. He knew better, but he did it anyway. He figured it was the smile that sent the farm boy over the edge.

Jay feinted a little to the left so the blow didn't hit him full in the face. Even so, the guy landed a pretty solid punch on his cheek. He could have kept his feet, but if he was going to get socked, he might as well play it to the full for Kate's sympathy. There was more than one way to win a fight.

❧ 7 ❧

Kate's father broke up the fight. Not that it was much of a fight. The only punch was the one Carl threw to deck Jay Tanner. That surprised Kate. If anybody was going to deck anybody, she figured it would be Jay knocking Carl down. A man like him, who had bounced around a lot, had to know how to defend himself. But he claimed not to want to fight and he stuck to his words. After Carl punched him in the face, he just sat on the ground rubbing his cheek and working his jaw a little. It had to hurt, but the funny thing was he never completely stopped grinning. Like it was all some kind of joke.

Carl was smiling too, proud of himself. A complete idiot. It was a good thing her father came out the back door when he did to stop the foolishness or another punch might have been thrown. Her punching Carl. She was that mad.

"What's going on here, Carl?" her father asked. At the sight of his frown, the friends who had been egging Carl on began muttering about needing to get home as they started back around the house. All the boys knew Victor Merritt was nobody to mess with when it came to his girls.

"Carl's lost his mind. That's what." Kate gave Carl a hard look.

"He was bothering Kate, Mr. Merritt. I wasn't about to let him mess with my girl." Carl kept his fists up like a fighter ready to go another round. He was acting like he thought Kate's father might grab his arm, raise it up, and declare him the winner.

Kate's father looked from Carl to Jay picking himself up off the ground.

"Sorry about this, sir," Jay said with an apologetic shrug. "I wasn't meaning to cause trouble. Kate and I were talking about the wedding. That's all."

"That's all, like heck," Carl shouted, his smile fading as Kate's father looked back at him. "You had your hands on her. I saw you."

Kate could feel the blood rising in her face. She hadn't been even close to this angry since she'd caught one of the neighborhood kids making fun of Lorena's name. And that was different. Just a silly little boy. Carl wasn't a little boy. He was simply acting like one. Like a kid on the playground claiming more than he had.

How could he think she was his girl? Sure, she went to the movies with him, but she never let him kiss her. They didn't even hold hands. She was going to have to tell him straight out how things were, but not here. Even as angry as she was, she didn't want to humiliate him in front of

Jay Tanner and her father. They'd been friends too long for that.

She stepped in front of Carl and stared him right in the face. She kept her voice tightly controlled. "Go home, Carl. I can't talk to you right now."

"You could talk to him." Carl's words were harsh, accusing.

"I can talk to anybody I want to, but right now, I don't want to talk to you."

"But you're my girl, Kate. I had to take up for you." He reached out to grab her arm, but she stepped away from him. He held his hand up in the air a moment before he dropped it to his side.

"I'm not your girl, Carl." For a minute she almost felt sorry for him as his shoulders drooped and he got a whipped dog look. But then he brushed her words aside as though they didn't mean a thing.

"Aw, Kate, everybody knows we're getting married. That it's just a matter of time."

Kate shut her eyes and blew out a long breath. Without looking, she knew Jay would be watching them with that same grin, like he'd found the sideshow at the Rosey Corner circus. She was glad when her father stepped up to put his arm around Carl's shoulders.

"Kate's right, Carl. You better go on home. The two of you can talk this out after tempers settle down a little." He had a sympathetic look on his face as he turned Carl away from Kate. Like he was feeling his disappointment instead of thinking the man was a complete idiot the way Kate did.

"But Mr. Merritt, you know it's true. She's been my girl forever." Carl peeked over his shoulder toward Kate.

Kate's father kept walking him toward the front yard. He sounded almost sad when he said, "Later, Carl. Now's not the time or the place."

They moved on around the house, her father's voice calm and Carl's voice taking on a whiny sound. That left her and Jay Tanner alone again. She waited for him to say something, but he was silent. The voices of the women in the kitchen drifted out to them. No words, just the easy sound of family.

Aunt Hattie laughed, and Kate wished she was inside with them instead of standing out in the middle of the backyard, wondering what to say to Jay Tanner. Because Carl was right. He had been holding her hand, and she hadn't minded at all. She hadn't even minded when he asked to kiss her.

How could her world get so totally turned upside down in one short day? And mixed up. Grieving over Mike promising his life and love to Evie one minute. Happy for Evie the next. And now ready to let a man she'd just met kiss her when she'd never once turned her face up to invite a kiss from Carl. Carl, who thought she was his girl. Carl, her friend she'd let think she was his girl.

She bent her head and breathed out a whisper of a sigh. Maybe she was the one being the idiot instead of Carl.

"Are you all right?" Jay asked.

She glanced around at him. He'd picked up his coat, but he hadn't moved any closer to her. The grin was gone. In its place was a different look. A wondering look. Like he was waiting to see what she was going to do next.

She pushed a smile out on her lips. "I think I should be asking you that. You're the one with the shiner."

He winced a little when he touched his cheek below his eye. "The boy packed a better punch than I expected."

"Why'd you let him hit you?"

His lips turned up in a smile to match hers. "You did see how much he enjoyed it, didn't you?"

"So you were simply doing your good deed of the day?"

"Something like that." His grin traveled up to his eyes. "I guess my trouble was that I could see Mike standing behind him, shaking his head at me. Saying 'Not on my wedding day.' But somehow when Mike tries to keep the peace, it works. When I try it, I end up on my backside looking up. I was glad your father came out. I wasn't sure how much longer I could be so peace loving."

"I didn't see much peace."

"We can only keep our side of the peace. We can't make the other side do the same. Or so Mike used to tell me when I was fighting my way through school. All that turn-the-other-cheek stuff. Nothing about that promises we're not going to get smacked upside the head again, but I think there are limits to my peacekeeping." He turned his face to the side. "How bad does it look?"

Kate stepped over to him and gingerly felt the swelling below his eye. "Looks like you could have a black eye."

"Won't be the first. And probably not the last." He captured her hand before she could pull it away. "Not a bad price for holding a pretty girl's hand."

"You're a charmer, aren't you?"

"I wouldn't mind charming you. You're an interesting girl, Kate Merritt."

He wasn't smiling now as he stared straight into her eyes. Charming her without a doubt. She felt a little breathless again, the way she had earlier when he'd asked to kiss the sister of the bride. "Interesting? That's not what I expected a charmer to say."

"You'd rather I say you're beautiful?"

"That's a nice word to hear." She told herself to pull her hand away and step back, but she liked it where she was standing.

"All right, you are beautiful, Kate Merritt, but interesting is better. Pretty girls are a dime a dozen, but an interesting girl, she just plants herself right in the middle of your mind and stays there."

He was altogether too close to her. She moistened her lips before she said, "And what makes me so interesting?"

"I don't know, but I wouldn't mind finding out."

"If you think I'm interesting, you must have a reason to think that."

"You're getting me mixed up with Mike. He's the one always looking for answers. Finds them too. But me, I don't need everything explained. Sometimes I just know." He pulled her hand up to lightly brush the tops of her fingers with his lips while keeping his eyes on hers. "Like now."

"What do you know?" Her voice was barely a whisper.

"That you want to let me kiss you, but you think you shouldn't."

Behind them the screen door slammed and broke the spell. Kate jerked her hand away from his. "You're the interesting one, Mr. Tanner. The way your imagination works overtime like that." She laughed a little. "But if you knew me better, you'd know that if I wanted to do something I'd do it."

"Interesting." A smile lit up his brown eyes. "First you won't elope with me and now you won't let me kiss you. For no better reason than you don't want to. You know how to hurt a man.

Maybe I should go hunt up Carl so we can compare broken hearts."

"I seriously doubt you've ever had a broken heart, Mr. Tanner."

"You call me Mr. Tanner again, I might." He laughed. "My name's Jay. Look, I took a punch for you. That surely earns me the right to be on a first-name basis with you." His voice softened a little as he added, "Kate."

The sound of her name reached out and touched her. Made her heart start beating a little too fast again. She'd never heard her name spoken exactly like that. She laughed a little to cover up how unsettled she was feeling. "All right." She hesitated a bare second, then said, "Jay."

Kate had almost forgotten the slammed door until Aunt Hattie called to her. "Katherine Reece."

The little black woman, hands planted on her hips, was standing on the back porch, staring out at them. Kate could see her frown all the way across the yard. "What you let happenin' out here? Your daddy tells me somebody might be needing some doctoring."

"Tell her I'm fine," Jay said.

Aunt Hattie moved a few steps closer and motioned toward them. "You must not be too fine if you have to tell somebody to do your talking for you. Now get yo'self on over here and let me see to that face. Least we can do for Pastor Mike's friend."

"No sense arguing," Kate said. "When Aunt Hattie sets her mind to doctoring, you're going to get doctored. Like it or not." She put her hand through Jay's arm and turned him toward the porch. "She's gentler than she looks."

"Ain't a thing gentle about me." Aunt Hattie went back up on the porch to wait for them. " 'Cepting my hands. The good Lord give me healing hands. I's the first hands to hold this one here." She pointed at Kate.

"And my daddy too." Kate grinned as she stepped up on the porch beside Aunt Hattie. "A lot of people in Rosey Corner owe their first breath to a smack from Aunt Hattie."

"I never smacked none of my babies. Better ways to get things done than smacking somebody." Aunt Hattie turned her frown from Kate to Jay's shiner. "But looks as how somebody's been doing some smacking."

"I think it was more like punching." Jay sat down obediently on the porch bench Aunt Hattie pointed him toward. "I'm fine. Really, Mrs.—" He hesitated. "If anybody told me your name, I've let it get away from me."

"Johnson. Hattie Johnson, but nobody calls me Missus nothing. I'm Aunt Hattie to one and all in Rosey Corner." Aunt Hattie leaned closer to peer at Jay's cheek. "My eyes ain't as good as they used to be, but it ain't hard to see you got some lump there."

"Yeah, I didn't dodge quick enough." Jay laughed, then winced. "But it only hurts when I smile."

She touched his cheek and looked around at Kate. "Run fetch me a pan of cold water and a rag. And bring a chunk of ice out of the icebox if we didn't use it all for that funny-tasting concoction your sister had us make. Strangest stuff I ever put in my mouth. I tol' her she oughta let me make my lemonade, but ain't no tellin' that one nothing. Not one thing."

By the time Kate got back with the water, Jay had worked his charms on Aunt Hattie. Her every wrinkle was smiling. She wrung the rag out in the cold water and dabbed Jay's cheek. "You done remind me of my boy, Bo. He was always making people laugh too. And your eyes, they set me to remembering his."

"Not a black eye like this, I'm hoping. He wasn't a fighter, was he?"

"No, indeed. My Bo was a baseball player. The best shortstop the Negro League ever saw, and he could swing that bat. Could hit the ball out of the park easy as pie." Aunt Hattie straightened up to her full four feet and ten inches and looked out toward the back fence as though watching one of those balls fly into the sky.

Jay followed Aunt Hattie's gaze, so he didn't see the look Kate shot at him or the little shake of her head. He asked, "He still hitting the long balls now?"

"Could be up in paradise. The Good Book says things will be finer than we can imagine when we get up to them other shores. I figure that means we's gonna get to do things we enjoys, don't you?" Aunt Hattie turned back to her doctoring. "And you don't have to be worrying, Kate, I ain't mindin' talking about my Bo. It's a good thing, not a bad thing to be able to say my boy's name and to brag on him some. He's done been gone these many years. Lost him in France in the war."

"I'm sorry, Aunt Hattie." Jay looked genuinely sorry as he put his hand overtop the wrinkled hand probing his cheek.

The man was good at grabbing hands, but Aunt Hattie didn't look as if she minded. Kate couldn't honestly say she had minded either. But she should have minded. She shouldn't have let him think he could charm her as easily as a little girl or an old woman. Then again, she wouldn't have thought Aunt Hattie would be easy to charm. She generally saw through anybody's pretenses. She never let Kate get away with the first thing around her.

But now it was past time to get everybody back on track. The sun would be sinking below the horizon soon, and Jay Tanner needed to be on his way to wherever his wanderlust took him next. That thought gave her an unhappy twinge, but she ignored it. "You want me to wrap this ice in a towel? I'm sure Mr. Tanner is anxious to get on the road."

Jay winced a little at her words. "I thought we were on a first-name basis, Kate."

Kate acted like she didn't hear him as she slid her eyes over to Aunt Hattie. "I can make an ice pack for him to hold on his cheek while he's driving."

Aunt Hattie looked at Kate with her eyebrows lifted, then back at Jay. "You as anxious to be on the road, Mr. Tanner, as it appears Kate here thinks you is?"

"Come on, you two. Mr. Tanner was my daddy. I answer to Jay or simply Tanner if Jay won't fit your tongue right." His smile was back, sparkling the charm out on Aunt Hattie. "As to moving on, I've had the offer of work here, so being between jobs, I thought I might just settle in for a week or two. I figure President Roosevelt is going to catch up with me with a draft notice anytime now. Might as well enjoy a little sunshine here in Rosey Corner first."

He shot a grin up toward Kate. A kid's grin. The kind of grin Tori used to give Kate after she'd talked her into going fishing. A pleased and somehow hopeful look, like she was sure this time Kate would at last start thinking fishing was as much fun as she did. Kate thought it better not to think about what Jay was hoping she'd decide was fun, but that didn't keep her heart from doing a funny bounce and her lips from tingling.

Aunt Hattie wrapped the ice in the towel and held it to Jay's jaw. "Pastor Mike hire you on to help him in his preaching job?"

Jay laughed out loud and then groaned a little as he touched his cheek. "I gotta remember not to laugh, but me doing any kind of preaching is pretty funny."

"You thinkin' the Lord can't use you?" Aunt Hattie stood back and put her hands on her hips again to give him a fierce stare.

"I'm thinking he wouldn't want to. I'm not good enough for that."

"Ain't none of us good enough. We's all broken vessels that the Lord can make whole to do whatever he intends us to do." Aunt Hattie narrowed her eyes on him. "You just keep in mind, Jay Tanner, that the Lord can hit a mighty straight lick with a mighty crooked stick."

Jay shifted a little uneasily on the bench, as though finally at a loss for words. Kate almost felt sorry for him. She'd been in his spot often enough, pinned down by Aunt Hattie's sharp eyes demanding she be a better person than she knew how to be. Kate took pity on him and tried to change the subject before Aunt Hattie got really wound up preaching.

"My mother didn't offer you a job at the store, did she? She might do that if she thought you'd keep talking poetry with her." Kate smiled at him.

"Maybe there will be some time for that too. A man will need to wet his whistle with a soft drink now and again." His smile eased back out on his face. "But no, it was Graham Lindell who offered me a bed and a job. Seems he's taken on a bigger painting job than he wanted."

Aunt Hattie chuckled and leaned back over to hold the ice higher on Jay's cheek. "That Graham Lindell." She looked over her shoulder at Kate. "Looks like he's up to something. And from the look on your face, I'm thinkin' you might not mind."

"I have no idea what you're talking about, Aunt Hattie." Kate willed herself not to blush. But she did know exactly what Aunt Hattie meant and exactly what Graham was up to as well. It appeared Jay Tanner had charmed Graham too.

 8

Carl was on the front porch when Kate, her mother, and Lorena finally walked home after helping Aunt Hattie clean up. Her father had come home earlier, but he wasn't keeping Carl company. He was probably out back milking the cow. Tori wasn't anywhere to be seen either. No doubt she was off walking in the twilight with

Sammy and dreaming about the day they could follow Mike and Evie down the church aisle. Carl was all alone, sitting stiff and straight on the swing, his feet planted on the plank floor to keep the swing from swaying the slightest bit.

It was plain he was stewing about her talking to Jay Tanner. Actually Carl had been right. She had been close to doing more than talking, but Kate wasn't about to admit that to Carl. Or to Jay Tanner either. If she ever saw him again. Jay had held Aunt Hattie's ice to his cheek for a while before saying his goodbyes and heading down to the church for his car. He hadn't asked the way to Graham's room above her father's blacksmith shop.

In spite of what he said, she couldn't see him staying there. Not really. What she could imagine was him laughing all the way down the road as he drove toward whatever town was next on his list. Rosey Corner was no more than an amusement for him. She was no more than a challenge. One she'd almost shamelessly let him win. Just the thought of it made her cheeks burn.

She wasn't happy to see Carl. She was tired. She was unsettled. She had no idea what she was thinking or how she was feeling. Not the best time to let an old friend down easy.

When he saw them coming across the yard, he jumped to his feet, making the swing jerk up and down on its chains. On the porch, her mother squeezed Kate's arm in a silent gesture of under-standing before she nodded at Carl and hustled Lorena past him into the house. Kate wanted to follow them, but unpleasant things couldn't be avoided forever. Toilets had to be cleaned out, floors scrubbed, and fishing worms squished on hooks. And she'd rather be doing any of those than facing Carl Noland on her front porch at that moment.

He was frowning. Obviously mad at her but at the same time looking uneasy. He didn't seem to know what to do with his hands as he stood like his shoes were tacked to the porch and peered over at Kate. She knew he was expecting her to say something to smooth down his ruffled feathers, but the only words that came to mind were "Go home." She couldn't say that. Not without at least an attempt at being nice.

A full minute ticked past after the screen door bounced closed behind her mother and Lorena. She had to say something.

"Carl . . . ," she started, as though she needed to let him know she remembered his name. Normally words didn't desert her so completely. She rubbed her thumb and fingertips together and wished for a pen and paper. It would be easier to write him a letter explaining everything than to tell him face-to-face.

The frown lines between his eyes deepened. "Kate, what's going on with you?"

He stepped toward her and she had to force herself not to back up. She motioned toward the swing. "You want to sit down?" She was delaying.

"No, I don't want to sit down." His voice rose until it wasn't much below a yell.

Kate looked toward the house. Sound would slide right through the open windows and door, and while she didn't care what her mother and Lorena heard, Carl might. "Then, let's walk out in the yard where we can talk." She nodded a little toward the screen door, and his face colored up.

Neither of them said anything as they moved across the dusty yard toward the maple tree. A rope swing hung down from one of the branches, and Kate wished Lorena was on it, begging Kate to push her even though she was plenty big enough to keep the swing going by herself. Kate didn't mind pushing her. It seemed to release something inside them both, a tandem of movement that was like poetry in motion.

A few of the maple's leaves had already turned a bright yellow that reflected the last rays of the setting sun and shed a golden light under the tree. To break the odd silence between them, Kate said, "The leaves are beginning to turn."

"I don't care about the stupid leaves." Carl whipped his hand through the air as though knocking away her words. His voice was tight. "Don't think you can just start talking about stuff like nothing's wrong."

Kate's insides clenched up. The day was beginning to feel two weeks long. Too much had happened. Evie and Mike. Jay Tanner. And now Carl with a storm darkening his face and demanding what she couldn't give him. She looked away from him out at the lilac bush her mother loved, losing its leaves now. Her eyes slid to the rosebush she'd jumped over a thousand times just to prove she could. Peony bushes and irises lined the yard fence and were forbidden territory when they were playing hide-and-seek. The clothesline on the other side of the yard had given them plenty of practice ducking and swerving during tag.

"We've had a lot of good times in this yard," Kate said. "You remember the time you hid up in this very tree and we couldn't find you? You said you stayed up there hiding for the longest time even after we gave up and went inside."

Carl looked up at the tree branches over his head. "I wanted you to find me."

"But we didn't." Kate let her eyes come back to Carl for just a second before she looked away again. "We thought you'd gone home."

"I don't give up easy. Not when it's something I want."

"I know." Kate studied the hard-packed ground under the swing where the grass had long since been worn away. The words she needed to say were backing up in her throat. She did like him.

That made it hard to say what she had to say. He was going to be hurt. Even now he was hurt. She could feel him staring at her, and while she didn't allow her eyes to travel back to his face, she had no trouble imagining the look that would be there. A little-boy look of betrayal, of the others not playing the game right, of being stuck up a tree and nobody caring enough to find him.

"What's wrong with you, Kate?" His voice was softer now.

Kate pulled in a long breath and let it out. She looked straight at him. She couldn't put it off forever. She was the sister who took care of whatever needed taking care of, whether that was Evie making it through getting married or Lorena learning her multiplication tables. She handled things. She'd have to handle this.

"I'm sorry, Carl. I do like you."

"Like me?" His voice came out in a funny squeak. He stared at her a minute, then ran his hand through his hair as if that might help him take in her words. The pomade he'd used to slick it down now left it sticking up in a mess.

Yesterday she could have smoothed it down with a laugh. Today that wasn't possible. Why were thoughts of love always getting in the way of friendship? It didn't have to be that way. Didn't she love Mike? Foolishly. Stupidly. But that didn't keep her from welcoming his friendship, even if romantic love was out of the question.

"We've been friends forever, Carl. I don't want to spoil that now."

"I love you, Kate. I've known we were going to get married ever since we were kids." He was peering at her as though he didn't quite know who she was. "Just the way you told me your father loved your mother. You remember telling me that, don't you? How your father was in love with your mother and then she realized she was in love with him too."

Kate held in the sigh that wanted to escape her as she looked down at the satiny bridesmaid dress she was still wearing. She tried to smooth off a spot of white cake icing, but it wouldn't rub off. She should have taken clothes with her to Aunt Hattie's to change. She should have stayed out of Aunt Hattie's backyard. She should have done a lot of things differently.

She met his eyes. A person couldn't be a coward about some things. "But I'm not my mother and you're not my father, Carl. Things don't always happen that way."

"What are you trying to say, Kate? That you don't love me? We've been going out for two years."

"I do love you, Carl, but not the way you want me to. I love you as a friend. A very dear friend." She said the words as gently as possible.

Carl made a sound as if she'd punched him in the stomach. He blinked a couple of times and lowered his eyes to the ground.

Kate reached toward him but then pulled back her hand. "I'm sorry, Carl. I can see you're hurt, but I can't change the way I feel."

"Is it because I've never officially proposed? I've been waiting for the right time, but maybe I shouldn't have." He went down on one knee and grabbed her hands.

She tried to pull him up, but he wouldn't let her. "Carl, please don't do this."

He acted as if he didn't hear her. "Kate Merritt, will you marry me?" Without waiting for an answer, he rushed on. "You have to love me. You have to marry me."

She gave up trying to get him to stand up and instead slid her hands free of his. "I can't, Carl. You deserve a girl who loves you the right way. Somebody who wants to be with you forever."

"But that's you, Kate." He looked up at her like a dog that was being whipped without any idea why.

She didn't say anything. What more could she say? He didn't want to hear her refusal. After a minute, he grabbed hold of the swing rope and clambered to his feet. A dreadful silence fell between them while he waited for her to take back her words. She didn't slide her eyes away from his the way she wanted to, but met his look. It was the least she could do.

At last he said, "I figure I might get my draft notice soon. I thought we could announce our engagement now before I join up, and then Pastor Mike can tie the knot for us after I finish basic training. They usually give a guy a little leave before they assign him to a base somewhere. I hear they're sending a lot of the guys west to California. You could go with me. You'd like California. You're always talking about wanting to see somewhere besides Rosey Corner."

She felt sorry for him, but a spot of irritation was growing inside her. Her voice wasn't as kind as she said, "We're not getting married, Carl. Not now. Not then. Not ever."

Anger flashed in Carl's eyes. "It's that fast-talking pretty boy, isn't it? He's come in here and turned your head. Got you forgetting who you are."

"And who am I?" Her anger was rising to match his.

"Somebody who thinks she's better than the rest of us. Like the world is going to stop and let you climb on anywhere you want. Well, it's not. You're just a small town girl from Rosey Corner who doesn't know half what you think you know." He spit the words at her.

She tried to back away from him, but the tree trunk stopped her retreat. She pulled in a breath and did her best to sound in control. "I think you better go home, Carl."

His face got even redder until he looked ready to explode. The words did seem to explode out of him. "I'll go home, all right. Right after I do something I should have done a long time ago."

"We're through talking, Carl." She pushed away from the tree to move past him, but he clamped his hands down on her shoulders.

"Through talking, but we're not finished. Not by a long shot. You want a man who just grabs what-ever he wants no matter what, then that's what you're gonna get."

She tried to jerk away from him, but he was too strong. He shoved her back against the tree, stepped closer, and mashed his mouth down over her lips. She tried to twist away from him, but his hands on her were like iron. So instead she froze and became part of the tree, stiff and unmoving. Carl didn't seem to notice as he shut his eyes and kept moving his lips against hers.

When at last he lifted his head, she stared straight at him with disgust. "Turn me loose or I'll scream."

He flinched a little at her words and dropped his hands off her shoulders. "You were supposed to kiss me back, Kate."

"That was no kiss. That was an attack." She glared at him and pointed toward the road. "Goodbye, Carl."

"You can't just say goodbye like it's over between us."

"Goodbye, Carl." Her voice was icy.

Anger and sorrow warred in his eyes. The anger

won. "Everybody always told me you were just like your granddaddy—cold, all drawed up inside yourself, not caring about nothing but what you wanted, but I didn't believe them. I didn't want to believe them. But maybe they were right. I gave you your chance. Believe me, there's plenty of other girls who know how to kiss a guy."

She kept her face blank as she met his stare. She refused to let him see how his words were like stones thrown at her heart. Who were these people telling him that? Everybody.

His face changed. The sorrow pushing in front of the anger now. But he didn't take back his words. Instead he turned on his heel and stalked away. She didn't move until he was out of sight up the road. Then she lifted up her dress tail to wipe off her mouth. Her lips felt bruised, her spirit wounded.

She dropped down in the swing and pushed her feet against the ground to launch herself into the air. She was glad for the wind against her hot face. Glad it was blowing her hair free from its pins. She leaned back to pump the swing higher. She wanted to be free of gravity, to float in the air with nothing to stop her flight. She imagined Carl's words blowing away from her, being lost forever. He was angry. She understood that. Maybe it would have been better if she'd simply kissed him. A parting gift. What if he was drafted? She should have told him she'd pray for him.

Up and back through the air her thoughts went.

But she couldn't swing forever. Twilight was giving way to darkness. Already the lights were on in the house. She'd have to go in. And then Lorena was running down the steps and across the yard toward her. Her beautiful little sister. Surely, Lorena was proof that she cared about somebody besides herself. She let her feet skip against the ground to stop the swing.

"Mama sent me to tell you to come in," Lorena said.

"All right." The swing was stopped now, but Kate didn't stand up.

"Are you okay, Kate?"

"Some people don't think so. What do you think?"

Lorena ran closer to wrap her arms around her. "I think you're perfect."

"Nobody's perfect." Kate stood up and pulled her close. She was getting so tall.

"Nobody but Jesus." Lorena peeked up at Kate. "But you're real close."

"If only," Kate said with a little smile.

"Did you and Carl have a fight?"

"You could say that."

"He's just mad 'cause you talked to Tanner. Did he really give Tanner a black eye?"

"Yeah, he really did." Kate gave her head a little shake as she looked down at Lorena.

"Poor Tanner." Lorena made a sad face.

"He'll live through it," Kate said. "If I were you, I wouldn't waste too much time worrying about Mr. Tanner. He can take care of himself or I miss my guess."

"Why'd he let Carl hit him then?"

"Maybe he caught him by surprise." A lot of things were catching Kate by surprise, so why not everybody else?

"You going to make up?" Lorena asked. "You and Carl."

"I don't know. Maybe not." Actually she did know. She breathed out a sigh. "Probably not."

"Good." Lorena tightened her lips together and gave a curt little nod.

"Good?" Kate frowned down at her. "I thought you liked Carl."

Lorena shrugged her shoulders. "He's okay. But did you hear him trying to sing this afternoon? He was awful. You don't want to marry somebody who can't sing."

"You silly goose," Kate said, but she couldn't keep from laughing as she flipped her hand through Lorena's curly hair. The laugh freed up something inside her and let Carl's angry words fade into the background of her mind. She wouldn't worry about what everybody was saying. She'd only worry about whether they could sing.

"I mean it." Lorena had a serious look on her face.

"What about Evie and Mike? He can't sing a lick."

"True," Lorena said a little regretfully. "But Evie doesn't care that much about singing anyway. And Mike preaches, so that makes up for not singing, don't you think?"

"I have no idea. You're the one doing this thinking, but I'm thinking love might matter more than singing ability."

"Love songs are the best." Lorena put her hands together up under her chin and got a dreamy look.

"I guess when you start getting stuck on boys, we'll have to get them to audition. You monkey." Kate poked her in the ribs to make her giggle. "Come on. Mama's peeking out the door wondering where we are."

Halfway across the yard, Lorena said, "Do you think Tanner can sing?"

"Who knows? But it doesn't matter. He's way too old for you."

"Not for you."

"I don't need you matchmaking for me, young lady. I can find my own fellows."

"But he was fun. Didn't you think so?"

"I bet he can't sing," Kate said, just to bother Lorena.

"He might be able to sing." Lorena sounded hopeful, then wistful. "You think we'll ever see him again?"

"I don't know. Maybe. Maybe not."

"I wish we would," Lorena said. "Don't you?"

"Maybe he'll come back in ten years looking for you. By then, you'll be all grown up and so beautiful he wouldn't be able to resist you." She put her arm around the little girl's shoulders and gave her a hug as they climbed the porch steps. "And he'll have taken singing lessons."

"He'll come back before then. He'll come looking for you."

Kate laughed, but the idea of seeing Jay Tanner didn't sound so bad. Instead a little thrill tickled through her.

She had to be out of her mind. Completely.

 9

Jay liked painting the boards on the old house. Back and forth. Dip the brush in the paint and swipe it against the wood. Back and forth. No thought required. His mind was free to wander anywhere. To wherever he'd left off reading before they'd hauled off to Mrs. Harrelson's house that morning. To the cities in the headlines in yesterday's newspapers that Victor Merritt brought to Graham Lindell each day.

Not that Jay wanted to think too much about the headlines. Bombs exploding. Planes going down.

Russians under siege. People dying. President Roosevelt kept promising to keep them out of the war, but he'd put troops in Greenland. Factories were turning out tanks for the Allied troops. Men were being drafted. Seemed to Jay the country was poised on the brink of falling into the conflict no matter what the politicians were saying. From what he read and heard, the average joe wasn't all that anxious to jump into the war. It was fine to supply the guns and ammunition, whatever it took, to stop the Germans, but that didn't mean they had to go over to do the shooting themselves. Let the English fight the war. They'd cheer them on from this side of the ocean.

He would have to go. Not to the war. Not if the president kept his word. But to serve. The draftees had to sign up for a year in the Army. A year wasn't so long. It wouldn't be pleasant. Not easy like standing in the sun slapping paint on a house, but he could do a year. He'd have to, since he figured it was only a matter of time before a draft notice caught up with him. Other men his age and younger were already being tapped on the shoulder by Uncle Sam. Even here in peaceful little Rosey Corner. Graham told him Carl Noland had joined up with the Navy before the draft could grab him. He was heading out for a training camp next week.

Jay dipped his brush in the paint and smoothed it on the rough board. The skin under his eye was still a funny purplish green from the punch he'd let that hayseed land on him. If he had it to do over, he might duck away from the guy's fist and land his own fist in the farm boy's midsection. That would have taken the air out of his overinflated sails. Help toughen him up for what he was sure to find in the service.

The early October sun reflecting off the white boards was heating up, and he looked around for a shaded spot that needed painting. Just till the sun began heading toward the horizon. But Graham had already grabbed the spot under the tree. Jay watched him a minute and wasn't sure but what he might be painting the same planks over again instead of moving out into the sun or climbing up a ladder. The man's old dog had scratched out a fresh hole back in the deep shade and was settled in behind him.

Jay was beginning to think Graham had been painting on this very same house all summer, but Mrs. Harrelson didn't seem to mind. She brought them ice water a couple of times a day and sometimes dragged a metal lawn chair around to sit and watch. Graham said she'd been a widow for three years. Jay was wondering if she was trying to snag a new husband in Graham, but when he suggested that, the man laughed and shook his head.

"My marrying days are long past. Poe and me, we're too old to learn new ways."

"Then it might be you ought to tell Mrs. Harrelson that, because I think she has a twinkle in her eyes when she's looking your way," Jay told him.

"Long as that twinkle don't catch fire. That happens, me and Poe, we'll be heading for the woods."

Graham was an interesting companion and the dog wasn't too stinky. Jay didn't regret the week he'd spent in Rosey Corner. It hadn't been so bad except for the black eye and the blisters from the paintbrush and the wasp stings on his ear from not swatting fast enough when he disturbed a nest up under the eaves of the house. Those kinds of things or worse could happen anywhere.

He did regret that Kate hadn't come around. He'd thought she would just out of curiosity. She knew he was still there. He and Graham went to the store for pop and bologna sandwiches at noon. Mrs. Harrelson didn't have enough of a twinkle in her eye to feed them lunch. But each time they went in the store, Kate kept disappearing back in the stockroom or out the front door with a box of groceries or who knew where. Anywhere but where she would have to say hello to him.

He might have begun to wonder if he'd lost his touch with the girls if some of the other Rosey Corner lovelies hadn't started finding reasons to walk past Mrs. Harrelson's house a few times a day. But not Kate. She wasn't the average girl. Already nineteen going on twenty and not worried about no ring on her finger. So not worried she'd sent her longtime beau packing. Off to the Navy without so much as a tear or so, one of the girls had told Jay the day before.

Alice, that was the girl's name. She claimed to be going on eighteen, but Jay had his doubts. He always moved over nearer to Graham when she sauntered up to the house. She was at that dangerous age, ready to leave behind being a kid but too young to really know what it meant to act like a woman. He didn't need that kind of trouble. But the girl wasn't happy simply flashing her eyes at him. She was a talker. Words spilled out of her like water through a sieve.

So he wasn't glad to look up and see her coming toward the house for the second time that day. Graham must have seen her coming too, because he actually grabbed a can of paint and climbed up the ladder to get away from talking to her. Jay didn't have any choice but to steady the ladder for the older man, which left him standing there, his ears way too open to the girl's chatter. She talked about everybody, but she kept coming back to Kate and the hayseed farm boy.

"Nobody understands it. We were all ready as anything for them to have a double wedding with Evangeline and Pastor Mike. But then that Kate goes and breaks poor Carl's heart." Alice pulled a sad face. "Broke it bad. But then, nothing Kate does surprises any of us."

"What's she done? Besides breaking Carl's heart?" Jay glanced over at her. She'd found some lipstick and smeared it on a little too thick. That plus the two bright spots of rouge on her cheeks made her look a little clownish. She wasn't bad looking, but she'd managed to completely hide that fact. Part of the problem of being too young.

She must have taken his question as a sign of interest, because she stepped closer and raised her eyebrows at him. "What hasn't she done?"

Jay thought about letting go of the ladder and retreating, but the ladder was worse than wobbly. It was one thing for him to take a chance of spilling off it, but if Graham fell, he might break his neck. The man wasn't all that old, but he wasn't all that young either. So Jay kept his hold on the ladder and on his smile as he tried to get the girl to put some space between them. "If I was you, I'd move back a ways. Graham can be sloppy with his paint. Some of it might splatter down here and ruin your dress."

Graham was acting like he was so busy painting he wasn't hearing what they were saying, but a couple of spots of paint landed on Jay's arm. Jay bit the inside of his lip to keep from grinning as he went on. "See? Not the best place to be standing. Could be Graham might even fall down on top of us, paint and all. This old ladder is pretty rickety."

"Oh, it looks plenty strong." Alice didn't give the ladder a glance. Her light brown eyes were fastened on Jay as she scooted a little closer. "But don't you want to know about Kate? You looked pretty interested at the wedding. Leastways Carl must have thought so." She brushed against his arm casually almost as if by accident, but there wasn't anything accidental about it.

Jay shifted to the side. If she moved after him, poor Graham would have to take his chances with the shaky ladder, because Jay would be in full retreat. "Just a little misunderstanding, that's all. Happens sometimes."

"And look what it got you. A black eye, poor thing." She reached toward his face, but Jay looked up to check on Graham just in time to avoid her fingers touching him. She let her hand settle on the ladder below his. "All because of Kate."

"She didn't sock me. Carl did."

"But she caused it. That's Kate. Always in the middle of any trouble."

"People have trouble here in Rosey Corner?" Jay laughed and tried to lighten the conversation. "Mike told me everything came up roses here."

"Oh well, that's what preachers are supposed to say."

"Really? I thought they were supposed to tell you what you were doing wrong and straighten you out. Get you back on the right track and all that kind of thing." He looked up. Graham was painting away, as industrious as he'd seen him all week.

"Well, some people are harder to keep on the right track than others." She leaned up against the ladder. "People like Kate."

Jay was letting go of the ladder to step back just as several large splatters of paint came raining down from above. Alice shrieked a little when a big blob of paint hit her right on the top of her head.

"Oops. Sorry, Alice," Graham called down to her. "I must've dipped out too much paint."

Alice gingerly touched the top of her head and then stared at the white tips of her fingers. It was all Jay could do to keep from laughing as he rubbed a splatter of paint off his own cheek onto his shoulder. "You better go on home and try to get that out, Alice."

Graham clambered down the ladder. He stopped on the second rung and peered at Alice's head. "Now don't you be worrying about that none, Alice. White hair looks right pretty. Mine's been that way for years." He stepped down to the ground and ran his hand through his hair. That made it stick up in even odder angles than usual and added a few streaks of white.

"Don't you have some kerosene here?" Alice asked.

"Nope." Graham lied with no hesitation. "Not a

bit. Me and the boy here, we don't mind being polka-dotted. We'll take a bath afore church on Sunday and get to looking respectable again." Graham glanced over at Jay. "Right, Jay?"

"Not much sense cleaning up while there's more painting to do." Jay picked up the paint can and brush and stepped away from the ladder. He wanted plenty of space between him and Alice.

"You could at least offer to wipe it out of my hair since you let the paint hit me." She directed her words over toward Jay.

"Well now, it wasn't the boy's fault. I was the one who spilled the paint on you," Graham said. "I can give it a try cleaning it off your head if you want me to." He jerked a handkerchief out of his pocket that looked like it might have been in that same pocket since last summer. He shook it a little, but it stayed bunched up, the cloth stuck together by who knew what.

Turning a little pale as he stepped toward her, Alice held up her hand to stop him. "That's all right. I'll run on home and let Mother help me." She peered around Graham to waggle paint-covered fingers at Jay. "I'll see you around, Jay."

"Sure thing." Jay gave her a quick look and went back to painting.

"You tell your mama how sorry I am," Graham called after her.

Jay waited until Alice was out of sight before he looked around at Graham. "You shouldn't ought to tell her to lie to her mother like that. You aren't one bit sorry."

"That's where you're wrong. I am sorry. Truly sorry I missed her nose. That's what I was aiming for."

"That wasn't very nice of you." Jay swallowed his smile.

"I'd heard all I wanted to hear of her nonsense." His voice was almost a growl as he went on. "Talking about our Kate like that."

Jay didn't say anything as he kept brushing on paint. Obviously Kate was good at getting people fired up. Thinking about her got him a little fired up too. But he didn't think he could claim her as his Kate the way Graham was doing.

"Come on over and take a break." Graham took a swig from the water jug and settled down in the shade next to his dog. "Maybe no more Rosey Corner hopefuls will be dropping by to make eyes at you for a spell."

"Mrs. Harrelson may come out to make eyes at you." Jay laid the brush on the top of the paint can.

"Nope. She's gone to Edgeville for more paint."

Jay took a drink and dropped down in the shade beside the old man. He looked back at the house. "How long you been painting on this house?"

"Oh, I don't know. I ain't one to count days. A job takes however long a job takes."

Jay squinted his eyes to count the unpainted

planks. Most of them in the full sun. The other side and the front were finished, but the back hadn't felt the first brush of paint yet. "How much longer you think this one might take?"

"It depends." Graham plucked up a broad piece of grass and put the end of it between his lips.

"On what?"

"Lots of things. The weather. If Mrs. Harrelson can afford to keep buying paint. You."

"Me?"

"How long you intend on sticking around. Whether you're one of those boys who ain't got no finish to him."

"No finish?" Jay turned to stare at Graham. "What are you talking about?"

Graham didn't seem bothered at all by Jay's frown. "How many jobs you quit in the last couple of years?"

"None that mattered whether I kept on with them or not. Anybody can dig a ditch or sling hash."

"Or paint a house."

"Or paint a house," Jay agreed.

"Never doing anything important gives a man a certain freedom. That's for sure. 'Cepting any job can be of some importance to somebody. Even painting a house. Mrs. Harrelson is right proud of the way it's looking, and in spite of myself, I'm admiring the job some too. Especially now that you're here to paint the eaves where the wasps hide out." He looked over at the house and chewed on his grass stem a minute before he went on. "I had a house. Bigger than this one here. Painted it once. Back before my folks passed. Didn't take me but a few weeks. I was young then. Younger even than you."

"Where is it? Here in Rosey Corner?"

"It was. It burned up some years back. When the woods over yonder burned." Graham waved toward the west. "The trees are coming back, but the house, it's gone forever."

"Tough luck for you," Jay said.

"Oh, it wasn't so bad. My memories didn't burn up. I worried some that might happen, but it didn't. And I made it out with the girls. Thanks to Poe here." Graham reached over and touched the dog's head. The dog opened his eyes and flapped his tail a couple of times against the dirt.

"The girls?"

"Kate and little Lorena. Maybe I'll tell you the story someday if you stick around long enough."

Jay wiped the sweat off his forehead with his shirttail and then stretched out on the ground with his hands under his head. "You could tell me now. While we're cooling off and watching the paint dry." Graham was an entertaining story-teller.

"Naw, you haven't earned that story yet."

"I have to earn stories?" Jay rose up a little to give Graham the eye. "I think we might have a

121

problem here. I thought I was working for cash."

Graham waved his hand. "I told you I'd give you half what I got. The stories are bonus. For both of us. Everybody round here has heard my stories way too many times. They're done tired of hearing how far Aunt Hattie's boy could hit a baseball or how me and Nadine were about the onliest ones not to get the flu back in '18. We about wore ourselves out tending to the sick. 'Course Victor was over there in France then, fighting the war."

Jay relaxed back down on the grass. He might never get the first dollar for this job, but sometimes it was good to simply stop awhile. "But what about Kate and the little sister?"

Graham didn't answer his question. Instead he took the stem of grass out of his mouth and fastened his eyes tight on Jay. "You seem awful interested in Kate. Egging on that gossipy Alice to talk about her."

"I was just trying to stop her thinking about stepping closer to me. Let me tell you, the next time she comes, I'm the one up the ladder."

Graham laughed. "You do seem to be drawing the female attention."

"Maybe it's you. Not me."

"That's a thought," Graham said.

An easy silence fell between them as a bee buzzed past and a mockingbird started running through his repertoire. Jay had almost dozed off when Graham spoke up again. "Thing is, the only girl who used to come around to make conversation while I was painting hasn't come near me all week."

"You mean Kate." Jay kept staring at the leaves above him. One shook loose in the breeze and floated down to land on his stomach.

"The two of you seemed plenty friendly at the wedding, but now she don't seem to want to let her eyes fall on you." Graham leaned forward and plucked up a new piece of grass. "You know any reason for that to be so?"

Jay chose his words carefully. He could move on down the road, but he liked Graham. He didn't want to part on bad terms, and it was easy to see he was Kate's champion. "Maybe she doesn't like looking at shiners."

"That could be it," Graham said. "It ain't a very pretty sight. Colorful and all as it is. But I'm thinking it might be something that happened before the black eye. What'd you do to scare that girl?"

Jay decided to be honest. "I asked her if I could kiss the sister of the bride, but then I got socked in the eye instead of kissed."

"But not by Kate."

"No, not by Kate."

"And now she's avoiding you like the plague." Graham's voice was low, almost like he was talking to himself.

"You could say that." Jay stared at the sun slipping through the leaves. If they didn't get up and start painting again soon, the day was going to be gone. But then Graham was the boss of this job, and if he wanted to talk about Kate, that was okay with Jay. He wanted to know more about Kate. That's why he was still in Rosey Corner. "Maybe she thinks I'm the one who's scary."

"Could be. Could be. Kate likes to think she can handle things." Graham looked over at Jay. "The question is, what are you going to do about it?"

"I don't know. What do you think I should do?" Another leaf came floating down to land on his chest. If he kept lying there doing nothing long enough, he might get covered up.

"Maybe nothing. According to whether you have honorable intentions."

"I wasn't thinking about marriage. Just a movie and maybe another slice of her mother's brown sugar pie."

"Nadine's pie is worth the trouble of taking a bath for Sunday dinner. That's for sure." Graham pushed himself up off the ground. "Guess we'd better paint another plank or two."

"Right." Jay stood up too, but before he could pick up his paintbrush, Graham stepped in front of him.

"Kate's one of a kind. You keep that in mind and don't be doing nothing I'm going to regret."

"You?"

"For making you this business deal. Seemed the thing to do at the time, but that was before I knew you might be a guy with no finish to you."

"I'll finish this job with you."

"Maybe you will." Graham gave him a hard stare, then he pointed up over their heads. "I lack some up there. Had to come down when I spilled that paint."

❦ 10 ❦

"So, Victoria tells me you threw over Carl." Evie smoothed out the skirt of the green dress she'd just unfolded and hung up on the hook behind the bedroom door. The dress was new. She looked around at Kate and snapped her fingers. "Just like that, she says. And look what that got you. Nowhere to go on a Saturday night."

It was the first time Evie had been home since the wedding. Now the house was in a stir as they figured out where Kate, Tori, and Lorena were going to sleep since they were giving over their bedroom to Evie and Mike. Mike had spent a lot of nights at the Merritt house, but he'd always slept on the couch—a visitor. He said he would again, but Evie stamped her foot and said absolutely not. Mama agreed with her. Even if it did cause an uproar.

Some things didn't change and Evie getting her way seemed to be one of them. Being married only made her a kind of honored guest with even more than her normal privileges. Next weekend Kate would take Lorena and go spend Saturday night with Aunt Gertie. Let Evie take over the house again. But tonight, Kate had been anxious to see her, to find out if she liked being married. To find out how it felt to be married. To find out if she herself was going to feel different.

She wanted to feel different. Mike was her sister's husband, a friend, her preacher. That was all. She'd been telling herself that for months, and this last week it seemed to finally be taking root in her head. When Mike's car had rolled into the yard that afternoon and he and Evie climbed out, Kate had simply looked at him with a weird kind of regret that she'd never find a man as good as Evie had.

That was Evie. Using her looks, claiming things to be her right as oldest daughter, demanding the best of whatever was up for grabs. Sometimes they fought about it, but Kate generally gave in. Life had always been easier that way. Besides, Kate was the middle sister—the one who had to make sure everybody got along.

But she had expected Evie to be different after she was married. Easier. Gentler. Not so ready to poke Kate with barbed words. To maybe be the one person besides Mama who understood about

Carl. All week at the store, people had been giving Kate the eye and stepping a little back from her like she might have something contagious.

Her mother told her not to worry about that. She said people were just surprised. That sometimes people got the wrong ideas in their heads about what ought to happen. Even though her mother understood and agreed that Kate couldn't marry Carl just because everybody in Rosey Corner thought she should, it was easy to see she was feeling sorry for him too. Everybody was feeling sorry for Carl.

Kate thought somebody should feel sorry for her. But it wasn't looking as if she was going to get any sympathy from Evie either. They were alone in the bedroom. Mike had gone to check on one of the elderly deacons, Mr. Blackwell, who'd been feeling poorly for a few weeks. Lorena and Tori were in the kitchen helping Mama get supper on the table. Kate had wanted these alone minutes with Evie to talk, but not to talk about Carl.

She sat down on the edge of the bed and ran her hands over the quilted spread. Aunt Gertie had cut the pieces out of old dresses and shirts. Kate's finger paused on a square of faded red. All that was left of a favorite dress when she was Lorena's age. She'd worn it until there were holes under the sleeves. But it had been Evie's dress first. Everything was Evie's first.

Kate held in a sigh as she said, "Carl wanted me

to marry him." Evie would have to hear the whole story and then tell her how she should have done it better.

"No surprise there. The two of you have been dating for years." Evie unclipped her earrings and dropped them in a dish on the dresser. She peered into the mirror, then picked up a brush to smooth out the ridges her hat had left in her hair.

"We've been friends for years. I never thought we were dating."

Evie paused in her brushing to stare at Kate's reflection in the mirror. "Come on, Kate. You knew he didn't think that. The boy's been crazy about you forever."

"You're right. I should have told him sooner. But I like Carl. It was fun doing stuff with him."

"Kissing stuff?" Evie raised her eyebrows at Kate in the mirror.

"No, of course not." Kate frowned back at her.

"You're almost twenty, Kate. Surely you've done some kissing." Evie started pushing little waves into her hair with her fingers.

"I've never met anybody I wanted to kiss." That wasn't exactly true, but she couldn't very well tell her sister how most of her teenage dreams of kissing starred her new husband. Then again there was that moment of temptation with Jay Tanner, but no way was she going to let Evie know about that. Everybody had a weak moment now and again that meant nothing.

"Oh, but kissing is so divine." Evie sighed and hugged the brush up against her chest. She spun around in a circle before plopping down on the bed beside Kate. "It is all so divine." She lay back on the bed and stretched her arms over her head with a blissful look on her face.

"So your wedding night was all right? You weren't scared?" Kate looked at her. "When Mama gave us the talk, you acted a little nervous."

"I know. It all sounds so . . ." Evie hesitated, a flush coloring her cheeks as she sat back up. "I don't know, so something when you talk about it. But when you're with someone you love, it turns into something divine. Two becoming one like the Bible says."

"Good. I'm glad you're happy, Evie." Kate reached over for Evie's hand. "Really glad."

"You're not jealous?" Evie leaned in front of Kate to look straight into her eyes.

"No. Why would I be jealous?" Kate frowned a little.

"Because I'm in love and you're not. Because I found out about all this first."

"You're oldest. You were supposed to get married first."

"Because there's only one Mike."

"You're right there." Kate kept her voice even. "Mike is a great guy and I may never find anybody half as nice as him, but can you really see me as a preacher's wife?"

Evie giggled. "Or me either, for that matter."

"But that's what you are now. Mama says it won't be an easy spot for you, and she should know. Being a preacher's daughter like she was."

"I know, but I'll figure it out. With Mike's help and Mama's." Evie squeezed Kate's hand. "And yours. If those church ladies give me trouble, I'll let you straighten them out."

"I can do it."

They both laughed then, sharing unspoken memories of all the times Kate had been in hot water with the church ladies for being too ready to speak her mind. Kate's laugh faded away. "The church ladies aren't too happy with me now. They were all set to eat wedding cake again with Carl and me. Now he's going off to the Navy and everybody thinks I'm heartless."

"Heartless Kate." Evie was still smiling.

Kate dropped her head so Evie wouldn't see how those words hurt her.

Evie put her arm around her shoulders and gave her a little shake. "I didn't mean it, you nut. You have the biggest heart of anybody I know. Except Mike, of course. But you, Kate, you love everybody. Just look at Lorena still thinking you're an angel half the time. And what about Graham? Anybody who can love that old man and his mangy dog has to have a big heart."

"Graham's a great guy."

"Yeah, I know. You've been telling me that for

years." Evie rolled her eyes. "He needs to take more baths, is all I'm going to say."

"Well, that could be. But he says Poe doesn't care how he smells." Kate stared down at her hands and pushed out her next words. "Do you think that's the way I'll end up? Never finding somebody to love?"

"Good golly, no. You'll find somebody right for you someday, Kate." Evie stood up and pulled Kate to her feet. "And then you'll know what I'm talking about. How loving somebody can make you feel like you're floating on butterfly wings." She laughed again and spun Kate around with her. "Divine. I think that's going to be my new favorite word."

Just then Lorena pushed open the bedroom door and ran in, her face lit up with excitement. "Kate! Kate! Tanner's here. Mike brought him home with him."

"Tanner?" Evie looked puzzled. "Have you gotten a dog?"

Lorena put her hand over her mouth and giggled.

"What's so funny?" Evie asked.

"No dog, although Lorena would like that. She means Jay Tanner, Mike's friend. His best man at the wedding." Kate tapped her finger against Evie's forehead. "Remember? Dark hair, brown eyes."

"Devil-may-care look. Not the kind of guy I thought would show up as Mike's best friend, I have to admit. I guess I didn't remember his name." Evie frowned a little at Lorena. "Why are you calling him Tanner?"

Lorena slid her eyes over to Kate as she said, "He told me to."

"And I told you Mr. Tanner would be better." Kate gave her a stern look.

Lorena ducked her head, but her grin didn't disappear.

"What's he still doing here? I thought Mike said he was on his way to Chicago or somewhere to look for work," Evie said.

The men's voices were drifting back to them from the porch where they must have settled down to talk. Kate's father laughed, and then there was the familiar sound of Mike's voice and the lower tones that belonged to Jay Tanner. Kate's heart did a funny little chug at the sound. She'd been avoiding him all week, but she couldn't very well slip out the back door and run away from her own house. She'd have to sit at the supper table with him looking at her and remembering how she'd almost let him kiss her.

"He found work here." Kate kept her voice casual. "He's helping Graham paint Mrs. Harrelson's house."

Lorena laughed again. "Tanner says he doesn't think Graham's too interested in getting the job done. He says Graham must be sweet on Mrs.

Harrelson. Either that or he likes the sugar cookies she's been baking for them."

"I'd bet on the sugar cookies," Kate said. "Graham's not about to let any woman catch him."

"No," Evie agreed, wrinkling her nose up. "He might have to take a bath."

The screen door slammed and then Mike was calling, "Where's my beautiful wife?" He came back into the bedroom, his face lighting up at the sight of Evie. He grabbed her close to him and dropped a kiss down on her lips as though they'd been apart for days instead of less than an hour.

She pushed him back. "Mike, the girls."

He looked at Kate and Lorena and then lowered his voice to a stage whisper as he turned back to Evie. "You did tell them we're married, didn't you? Oh that's right. They were there."

"Oh, stop being silly." Evie hit him lightly on the arm.

"Never will I stop being silly over you." He was staring straight into Evie's eyes.

Kate could see Evie almost melting against him. She put her hand on Lorena's shoulder. "Maybe we'd better go see if Mama needs help setting the table. Did you tell her we had an extra guest or is Jay staying to eat?" Kate looked at Mike.

"Of course he's staying," Mike said. "I told him your mother might have made a brown sugar pie."

"Nope," Lorena said. "Apple dumplings."

"Even better. He'll think he's died and gone to heaven," Mike said. "He says he's been living on bologna and beans. I figured he'd been down here begging supper every night, but he says not. Says he's just been hanging out with Graham and his old dog. But Graham was headed out to the woods to sit on a log somewhere and pretend that Poe wasn't too old to track down a raccoon tonight. So Jay was at loose ends."

"He didn't want to go hunting with Graham? I can't imagine why not."

"Me either," Kate said, with none of Evie's sarcasm. She wished she were sitting on that log beside Graham, listening to his stories while they waited for Poe to start baying somewhere in the woods.

Mike laughed. "Jay never was one much for hunting four-legged creatures. He was more interested in girl chasing. Come to think of it, I'm surprised some girl hasn't already made eyes at him and talked him into taking her somewhere. Jay's never had trouble getting girls. Keeping them maybe, but not getting them."

Lorena piped up. "Oh, the girls have been after him. Graham says they've been parading past Mrs. Harrelson's house every afternoon, but Alice Wilcher is the worst. Graham said he had to drop paint on her head the other day to get rid of her."

"Drop paint on her head? How did he manage

that?" Kate tried not to laugh, but the thought of Alice with paint running down her head was too much. Alice's father was a lawyer in Frankfort, and she was always letting everybody else know how much better her things were than anybody else's. So maybe she had some better shampoo.

"I don't know. But he did. Said she was a mite upset." Lorena laughed too.

"You two are terrible," Evie said. "Poor Alice." But she couldn't keep from laughing with them.

"Girls, girls," Mike called them down with a smile that gave lie to his words. "Show a little compassion. Alice isn't that bad."

"Oh yes, she is," Kate and Evie said in concert.

"I hear compassion has been in short supply this week around here anyway." Mike looked straight at Kate.

"Oh?" Kate knew what he was talking about, but pretended not to. If it had been anybody but Mike, she would have said she didn't want to talk about it, but you couldn't tell a preacher that, or a new brother-in-law.

"I hear you gave poor Carl the old heave-ho. His mother ran me down at Mr. Blackwell's. She says he's feeling pretty low about leaving for the Navy and other things too, I'm thinking." Mike lifted his eyebrows in a kind of unspoken question.

"I'm sure he'll tell you all about it, and if he doesn't, plenty of others here in Rosey Corner will be delighted to let you know all about your heartless sister-in-law." Kate couldn't keep an edge of bitterness out of her voice.

"Maybe I'd better squeeze out some time for a talk with you too." Mike had his pastor face full-on.

"I'm fine, Mike." The last thing Kate wanted to do was talk about her love life or lack of one with her new brother-in-law. "Really."

"She is, Mike," Evie said. "And if she needs to talk, I'm here."

"Me too," Lorena added, wrapping her arms around Kate's waist.

"The Merritt sisters. Arms linked, an invincible force against the world." Mike shook his head as he turned Evie toward the door. "Come on. Jay will think I got lost. Then again, he might not have even noticed. He and your dad were talking H. G. Wells."

Evie groaned, but Kate hoped they'd keep talking science fiction books. Creatures from the deep or outer space were better than everybody wanting to know about Carl. Or her.

She started on back to the kitchen, but Lorena grabbed her arm and pulled her toward the porch. "You've got to say hello. Tanner asked about you as soon as he got here."

"That he did." Mike's smile faded a little as he looked at Kate like he'd just thought of something that was worrying him. Like maybe there might not be enough apple dumplings for everybody.

Kate lifted her chin. She wasn't afraid to look Jay Tanner in the face again. She had no idea why her throat was feeling tight and her heart was beating up in her ears. She had absolutely no reason to feel nervous. For one thing, she had no intention of being alone with him again. That way she couldn't be tempted the way she'd been the day of the wedding. The best way to stay out of trouble was to avoid it. That's why she'd been doing a disappearing act every time she caught the first glimpse of Jay Tanner all week. That's why she hadn't been to see Graham once even though she missed talking to him. That's why she was plastering a smile across her face now when she couldn't go out the back door and stay out of sight of his laughing brown eyes. She'd never been around a guy who made her feel so uneasy.

The book talk didn't keep him from standing and fastening his eyes on her as soon as she stepped through the door. Lorena tugged her across the porch toward him.

"See, Tanner. I told you she was here." Lorena looked back at Kate. "He thought you might be off on a date or something."

"Not tonight." Kate smiled politely as she met his eyes. She couldn't just stare at the floor all night. "So glad you could come join us for supper, Mr. Tanner."

"Mr. Tanner?" Mike laughed behind her.

Jay laughed too, but he didn't shift his eyes from Kate to Mike. "Miss Merritt and I have a very formal relationship. Comes from meeting at a wedding all dressed up in fancy clothes, I suppose. But I did think we'd decided to be on a first-name basis."

"Just trying to set a good example for Lorena," Kate said. "She seems to keep forgetting the mister in your name."

It got too quiet on the porch then. An uneasy quiet that matched the unease inside Kate. Even her father was looking at her like he was noticing something about her he hadn't ever seen before. The only one who didn't seem bothered was Lorena. "Daddy says it's okay if Tanner says it's okay."

"Birdie and I have an agreement on names." Jay flashed a look between Lorena and Mike and then settled his eyes back on Kate.

Lorena giggled. "Evie thought I was talking about a dog when I said Tanner was here."

Jay laughed, an easy sound that somehow reached out and made the uneasy feeling vanish. "Tanner. That is a good dog's name. I'll have to remember that if I ever get an old hound like Poe. Or could be, I'll get a girl dog and name her Birdie."

"I wish I had a dog," Lorena said. "I'd name him Scout."

"Maybe someday, Lorena," Daddy said. "If we

put up a fence to keep him off the road. Cars go by here too fast."

Lorena pulled a sad face. "Poe doesn't get run over."

"Poe never leaves Graham's shadow," Kate said. "You know that."

"I could teach Scout never to leave mine." She looked over at Daddy.

Kate noted the beginning of a worried frown on his face. He didn't like to deny Lorena anything. "Dogs aren't always that easy to train, but like Daddy says, someday." She put her hand on the girl's shoulder. "We'd better go help Mama now."

Her mother put the extra leaf in the kitchen table to make it bigger, but they were still elbow to elbow as the nine of them sat around the table. Sammy and Tori had been over at Graham's pond fishing, but showed up in time for supper. They didn't have enough chairs, but her father brought in a milk can and Lorena perched on its top at the corner of the table right next to Jay Tanner. She was captivated by him. Completely captivated.

Talk and laughter filled the kitchen. Nobody seemed to mind being a little crowded or that the heat from the cookstove lingered in the air. A kind of sparkle of happiness hung over the table. A growing family together. A visitor welcomed. Kate didn't say much. She simply soaked in the good feel. There'd been times not too long ago when meals weren't always easy. That was before her father quit drinking.

Kate hardly ever thought about those times anymore. The times when she'd had to help her father into the house and to the couch after he'd been out drinking. She looked at her father at the head of the table now, smiling, proud, sober for good. Her parents had forged a new and stronger partnership of love after they'd taken Lorena into the family. And now they were taking Mike in, and not so far from now, Sammy would be marrying Tori. They were planning on the day after Tori graduated from high school.

Tori would probably beat her to the altar. Maybe Lorena too. In spite of Evie saying that Kate would find the right man to love, Kate had no assurance that would ever happen. Not as long as she stayed in Rosey Corner, and how could she leave? She belonged in this place. She wasn't someone like Jay Tanner, who could drift from place to place because he had no roots. She had roots. Deep roots.

As if he knew she was thinking about him, his eyes settled on her. Then Lorena was slipping off her makeshift chair and coming around to put her hand on Kate's arm. "Please, Kate. Say you will. Please."

Kate had been so deep in her own thoughts that she hadn't paid attention to what was being said at the table. "Say I will what?"

"Go to the matinee tomorrow. Tanner says he'll take me, but Mama says I can't go unless you go too." Lorena jerked on Kate's sleeve. "You have to say yes. They're showing that new movie, *The Maltese Falcon*. You said you wanted to see it and now you don't have Carl to take you." Lorena made a little face. "Guess I shouldn't have said that. But please, Kate. Please, pretty please."

Kate looked across the table at Jay.

"It's just a movie." He shrugged a little.

She could feel the others watching her with some of that same uneasiness that had been out on the porch. She decided this time she'd be the one to make it go away. "Sure, why not? Sounds like fun."

Jay smiled and everybody started eating the apple dumplings again. The only one whose smile didn't come back right away was Mike. He was looking at Jay with the nearest thing to a frown Kate had seen on his face for weeks.

When they finally pushed away from the table and her father and the other guys headed out to the porch, Mike hung back to hand Kate his dirty plate. "Maybe we better have that talk after all, Kate. Think you can show up a few minutes early to church in the morning?"

"I guess." Kate stacked his plate on the others she was taking off the table. "But Mike, I couldn't marry Carl. I know everybody feels sorry for him and thinks I led him on, but I didn't.

Not really. I kept telling him we were friends."

"This isn't about Carl. There's something else I need to talk to you about." He kept his voice low, as though he didn't want anybody else to overhear them.

"Why can't we just talk here?" Kate piled some forks and spoons on the plates.

"Some things are easier to talk out when nobody else is around."

Kate gave in. "All right. I'll be there." Kate had been called in for stern lectures and prayers plenty of times while her Grandfather Reece was the preacher, but never before had Mike thought it necessary to pray over her. Then again maybe this was nothing to do with her, but something about Evie. Something he needed to know to keep Evie thinking divine thoughts.

Could things get any more uncomfortably confusing?

❦ 11 ❦

"I should have let Evangeline talk to you." Mike shifted his eyes away from Kate's face and ran his fingers over the Bible he was holding.

Kate had shown up early for church the way he'd asked and found him waiting for her out by the rock fence between the church and the cemetery. Not exactly a private spot, but his church members knew not to bother Mike if he was under what they called his praying tree.

Mike had on his pastor face, the one everybody in Rosey Corner loved. A kind face. Not condemning. Concerned. Mike loved his people. Faults and all. He worked hard to help them figure out ways to get past those faults and begin a better Christian walk, but he didn't make anybody feel that a backward step was going to end any chance of God loving them.

But now standing with her in the shade of the big oak, he seemed at a total loss for words. She'd heard him pray plenty of times, though not usually for her and her alone. His words were generally simple but sincere. Something like Aunt Hattie's prayers but with a touch of preacher formality in them. Aunt Hattie had a way of raising her eyes toward the sky and talking to God like she could see him sitting right there on his throne chair, bent down listening.

Kate was beginning to wish Aunt Hattie was standing there in the shade of Mike's prayer tree with them. She'd get things going. Kate tried to think of what Aunt Hattie might say, what Bible verse she'd pull out to bring the Lord's words into the conversation, but nothing came to mind. Instead Kate waited while Mike shifted uneasily on his feet and stared out toward the cemetery.

Finally she couldn't keep from prodding him. "Is it something about Evie? Has she been wanting to buy too much? She's sometimes not too sensible about money." Kate was fishing for something.

Mike looked back at her and smiled. "No, no. I don't care what Evangeline buys. I'd get her the moon if I could."

"Then what are you wanting to talk to me about? If it's not Carl and it's not Evie." Kate frowned up at him. People were showing up for Sunday school and sending curious glances back their way.

"I should have talked to Jay instead of you." He let out a long breath. "This is making me feel like a heel."

"What do you mean?"

"I mean that I love Jay like a brother, but that doesn't mean I'd want my sister to fall for him." Mike placed his hand on her shoulder and fastened his eyes on her face. "Jay's not your settling-down kind. I don't want you to get hurt, Kate, and I think that could happen if you start going out with Jay."

"The movies weren't my idea." Kate didn't shy away from his look. "That was Mama giving in to Lorena."

"I know that. Your mother doesn't know Jay either."

"What's so bad about him?" Kate was curious

now. Jay had told her Mike was his best friend, but he wasn't sounding much like any kind of friend. "I could tell right off he was a charmer, and I didn't figure there was any way he'd stick around here at all. But then he did. Graham seems to like him well enough."

"Everybody likes Jay. Well, everybody except the ones who want to punch him in the face the way Carl did."

"You can't blame Jay for that. Carl was imagining things that weren't happening," Kate said. "Jay didn't do a thing to provoke him. In fact, he stood there and let Carl sock him without putting up the first bit of fight. Said he was trying to keep the peace the way he knew you would be doing if you were there."

"You think I'm sounding disloyal to a friend, don't you?" Mike didn't wait for her to answer as he pulled his hand off her shoulder and ran it through his hair. He was going to need a comb before he got behind the pulpit. "I guess I am, but my first loyalty, after the Lord, is to Evangeline and my new family. To you and Victoria and Lorena."

"You didn't marry us all, Mike. Just Evie."

"But you're my sisters now the same as you're Evangeline's. Jay has left a string of broken hearts everywhere he's been. He can't commit to anybody or anything. It has to do with the way he was raised. Farmed out to an aunt and uncle who thought he was nothing but an obligation. He's never truly trusted anybody."

"Not even you?"

"Not enough." A worried frown wrinkled the skin on Mike's broad forehead. "He shuts his ears when I tell him about God's love. He doesn't want to hear it. He says he doesn't need the Lord." Mike's frown got deeper, more concerned. "You don't want to tie yourself to a man like that. A man who's afraid to love God or anybody else."

"I'm not going to fall for Jay. I've made enough mistakes in love already." Kate wished those last words back, but if Mike had any idea that they might refer to him, he didn't show it. He had probably forgotten her juvenile confession of love long ago. She went on quickly to put those words behind her and out of both their minds. "Now, Lorena might be a different matter. I think she's completely smitten. That's the only reason I'm going to the movies. To make Lorena happy." She smiled up at Mike, hoping he would let the whole matter drop.

"You won't always be able to shield Lorena from unhappiness." He gave his head a little shake. "But that's a different sermon for a different day."

"And you need to go get ready for your sermon for this day. Everybody will be anxious to hear if being married has made you a different preacher," Kate said lightly.

"Being married makes you a different everything." Mike smiled, but then his smile faded. "Just be careful who you give your heart to, Kate. I, and Evangeline too, we want you to be happy. The way you want Lorena to be happy."

"Didn't you tell us once that the word for 'blessed' in the Bible could be translated happy? Happy are the children of God." Kate felt a little embarrassed. "I don't know if that's really in the Bible or not."

"It's in there dozens of times in a dozen different ways. The Lord wants to give us the desires of our heart. Evangeline and I will pray that you will find the man the Lord has in mind for you." He had on his pastor's face again. "Prayers are answered."

"But not always as we expect."

"The Lord knows best."

Those were words she knew better than to argue with. The Lord did know best, and he had chosen Mike to deliver his message to the people. To her. It always amazed Kate how quickly Mike could change from being just Mike to being Pastor Mike. Even his voice changed, got deeper and fuller when he let the Lord's truths flow through him out to his Rosey Corner sheep. He knew them all well by now, after five years of standing in their pulpit and putting his feet under their Sunday dinner tables. He'd prayed by their sick beds and preached the funerals of those who'd crossed the great divide.

Kate knew them all too. In a different way. She'd grown up in the church. Believed and was baptized by her grandfather years ago. She belonged here. But when she and Mike stepped away from the shade of the tree to join the people congregating in the front yard and she saw Carl coming up the walkway with his mother, she wished she could be anywhere but here. Carl was staring straight at her, defiant in his anger. She squared her shoulders and kept walking. Nobody had ever accused Kate Merritt of being a coward. She wasn't about to let them do so now.

"Will wonders never cease?" Mike whispered under his breath as they moved toward the church steps. "I never expected to see him sitting in a Rosey Corner church pew."

"Who?" Kate asked, but then knew without him answering.

Jay and Graham were coming up the walk behind Carl. She sent up a quick prayer that Carl wouldn't spot Jay and start a fight right in the middle of the churchyard. Jay didn't look worried as he shot an amused smile her way. Rosey Corner was obviously proving very entertaining for him.

"I hope the good Lord gives me the right message," Mike said, more to himself than to Kate.

"You'd better hope Carl doesn't forget he's at church and try to punch Jay again," Kate said.

"He had the crazy idea Jay was the reason I told him I couldn't marry him."

"Was he?" Mike had on his pastor face again.

"No. Carl was the reason I couldn't marry Carl."

Kate wished she could go on home or, even better, keep walking past her house to Lindell Woods. At least there nobody would be staring at her like she was Delilah betraying Samson. Without waiting for Mike to say anything more, she rushed up the steps and into the church. Maybe she was a coward after all. She wanted no part of whatever might be going to happen in the churchyard. Instead she'd sit inside and hope Mike was as good at keeping the peace as Jay thought he was.

Kate was glad when her mother slipped into the pew beside her and squeezed her hand. Her mother always understood. It was a gift she had. Lorena scooted in between them—her favorite spot with Mama on one side and Kate on the other.

She had an excited gleam in her eyes when she whispered to Kate, "He's here. Did you see him?"

"I saw him," Kate said.

"Do you think he'll come sit with us?"

"You know Graham never sits this close to the front. He likes the back row and Jay will sit with him."

Lorena looked disappointed for a flash, but then

her face was shining with excitement again. "I can't wait until this afternoon. Can you?"

"Shh, we're in church." Kate hushed her to keep from answering. The thing was, she did feel a tremble of excitement when she thought about the movies that afternoon. Something she'd never felt with Carl. Something Mike had just been warning her against feeling. A warning she knew she should take seriously. But at the same time, she couldn't quite stop thinking about Jay.

She peeked over her shoulder at the other people coming into the church to settle into the pews. Jay was watching her, waiting for her to look his way. Ready to laugh. Refusing to take life seriously in spite of his eye still showing evidence that sometimes life could knock him down. She quickly turned her head around, but not before she saw Carl staring at her from across the church aisle.

She felt sorry for him. In spite of the way he had forced a kiss on her. In spite of the way he had turned her into the villain of the piece. She felt sorry for him the same as everybody else in Rosey Corner. She didn't want to, but she did. And now he was going off to who knew where with the war clouds thickening. Why in the world had he decided to join the Navy? German submarines were sinking ships without paying any attention to what flag might be flying on their mast. Navy men were on ships.

Somebody had come in the store a couple of days back and said Carl claimed to want to see the world. Kate knew the words were intended for her. She'd be stuck in Rosey Corner, measuring out beans or slicing cheese and bologna while he'd be seeing the sights. The same places she'd read about and wondered aloud about to him many times. Kate stared down at her hands as Mr. Jackson stepped up behind the podium to announce the number of the first hymn. Sometimes life could throw a left hook that didn't leave marks on the outside, but bruised plenty on the inside.

The songs ended. The offering plates were passed. Mike stepped up to the pulpit and opened his Bible. For a moment, he looked uneasy, but then he made a joke about being glad to welcome Mrs. Champion to Rosey Corner Baptist Church for the first time. Evie blushed prettily right on cue and a laugh rippled through the church. Mike laughed too and kept smiling as he added how glad he was to see Jay there.

Then without further ado, he switched over to his pastor voice and began preaching about Saul on the road to Damascus. He told the story with power and gentleness both. "That's how it is with each of us. Every man, woman, child. We begin our journey of life one way and somewhere along that road we are all confronted with the Savior. While we might not be struck physically blind as Saul was, we are all blind in spiritual ways until we open our eyes to Jesus and let him take control of our hearts."

Kate listened, glad that it was always Pastor Mike she saw behind the pulpit. A man sharing the Word of God. She wondered how Evie saw Mike this morning now that she was his wife. And Jay. Would he think Mike was preaching the message for him? Wasn't that how it was supposed to feel when a person was hearing a sermon? Weren't the preacher's words supposed to be convicting each heart in whatever way they needed? But according to Mike, Jay had never wanted to hear the gospel. Yet he was sitting in the church now, hearing the gospel preached by his best friend.

Sitting on a church pew didn't necessarily mean he was hearing the Word. Wasn't she sitting there wondering about everything except how she should change to be a better Christian? She should have pretended she was sick and headed out for those trees.

She was glad when Mike announced the invitation hymn. She wasn't as glad when Mrs. Noland stepped out into the aisle on the first verse and grabbed Carl's arm to pull him along down to the front with her. After a whispered conversation with Carl's mother, Mike held up his hand to stop the singing.

"Our brother, Carl Noland, will be leaving for the Navy on Tuesday. We all know that while our country is maintaining a neutral stance, things are very dire overseas. As Carl's church family, we can covenant to pray for him and all the soldiers being drafted into service." Mike looked very serious. "While Mrs. Taylor continues to play, I know you will want to come up and let Carl know you will be supporting him with your prayers."

Kate stood up with everyone else and joined the line going down to speak to Carl. What else could she do? She reminded herself once more that she wasn't a coward. But her heart was beating too hard even before she stepped up in front of Mrs. Noland. With a scowl on her face, the woman yanked her hand back when Kate reached toward her. Kate kept her hand suspended in the air, not sure what to do next. Her mother put an arm around her and scooted her on over in front of Carl.

A sudden silence fell over the church. Everybody knew Kate had thrown Carl over.

Mama kept her arm firmly around Kate's waist as she reached out and grasped Carl's hand with her free hand. She filled the void. "We're proud of you, Carl, for stepping up to serve your country. We'll keep you in our prayers."

Kate looked straight at Carl. She hated being the reason for the hurt anger in his eyes. She wanted to forget how he'd shoved her against the tree and forced a kiss on her. She wanted to go back to when they were wading in the creek catching frogs. To any time before last Sunday. She managed to smile and whisper, "We will."

She was turning away when he grabbed her arm. For a minute she thought he might be going to apologize for the way he'd acted, but instead he said, "I'll send you a card from Hawaii."

"Is that where you're going?" Kate kept her voice even.

"Maybe. After training."

"I've read it's beautiful there."

"One thing sure, it's far from Rosey Corner and some place you'll never go." The corners of his lips turned up in what was closer to a grimace than a smile. "You could have, but you passed up your chance. You passed up your chance for a lot of good things."

Kate's mother began to ease her away from Carl. Kate hesitated. A week ago she could have hugged Carl, kissed his cheek, and wished him all the best, but not now. So she merely touched her hand on his arm lightly and said, "Goodbye, Carl."

Her words carried a sad echo of the angry goodbye she'd told him a week ago. Some things couldn't be changed.

❧ 12 ❧

Jay didn't go forward to shake Carl's hand. He was tempted to, but there were times when even somebody like him had to exercise good sense. The farm boy had packed quite a punch, and Jay didn't need another black eye. He did want to be able to watch the movie that afternoon, or at least watch the girl with him at the movie.

He'd been watching her all morning. Blatantly, before Mike went to preaching. Covertly during the sermon. He listened with half an ear to what Mike was saying. He figured he was pushing the Scripture words right at him, but no way was Jay expecting any Damascus Road turnarounds in his life. Maybe if the Lord did speak out loud to him, blind him with light, he'd be like Saul and ready to pay attention. But Jay had doubts the Lord was all that worried about converting him. Saul was a different matter. The man got a new name and went on to write half the New Testament.

Jay had spent plenty of hours in church with his aunt and uncle. He'd heard hundreds of sermons and seen all those pictures of the good Lord knocking on doors and wanting to come in. Jay figured his heart door was too thick for him to hear any knocking. That was okay. A person needed a tough heart. He'd found that out soon enough after his mother died.

But his heart was feeling some softer every time he looked at Kate. She hadn't looked back toward him but once, and that time she'd flipped her head back around and brushed her hand through her hair as though to knock his eyes off her. That wasn't about to happen. In fact, his eyes were so ready to settle on her that he was beginning to think maybe he should pack up his things and hit the road. She had him feeling like he might be tiptoeing around quicksand.

When Mike called for everybody to go up and pray for the hayseed, Jay stepped to the back of the church. Graham shrugged his shoulders a little and joined the queue going forward. Kate stepped out into the line too, her step a little hesitant, but her mother and the kid sister pushed her along with them. The tension was palpable in the church when she stepped up to the hayseed's mother. No forgiveness on that woman's face. Then Carl grabbed Kate's arm to keep her from turning away from him.

For a second, Jay wondered if they were going to hear an impassioned proposal right there at the church altar to try to force Kate's acceptance. An uneasy silence fell over the church. About halfway down the aisle, Graham's shoulders stiffened and his head came up like his old dog catching a scent of trouble in the air. Across the church, Kate's father turned away from the man beside him to stare down toward the front of the church too. Jay leaned back against the wall behind the back pew and tried to look relaxed. There wouldn't be any need for him to rush down to Kate's aid with both Graham and Mr. Merritt ready to do battle for her.

The farm boy's voice was too loud, his words harsh. He wasn't about to let Kate off easy, letting her know, letting the whole church know, she'd lost her chances with him. Jay couldn't hear her words back to Carl. They were too soft, but the whispered echo of regret wasn't hard to hear. That was the trouble with being well loved the way Kate was. The way Mike was. People like them struggled when somebody was mean-spirited. The same kind of things rolled right off Jay. He didn't have to be liked.

He did tighten his hand into a fist and think about how he owed the hayseed a punch in the nose. But not in Mike's church. Not when the man was up there collecting prayers before going off to the Navy. Jay stretched his fingers out and shook them a little. The best thing for him to do was step outside. Let whatever happened happen. It was none of his business.

But he couldn't keep from smiling a little as he heard Kate telling the man goodbye. There was a final sound to it. A sound Jay liked. A sound that seemed to release the church people to start talking again. At the door, Mike began to shake the hands of the people who'd already talked to the hayseed and his mother and were headed out.

Jay waited his turn. Mike grasped his hand and gave him his preacher talk. "So glad to see you here this morning, Jay."

"Couldn't pass up the chance to hear my buddy preach."

"Did I do it right?"

"You're asking me?" Jay laughed and pulled his hand free. "You better ask the man upstairs that question."

"But it's the men down here who have to hear." Mike's eyes probed Jay's face. "That's why the Bible stories are there for us. So his Word won't come back void."

"I'm sure your words reached those they were supposed to reach," Jay said easily. He'd survived a lot of one-on-one sermons from Mike. He didn't mind. It was proof his friend cared about him. That didn't mean Jay had to rush down a church aisle and pretend something that hadn't happened.

Mike pressed his lips together for a second before he said, "Someday you may come face-to-face with the Lord the way Paul did and be unable to shut him away."

"Who knows, Reverend? You could be right."

"No could be about it. I am right about that. Be

assured the Lord will never give up on you and neither will I." Mike gave Jay a hard look, but then his smile was popping out again for the person next in line. Jay had had his handshake and word with the preacher.

That was fine with Jay. He was ready to be out in the sunshine, but once out there he didn't hang around to wait for Graham or to see if he might wangle an invite to the Merritts' Sunday dinner. He didn't belong there in the churchyard among all the families clustered in groups, planning their times together. He didn't belong anywhere except maybe in his car out on the open road.

But he did keep his promises and he'd promised Birdie a movie.

They were on the porch waiting when he showed up at their house a couple of hours later. As soon as he killed the motor, Birdie ran down the porch steps toward his car, excitement practically exploding out of her eyes. Kate didn't show the same eagerness, but she was smiling. She didn't appear to be hanging on to any lasting effects from the hayseed doing his best to humiliate her in church.

It was a half hour's drive to Edgeville. Kate made sure to put the kid between them on the car seat and then at the movies. She was keeping him at arm's length.

Birdie didn't notice. She was full of chatter in the car that covered up any awkwardness between

Jay and Kate and then entranced by the movie. Jay was entranced too. Not by the movie. He barely noticed the actors moving across the screen. The girl two seats over was the one grabbing his eyes. He watched her face in the flickering light from the screen and had the feeling she knew he was watching her instead of the movie, but she kept her eyes on the screen. Very casually, he draped his arm over the back of the kid's seat and let his fingers graze against Kate's shoulder on the other side of Birdie.

She didn't shift in her seat away from him. A good sign. But a sign of what? That she liked his touch or that she was so engrossed in the movie she didn't even notice? The kid squealed and covered her eyes as one of the actors on the screen almost got shot. Kate leaned over to whisper something to her, and her hair brushed against his hand. A tingle shot through his arm straight to his heart.

He jerked his hand back almost like he'd been burned. And he was playing with fire. He'd done that as a kid. Experimented with what he could feed into a fire to make the flames flash up brightest. He wasn't a firebug. He'd never wanted to set any buildings on fire or anything like that. Not even old haystacks that a lot of the other boys had thought were simply waiting for their matches. He just wanted to know what would make the fire burn hottest or what would make the blackest smoke. He'd lost his eyebrows once to the idiotic idea of pitching a pint jar of gasoline on a fire, but he'd learned. He'd always had to see things for himself, learn it on his own. No matter the cost.

But some lessons in life carried too big a price. Could be he should just keep hands off. Could be he should take these two girls home after the movie and keep riding on down the road. He could feel Kate looking at him, wondering about him. He rubbed his arm as if he'd had a muscle spasm. And maybe he had. Some teacher once told him that the heart was a muscle.

She leaned toward him behind Birdie, who had scooted forward in her seat to make sure she didn't miss a minute of the scene. "Are you all right, Jay?" she asked.

He thought it might be the first time she'd used his first name without hesitation, and he felt another jolt of unfamiliar feeling slam through him. "I'm fine." He kept rubbing his arm. "Just had a twitch in my arm. All that painting, I guess."

Birdie looked around to fiercely silence them. "Shh!"

Kate put her fingers over her lips to hide a smile that even in the darkened theater set her eyes to sparkling. She looked back to the screen, but he didn't. Nothing on that flickering screen could be anywhere close to as fascinating as her. Some-how, before he drove away from Rosey Corner, he was going to get that kiss she'd wanted to give him after the wedding. All he needed was to get her by herself without the kid being a buffer.

It almost happened on the drive home. Not getting the kid from in between them. Kate had made sure Birdie scooted into the middle again, but the kid had started nodding off before they were two miles down the road.

Kate put her arm around the girl and let her lean back against her. She smoothed the dark curls out of the kid's face as she said, "She didn't sleep much last night. Too excited about everything that was happening. Evie and Mike being there. You taking her to the movies. Sleeping on the floor. We let Tori have the couch since Lorena thought sleeping on the floor would be fun. She found out the floor didn't have much give, even though we put down every blanket we could find for a pad." Kate looked over at Jay. Her hair was blowing back from her face. "Evie and Mike had our bedroom."

Her cheeks pinked a little, and she looked down at her hands as if she thought she shouldn't have mentioned the bedroom. Not when talking about the newly married couple. He pretended not to notice.

"So how does your sister like being married to my friend, Preacher Mike?"

She looked up at him with a little frown. "Is that what you call him?"

"Sure, why not? He's earned the title, and you folks here in Rosey Corner seem happy to hear him preach."

Jay smiled over at her. He wished they were parked somewhere in the shade. He wished Birdie was asleep in the backseat. He wished Kate was scooted over beside him where he could put his arm around her and breathe in her scent. Most of all, he wished he hadn't made her think of Mike. He wanted her to be thinking about him, not Mike. He hadn't forgotten that look he'd seen on her face during the wedding.

"Evie's wanting him to look for a bigger church."

"Women. Ready to start changing a man as soon as they say 'I do.'"

"Well, nobody expects Mike to stay in Rosey Corner forever. Not like my grandfather Reece did."

"Why not?"

"Why not what?"

"Why not stay in Rosey Corner?" Jay glanced over at her.

"Our church is too small to pay a preacher enough to keep him going. At least not one with a family. Evie wants to have a house, new furniture, children someday."

"Sounds like Mike better get busy."

"Evie's got a job. A good job. She went to business school, so she's not depending on Mike

163

to do it all, but Evie's not a small town girl. Even if she did grow up here. She's always wanted to get away from Rosey Corner to somewhere bigger. Somewhere where the action is."

"Sometimes the action's not all it's cracked up to be," Jay said.

"But aren't you planning to go to Chicago?" She peered over at him.

He kept his eyes on the road. "I was thinking about it before I got a better offer painting houses."

She laughed. It was a good sound. An easy sound. "Is Graham even paying you?"

Jay laughed along with her. "Sure he is. We made a business deal."

"He's been painting that house since August."

"I like a man who takes pride in his work." Jay saw a place to pull off next to a stand of trees and eased his car over into it. Birdie stayed slumped against Kate and showed no sign of rousing when he killed the motor.

Kate looked around. "Why are we stopping?"

"The car gets hot. Needs to cool off."

She leveled her gaze on his face. "Do you always lie so easily?"

He turned his ear toward the motor. "You don't hear it steaming out there? The thing's liable to blow up."

She called his bluff. "Then maybe we'd better get out."

"Okay. The car's not hot. I just wanted to be able

164

to look at you while we're talking. I like looking at you." He slid his arm along the back of the car seat toward Kate, but stayed his hand before he touched her. He wanted to, but she wasn't putting out any of the welcoming vibes he'd felt in the movie theater.

"I'm not pretty. Not like Evie or Tori or even Lorena." She looked down at the sleeping girl and gently touched her hair. "She is so beautiful. Me, my hair won't curl and my eyes don't even know what color they want to be. First green, then sort of blue."

"And sparkling like sunlight on water." Now Jay did touch her cheek with his other hand to turn her face toward him. "I like your eyes. I like looking at you," he repeated. "I like talking to you."

She leaned away from his fingers. "You probably say that to all the girls."

He pulled his hand back. He had the feeling the kid was awake and only keeping her eyes closed pretending to sleep now. Enjoying eaves-dropping. That was okay. It could be that he was going to have to win them both over to ever get anywhere with Kate. "Only when it's true," he said.

"All right then. If you want to talk, talk." She seemed to be daring him to come up with some-thing that would make her want to listen.

He twisted in the seat a little and draped his left arm over the steering wheel. "So what about you, Kate Merritt? You planning to stay in Rosey Corner all your life?"

"It's all I know."

"All you want to know?" he asked with a lift of his eyebrows.

She didn't answer him. "It's nice here. My family is here. Mama needs me to help with the store, and others need me around too." She gently touched Lorena's hair. If she knew the kid was awake, she didn't give any sign of it. "I wouldn't want to leave forever."

"But maybe for a while?"

"I wouldn't mind going to college. Nobody in my family ever has. Well, Evie went to the business school, but that's not what I want. I want to study literature and history. I want to find out about things I don't even know are out there to find out about." She got a faraway look on her face.

"Then you should do it."

She let out a whisper of a sigh. "Some things are easier to dream about than to do."

He couldn't argue against the truth of that. He'd long ago stopped bothering to even dream about his future. No sense building castles in the air that were going to disappear in the first breeze of reality. But things were different for her. "Dreams can come true. Just ask the songwriters."

She smiled a little, but she couldn't seem to hold on to it as she stared straight at him. "Do you think the president will keep us out of the war?"

He didn't know how they jumped from dreams coming true to worries about the war, but then the war shadow hung over them all. "I hope so," he said.

"But you don't think so."

"I don't know. How can any of us know what will happen tomorrow? But either way I think I'll be getting a call from Uncle Sam. As soon as he can find me."

"Sometimes it seems as if everything's just on hold. That we're all waiting, for what I don't know. But it's not good."

A tear eased out of the kid's eye and made a path down her cheek. He reached over and brushed it away. "Hey, Birdie, no fair crying in your sleep. We're out for a good time, remember?"

Kate hugged her. "You little rascal, have you been playing possum on us?"

The kid couldn't keep from giggling then as she opened her eyes and looked up at Kate. "I wanted to see if you'd kiss him."

"You silly goose." Kate poked her in the ribs, but Jay noted a flush warmed her face.

He grinned a little. "I wanted to see if she would too, Birdie. But there was this kid in the way."

"Sounds like that was a good thing," Kate said.

The kid giggled again and sat up. "Are we home?"

"Nope, the car got hot and we had to let it cool

off," Kate said without a moment's hesitation before she looked over at Jay.

"Yep," he agreed. "But now I've got a hankering for some ice cream. Any place around here sell it?"

"Not on a Sunday. Everything's closed up. We might have gotten some in Edgeville if we'd thought about it sooner."

He started up the car and turned it back toward Edgeville. "Point the way."

"That's crazy. We're over halfway home," Kate said, but she was laughing.

"Everybody should be crazy at least once a week. Right, Birdie?"

"Right, Tanner."

"Right, Kate?" He looked over at her. She was laughing. She might not know it, but she was beautiful.

"Right, Tanner," she echoed Birdie. Something about the way she said it was almost as good as a kiss.

❧ 13 ❧

Kate breathed out a sigh of relief as she watched Evie and Mike's taillights disappearing down the road back toward Frankfort after church Sunday night and was instantly ashamed. How could she be glad to see her sister leaving? But she was. A married Evie was even harder to put up with than an unmarried Evie. It was like she thought being married made her know more about everything now. In truth, she did know more about being married than Kate. She knew about a husband cleaving to his wife. She knew about love. Kate didn't even know about kissing.

She could know. From experience. Jay Tanner had been ready to kiss her. She was almost sure of that, but Kate had pushed Lorena between them and kept her there. A sensible decision, but sometimes having good sense was overrated. Maybe kissing was too. She thought about Carl mashing his mouth down on hers and felt a little sick. But that hadn't been a loving kiss. Carl had been angry. He was still angry.

It would be easier if she could stay angry with Carl. She had reason enough. The kiss for starters. Then the words he'd thrown at her in church that morning. Words he'd hoped would hurt her. But she didn't want it to be that way. She didn't want Carl to hate her, but she didn't want him to love her either. Why couldn't he see that being friends was best?

Then again, maybe she was the one not seeing things right. Everybody seemed to think she was the problem instead of Carl. Maybe she was. Maybe she should have agreed to marry him. As Evie pointed out, she was never going to find another man like Mike. And Mike was taken.

She could have said yes last week and stood up with Carl this very day in church before he went to the Navy. She could be a married woman just like Evie, and packing to follow her husband to wherever he was sent in the service. Mrs. Carl Noland. She pushed away the thought as a shudder ran through her. She could have never married Carl. Never. But friends—they could have stayed friends forever. She did care about him. She did want him to be safe. She just didn't want to follow him anywhere. Not even to Hawaii.

He'd intended to wound her with that. She'd been talking about Hawaii, that group of islands the United States claimed as a territory way out in the middle of the Pacific Ocean. A paradise half a world away with sunshine and volcanoes and pineapples. She'd read a book about the islands after she'd seen something in the newspapers about a military base there. She'd told Carl about it. How a man joining the service would have to want to pick that over the military base that was being built up in Greenland. Sunshine and beaches instead of snow and icy winds.

Not that any of that mattered when war clouds were edging ever nearer. The bases were there to protect the mainland. To keep the war away from American shores. But overseas people were dying. That wore on Kate's mind. Sometimes she couldn't keep the newsreels of bombs exploding over England and Hitler's army doing their odd goose-step march from playing over and over in her head. And now Carl might be in those news-reels.

Another sigh escaped her just as her mother stepped up beside her on the porch and put her arm around her waist. "Sorry to see her leaving?"

"No," Kate said.

Her mother laughed softly. "My honest Kate. I've never had to probe beneath your words to see what you were really thinking."

"I didn't mean that the way it sounded." Kate tried to soften the harshness of her word. "I'm glad Evie's so happy."

"And Mike too. He was practically beaming today," her mother added, tightening her arm around Kate. "He's been waiting for Evangeline to be ready to walk down the aisle for a couple of years now."

"She wanted things to be right."

"That she did. Evangeline always has a picture in her mind of how things should be."

"Is that bad?" Kate turned to look at her mother in the light spilling out from the front window onto the porch. She had the shadow of a frown on her face as she kept staring at the road where the car had disappeared from sight. A look Kate had seen often enough over the years when her mother was concerned over one of her daughters.

"Not bad, exactly. But I wouldn't be surprised if she cheats herself out of some happiness now and again when life won't live up to her expectations. Then again, life can be a stern teacher." She looked at Kate. "Come sit on the swing a minute."

The night air was beginning to cool, surrendering the gathered warmth of the October day. For a few minutes, they sat quietly, listening to the crickets and tree frogs that were enjoying the way summer had lingered over into autumn. Kate could hear her father inside, reading to Lorena. She could read any book she picked up now, but she still wanted to be read to every night. Something Daddy loved as much as Lorena did. Kate concentrated on listening closer for a minute and recognized Jules Verne's *Around the World in Eighty Days*. The familiar words of the story wrapped around her like a hug as she wondered how many times her father had read that story.

Tori and Sammy were on the couch, listening too. Kate could see them through the window, sitting close, holding hands, belonging together in spite of how different they looked. Sammy with his sandy hair and freckles. Tori with her black hair and ivory skin. At fifteen, she was already prettier than Evie and more settled than Kate. She knew what she wanted in life. To finish school, marry Sammy, and have a family. Until then, what made her happiest was yanking her hair back in a careless ponytail and going fishing with Sammy. She didn't look into the future and wonder if her life was going to matter. She'd already found what mattered to her. Sammy, home, and family.

Home and family mattered to Kate too. Just sitting beside her mother, watching Tori and hearing her father read to Lorena made her heart swell. She couldn't imagine not being here, but then that wasn't exactly true. She could imagine. She was bedeviled with imaginings of what might be. Of what she might be. Or should be. She wanted to be like Tori and be content with her place, but she wasn't. She was adrift in her own mind, lost on a sea of possibilities that was teeming with difficulties.

Her mother finally broke the silence between them. "I love hearing your father read to Lorena. I fell in love with him while he was reading aloud. I used to tell him that with his voice he could have been an actor."

"Or a preacher."

That brought a laugh. "Heaven forbid. I was a preacher's daughter. I have to admit to being eternally grateful your father never heard the call to preach."

"Is it that hard to be a preacher's wife?"

"Maybe. Maybe not." Mama set the swing to swaying a bit. "But I've often thought to be a good preacher's wife, a woman needs to have a calling the same as her preacher husband."

"You think Evie has a calling then?" Kate couldn't keep the doubt about that out of her voice.

"Not one she's aware of yet, but the Lord has a way of helping people change. Evangeline has much to learn, but she wants to be a good wife to Mike. Some things might be hard for her at first, but I think she may find a calling in time." Mama looked out toward the road as if sending a prayer after Evie. "And being a preacher's wife is surely much different from being a preacher's daughter. I was never able to please my father, much less his congregation. Mike is very pleased with Evangeline, and his evident love for her will be like the prime for a pump and bring forth love from his church people."

"People here already love Evie."

"They won't stay here." Kate's mother spoke the words flatly. "He loves our church, but he's ready to move on. As is Evangeline."

"That makes me sad."

Her mother reached over and squeezed her hand. "One of the sure things in life is change, my dear daughter. Everything changes."

"Everything?" There, swaying back and forth on the swing with her mother the way she had hundreds of times and hearing her father's voice reading Jules Verne's words aloud, it seemed as though nothing would ever change.

"Everything but the Lord. He's the same yesterday, today, and forevermore, but it's not like that for us. Even when things seem the same, they're changing. You girls are getting older, growing toward your futures. Things can happen to change everything."

"You're thinking about the war over there."

"Over there." Kate's mother let out a long breath that carried the sound of sadness. "Your father went over there in the war that was to end all wars and now look what's happening. The whole world has gone to war."

"Not us. President Roosevelt promised he wouldn't send our men overseas in a speech just last week."

"We can only pray he can keep his promise. And maybe we are far enough away from the conflict that we'll be able to simply change the course of the war by supplying the Allies." Kate's mother squeezed her hand again. "But let's not talk about war. We can't do anything to change what's happening right now, and war talk is hard for your father. He can't stand the thought of the boys having to go fight the way he did."

Kate lowered her voice to a near whisper. "He won't start drinking again, will he?"

"You don't have to worry about that," her mother said with no hesitation. "I don't think anything could send him back down that path. Thank the Lord. But the war over there does worry him. Carl today worried him."

"You and Dad wanted me to marry Carl, didn't you?"

"No." Her mother gave her hand a little shake. "Why would you think that?"

"You like Carl."

"Well, yes, but we would never want you to be tied to a man you didn't love with all your heart. We just want you to be happy." Her mother studied her face in the soft light before she went on. "But we did both understand that Carl was upset and nervous about his future. That's why he did what he did this morning in church, trying to make you feel bad."

"I did feel bad."

"I know."

Again silence fell over them, but this time it didn't seem quite so easy. The swing's chains groaned a little under their weight as they kept it rocking back and forth. Inside Lorena laughed. The sound reached out and made Kate want to be inside with her listening to Daddy read. She sat forward in the swing to stand up, but her mother put a hand on her arm.

"Wait, Kate. We need to talk."

Kate started to say she thought they had been talking, but it was plain her mother had more to say. Kate flashed back through the day, trying to remember if she'd done something wrong, but nothing came to mind other than Carl. They'd already talked about him. She leaned back, but stayed stiff.

"Don't act so worried," her mother said. "I'm

not going to fuss at you about anything. You're an adult and can make your own decisions now."

"But . . . ," Kate said for her mother, because she heard the word in her hesitation.

"You're right. There is more." Mama pulled her hand away from Kate's and smoothed the folds in her skirt. It was a way she had of getting her thoughts organized. "Mike talked to me this afternoon while you were at the movies."

"What about?" Kate asked, but she knew. The same thing Mike had talked to her about that morning in the churchyard.

"Jay." Mama hesitated again as if waiting for Kate to say something, but Kate stayed silent this time. So after a moment, she went on. "Mike's worried you might be falling for him and he doesn't think that's a good idea."

"It's Lorena who's head over heels. Not me."

"Lorena does like him. I like him. Your father likes him."

"It's only his best friend in life who doesn't like him."

"Now, don't be mean." Mama gave Kate's arm a little tap. "Of course, Mike likes Jay. It bothered him to tell me what he did, but he doesn't want you to get hurt. He says Jay is not the settling-down type. That he has girlfriends in every town he's been in. And I can see why. A good-looking boy like him."

"He's a charmer, for sure," Kate agreed, careful

177

to keep her voice casual. "That was pretty plain from his first hello here before the wedding."

"But nobody expected him to stick around after the wedding."

"Graham talked him into it."

"And that's what you have to wonder about." Mama turned to look straight at Kate in the dim light coming from the window.

Kate met her look. "What do you mean?"

"About what Graham was thinking when he offered him a job and a roof over his head."

"That he can't climb ladders like he used to and he wanted to get that house painted before winter?" Kate suggested with a smile.

"That's a definite possibility." An answering smile flashed across her mother's face. "But then it could be he was playing matchmaker."

"Matchmaker?" Kate frowned a little and shook her head. "Not Graham."

"I don't know. Good-looking boy blowing in from somewhere outside of Rosey Corner. A touch of the mysterious to make him more interesting. Carl not right for you in Graham's eyes."

"And mine," Kate said. Then she laughed and grabbed her mother's hand. "But Graham is no matchmaker. He was just charmed by Jay the same as the rest of us."

"Us?" Her mother lifted her eyebrows at Kate.

"Well, you. I've not been charmed. Simply entertained. And a little surprised. I never expected Jay to stick around Rosey Corner this long either."

"But he did. I think that may be because of you."

Kate was quiet a minute before she said, "Are you telling me I shouldn't see him again?"

"No. You're not a child. You can see who you want. All I'm telling you and all Mike's telling you is to be careful."

"Don't worry, Mama." Kate leaned over and kissed her mother's cheek. "Jay will be heading on down the road again soon, and then we'll probably never see him again." Kate was surprised at the way those words bothered her.

"You may be right. Just make sure he doesn't take your heart with him." She put her hand on Kate's cheek. "Hearts are hard to get back once you give them away."

"I'm glad you didn't want to get your heart back from Daddy."

"Never."

"Not even when . . ." Kate let her thought stay unspoken. She shouldn't have brought up those bad years before her father quit drinking.

"Never means never, Kate. For better or for worse. In sickness and in health. When your father and I made those promises to each other, we meant them. And that's all we want for you girls. The same kind of love that will endure whatever life throws your way."

Kate smiled and tried to lighten the moment. "Well, one down. Three to go."

"Maybe two down. Victoria seems pretty set on her choice." Mama peered past Kate toward the couple on the couch inside. "Look at them. Both so young. Your father says he knew he loved me when he was that age and even younger."

"You think she's too young?"

"Victoria knows what she wants." Her mother stood up and reached a hand down toward Kate to pull her to her feet. "You'll find your dreams too."

"If I knew what those dreams were," Kate said.

"You do know, Kate. Your problem is figuring out which to do first." Her mother caught both her hands and held them. "Think about it. What would you do if you could do anything in the world?"

"You mean like go around the world in eighty days?"

Her mother gave her hands a shake. "Be serious."

"Go to college." The words spilled out. She'd never spoken them aloud to her mother. There wasn't money for college. "I know there's no way and I can't, but there's so much I don't know yet. That I want to know."

"My Kate, always reaching for more. But if you can dream it, it can happen."

"I don't see how."

"Nor do I right now, but the good Lord can sometimes open unseen doors to us to give us the desires of our heart." She squeezed Kate's hands and turned her loose. "Let's go in and listen to Phileas Fogg. Talk about an impossible dream. Jules Verne came up with some interesting ones in his stories."

Kate trailed after her into the house. College was only the beginning of her impossible dreams. She thought of her notebooks full of scribbled stories and wondered if those stories would ever be in a book like Jules Verne's for people to read aloud in the night.

❧ 14 ❧

The sunshine-filled days of October kept going. A few nights carried a nip in the air that began to color the leaves until just walking up to the store to help her mother was a treat. The red and gold leaves were bright against the deep blue of the sky. Cotton clouds floated above them. The talk at the store was more about the World Series and Joe DiMaggio's hit total for the baseball season than the war. People did talk about how Carl's mother was worried sick about Carl going off to the Navy, while sometimes casting a curious eye toward Kate, but she simply pretended not to notice.

She was getting very good at pretending. So good that sometimes even she didn't know when she was pretending and when she wasn't. She laughed with the people at the store as she measured out their beans or penny nails. She talked her mother into emptying a couple of shelves for books—not to sell, but to exchange or loan out like a tiny library. When her father wasn't at the store, she pumped the gas or tried to. Most of the men jumped out of their cars to do it themselves after she set the pump. They did let her wash their windshields while they filled their tanks.

In ways, everything was the same. In other ways, everything was different. Evie was Mrs. Mike Champion, the preacher's wife. Carl was gone. Alice Wilcher did her best to jab Kate with every tidbit of news about Carl when she came into the store. That didn't bother Kate as much as the way the girl went on and on about Jay Tanner. It was more than plain that Alice had succumbed to Jay's charms. She hinted that the feelings were mutual.

"A girl knows," she told Kate on Friday morning when she stopped by to get a loaf of bread for her mother.

"Knows what? The kind of bread her mother wants?" Kate smiled to take some of the bite out of her words. But the fact was, she'd never been overly fond of Alice Wilcher. The girl was only a little older than Tori, but half the time she acted as if she didn't have good sense. Now thinking she was going to catch the eye of Jay Tanner was proving that triple.

But then, maybe it was Kate who was fooling herself. Maybe Jay did like Alice or at least was leading her on enough to make her one of the brokenhearted girls he would leave behind in Rosey Corner.

"Very funny." Alice gave Kate a look before going on airily. "What a girl knows is when a man is interested in her. She can sense it."

"So you and Jay been doing things together?" Kate kept her voice neutral as she straightened the candy bars next to the cash register. A last-second temptation for their customers. The penny candy and bubblegum were on the other end of the counter.

"I see him every day after school." Alice fluffed up her hair.

"I guess you've been going by Mrs. Harrelson's then. Do you think Graham will ever get that poor woman's house painted?" Kate tried to change the subject. Let Alice have her fantasies. What difference did that make to Kate? She had plenty of her own, none any truer than Alice's.

"Oh, I'm sure they will, now that Jay's there doing most of the work. He's always up on the ladder painting the hard-to-reach places while that crazy old Graham watches more times than not."

"Graham's not as young as he used to be."

"He's not the only one." Alice gave her a pointed look as she waited for Kate to ring up the bread. Kate's mother was in the back of the store helping old Mrs. Jenkins gather up the groceries she needed. Lorena was playing jacks in the back room. If Kate stopped to listen, she could hear the jack ball bouncing against the floor.

"Are you talking about me?" Kate managed a laugh as she took Alice's money.

"Well, you have to admit that most of the girls your age here in Rosey Corner are married. And look at Ruth Ann Wilson with one baby already and another on the way."

"Ruth Ann told us she was expecting again the last time she was in the store." Kate picked Alice's change out of the cash register drawer. She took her time while silently repeating her mother's rule to always be nice to the customers, whether they deserved niceness or not. "Her little girl is cute as can be. Ruth Ann lets me hold her while she gets her groceries."

"I didn't figure you liked babies."

"Oh?" She handed Alice her change and put the bread in a sack. "Why in the world would you think that?"

"The way you spurned poor Carl and after the two of you had been a couple since forever."

"We were friends. Never a couple." As soon as the words were out of her mouth, she was sorry she'd wasted her breath on Alice.

"You must have forgotten to tell Carl that." Alice dropped her change down into her coin purse.

"Maybe I did." Kate gripped the edge of the counter. She needed to keep her hands occupied before she grabbed an onion or something to throw at Alice's head. "But some things you just think people should know."

"Are you saying you never led Carl on? Made him think you were going to marry him?"

Kate relaxed her grip on the counter. She brushed her hands over the smooth wood as though clearing spilled flour from its surface. "What I'm saying is that I never thought we were a couple. You'll have to ask Carl what he thought."

"Well, now, that won't be too easy, will it? Although I did promise to write to him. Several of us at school did, since we figured you wouldn't be writing him and the poor boy, going off to the service and all."

"That's really nice of you, and I'm sure Carl will find a girl to make him happy." Kate kept her smile steady as she fixed her eyes on Alice's face. She'd never noticed before how there was something slightly off center about the girl's nose. Maybe from poking it in everybody else's business. She might have kindly advised Alice of that fact, except her mother and Mrs. Jenkins were coming toward them. So instead she said, "Maybe even you, after you write him all those letters."

Alice laughed a little as she picked up her sack. "I'd rather have my boyfriends closer to home than . . ." She hesitated. "Where did he say he might go?"

"Hawaii," Kate supplied.

"Right here in Rosey Corner suits me better." Alice's lips turned up in a smirk. "Where Jay Tanner just happens to be."

Kate's mother gave Kate a warning look as she set Mrs. Jenkins's basket of groceries on the counter.

Mrs. Jenkins, who couldn't hear thunder, peered toward Alice and said, "A tanker blew up? Here in Rosey Corner? I knew putting gasoline in tanks was a bad idea."

Kate bit her lip to keep from smiling as she turned away from Alice and began ringing up the old lady's groceries. Mrs. Jenkins was a sweet little woman, but conversations with her could fly off into some weird directions. Kate let her mother handle this one.

She patted Mrs. Jenkins's hand. "No, no, Stella. Nothing's blown up. Yet." Kate's mother sent another look Kate's way, before smiling over at Alice. "How's your mother, dear? I haven't seen her out for a while."

Alice answered with as few words as possible as she hurried out the door. Maybe worrying about those gas tanks out in front of the store blowing up.

Kate picked up the groceries to carry them home for Mrs. Jenkins. There was no way the little woman with her shoulders humped over from her many years could carry them herself. Lorena deserted her jacks game and caught up with them out on the road. She liked Mrs. Jenkins.

Mrs. Jenkins put her hand on Lorena's head and asked, "Where were you hiding? I didn't see you at the store."

"I was in the back room," Lorena said.

"You were on the moon?" The old lady leaned her whole body to the side to peer up at the sky. "How was it up there?"

Lorena giggled and then shouted toward Mrs. Jenkins's good ear. "Very bright. All aglow like a million lightning bugs."

"Bugs. Crawly old things. I never was one to question the good Lord's design, but if I was, I'd wonder why he gave bugs so many legs."

"That's a good question," Kate said.

"Squash 'em. Yes, that's what I do." The old lady banged her cane down on the road.

After they got Mrs. Jenkins and her groceries home, Lorena tugged Kate in the opposite direction from the store. "Come on. Mrs. Harrelson's house is right down the road."

"Mama might need us back at the store," Kate said.

She'd managed to avoid Jay Tanner all week while Mike's warning echoed in her head. A

187

warning underlined by her mother. *Be careful. Don't be charmed. Avoid heartbreak.* Excellent advice that she was ready to follow. She had no intention of continuing to trip up on the path of love the way she already had with her impossible yearning after Mike. That had been a childish feeling she'd allowed to stick around in her heart way too long. So now she was doing some inner housecleaning, stripping away every wrong thought that might give her trouble. She wasn't about to move equally hopeless and foolish feelings into her heart to take their place.

But Lorena didn't know any of that. She just knew the sun was shining and they were three houses away from Mrs. Harrelson's. "I've got Graham's favorite hard candy. Tanner likes it too."

"Well, go on and take it. I'll see you back at the store."

Lorena clung to Kate's arm. "Graham's been asking where you've disappeared to. Says he hasn't seen you in a gazillion days." Lorena grinned. She liked talking like Graham. Then she looked on down the road and her smile faded as her voice took on a pleading tone. "Please go with me, Kate. You know I don't like going past that house."

Lorena slid her eyes toward Ella Baxter's house where she'd spent several very unhappy weeks years ago.

"You don't have anything to worry about with

Mrs. Baxter now. Nobody will ever take you away from us again." Kate put her arm around Lorena and hugged her close against her side.

"I know, but I still don't like walking past that house by myself."

"But you do all the time, don't you?"

Lorena shook her head a little. "Uh-uh. Not unless Graham's with me. Or Fern or you. Please! Mama said we could."

"Oh, all right."

Kate gave in. Her mother would be closing the store before long anyway, and she did miss Graham. Nobody had said to avoid Jay completely. Just to be careful. It would surely be easy to be careful with the sun shining bright and Lorena and Graham right there beside them. Could be Alice Wilcher would be there too, making plans for her and Jay.

Kate started to smile at the thought, but then a funny feeling jabbed her. A poke of jealousy. If Lorena hadn't been clutching her hand so tightly as they hurried past the Baxter house, Kate would have turned and gone the other way. Any way but toward Jay Tanner.

Lorena let out a relieved breath when they got to the other side of the Baxters' yard and then started pulling on Kate's hand until they were both almost running. The way they had from the church to Grandfather Merritt's house after the wedding. Laughing. With Jay.

"Well, look here. If it isn't my two favoritest girls in Rosey Corner come to help us do some painting." Graham was holding the ladder while Jay was painting the top planks. He looked up at Jay. "Come on down and take a break. We've got company."

"We keep taking breaks, the snow's gonna fly before you get this house done," Jay said, even as he unhooked his paint can from a rung of the ladder to do as Graham said.

"Snow's white. Mrs. Harrelson won't notice a bit of difference." Graham winked at Lorena and then looked at Kate. "Where you been, girl? I had about decided you'd left the country."

"Lorena and I have been up on the moon," Kate said with a laugh. Behind Graham, the ladder wobbled precariously as Jay began climbing down. "Don't you think you should steady the ladder a little?"

Graham waved his hand in dismissal. "The boy's nimble. He could jump from there and land on his feet like a cat."

"But he might spill the paint." Kate shot a worried look up at the paint can. "On us."

"Wouldn't be the first time some paint got spilt," Jay called down to her. "Could be you should back up a little."

Kate reached to pull Lorena away from the ladder, but she had already taken off toward where Poe was stretched out over in the shade. Graham shuffled after her just as Jay skipped the last couple of rungs on the ladder and landed right in front of Kate. By design, if the smile in his eyes was any indication. His face was speckled with paint and white streaked the black hair sticking out below his cap. She breathed in the mingled scent of sweat, paint, and the outdoors. A different odor, but one that wasn't entirely unpleasant. She thought she should step back, but her feet seemed stuck to the ground.

"Hello, Miss Merritt."

Her heart did a funny bounce something like the ladder had a minute before. "Tanner," she said.

His smile slipped down from his eyes and curled up his lips. "I'm glad you didn't stay up on the moon. You and Birdie."

"Right. Lorena. I better see where she went." Kate started to look around, but Jay reached up with his free hand and put his finger under her chin to turn her face back toward him.

"She's busy scratching Poe's ears. Can't you hear his tail flapping against the ground?"

"No." All she could hear was her heart pounding up in her ears. But this was crazy. Absolutely as crazy as talking to Mrs. Jenkins and wondering where the conversation was going to shoot off to next.

"Well, it is."

"She likes dogs," Kate said.

"She does."

"You have paint spots all over your face." She didn't know why she said that. Maybe because she couldn't take her eyes off the face those paint spots were on.

"I know, but I've been told I clean up pretty good." His finger was still under her chin. "You think if I can get the paint off, you might go for a walk with me later?"

"Where would we walk?"

"Back up to the moon if you want."

"Lorena will want to go too."

"She can show us the way."

"Mike says I shouldn't." She wished the words back as soon as they were out of her mouth.

"Mike?" A shadow of a frown flashed over his face, but then was gone. "Big brother watching out for us."

She didn't say anything. She'd already said too much.

"Well, for you anyway." His smile came back. "Okay, so we know what Mike says, but what do you say? A little stroll through Rosey Corner with Graham's favorite girls. You want him to, I'll talk him and Poe into coming too. That ought to be enough chaperones for you."

"I don't need a chaperone."

"No," he said as he ran the back of his fingers across her cheek before he dropped his hand away from her face. "No, you don't. But maybe I do. So how about I come by your house around six?"

"Six sounds fine." Her cheek tingled along the path his hand had touched on her face.

"Good. You bring the trumpets and I'll bring the drums and we'll have a parade the likes of which Rosey Corner has never seen."

15

Sunday morning when Jay woke up to the sound of the old dog's foot thumping the floor as he scratched at his ear, he was a little surprised to find himself still in Rosey Corner sleeping on Graham's extra cot. Every plank of Mrs. Harrelson's house had been painted at least twice, but Graham didn't seem in any hurry for Jay to move on.

Jay wasn't in any hurry to move on down the road either. Not while Kate Merritt was smiling his way, and she was. In spite of how Mike had warned her about him. Jay wanted to be mad about that. He didn't know exactly what Mike had told her, but he could imagine. Stay away from Jay Tanner. He's not the kind of guy you want to invite into your life. So what if he'd be willing to do anything for a friend. Loving him like a brother was one thing. Thinking about your sister keeping company with him was a whole different kettle of fish.

Mike did love him like a brother and that's why Jay couldn't really be too sore at him. Not even later that day when he hunted Jay up on Sunday afternoon to look him straight in the eye and tell him he wasn't good enough for his new sister. Maybe not in those exact words, but the message was plain enough. One thing about Mike, he didn't lack courage to do whatever he thought right, come what may. And he always knew what he thought was right.

That's where Jay struggled. Knowing what was right enough to fight for. He could fight and had more times than he liked to remember. But he couldn't remember very many of the reasons mattering. Instead it was some guy having too much to drink. A jealous boyfriend. A stupid dare. Or simply to prove he was tougher than the man standing in front of him, whoever that might be. His father. His uncle. A complete stranger. Mike.

He didn't punch Mike in the nose when he said it would be better if Jay didn't try to keep company with Kate. He curled his fist and thought about it, but Rosey Corner must have settled a peace blanket over him. Besides, nobody went around punching out preachers when they were telling the truth. Jay wasn't good enough for Kate. He wasn't good enough for any girl, because

Mike was right. He had a failing. A spiritual lacking. Hadn't his aunt told him so over and over? She'd said some were born with the mark of Cain, with no way to please the Lord or anybody else.

Back in their school days, Mike was always telling him how wrong his aunt was. He claimed the Lord didn't keep score, that he thought every man was worthy of love. But now it was appearing as if Mike maybe had kept score and wasn't all that sure about Jay after all.

"I don't want to see Kate get hurt. She's extra vulnerable right now," Mike said. They were in the churchyard under a big old oak tree next to the graveyard. Mike had asked him to walk down to the church with him after he came knocking on Graham's door.

"Why?" Jay asked. "Because she thinks she's in love with you?"

Mike frowned. "What in the world are you talking about?"

"You saying you didn't know that?" Jay leveled his eyes on Mike.

"She used to have a crush on me, but that was a long time ago." Mike waved his hand dismissing Jay's words, but a stain of red settled across his cheekbones to tell Jay he did know. "I was talking about all that with Carl."

"I think Carl is out of the picture now." Jay leaned back against the rock fence that separated the graveyard from the churchyard and looked off down the road. "Actually it's pretty plain that poor old Carl was never really in the picture. He just didn't know it."

"I didn't ask you to walk down here to talk about Carl." Mike hesitated a few seconds before adding, "Or me."

Jay ran his hands over the rough surface of the rocks on top of the fence. They were cool in the deep shade under the tree. He fastened his eyes back on Mike's face. "I get the feeling you're wishing you hadn't asked me to come stand up with you at your wedding."

Again Mike hesitated. A hesitation that stabbed Jay.

"I didn't say that." Mike reached out and put his hand on Jay's shoulder. "You're my brother, Jay. You'll always be my brother. But Kate, well, you have to know Kate to understand. She thinks she can fix everything. She might decide she can fix you."

Jay breathed out a little laugh. "And we all know that's not possible."

"I didn't say that either." Mike gripped his shoulder and gave it a little shake before he pulled his hand away. "But the one who has to do the fixing is you. With the help of the Lord."

"What is it you think needs fixing the most?" Jay picked a piece of moss off the rocks before he looked up at Mike. "About me."

Mike grinned, trying to take a little of the tension out of the air between them. "You want me to make a list?"

"Might be helpful." Jay pushed away from the fence. "Look, Mike, I like it here. Graham's got some good stories. Your new mother-in-law makes a great pie. I even like the sound of the hammer shaping iron when Mr. Merritt is working in his blacksmith shop, but I'm not going to stay around for long. Kate's way ahead of you in holding me at arm's length. You don't have a thing to worry about." Jay gave him a sideways smile. "Nothing but a new wife and a church full of people watching to see if you're going to stub your toe and say something you shouldn't."

"That's plenty to worry about." Mike believed him if the relief flooding his face was any indication. "Why don't you hang around down here with me? It'll be church time again soon. I've been preaching through the book of Job on Sunday nights."

Job. That's all he needed. To hear about how God had let the devil knock down a man who was living right. The good Lord lifted Job back up, gave him back his good life. But Job had passed the test. Jay couldn't get the first answer right.

Jay pushed a smile out on his face. "Job. Sounds interesting. Maybe I'll come back down nearer to church time."

They both knew he wouldn't, but Mike

pretended he might. "Great. I'll bring you a piece of Nadine's pie."

Jay left his friend under the tree in the churchyard. He didn't look back. He didn't need to in order to know Mike would be standing there in the shade, his hands jammed down in his pockets, his head bent, maybe praying for Jay's soul. What was it Mike had said about Kate? That she thought she could fix everything. Mike could have been talking about himself. But then, preachers were supposed to fix things. Keep church members on the straight and narrow. Keep them safe from the wolf in sheep's clothing.

Jay walked back up the road toward the blacksmith shop with the words echoing in his head with every step. *Not good enough. Not good enough.*

He didn't climb the steps up to Graham's room. Instead he got into his car and drove to Edgeville. It was Sunday, but a man who knew his way around, a man who wasn't good enough for church people, a man like that could always find a drink or two to keep from thinking too much.

He didn't go back to Graham's that night. He slept in his car in the very spot where he'd pulled over to talk to Kate the week before. Mike was right. He wasn't good enough, but that didn't keep the girl from walking through his dreams, awake or asleep.

The moon was waning, and not quite as bright

as it had been on Friday when they had made their parade through Rosey Corner. He'd pretended the drum rolls, and Kate had circled her hands against her lips to make a horn. The kid had grabbed a stick and marched out in front of them to lead the parade. He hadn't expected to walk in the moonlight alone with Kate. She was good at keeping Birdie between them. He didn't mind. It was enough being there with them. Feeling like he might belong.

They'd stopped at her Aunt Gertie's house and sat on the porch awhile to visit with her and her husband, Wyatt. Gertie brought out sweet iced tea and cookies for them while they talked about books and baseball and cars and whether saving tinfoil gum wrappers could make a difference in the war overseas.

By the time they headed back to Kate's house, it was going on ten o'clock, but the moon was casting a silvery light over everything. They were almost back to Kate's house when the woman stepped out in front of them. Graham's sister. Fern. It wasn't the first time he'd felt her eyes on him. She stood back in the trees and watched them paint on Mrs. Harrelson's house now and again. Graham said not to pay any attention to her, that she wasn't a talker, but she did like looking things over.

There in the middle of Rosey Corner, she moved out of the shadows into the moonlight, silent and stiff like a soldier guarding the path and ready to stop anyone who didn't know the password.

When Birdie saw her, she squealed and ran to throw her arms around the somber woman's waist. "Fern! You should have come and joined our parade earlier."

"I saw you." A trace of a smile slid across the woman's face and disappeared again like a crawdad skittering between rocks in a creek. She was wearing bib overalls over a dark plaid shirt that blended in with the shadows. Untidy spikes of gray hair poked out from under a dark cap. She briefly touched the girl's back before Birdie stepped away from her.

"It was fun, wasn't it, Kate?" Birdie peered over her shoulder at her sister.

"It was," Kate said, but some of the ease was gone from her voice. "But could be we looked kind of silly to anybody watching."

"Nothing wrong with being silly. People been thinking I'm silly in the head since before you were born." Fern shifted her eyes from the child to Kate. "Shouldn't always be worrying about what others think. Can't build any castles like that."

"You're right, Fern," Kate said.

"Fern's always right," Birdie added with a giggle. "Aren't you, Fern?"

"Right enough for somebody silly in the head." The woman shifted her stare to Jay. "What about you? Brother says that woman's house is finished. You leaving?"

Birdie and Kate both went suddenly still, almost as if they were holding their breaths to see how Jay was going to answer. "Not tonight," he said easily.

The woman stepped closer to him. "Brother says your name is Jay. Like the bird. Mine's Fern. Like the plant."

"Hello, Fern." For a minute he thought she might reach out her hand to shake his, but she didn't. Instead she moved another step closer. He didn't back away from her as she squinted her eyes and stared at him, their faces only inches apart.

"You're good-looking like him."

"Him?" Jay asked.

Beside him, Kate started to answer, but without turning her head, Fern cut her off. "My question, not yours. Him. The one I wanted to marry."

"But you didn't."

"How do you know? Brother tell you that?"

"No. I thought you sounded sad when you said it."

"Marrying can make you sad too. Sometimes sadder than not marrying." Fern made a noise that might have been a laugh. "But I don't know if we'd have had that kind of sad. He died. Maia died with him."

Jay glanced over at Kate, but she was watching

Fern with wary eyes as she stepped up behind Birdie and put her arm around her. Jay hesitated, not sure he should ask any more questions.

The woman suddenly poked him in the chest with the point of her finger. "Go ahead and ask. You want to."

"All right then." Jay stood his ground even though the woman's shoes were practically nudging against his toes. "Who's Maia?"

"A girl who lived a long time ago and lost everything." There was no doubt about the sadness laced through her voice this time.

"Fern, does Aunt Hattie know where you are?" Kate asked softly.

Fern made the noise that might have been a laugh again, but she didn't look over at Kate. She kept her eyes straight on Jay's face. "See. She thinks I'm silly in the head too, but she's better than most. Me and her, we take care of the little girl."

"I'm not little anymore," Birdie spoke up.

"Little enough." Fern glanced over at her. "Still need taking care of." Then her eyes were boring into Jay again. "You remember that, Jay like the bird. Don't you do nothing to hurt our little girl." She poked Jay in the chest again. "You remember that."

Jay finally stepped back from her. "Yes ma'am, Miss Fern like the plant. You don't have to worry about me."

She leaned forward and scowled first at him, then at Kate. "Hattie don't worry about me. She understands freedom. Could be, someday you will too. If you ever break loose."

"Break loose of what?" Kate asked.

"That question's for you. Not me." As quickly as she had stepped out of the shadows, she stepped back into them and disappeared.

"Bye, Fern," Birdie called after her.

They stood silent for a moment where she'd left them, but Jay couldn't hear her leaving. It was like she dissolved into the trees alongside the road.

"Welcome to midnight in Rosey Corner," Kate said. He could tell she was smiling even before he looked over at her.

"It's not midnight," Birdie said. "Is it?"

"No." Kate laughed. "But midnight's when the spooks come out."

"Fern's not a spook," Birdie said stoutly.

"Of course not. I shouldn't have said that." Kate leaned over and kissed the top of Birdie's head.

"What should you have said?" Jay asked as they began walking again.

"That Lorena may be the only person in the whole world Fern loves and who loves her back."

"What about Graham?" Jay asked.

"She endures Graham. And Graham does what he has to in order to take care of her. It's easier than it used to be, since she does sometimes sleep at Aunt Hattie's house. But when the moon is full . . ." Kate let her words trail off.

A shiver crawled up Jay's spine and he couldn't keep from glancing over his shoulder to make sure Fern wasn't sneaking up on them again.

Kate laughed. "She won't hurt you. She doesn't even carry her little hatchet around with her these days. Not unless she's going out in the woods where some of the cedars are coming back after the fire we had several years ago."

"She makes cedar palaces," Birdie said. "I'll show you one of them if you want me to."

"Maybe someday," Jay said. "But who was the Maia she was talking about?"

"Maia." Kate sighed a little and all the teasing went out of her voice. "She told me once that's what her true love called her, but he died in a tragic accident before they could get married. I've seen a portrait of her when she was young. She was beautiful."

"Fern?" Beautiful didn't seem to be a word anybody would use to describe the woman he'd just seen.

"Yes, Fern," Kate said. "All that was a long time ago. Graham says she almost died during the influenza outbreak in 1918 and hasn't been the same since. Or who knows? Maybe it was her broken heart that changed her."

"I like her the way she is," Birdie said.

"Yes. Yes, you do." Kate reached out and

squeezed Birdie's hand. "But enough about sad things. We're not walking to a dirge. We're marching in a parade." She cupped her hands and put them to her mouth to make a horn sound.

He had jumped in with a rat-a-tat and Graham's sister was forgotten. Magic had seemed to mix in the moonlight until Jay wondered if he might be dreaming it all. The strange woman. Rosey Corner. Kate. The cute little sister who broke out in song with no urging. The easy laughter between them.

Now Mike wanted him to wake up from that dream. To knock back the good feelings and remember he wasn't good enough. His best friend, Mike. He hadn't actually said those exact words out loud. But he had wanted to put up a barrier between Jay and Kate. It didn't matter if the words were spoken aloud or not. They were there—in both their heads.

At dawn he started his car and drove back to Edgeville. He'd find a map and move on. He didn't have any reason to go back to Rosey Corner. Clean breaks were always the best. Just disappear. He hated not telling the kid goodbye. He liked Birdie. And she'd already had too many people disappearing from her life. Graham had told Jay her story. How she'd been dropped on the church steps like an unwanted puppy. How she knew her name and that was about all. How she believed someday her parents would come back.

He could tell her things like that didn't happen. Nobody came back. Now he wouldn't be coming back. What was it Graham had said about him? That he wasn't a finisher. That wasn't exactly true. He did finish things. By chopping them off clean.

He stopped at the first eating place he came to. A rundown shack with a sign promising home cooking. He was finishing his plate of eggs and bacon when a man in overalls came in looking for help putting up a late crop of hay. A day's labor for some more coin in his pocket. A good enough reason to not put more miles between him and Rosey Corner until tomorrow. In fact Mr. Franklin's farm was back toward Rosey Corner. Jay tried not to think about that as he forked hay up on the man's wagon, but the place pulled at him. Kate pulled at him. The kid pulled at him.

As the sun was beginning to sink in the west, they hauled the last load into the barn to leave on the wagon until morning. The farmer had milking to do. When Jay jumped down to pull open the barn doors, a black pup ran out to bark at the horses pulling the wagon.

"Dang fool pup." Mr. Franklin tightened his hold on the reins. The horses threw up their heads and shifted their feet uneasily as the dog nipped at them. "Whoa!"

One of the horses lifted a hoof and easily kicked the pup aside. The pup yelped and scurried over to hide behind Jay.

The farmer leaned over to spit on the ground. "Should've shot that worthless mutt when it first showed up last week."

"Not your dog then?" Jay picked up the trembling pup and cradled it against his chest. The pup's tail began wagging as he licked Jay's chin. "He's friendly. What do you think he is? Some kind of shepherd mix?"

"Don't know. Don't care. It ain't staying around here. Not alive anyhow."

"How about I take him off your hands?" Jay said.

"Suits me."

Jay held onto the pup while the farmer paid him and offered Jay a job repairing fences the next day if he wanted to come back. "But don't bring that pup. It ain't nothing but trouble."

"Don't worry, boy," Jay said as he put the pup in his car. "People been saying the same about me ever since I can remember."

At the end of the farmer's lane, Jay turned his car back toward Rosey Corner. "Old Poe won't know what hit him, will he, boy? But it'll just be for a day or two till I can take you to Birdie. She's going to love you."

He smiled as he drove. And he was going to love having a reason to show up at the Merritts' house again. He might even have to hang around long enough to build a pen for the pup. He might not be good enough, but maybe the pup would be. Something to remember him by.

❧ 16 ❧

"Graham came in the store on Monday, earlier than most days. He was alone. "How's business?" he asked.

"Seeing as how you're the only customer in the place, I guess that depends on what you're buying." Kate smiled and peered out toward the door to see if Jay was following him in.

Ever since Friday night, smiles had come easy. A moonlit parade through Rosey Corner had proven to be a spirit lifter. Even with Fern's spooky appearance out of the gloaming. Kate ought to be used to that by now, but sometimes it still startled her and made her jump. Something that always brought that shadow of a smile to Fern's face.

Jay had been a little spooked by Fern too, even though he pretended not to be. Kate knew exactly how he felt when he looked over his shoulder after Fern disappeared back into the shadows. The shivers up the back that could come from feeling eyes watching from the trees. She doubted he'd ever met anyone like Fern the plant. Thinking about it, Kate's smile got a little bigger.

Graham picked up a chocolate bar and a banana

and then added a can of mackerel for Poe, who had plopped down out by the front door to wait for him. "Breakfast," Graham said. He pulled back the banana peel and took a bite. "Put it on my tab. I ain't too far behind on paying, am I?"

"No, you paid Mama last week, remember?" Kate pulled out the ledger from under the counter and thumbed through the pages to find Graham's name.

"That's right. So I did. Where's your mama?"

"Daddy borrowed Uncle Wyatt's car to take her to Edgeville to pick up some stock." She licked the pencil lead to make it write darker and wrote down the cost of Graham's purchases.

"Victor needs to break down and buy a car."

"I think he would if he didn't feel it would be betraying every horse he ever shod."

"Plus he'd have to let you girls drive." Graham took another bite of banana.

"I can drive. I drive Mike's car sometimes." Kate closed the book and stuck it back on the shelf under the counter.

"But you only drive it here around Rosey Corner. Not off to some big town or anything."

"I might get my own car someday," Kate said.

"I fully expect you to or to meet a fellow who has one. Then you're liable to drive clear across the country to who knows where." He finished off the banana and pitched the peel into the trash can. "Speaking of driving clear across country, I don't guess you've laid eyes on Jay lately, have you?"

"Not since Friday night. I was wondering where he was." Kate looked past Graham toward the door again. "But then I heard you finally finished up Mrs. Harrelson's house. Did that dissolve your business partnership?"

"Could be. Or maybe Preacher Mike made him a better offer."

"Mike?"

"He came by to see him Sunday. The two of them went for a walk. I heard the boy's car start up not long after that, and I ain't seen hide nor hair of him since."

"Oh." Kate felt a sinking feeling, and her smile that had come so easy a few minutes ago was now straining her lips. Mike must have told Jay to leave. But surely he wouldn't have left forever without even saying goodbye. If not to her, then at least to Lorena. He'd acted as though he really cared about Lorena. And Graham. And her.

Graham huffed a breath of air out his nose. "I'm hearing a pile of words under that oh. You want to share any of them with me?"

"I don't know." Kate kept her eyes away from Graham as she ran her finger along the top of the cash register. Dust had a way of gathering there. She brushed her hand off on her apron and looked back at Graham, who was still watching her and hadn't even opened his chocolate bar yet. "Really, I don't. Except last week Mike told me it would be better if I didn't get too friendly with Jay. Maybe he told Jay the same thing yesterday. That he shouldn't get too friendly with me. Or maybe Alice Wilcher."

"That Alice could run a man off all by herself." Graham tore off the candy wrapper and took a bite. He looked to be thinking hard while he chewed. "So you think Preacher Mike might have done some preaching."

"That's what preachers do." Kate blinked a couple of times. She swallowed hard and forced out more words. "But we all knew Jay wasn't going to stay around long. He helped you finish Mrs. Harrelson's house. Maybe that was all we could expect."

"You could be right. Could be I shouldn't have offered him a bed in the first place, but I liked the boy."

"Everybody likes Jay." Kate grabbed a rag to rub off the counter. It wasn't dirty, but she needed to be doing something. Anything but looking at Graham.

"Even you?"

"Even me."

Graham watched her trying to scrub holes in the counter. At last he said, "The boy might not be gone forever. He might come back."

Kate shut her eyes a moment and then looked

straight at Graham. "Probably be better if he didn't." She didn't bother trying to smile. He knew her too well to be fooled by a fake smile.

Graham broke off a piece of his chocolate bar to hand to her. "One thing you can count on is that life keeps rolling along no matter what happens. As long as you're still breathing, there's a chance for happiness around the next corner."

"But what if you don't ever turn any corners and just keep standing in the same place?"

"There's all kinds of corners to turn. Me, I haven't been out of Rosey Corner since I don't know when, but I'm always heading around happiness corners. Out in the woods with Poe. Catching fish with Victoria and Sammy. Watching Victor bend a piece of iron into some fanciful shape. Hearing that little Lorena giggle at one of my stories. Sharing a chocolate bar with you." He reached over and touched Kate's hand. "But your corners won't all be here in Rosey Corner. You'll be going around some different corners."

"When's that?"

"When you're ready."

Kate found her smile again then. Not the easy one from earlier, but one Graham would understand. "Thanks, Graham. You and Poe are the best friends a girl could have."

After he left, the store seemed too empty with no new customers coming through the door. Monday mornings were always slow, but she couldn't just stand there and stare at the empty doorway. She grabbed the broom and headed outside to sweep away the leaves that had gathered overnight on the concrete slab in front of the store.

She sent the leaves flying with her broom. It was good that Jay Tanner was gone. Jay Tanner wasn't her happiness corner. He wouldn't have brought her anything but trouble. She didn't have the first reason to feel sad. She hadn't known the man but a few weeks. Hardly at all. Mike did know him. He knew him so well that he'd not only warned her but warned her mother as well. *Keep your daughter away from Jay Tanner.*

Kate paused in her sweeping for a moment and stared toward the church. She could just see its white siding through the trees. Whatever Mike had said to Jay on Sunday had made him leave. Mike would be glad. He'd think he solved the problem that in some ways he'd brought to Rosey Corner by asking Jay to be his best man. But the problem was, Kate wasn't glad the problem was solved.

From the other direction she heard children playing. Morning recess time at the school. Lorena would be running out to play with the other kids. In Edgeville, Tori and Sammy would be going to classes at the high school. In Frankfort, Evie would be sitting at her desk typing letters for her boss.

Kate shut her eyes for a minute and thought about her own fingers touching the keys of a typewriter. Not typing letters for some boss, but typing up her own stories. She'd read that stories had to be typed before magazines would consider them for publication. Double-spaced. She'd gotten a book from the library about writing. But her stories were still in notebooks under her bed. Untyped. Unread. Unready.

She sighed and began sweeping again even though she'd already cleared away the leaves. Some dreams were too big. Maybe it was time for her to be sensible about that too, the same as being sensible about Jay Tanner being gone. Her mother needed her help at the store. Rosey Corner needed a store where people could get the things they wanted. In time, she could go get a job in Edgeville or maybe even Lexington, but right now she needed to be in Rosey Corner.

She shouldn't even be thinking about her stories when so many bad things were going on in the world. If she wanted to think about writing, she should think about writing news reports or letters to lonely soldiers. But wait. Alice Wilcher and her friends were doing that. At least to Carl. That was good. She couldn't write to Carl. Not now. She couldn't even write to Jay Tanner. Who knew where he would go from here? The only person who might know that would be Mike. Mike who had fixed things by making Jay leave.

What would she tell Lorena? The sound of the schoolkids playing drifted down toward her. A happy sound.

A Ford slowed on the road and turned into the store. Kate was glad when the woman eased up to the gas pump. Mrs. Moore rolled down her window and asked for two dollars' worth of gas. While Kate set the pump and turned the handle to start the gasoline flowing, she asked the woman how she was doing.

"Oh, honey, not too well." Mrs. Moore sounded near tears as she looked back toward Kate. "My nephew over in Franklin County got drafted. He's a good boy, got a girlfriend and a good job. But my sister says he has to go to the Army. She sounded worried sick in the letter I got Friday. This is the first chance I've had to go see her. I haven't been off the farm for over a week. Didn't even make it to church yesterday. Harold had a cow down and you know what the Bible says about an ox in the ditch. Anyway we don't have a radio. No way to get any news. Do you know how things are going over there?"

Before Kate got any words out in answer, Mrs. Moore took a quick breath and went on talking. "I don't know why the president is drafting our boys. We aren't in the war." She dug in her lap and came up with a limp handkerchief to dab against her eyes.

"He says he won't be sending them overseas,

Mrs. Moore, so I'm sure your nephew will be all right."

"But the war's still going on, isn't it?" Mrs. Moore poked her head out the window to peer back at Kate pumping the gas. "Are the Allies making gains? England hasn't fallen to the Germans, has it?"

"No, they're holding their own. But the news isn't good. Lots of bombings and ships going down." Kate finished pumping the gas and stepped up to the window while Mrs. Moore fumbled for her purse. "You want to buy a newspaper? We have a couple of issues left in the store. You might catch up on the news that way."

"No, no, honey. Harold wouldn't want me wasting good money on what he calls old news. And I guess it is by the time the papers come out. I keep hoping they'll bring the electric lines out our way so we can get a radio, but we live so far out. No telling how long it'll be before that happens."

"Maybe it won't be all that long." Kate kept a timbre of sympathy in her voice as she waited for Mrs. Moore to pay her. "We'll keep your nephew in our prayers at church. We've been praying for all the boys joining up with the Army."

Mrs. Moore handed Kate a couple of bills. "Have some boys been drafted here too then?"

"A few. Carl Noland joined the Navy last week. He left last Tuesday."

"Oh, I am sorry, honey." The woman teared up again. "He's your fellow, isn't he? No wonder you were looking so sad when I pulled up, and now I've just been loading you down with my troubles when you've got enough of your own." As she reached out the window to give Kate's arm a gentle pat, her eye must have caught sight of her watch. "Good gracious, is it that late already? I'd better hurry or I'll just have to turn around and drive back as soon as I get to my sister's house."

"Carl and I were only friends," Kate said, but Mrs. Moore wasn't paying any attention as she pressed the starter button and the engine rattled to life.

"Thank goodness this old heap started. I've been telling Harold we need a new one, but he doesn't listen to me." She looked back over at Kate. "I'll pray for your fellow every time I pray for Jerry. That's my nephew. Jerry Sanders. I think prayers need names, don't you?"

She didn't wait for Kate to answer as she turned her eyes forward, shifted the car into gear, and with a little jerk, pulled back out on the road.

"He wasn't my fellow," Kate said into the exhaust fumes. Was that her lot in life? To be talking to the taillights of cars disappearing down the road out of Rosey Corner? She hooked her hair behind her ear. Her hand smelled like gasoline.

Inside she set the broom in the corner and put

the money in the till. Then she went into the water closet to wash the gasoline off her hands. Her mother had put water in the store two years ago. It was not only a convenience, but a customer draw as well. Kate was convinced that some people came in just to use the flush toilet, but then felt like they had to buy something before they left. Made for a run on the penny candy.

She stared into the little oval mirror over the sink. She didn't look sad. Of course she didn't. She had no reason to look sad. A little worried maybe. She was going to have to think of a way to tell Lorena her Tanner had left town without so much as a fare-thee-well. But she didn't have to do that today. Sometimes in spite of how people claimed bad news traveled fast, it could wait. Maybe she'd figure out a way to wait until next weekend. Let Mike tell Lorena. He was the preacher.

"You're one mixed-up girl," Kate whispered to her reflection. "But you better get this one thing straight. It's a good thing that Jay Tanner drove away from Rosey Corner before you did something stupid like fall in love with him. A very good thing."

Out in the store, the bell over the door rang. Another very good thing. It gave her a reason to quit looking in the mirror. It gave her the chance to quit thinking about Jay Tanner driving his Nash on down the road. Away from her.

Supper was over, the dishes put up, and the chapter of *Around the World in Eighty Days* read when a car drove into the yard. Lorena already had on her nightgown. Kate hadn't told her Jay was gone. She hadn't told anybody. It didn't seem necessary just yet. Keeping quiet about the truth wasn't exactly a lie.

"Who could that be at this time of the night?" A worried look wrinkled Kate's mother's brow. "Can't be good news."

Kate's father laid down his book and stood up to peer out the window at the lights. "Don't be borrowing trouble before it comes, Nadine. Probably just somebody who forgot to come by the store before you closed. You know how some people are. Think you keep a stock of everything down here at the house. I'll see what they want."

The lights went out as the motor died. Kate followed her father to the door. For some reason her heart was up in her throat. She wasn't afraid, but she was something. Then a flurry of barks sounded from out in the yard. Not big dog, deep barks, but yips. Lorena pushed past her and ran barefoot off the porch.

"It's Tanner," she called back as she ran across the yard. "And he's got a puppy."

"That boy's bringing us some trouble," Daddy said. But he didn't sound cross. He sounded almost as anxious as Lorena to get across the

219

yard to see exactly what Jay had in his arms as he got out of his car.

Kate leaned against the porch post and waited. So she felt more than saw Jay looking straight toward her, and she couldn't keep from smiling. The easy smile that wasn't a bit of a strain to her lips, and she wondered if she might be rounding one of Graham's happiness corners.

"A pup. That's all we need." Her mother stepped up beside Kate.

"Lorena will be happy," Kate said.

Her mother must have heard the smile in Kate's voice. She put an arm around her for a moment as she said, "Maybe Mike's wrong."

"He just brought a pup to Lorena."

"So it seems," Mama said. "Come on. Let's go see what trouble looks like."

Lorena already had the furry black puppy in her arms, giggling as she let it lick her face. Tori was laughing too as she touched the pup's head.

"I brought Birdie something." Jay grinned at Kate.

"I see him," Kate said. "Looks like trouble."

"Trouble. That's him all right. Been nothing but trouble since I laid eyes on him. Poe let me know right off that absolutely no way was he going to let this fur ball of energy close to him. You ever hear a coon dog baying in a small room? Hard on the ears. So Graham said maybe it wasn't too late to bring the pup on down here so we could get some sleep." Jay looked at Kate's father. "I'll come build a pen for him tomorrow if you'll let Birdie keep him."

"Please, Daddy, I can keep him, can't I?" Lorena shifted her eyes from Daddy to Mama. "I'll take care of him. I promise. Kate will help me, won't you, Kate?"

Then everybody was looking at Kate, and she couldn't stop smiling as she took the puppy from Lorena. His whole body seemed to be wagging. "He's very cute," she told Lorena. "But I think Mama and Daddy are who you need to convince."

Lorena grabbed Mama's arms and jumped up and down, as excited as the pup. "Please, please, please!"

"Calm down, Lorena, before you hurt yourself or somebody else." Mama put her hands on Lorena's shoulders to stop her hopping, but she was smiling.

Then Daddy reached for the pup. "Let me see that wonderful critter." He held him up in front of his face. The pup's tail kept going a mile a minute and he began yipping as though pleading his case with Daddy. "Yessir. One fine animal." He handed the pup back to Lorena. "So what are you going to name him?"

"Trouble," Lorena said without hesitation. She laid her cheek down on the puppy's head and he snuggled closer to her.

"I thought you had picked out the name Scout for your first dog," Kate said.

"But Tanner called him Trouble. That sounds even better than Scout."

"I guess that's what we were all calling him. Trouble." Daddy groaned a little, but he was smiling too. "I've got a bad feeling he's going to live up to his name."

Jay laughed. "I guess everybody needs a little trouble in their life." But he wasn't looking at Lorena and the pup. He was looking straight at Kate.

❧ 17 ❧

The pup did live up to his name. Trouble. But at the same time Kate couldn't keep from smiling when he looked up at her with his head cocked to the side as though puzzled about why she was fussing at him. Weren't shoes made for chewing? Magazines for shredding? Socks for attacking? Holes for the digging?

Trouble had the black wavy coat of a shepherd dog, even to the flashes of white on his neck, but he had the bay of a beagle. When anybody remarked on the pup's feet that looked too big for the rest of him, Kate's father would shake his head and say the dog would end up eating them out of house and home if he grew to his paws. The pup did do his best to eat everything in sight and wasn't above snatching an extra snack anytime a bit of food was left untended.

The first few days he chased the chickens until feathers were flying all over the backyard, and Lorena or Kate would have to grab him and tie him to the clothesline post. Finally the rooster and several of the feistier old biddies ganged up on the pup and pecked him until Kate chased them away with a broom. That took care of his chicken chasing.

But the way he bounded up to those in his new family with his tail whipping back and forth in a frenzy of joy made up for the trouble he caused. Jay was true to his word and came the next day to make a pen for the dog. But by the time the pen was finished, it wasn't quite as essential. With a few licks and wags of his tail, Trouble won over Kate's mother. Before two days went by, the pup was under the table, hoping for a dropped crumb every time they ate. After supper, he sat attentively at Kate's father's feet and listened to him read as though he understood every word. The mournful howls that first night when they tried to put him out in the barn to sleep earned him a place under Lorena's bed. Trouble was one happy dog.

Kate felt some of the same unreasonable

happiness. A joy with facing each morning. A smile that slid onto her face at odd moments. She felt a little guilty about the good feelings coursing through her. After all, she hadn't quit reading the papers or listening to the news accounts on the radio.

The Nazis' siege of Leningrad was ongoing in an attempt to starve the city, while other German troops were marching on Moscow. The British were making a few gains in the deserts of Libya. Japan was in political chaos with a changing government. United States naval ships were being torpedoed. Eleven sailors died when the USS *Kearney* was torpedoed the middle of October, but worse news came on the last day of October when German torpedoes sank the USS *Reuben James* in the icy waters off the coast of Greenland. While some of the crew were rescued, dozens were unaccounted for.

Carl was still in California at a training camp, but the ships going down underlined the dangers he would face in the Navy. Mrs. Noland stopped coming into the store. She somehow tied Carl being gone to Kate turning him down. It didn't make sense, nor did it matter that Carl seemed to be having the time of his life. He wrote back to Alice Wilcher that California was something to see, with no end of beautiful girls who liked jitterbugging with him whenever he had a few hours' leave.

Alice came into the store the day after she got the first letter. "Carl wanted me to be sure to tell you thank you." She pulled the letter out of her purse and held it out toward Kate. "See? Right there."

Without a word, Kate gave the letter a quick glance. Carl's big loopy handwriting filled the page, all right, but she didn't bother reading any of his words.

Alice shook it a little. "You can read it if you want to."

"That's all right. If Carl wants me to read his letters, he can write them to me and not you." Kate picked up a few cans of orange juice and carried them back to stack on the shelves. She managed not to sigh audibly when the girl followed her. If only somebody would pull up to the gas pumps out front to give her an excuse to get away from Alice.

"You want me to write him and tell him that?" Alice folded the letter and stuck it back into her purse.

"I don't care what you tell him, Alice." Kate moved the cans around on the shelf to put the newer ones in behind the two already there. "I have no claim on Carl."

"That's what he wants to thank you for. He says he's glad you turned him down, because now he's free to see the sights with the girls out there." Alice's voice sounded a little dreamy as she went on. "Who would have ever thought about Carl being out in California? Wonder if he's met any movie stars."

"I don't know. You should ask him." Kate smiled with true sincerity as she turned to face Alice. "It's wonderful news that Carl is enjoying the Navy, and I'll be praying he stays safe and meets that girl of his dreams, because he's right. That was never me."

Kate's pleasant agreement momentarily robbed Alice of words. "Well," she spluttered, but she recovered as Kate stepped past her to get more cans to stock the shelves. "I hear Jay Tanner found a job in Edgeville. With some farmer. I never took him for a farm boy."

"Mike says he grew up on a farm."

Kate looked out the window, but no car was pulling up to the pump. No customers were coming through the door. Just her and Alice. Her mother was in the back room working on the books for the store, and Lorena was out walking Trouble. Kate could hear him barking and then Lorena yelling at him. Trouble in trouble. Kate smiled. Sammy had dropped Tori off at the store after school, but she hated waiting on customers. Mama had let her head home to start supper.

If Kate listened hard, she could hear her father's hammer shaping iron down the way. The sound wrapped warmth around her. An "everything's right in the world" sound. That wasn't true by any means now. Not with half that world at war. But Rosey Corner was far from the conflict. And Kate loved the sound of iron on iron. She wondered what her father was making. Something useful or something fanciful.

Her eyes went to the wooden keg full of iron pokers. Some were plain, nothing but a piece of iron curved at the bottom with a loop bent into the top. Others had handles shaped like horse heads or the iron was laced in intricate designs. The only person in Rosey Corner to take one of those fancy pokers home was Aunt Gertie, and Kate's mother wouldn't let her pay for it. But now and again a stranger passing through would stop for a soft drink and be entranced by the fancy pokers.

Kate picked up some cans of peaches to take back to the shelves. She hoped Alice would drift on out the door, but she trailed after Kate.

"I hear he's almost like one of the family down at your house now that he brought you that dog. It'll just get run over, you know."

Kate positioned the cans on the shelf just so. "Were you needing something, Alice? I'll be glad to help you find whatever it is if you have a list."

"I don't think we need anything today," Alice said with a wave of her hand. "I just came by to pass along a little friendly information."

Kate stayed silent, her face impassive.

"Maybe warning would be a better word." Alice

leaned closer to Kate and lowered her voice to a near whisper. "A friend told a friend of mine at school that Jay had been spotted at the roadhouse this side of Edgeville."

"There's no law against that. Your friend's friend must have been there too."

"But he says Jay was downing the booze like there was no tomorrow. Wouldn't it be funny if you got mixed up with a man just like your father?" Alice looked very pleased with herself.

"I'd be proud to end up with a man like my father." Kate's heart began to beat up in her ears as she hid her fists in the folds of her skirt. She couldn't sock a customer.

"Drunks aren't very dependable, but my mother says you all found that out the hard way a few years back."

It was good that Kate's mother came out of the back room at just that moment. From the stiff smile pasted on her face, Kate figured she must have heard Alice talking. "Why, Alice, how nice to see you. And you say you've heard from Carl? I'm sure he appreciates his letters from home."

"Yes, ma'am." A flush crawled up into Alice's cheeks to spread out around her pink rouge spots. She obviously hadn't thought about Kate's mother being in the back room to overhear her. She mumbled something about being needed at home and made a beeline for the door.

"She's just a schoolgirl, not much older than

Victoria." Kate's mother sounded almost as if she were talking to herself. "And I suppose she was just repeating what she heard at home."

"Alice has never had much sense." Kate shrugged her shoulders. Being mad at some people wasn't worth the effort.

"I know. Poor thing. She's pretty enough, but bless her heart, pretty isn't everything."

"I've almost got all the new stock on the shelves." Kate started to turn away. She didn't want to talk about Alice or Carl.

Her mother put her hand on her arm. "Was what she said true?"

Kate frowned. "About Daddy?"

"No, of course not. I know the truth about your father." Mama hesitated. "About Jay. Does he drink?" She looked worried.

Kate felt the same worry scratching around inside her. "I don't know, Mama. Not when he's been with us. But maybe that's something you should ask Mike. He'd know."

Her mother rubbed her forehead as though her head might be hurting. "Or it could be we shouldn't pay attention to gossip."

Kate smoothed her hands across the counter. "Did Mike say anything else to you about Jay?"

"Not much. Just asked if Jay had been coming around."

"What did you tell him?" Kate held her breath as she listened for the answer.

"What do you think?" Kate's mother said. "I said Jay stopped by the house most every day except on Sunday. He looked some bothered by that, but the truth is what it is. I love Mike. He's one of mine now. And he's our preacher and a good one, but he can't order the lives of his church people any more than my father could years ago. That was something Father could never accept. He was ever sure he knew the righteous way, the only way, and he expected people to do what he said. Especially me."

"But you didn't always." Kate kept her fingers moving across the counter, tracing out an invisible pattern.

"No, I didn't. Some decisions can't be made for others. Even by a preacher. Or a father." Mama put her hand over Kate's on the counter. "Heaven only knows, we all have to make our own mistakes and seek our own forgiveness."

"Evie would tell me that I'm making a mistake." Kate looked up at her mother.

"It doesn't matter what Evangeline thinks." Her mother's eyes were sharp on her. "What matters is what you think."

Kate's cheeks flushed. "What if you don't know what you think?"

Mama's lips turned up in a small smile as she squeezed Kate's hand. "Then you wait on the Lord to help you figure things out."

Kate stared down at the floorboards worn white

by hundreds of Rosey Corner feet. She pushed out the question that was swelling inside her. "How do you know when you're in love?"

With gentle fingers, her mother pushed a lock of Kate's hair away from her face. "A hundred ways. When your heart does a dance when you see him. When you don't think you'll be able to keep breathing if he goes away. When you'll do anything to be with him even if that means leaving everything you've known and loved."

"That's what you did for Daddy, wasn't it?" Kate raised her head to meet her mother's eyes.

"It was. Neither of our fathers approved our match, but in spite of them, we grabbed the time we had before he had to go to the war. I've never regretted that. Not once."

"Even when—" Kate started.

Her mother cut her off. "Even when your father was struggling with the drink. You know how hard that was for me, but I never regretted loving your father. That's the way love is, my Kate. When you truly fall in love, nobody will have to tell you. You'll know." She reached over and touched Kate's blouse over her heart. "You'll know here."

"What if it is Jay?" Kate asked softly.

"Do you think it is?"

"I don't know."

"Then it might be, and then again, it might not be. Because you will know. Love doesn't always come barreling down on you like a train engine.

Sometimes it sneaks up on you like spring overtaking winter. The chill winds begin to warm and suddenly the trees have leaves and the flowers are blooming. You will know."

Kate looked down at the floor again. But what if love wasn't as easy for her as it had been for Evie and her mother?

Mama put her fingers under Kate's chin and raised her head up to search her eyes for a long moment. "Have you kissed him?"

Another blush warmed Kate's cheeks as she shook her head a little.

"Then maybe you should."

Kate was glad when Lorena came rushing into the store to say Trouble had pulled loose from her to chase after a rabbit. Tears were streaming down Lorena's cheeks as she wailed, "He's gone."

Graham followed her in. "Now don't you worry, little Lorenie. I'll get Poe to hunt him up for you."

When they filed back outside, Poe kept his head firmly on his paws as he gave Graham the eye. It was plain he had no plans to do any dog hunting. Especially for some pup that was always tugging on his ears. Lost forever would suit Poe.

Kate took one look at the old dog and hurried back into the store to slice off a hunk of bologna. "I don't think we can count on Poe, but this should do the trick." She held up the bologna.

She ran with Lorena back to where she'd lost

Trouble. By then the rabbit had made it to a safe hiding place and Trouble was digging in Mrs. Alcorn's flower bed. Kate held out the meat, and ten seconds later, Lorena had hold of the rope still around his neck.

"You're the swellest," Lorena said.

Swell. Practical. Problem solver. Unless it was the problem of Jay Tanner. Why did she always think he might be a problem? Why couldn't she simply let the smiles break loose and enjoy the moment? Let him kiss her. He wanted to. She wanted him to. Maybe that was the problem. She wanted him to, but she didn't know how to let him know that.

❦ 18 ❦

Jay couldn't remember ever being so happy. At least not for such a long stretch of days. He'd had happy moments. Times when he'd hit the winning home run in a ball game back in high school or the day he got his car and took it out on the road. He'd rolled all the windows down and let the air rush past him. It was like nothing could ever stop him again or steal that feeling of freedom.

But he'd never gotten out of bed morning after morning ready to start whistling even when he was facing a day of picking corn or sawing wood. The work for Mr. Franklin was hard, but the old farmer was an easy boss. He didn't say much, but what he did say mattered. He was a bear of a man who never got in a hurry but kept plodding along until the job got done.

His little wife was his opposite in every way. Short, full of chatter, and never still when they went in for the noonday meal. She popped up and down out of her chair to get first this and then that. She didn't cook fancy, but she did cook plenty. Their daughter had married and moved off to Indiana. A son had gone west, met a girl in Texas, and had only been back to Kentucky to visit a couple of times since.

Every day Mrs. Franklin would be out of the house before the mailman's car was out of sight, hurrying down the long lane to see what he'd left. The cornfield ran alongside the lane, and Mr. Franklin would pause in his work long enough to watch her check the mailbox. The first few days he simply frowned and went back to picking corn, but then one day the little woman looked toward him and waved an envelope in the air.

A smile creased Mr. Franklin's face as he threw up his hand at his wife. "Good. A letter today." He bent back to his task, muttering, "Them kids could see their mother when she gets a letter, they'd write twice as much."

Jay pulled another ear of corn free from the

shuck and pitched it in the wagon. He could probably count on one hand the times he'd gotten a letter. Lately, no letters could catch up with him the way he moved around. It had been a simple wonder that Mike had tracked him down in Tennessee back before the wedding. Something his friend seemed to be regretting now.

That was the only shadow on Jay's happiness. Mike. He hadn't seen Mike since the day he'd preached at him in the churchyard. He didn't want to see Mike. Not if he was going to tell him how he should go away. So he stayed away from Rosey Corner and the Merritts' house whenever Mike and his bride were there.

Nobody seemed to question him disappearing to Edgeville on the weekends. He found plenty of places there to while away a little time. Road-houses kept their lights bright far into the night, where the music was loud, the dancing lively, and the drinks flowing to help the people forget war talk and draft notices. That was one letter Jay wasn't looking forward to getting, but he had registered his address with the post office. They could find him if his number came up.

But anytime he was away from Rosey Corner, he wished every minute that he was back there. Talking to Kate. Seeing both Kate and Birdie. It didn't matter that Kate still shoved the kid between them whenever they were together. Nothing seemed to matter much except finding ways to get that smile to sneak out on Kate's face and make her eyes sparkle. The pup had been a great idea. Even before that, Birdie was in his corner. She'd liked him from day one, but now that he'd brought her the dog, she thought he was grander than grand.

He liked the kid, and not just because of Kate. When Birdie heard him pulling into their yard, she always came running out of the house and was beside his car before the engine made its last heave and shuddered to a stop. She had pulled him into the circle of the Merritt family until he felt like he belonged at their supper table or in their living room listening to Mr. Merritt read aloud.

Jay's mother had read to him. He had almost forgotten that, but Kate's father's voice bringing a story to life made his own mother's voice echo in his memory. She'd read from a book with a worn blue cover that must have held a hundred stories. The thick weight of it had mashed down on his legs as he leafed through the pages to find the best stories. She'd been sickly even then, but she liked for him to sit by her in the bed. She pointed out words to him and explained their magic for telling stories so that he was reading even before he started school.

It had been years since more than a fleeting thought of his mother had lingered long in his thoughts, but somehow she seemed to hover around him whenever he was in the Merritts' sitting room. It was good remembering her love.

But as much as he liked Birdie, as much as he enjoyed the rest of the family, it was Kate who was putting the smile on his face when he got up in the morning and keeping it simmering below the surface all through the day. If he could have somehow blocked the war news out of Rosey Corner and gotten Mike to understand that he had turned a corner away from his wild days, things would have been near to perfect. He would walk through fire before he would do anything that might hurt Kate or any of her family.

He thought about hunting up Mike to tell him that, but Mike wouldn't believe him. Not unless he made some kind of big confession in front of God and man. He'd expect Jay to start occupying a church pew every time the church bell tolled. Jay had done that with his aunt and uncle. A big pretense of piety that had meant nothing. Once they left the church and went back home, things were the same. Nobody loved anybody, and when they went back the next Sunday, the pews were never any softer and neither were their hearts.

Then again, a church pew might not be too uncomfortably hard sitting next to Kate. Even with Birdie between them. But he kept thinking about Mike preaching straight at him. Mike expecting some spiritual proof to balloon up inside him, and if nothing like that happened,

Mike thinking he should be gone. He couldn't handle that. He'd just have to find another place to sit beside Kate.

But he hadn't considered the middle of Lindell Woods. Graham had been after him to go raccoon hunting ever since Mike's wedding. Jay kept putting him off.

"I hear you don't even hunt. Not really," Jay said when he started in on him the middle of November. The day had been nice, warm for the time of year, and Graham said it might be their last chance to go hunting until spring.

"Whoever told you that about Poe and me not hunting just don't know." Graham picked up his walking stick. Poe had his head up watching him with more energy than the old dog had shown since Jay had been there. "It's according to what you're hunting."

"I thought that was raccoons," Jay said.

"And sure, we like saying hello to the coons that pass along our way, and now and again Poe gets up enough energy to give them a little chase for old time's sake. He used to give these youngsters' grandpappies a run for their money."

"But you didn't kill them then either." Jay smiled at the man.

"Never did care much for killing things. Poe neither." Graham touched the old dog's head. "There's all kinds of ways to hunt and all kinds of things to be hunting. Sometimes we're simply out there hunting a little peace and quiet and maybe some memories. You come on with us tonight and you'll feel the deep of the night."

"The moon's practically full." Jay looked out the window where the moon was rising up above the eastern horizon. It looked twice as big as normal and had an orange glow.

"Just because there's light don't keep it from being deep in the night." Graham pulled on a jacket and stuck a candy bar and a sausage wrapped in newspaper down in his pocket. He turned to look full at Jay with his grin that meant he was about to say something out of the way. "The girls is going with us. I told them they'd have to leave their Trouble home, but that I might bring my trouble along."

"So I'm trouble now." Jay laughed. "Your trouble?"

"If I hadn't offered you a business partnership, you'd be off in Chicago now, so guess I gotta take blame for keeping you around. 'Course it could be you're troubling somebody else now." Graham gave Jay a knowing look. "Or maybe they're troubling you."

"Could be," Jay admitted as he pulled the laces of his shoes tight and tied them. He stood up to follow Graham out the door to see what he could hunt.

"Best grab your jacket. You might need to share it with somebody before the night's over."

Kate and Birdie were waiting for them at the edge of the yard. The pup, barking for all he was worth, was shut up in the pen Jay had built for him. With a growl rumbling in his throat, Poe looked toward the pup's pen and flapped his ears back and forth.

Kate laughed and rubbed the dog's head. "It's okay, Poe. He can't get to your ears. I promise."

As they headed across the field toward the trees, the pup's barks grew more frantic. Birdie looked back toward the yard. "Do you think Trouble will be all right? Maybe I shouldn't go."

"The woods is waiting for us." Graham put his hand on the kid's shoulder. "You can't let Trouble rule your life, girl."

"He'll stop as soon as we're out of sight," Kate assured her. "And if he doesn't, Daddy will take him in the house and let him sleep next to his chair till we get home. He likes Trouble."

"Liking trouble can get a feller in hot water," Graham said.

"Chasing trouble's even worse," Jay put in.

"Oh, you two." Kate blew out an exasperated breath. "If you don't stop it, we're going to change Trouble's name."

"Trouble by any other name is still trouble." Graham had a smile in his voice.

Jay laughed. "What would you call him if you didn't call him Trouble?"

"I don't know. How about Wisdom? Better to be

talking about what wisdom does than trouble," Kate said.

"Wouldn't work. You'd have to have another dog for that." Graham let his eyes slide over to Kate. "Nothing wise about Trouble."

"I give up." Kate threw her hands up in the air, but she was laughing.

They were all laughing. Behind them Trouble kept barking, but not quite so frantically. They pushed through some scrubby cedars and stepped into a different world where the trees towered above them and shadows drifted beside them like live things.

Jay eyed them, not sure they weren't alive. It had been a long time since he'd been in the woods after dark. But if live animals were skulking along in the shadows, they had little to fear from the invaders of their territory. The newly fallen leaves crunched under their every step. They weren't going to sneak up on anything this night.

"We love these trees," Birdie told Jay as she let her hand slide across one of the tree trunks that was so big it would take all of them holding hands to circle it.

"Old growth trees," Graham added with a hint of reverence in his voice. "Been here since way before us." He also laid his hand on the tree like he was greeting an old friend.

"Made it through the fire," Kate said.

"The fire was scary." Birdie moved over to

stand close against Kate. "I thought everything was going to burn up. Us too."

"But Fern and Graham got us out of the fire." Kate put an arm around her.

"Seems to me I remember Poe being the one to get us out of that mess," Graham put in. "You can always trust an animal to know the way out. 'Cepting maybe that Trouble. Not sure I'd be chasing after him with any kind of trust just yet."

Graham had told Jay the fire story just last week. How the flames had flashed through the dry cedar woods and very nearly cut off their escape route. He hadn't mentioned his sister, or much about the dog. Or even told what they were doing in the woods in the middle of a fire. When Jay had asked, Graham said some things had to be learned and not explained.

"So how come you were in the woods when it was on fire?" Jay asked now. A person learned things by asking.

"Fern was saving me," Birdie said.

"Saving you? From the fire?"

"No, from the rats." Birdie's voice shook a little. "I don't like rats."

Kate pulled Birdie closer to her and looked at Jay over the kid's head. "It's a long story."

"And one we don't have time to be telling right now," Graham said. "We're hunting, and if we keep jabbering, no respectable coon will come anywhere near us."

"Where are we going to wait for them to show up tonight?" Birdie whispered.

"I thought maybe we'd split up awhile and double our chances. The two of us and Poe will go over yonder a ways to the other side of the trees and Kate can stay here with the greenhorn."

"Hey," Jay protested. "I've been in plenty of woods."

Graham gave him a look. "Hunting?"

"Never hunted anything but trouble," Jay admitted.

When Birdie giggled, Kate let out an exaggerated sigh. "Trouble is safe at the house. We're not mentioning him again tonight."

Poe gave a funny growly bark as though he were disgusted with all their talk. He raised his nose in the air and then stuck it close to the ground before he ambled off. A few seconds later he was baying, a deep, throaty sound that filled the air.

"Now that's hunting." Graham grabbed Birdie's hand. "We better chase after him to make sure he don't get in trouble—oops, sorry, Kate—if he catches up to a coon he don't recognize. No telling what might happen then."

The two of them took off through the trees, Graham in a slow lope and Birdie stirring up the leaves underfoot as she ran alongside him. The dog kept baying.

Kate leaned back against one of the trees. "Hearing Poe always gives me chills up my spine."

"Good chills?" Jay stepped closer to her.

"Yeah, like sometimes when Lorena sings a song at church. The sound touches something inside me." She was silent a minute, listening again. "It's so natural, so right here in the woods. A dog on the trail of something."

"The something—the raccoon—probably isn't so happy to hear it."

"The chased and the chaser. I guess when you think about it that way, you're right. But I still like to hear Poe. Don't you?"

"As long as it's out here in the woods and not next to my bed. That dog can do some loud grumbling in his sleep."

He was glad a shaft of moonlight was shining on Kate's face so he could see her smile. He knew what was feeling so natural, so right. Her being there with him. It was the first time they'd been totally alone together since the wedding when the hayseed had spoiled their moment in that backyard. The Navy boy was clear across the country now. Jay and Kate were alone in the soft moonlight with Poe's baying growing more distant, taking Graham and Birdie away from them.

The only one who could spoil this moment was Jay himself. That thought made his hands suddenly sweaty as his heart began thumping in his chest. When in the world had a girl ever had him feeling so worried about how she was going to like his kiss? And he was going to find a way to kiss her.

She shifted her position against the tree trunk as though the bark had suddenly begun to poke her. Her smile faded and she looked away from him toward where Graham and Birdie had disappeared into the shadows. An uneasy silence settled between them while the natural sounds of the woods started up again now that the dog had moved away. An owl screeched in the distance. Leaves rustled as a squirrel or perhaps a crafty raccoon moved in a tree behind them. He was so close to her that he thought she might hear the pounding of his heart as they stood frozen in the moment, waiting for a sign to let them know what to do next.

None came, but Jay wasn't about to let this moment pass. He put one hand flat against the tree beside her head and leaned even closer to her. She slipped her eyes past his and looked down at the ground. He put a finger under her chin and tipped her face back up until she was looking straight into his eyes.

"Can I ask you something?" His voice sounded odd in his ears. Almost hoarse. Too full of feeling.

"I suppose so." Her words were a mere whisper sliding through the silvery moonlight to his ears.

What he wanted to ask was did she think she might ever be able to love him, but the words that actually came out were different. "How about we elope?"

"Now?" Her lips twisted a little as though she were trying to keep from smiling.

"Sure, why not? I've got gas in the car."

A smile broke across her mouth. "One of these days I'm going to scare you to death and say, let's go."

He didn't smile. Instead he kept staring into her beautiful eyes. "Please do."

Her smile disappeared, but she didn't look away. "You can't elope with somebody you've never even kissed." Her words were soft, hesitant, as though she wasn't sure she should speak them aloud.

"We can fix that easy enough."

He cupped her chin with his hand and bent down to cover her lips with his. At first she seemed uncertain, but then she stepped away from the tree into his embrace, her lips accepting his. Her hands slipped up around his neck, setting his skin on fire. Nothing mattered but her lips against his. Nothing. Absolutely nothing.

By the time he lifted his lips away from hers, he could barely breathe. He pulled her close against him and soaked in the feel of her in his arms, her hair tickling his lips. He'd never felt this way after kissing any other girl. But then he'd never kissed Kate Merritt before. But he did want to again. And again and again.

❧ 19 ❧

In the moonlight, under trees that ever made her want to sing, with the sound of Poe's baying music in the distance, had to be the perfect place and time for a kiss. A kiss she had practically demanded from him. A kiss that was so much more than she expected.

The touch of his lips set off such tremors inside her that she wasn't sure the ground hadn't suddenly begun shifting under her feet. She needed to grab hold of something to keep her balance, but instead of being sensible and leaning back against the sure and sturdy support of the tree behind her, she stepped straight into Jay Tanner's arms and lost herself in his embrace. Of their own accord, her hands reached up around his neck to touch his hair and pull him even closer. The heat of his body against hers started her heart pumping as if she'd just run all the way to the store and back. Every inch of her skin was deliciously awake and tingling.

When at last he lifted his head and broke the contact of their lips, she grabbed in a breath of air like a drowning person managing to get her head above the water. But it wasn't a bad feeling. Quite the contrary. She was ready to sink back into the lake of these feelings. She laid her head against his shoulder and could hear the blood pumping through him to match her own racing pulse.

He kissed her hair and her lips felt abandoned. She was sinking again and had no desire at all to grab for anything solid to hang on to. Instead she lifted her face up to let him capture her lips again. Feelings stirred awake within her that she had never even thought to imagine. She had once dreamed of being in love with Mike. A foolish fantasy. If this was the same and nothing but an impossible dream, the desire rose within her like a prayer to stay wrapped in the fantasy forever.

"I once danced in the moonlight."

Fern's voice shattered the spell over Kate, and she jerked back from Jay to look over her shoulder. Fern was watching them from the shadows, standing as rigid as one of the trees. Kate couldn't see her face, but she felt her stare.

Jay loosened his embrace enough to allow Kate to turn toward Fern, but he didn't let go. Instead he wrapped his arms about her waist and held her close against him. It seemed only natural to lean against his chest. A place that fit.

"Did it make you happy, Fern?" Jay asked as though it were the most natural thing in the world for the woman to appear in the night and catch them kissing.

"For a while." Fern stepped out of the shadows

closer to them. "That's all a person should expect. A little while of happiness."

"Sometimes a moment is enough." Jay brushed his lips against Kate's hair.

"Not for her," Fern said, staring at Kate again. "That one always wants more. Just like I did."

Kate found her voice. "Nothing wrong with wanting more of the good things."

Fern made the harsh sound that passed for her laugh. "Things like moonlight kisses."

"A fine thing," Jay said. "Like your dance in the moonlight."

To Kate's surprise, Fern lifted her arms up over her head and made a twirl around. For a few seconds, Kate was almost able to imagine the young, pretty girl she'd once been, dancing in the moonlight with her love, instead of the woman in front of her with barely combed gray hair and a shapeless dress hanging on her sturdy frame.

Fern's twirl brought her nearer to Kate and Jay so that when she stopped, she was close enough to poke her finger against Kate's arm. "Brother gave you this chance. He thinks you can learn to dance before it's too late."

"Maybe you can teach me," Kate said softly.

"Can't teach that dance. You have to learn it on your own." Fern poked her again, hard enough to leave a bruise. "If you hear the music. That's what matters. Hearing the music."

"Do you still hear it?" Jay asked.

"People think I don't. She thinks I don't." Fern pointed toward her, but Kate shrank back closer to Jay, who shielded her arms with his own before the woman could poke her again. Fern's lips turned up a bare bit.

"I know you were in love once," Kate said.

"Once." Fern's bare smile disappeared. "Death doesn't stop the music. Just turns it sad."

Before either Jay or Kate could speak then, she raised her head. "Brother's coming." Then, without rustling the first leaf or bush, she melted back into the shadows.

"Are you sure she's real?" Jay asked when they could no longer see her.

"She's very real." Kate rubbed her poked arm and listened for Graham and Lorena, but all was silent. Even Poe's baying had stopped. "And if she says Graham is coming, he is coming whether we can hear him or not." She started to step away from Jay, but he kept his arms tight around her.

"I'm not listening for Graham," he said. "I'm listening for music."

"Do you hear it?" She turned to face him. For sure, she was hearing something. A ringing in her ears. The pounding of her heart. The dry leaves above their heads rattling in the slight breeze. Was that music enough?

"I think I do." He slipped one arm around her waist and held up his other hand to capture hers. "The moonlight awaits. Shall we dance?"

He kept his eyes intently on hers as they waltzed in the open space between the trees, moving as one. They didn't speak. They let the moonlight music speak for them. When Jay began humming a tune, it perfectly matched the song burying itself in Kate's heart.

She didn't want the dance to ever end, but then Lorena and Graham came back and caught them gliding across the carpet of leaves as though they were on a polished dance floor.

Lorena stopped when she saw them and asked Graham, "What are they doing?"

"I can't right say," Graham said. "Except I'm pretty sure it don't have anything to do with hunting coons." He sounded extraordinarily pleased with himself, as if he'd just come up on a rich patch of ginseng.

Jay laughed and let go of Kate's hand to reach toward Lorena. "The midnight band began playing, so we didn't want the music to go to waste. Come on and dance with us."

"You too, Graham." Kate held her hand out toward him.

"Aw, Kate. I ain't danced in I don't know when. Since before the war."

"Then now's the time," Kate said. "Grab his hand, Lorena. He's not getting out of this."

Lorena laughed and tugged Graham over to join hands with Kate before she grabbed Jay's hand. "I didn't know you could dance, Tanner."

"Everybody can dance if they hear the right music."

"I don't hear any music," Lorena said. "Nothing but an owl over yonder."

"But you will hear it, Birdie. Someday, and then you'll dance wherever you are as long as there's moonlight." Jay looked at Kate and his smile started up the music again.

Evie and Mike didn't come home until Sunday morning the weekend after the raccoon hunting trip. They went straight to church from Frankfort. Mike was having to work on Saturday nights running the movie reels. To make extra money, Evie said. Starting up housekeeping cost money. And so did new dresses.

"Mike likes for me to look nice," Evie said as she changed after church and carefully laid out the new brown dress on the bed. "I brought a couple of my old dresses home for you and Victoria. You'll look good in this red one. And here's a green one Mama can take up for Victoria. That girl is too skinny." She pulled the dresses out of her bag and handed the red one to Kate. "You're a little taller than me, but I hear skirts are going to be shorter this winter anyway."

Kate held the dress up against her. It was a nice red with round, clear buttons down the front. "I don't remember you ever wearing this."

"Of course not. Why in the world I ever bought

a red dress is beyond me. Everybody knows a redhead can't wear red, but those buttons were so cute and it was dirt cheap on the bargain rack. I guess I thought I could go against the fashion sense, but fashion knows. I look awful in it, but you'll look good." Evie gave her the once-over.

Kate stared at her reflection in the dresser mirror. Maybe Jay liked red. She hadn't seen him since they'd danced in the moonlight on Friday night. He'd made himself scarce the way he always did on Saturdays and Sundays. Going to the roadhouses in Edgeville, if Alice Wilcher could be believed. Maybe dancing with some other girl there.

A sick feeling ballooned up inside her. While they'd been in the woods with Jay's arms around her, she hadn't felt any worry at all. It was right. Very right. The memory of his lips on hers made her feel like spinning or running outside and across the field to the woods. She'd done that yesterday. On the way home from helping her mother in the store, she'd made a detour through the woods and stood in the same spot under the trees.

But there was no moonlight. No music floating in the air. What had Fern said? That the music stayed if one truly heard it. But if Kate had any music in her heart, it was frozen by the thought of Jay hearing music in the Saturday night road-houses. Maybe asking some other girl to elope.

She'd been to a roadhouse once with Carl. He'd said it wasn't a rough place unless a person wanted to make it a rough place. But Kate had seen plenty going on. Drinking and fist fights and loud talk. Places like that could be where her father had gone when he'd walked down the alcohol road and then came home carrying the sickening odor of drunkenness with him. He'd left that behind, and Kate was glad when she and Carl left the place behind that night last year.

She didn't like to think about Jay doing all those things—drinking and talking too loud or dancing with who knew who. With real music playing in his ears. But wasn't moonlight music better? It had to be. Magically better. She shut her eyes a moment and heard Jay humming in her ear. The only reason he wasn't in Rosey Corner was because of Mike. It had nothing to do with him wanting to be at the roadhouse. Nothing to do with him being called by the drink the way her father had been years ago.

He'd be back in Rosey Corner tonight. After church. After he thought Mike was gone. She wouldn't see him, but she'd know he was sleeping on the cot in Graham's room over the blacksmith shop. Then Monday after he worked, his car would be pulling up into their yard. Lorena would be running out to greet him and Kate would have to wrap her arm around the porch post to keep from running behind Lorena to do the same. But she'd wait for him to come to her. To raise his eyes and fasten them on her face. Just the thought of it made her heart beat faster as she stared at her reflection in the mirror.

"Whatever in the world is the matter with you, Kate?" Evie grabbed her shoulder and gave it a shake to bring Kate back to the present. "You haven't heard a thing I've been saying."

"Sorry, Evie." Heat crawled up into Kate's cheeks as she grabbed a hanger to drape the dress over it. "Thank you for the dress. I'll wear it to church next week, unless you think the color might be too bright for church."

"You can wear red to church. At least to our church. It's not the devil's color or anything. But maybe not to a funeral."

"Why are you talking about funerals?" Kate frowned at her. "Has somebody died that I don't know about?"

"Well, no, but people do die, and as a preacher's wife, I'm going to be expected to make an appearance."

"I'm sure you'll be a great comfort to the bereaved." Kate rolled her eyes at Evie. "Making your appearance in your somber black dress with hat and shoes to match."

"A girl might as well look nice while she's doing what has to be done. There are a lot of those kinds of things a preacher's wife has to do.

Whether she wants to or not. Marriage is not all fun and games, you know."

Evie sounded so upset that Kate asked, "You and Mike have a fight?"

"No, no, nothing like that." Evie waved her hand to dismiss that idea as she sank down on the bed and stared at her hands. "But it's all so hard, Kate. Working all day and then coming home and having to cook and get the clothes washed and ironed. How can anyone expect me to be smiling all the time? But the church ladies do. They'd think something was wrong if I wasn't. Mike says I'm doing great, but he's so busy working extra hours and then studying the Bible and trying to come up with what the Lord wants him to preach." Evie looked up. "We don't ever have time to just go out and have fun anymore. I wouldn't have anywhere to wear that red dress even if I wasn't a redhead."

Kate sat down beside her and put her arm around her. "I'm sorry, Evie."

"Don't get me wrong." Evie's shoulders stiffened. "I love being married to Mike, but I'm just so tired lately."

"You think you might be in the family way already?"

Evie's eyes popped open wide. "Good heavens, no. We're taking precautions."

"Aunt Hattie says precautions can sometimes let you down."

"Not us. We're careful. We want to wait awhile before we invite a baby into our lives."

"I think it would be wonderful being a mother."

"You would," Evie said. "But it's better to line up a husband first."

"That would definitely be best." Kate kept her face turned away from Evie and got up to run her hands over the red dress.

"Maybe if you wear that red dress, you'll catch some fellow's eye," Evie said.

"Could be." Kate tried to sound nonchalant, but Evie knew her too well.

"What are you keeping from me, Kate Merritt?" Evie demanded.

"Nothing," Kate said.

"Turn around and look me in the eye and say that."

Kate turned around, but she didn't say anything. It was easy to evade the truth with her back turned to Evie, but not so easy face-to-face.

"You fell for him, didn't you?" Evie looked disgusted. "He brings you a dog and you fall for him."

"I haven't fallen for anything," Kate protested. "And he brought the dog to Lorena."

"A man like him can always find a girl's weak spot. He spotted yours right off. Lorena. You don't think he really likes Lorena as much as he pretends, do you?" Evie sounded exasperated. "He's a charmer, Kate. Pure and simple."

"I know," Kate said.

"Mike warned you."

"He did." She hesitated a moment and then added, "But I like him. We all like him. Maybe Mike's wrong. People can change." She stared hard at Evie. "And he does like Lorena. Don't you dare tell her that he doesn't."

"But he'll go away." Evie must have seen how that thought hurt Kate, because her voice softened. "And it's not even his fault. Mike says nobody loved him growing up and so he didn't learn about how to love anybody else."

"He loves Mike. At least he did."

"That's just it. When things get hard, he can stop loving. Do you think Mike would ever do that? Stop loving because things got hard?"

"No." Kate knew Mike. She knew he was faithful and believed in living right. A good man. She couldn't say the same about Jay. She wanted him to be a good man, but she didn't even know if he believed in God. He'd only shown up at church that one Sunday. She couldn't argue any of that with Evie. Instead she let out a long sigh and stared down at the floor so Evie couldn't see the tears that wanted to jump up into her eyes. She never cried. Never. And here she was, wanting to weep because Evie might be telling the truth about Jay Tanner.

"Aww, honey, I'm sorry." Evie wrapped her arms around her.

Evie being nice to her was too much. The tears spilled over. She wanted to run out of the room, out the front door, and across the field. If she was going to make a fool of herself weeping like some girl with no backbone like Alice Wilcher or even Evie who could cry over a broken fingernail, then she wanted to be alone where no one could see her.

"Shh, Kate. It'll be all right." Evie rubbed her hands up and down her back. "We'll make it all right."

"How?" Kate choked out the word.

"I don't know, but we'll think of something." Evie pulled back from Kate and peeked at her face. "We always do. You always do."

Evie was right. She did always think of something. Kate grabbed up her skirt tail and almost angrily wiped the tears off her cheeks. Evie didn't make things all right. Kate was the one who did that. She was the responsible sister who made sure everybody was all right.

But it was Evie who spoke first. "I'll talk to Mike. Maybe you're right. Love can change a man and it's easy enough to see that you're in love. I guess the question is whether he's in love. Did he tell you he was?"

"We've only been alone together once. Lorena is usually with us."

"Protection, huh?"

Evie did know her too well. "It seemed sensible, but then we went coon hunting with Graham."

"Graham? He's the one who got Jay to stay in the first place, isn't he?"

"He likes Jay."

"I know. You told me. Everybody likes Jay." Evie laughed. "That crazy old Graham. Can you believe that? Him matchmaking for you."

"I guess he figured I might never have the nerve to leave Rosey Corner to go find a fellow on my own."

"So he found one for you. Could be he should have talked to Mike first."

"Could be he thought if Jay was Mike's friend, he didn't need to."

"Maybe so," Evie agreed easily. "Where is Jay now? How come he's never here when we are?"

"Mike." There wasn't any reason not to be honest with her answer.

"I'll take care of Mike." Evie tapped her finger against her lips. "Thanksgiving is next week, isn't it?"

"Right." Kate looked at her a little warily, not sure she wanted to know what she might be plotting. "President Roosevelt set it for the third Thursday again this year."

"Heaven knows why he keeps wanting to change that around." Evie shook her head. "What was wrong with the last Thursday in the month?"

"I don't know. Somebody said it was so there'd be more shopping days before Christmas." Kate shrugged. "But what difference does it make which Thursday as long as our family is together?"

"Family and friends." Evie's face lit up. "That's it. That's our answer. Mama always asks half Rosey Corner to come eat with us on Thanksgiving. It'll seem natural as anything for Jay to show up too, and he and Mike can make up."

She said it like the two men could fight and make up the way she and Kate had always done. But then Evie had a way of wanting to believe there was an easy answer to every problem. Either that or she sank into despair of there being no answer at all. Maybe this answer could be an easy one.

Evie turned and peered into the mirror to fluff up her hair before she looked back at Kate with a smile clear across her face. "I can't believe it. My little sister is finally in love!"

"Tori's been in love with Sammy forever," Kate said.

"That's not the little sister I'm talking about and you know it." Evie poked Kate with her finger. "It's you I'm talking about. You who always pretended not to want to be in love. And now look at you. Head over heels in love."

"In something anyway," Kate admitted. She didn't know when she had ever felt so unsettled and unsure of what to do next.

"If not in love, in what?" Evie raised her

eyebrows at Kate. "Trouble? You haven't been that carried away, surely."

"Honestly, Evie, I'm not stupid."

When Kate frowned at what she was suggesting, Evie laughed. "You wouldn't be the first girl to be in trouble because she thought she was in love."

"I'm not in trouble," Kate said distinctly. But the surer she tried to sound, the more she doubted. Not in trouble the way Evie meant. But perhaps in trouble nevertheless. It would have been a lot safer if she could have fallen in love with Carl instead of someone she knew so little about. Someone who might break her heart.

She followed Evie out of the bedroom toward where the family was gathering in the kitchen. When had she become such a coward? Afraid of finding love? Maybe that was why she'd played at loving Mike so long. Safe, unattainable Mike. And dated Carl, a man she knew she'd never marry. Maybe she was afraid of what love might ask of her.

❧ 20 ❧

"We've done got up enough wood for the winter and the fences are in good shape. Not much left to do till spring." Mr. Franklin looked sorry to be saying the words to Jay as he handed him his pay the day before Thanksgiving.

"That's all right, sir. I didn't expect the job to last through the winter."

"The wife, she said to tell you about our spare room if you need a place to sleep till you find another job. You could help with the feeding and such for your keep. She's taken a liking to you, I guess." The old farmer looked down at the ground and then slid his eyes back up to Jay's face. "And you did get rid of that goldarned pup for me."

"That's nice of the two of you, but I've got a place with a friend right now. Although I have to admit the thought of Mrs. Franklin's cooking is tempting." Jay smiled as he pocketed the money.

Jay couldn't tell if Mr. Franklin looked disappointed or relieved. The man never let much expression slip out on his face, but his lips did turn up a bit as he said, "Always something on our table. The wife wouldn't mind you showing up for a meal now and again. And come planting season, I could use some more help if you're in the neighborhood."

"I'll keep that in mind." Jay shook the man's hand and waved at Mrs. Franklin, who was watching from the porch.

When he started to turn away, she scurried down the steps to stop him. She thrust a package into his hands. "Here's some of those cookies you like." Then she looked a little uncertain as she pulled a slip of paper out of her apron pocket. "And here's our address. You write us if you leave Rosey Corner so we'll know how you're doing."

"Now, Maddie, don't be bothering the boy to write you letters," Mr. Franklin said.

"You stay out of this, Alfred." She glared at Mr. Franklin with more defiance than Jay had ever seen out of her. "Everybody likes getting letters. The way things is going, it could be he'll get drafted and then he'll need somebody writing him." Her eyes came back to Jay. "Everybody needs a friend or two in this world."

"That's for sure." Jay tucked the address in his pocket, held up the cookies, and added, "Especially friends with cookies. The best kind, Mrs. Franklin."

His words brought a pleased smile to the little woman's face, and she surprised both of them by tiptoeing up to kiss his cheek. "You come back to see us now, you hear," she said, slipping her hand up to brush away a stray tear.

He looked in the rearview mirror at them as he drove down their lane. They were still standing watching him when he pulled onto the road, and he leaned out the window to wave one last time. Nice people. He felt kind of sad pressing on the gas and leaving them behind.

He didn't know what was the matter with him. Getting attached to people right and left when he'd always valued his ability to act friendly without letting anybody close to him. But now here in Rosey Corner he was collecting friends like a boy stuffing his pocket with pretty rocks. He'd done that as a kid. Stuck rocks in his pockets and carried them home. His mother had never minded. She'd exclaimed over his treasures when he'd shared them with her.

But once at his aunt's, everything changed. When she found his stash of rocks hidden away under his bed, she made him throw them all in the creek back behind the house. Even the round, smooth gray one with a ribbon of sparkle through it that was his mother's favorite. He'd gone back to the creek and found that one to hide in a hollow tree, but one day when he went by the tree to touch it, the rock was gone. Lost. The same as everything he'd ever cared about. All lost.

It was better to not have things. Better to not want to hold onto things. Things or people. People couldn't be depended on. They died. Or worse, they stopped caring. They told him to go away. Even Mike. To save Kate. From him.

Kate. How could simply thinking a girl's name make those bleak memories of things lost in the past vanish? Instead Kate was there in his mind. Dancing in the moonlight. Her lips touching his. Her fingers in his hair. A smile curled up inside him at the thought. He'd seen her since then. On Monday and Tuesday, but they hadn't been alone. She'd made sure the kid sister was in the middle of them again, but it wasn't the same as before. She wasn't really holding him away. It was more like she needed time to get used to the feeling of wanting him to kiss her. And she did.

He had an intuition for that, for knowing when a girl wanted his kisses. Sometimes he'd obliged the girl. More times he hadn't. No sense inviting unnecessary difficulties into his life. That was what girls generally turned out to be. But with Kate, he didn't care about the difficulties. He just wanted her in his arms again.

He couldn't deny it worried him if he let himself think about it. The way he felt. He didn't let people get to him. They could hate him. They could love him. They could ridicule or praise him. It had always been the same to Jay. He plain didn't care, because caring made him weak. He couldn't be weak. He'd figured that out while he was living with his aunt and uncle. Wanting somebody to love him was a giant step toward weakness.

He held everybody at arm's length. Even Mike, who was the nearest thing to a friend Jay had. There were times he'd wanted to do more than peek over the wall at Mike, times when he wanted to let down his guard, but he hadn't. And a good thing, since Mike had looked him straight in the eye and told him to go away. What kind of friend was that? Perhaps one who knew him too well.

Jay thought that's what he should do. Go away before he did something stupid like tell Kate he loved her or ask her to elope again. Moonlight and kisses could make a man lose his head. Especially when kissing a girl like Kate in that moonlight.

A girl could maybe lose her head too. Kate surely had when she'd the same as asked him to kiss her. Most every other time they'd been together, she'd seemed as uneasy with the whole idea of love as he was. And she'd known nothing but love in Rosey Corner. She didn't have the vaguest idea about how it would feel to be thrown away as a child the way Birdie had been. The way he had been. She thought she did, but nobody could know that unless it happened to them.

Birdie was young. She still had some fairy-tale notion that her parents would someday come back for her. At least he'd never had to flirt with that idea and be disappointed year after year. He knew he was on his own from the day his father had sent him away. But could be if an angel had shown up to love him and take care of him, everything might have been different. Maybe then he wouldn't be afraid to trust this feeling that kept expanding inside him instead of waiting warily for it to burst.

They had asked him to their Thanksgiving dinner. Not only Birdie and Kate, but Mrs. Merritt had made a special point of asking him. Graham was going. And that old black woman who doctored his eye after the hayseed socked him. Maybe even Graham's odd sister. The one who kept appearing out of the shadows. The one who'd been the reason for his dance with Kate in the moonlight. He owed her for that.

The problem was, Mike and his bride would be there too. Jay's hands tightened on the steering wheel as he drove past the first houses in Rosey Corner. He hadn't told Kate and Birdie he was coming, but he had let them think he was. Now though, he was thinking he should have headed for Edgeville instead of Rosey Corner when he pulled out of the Franklins' lane. Still, it was only right to let them know he couldn't come.

When he passed the blacksmith shop, a light was on in the upstairs room. Graham would be reading while he ate beans out of a can or maybe he'd have his ear glued to the radio to hear the war news or what was happening with the coal strike. He'd have an unopened can of beans set out for Jay too and maybe a can of peaches. Jay thought about stopping to run the cookies Mrs.

Franklin had given him up to Graham, but he didn't take his foot off the gas.

He drove on past the Merritts' store, all buttoned up for the night. But he didn't drive past the Merritts' yard. He'd been heading toward here ever since he'd gotten up that morning. Every thought, every breath had directed him to this place. Like he couldn't wait to get there. He thought this must be what it felt like to go home. To belong someplace. He didn't have the right to the feeling. It wasn't his home. But it was Kate's.

The pup started barking inside the house, and he'd barely stopped the car when Trouble and Birdie came flying across the yard.

"You're late. We thought you weren't going to stop by." The kid stepped up on his running board before he could unlatch the door. The pup was jumping up beside her, his toenails scratching against the car.

"I missed the story, didn't I?" Jay was surprised at the disappointment rising up inside him at that. He mashed it down. He wasn't a kid like Birdie who needed a bedtime story.

"Yeah, I'm sorry. Daddy waited awhile, but we really did want to find out what happened next."

"Guess you'll just have to tell me what crazy things happened to old Phileas Fogg this time. You or Kate." He looked past Birdie toward the porch. Kate was leaning against the post at the top of the steps, watching them the way she did

269

every time he drove into the yard. "If she comes out here to talk to me."

"You're not coming in?"

"Better not. I worked late at the farm, cleaning out the barn. Haven't had time to wash up, so I'm thinking you'd all be happier if I keep my stinky self in the car."

Birdie stuck her head partway through the open window and took a big breath. "Phew, you're right. You smell like the cow stall out in the barn."

"A good honest odor," Jay said. "But one I thought I wouldn't ever be washing off me again. Take it from me, Birdie. Never say never."

"Isn't he getting out?" Kate called from the porch.

"He says he's too stinky," Birdie called back to her.

Kate laughed and came down the steps to stand in front of the porch. Jay didn't know whether to wish her closer or not. If she caught a good whiff of him, she might never want to hug him again. He should have stopped at Graham's and washed up at the pump out behind the blacksmith shop.

"Well, tell him that Mama says we're eating at one o'clock tomorrow."

Birdie turned toward Jay again. "One o'clock. I can't wait. Mama's been making pies ever since she got home from the store. It smells heavenly in the kitchen."

"That's why I stopped by, to say not to look for me tomorrow."

Birdie's face fell. "You have to come. Mama made a brown sugar pie just for you."

"Maybe you can save me a piece and I'll come by later." He felt like a heel making the kid unhappy, but he'd feel like a bigger heel sitting across from Mike. He started to pat Birdie's hand on the window, but she jerked away before he could touch her.

"That's not the same." She hopped off the running board and glared at him with her fists on her hips. The pup's ears drooped as he hunkered down at her feet. "This is Thanksgiving. Everybody has to come eat together. All the family. Or you don't get any pie."

"I'm not family, Birdie," he said softly. He opened the car door and leaned out toward her. He didn't want to hurt her with his words, but he couldn't let her fantasize something that wasn't true. He wasn't family. He didn't have any family.

"But don't you want to be?" Her bottom lip was trembling.

"Wanting something and it being true are two different things," Jay said.

"If you want it enough, it can happen. You've got to believe, Tanner." Now there was no doubt she was on the verge of tears.

He slipped out of the car and stooped down on the ground in front of her. He didn't touch her, but instead stroked the pup. When he peeked up at her, he caught sight of Kate heading across the yard toward them. "I'm glad you believe it, Birdie. Now don't be mad at me. I'll make it up to you. Maybe we can go to the movies Saturday."

"I don't want to go to the movies." She stomped her foot. "I want you to come tomorrow. I want you to be part of my Thanksgiving family."

When he just looked at her without saying anything, she whirled away from him and ran to grab Kate around the waist. Kate pushed her away and leaned down to look in her face. "Whatever is the matter with you?"

"He says he doesn't want to come to Thanksgiving dinner. That he's not part of our family." The child's voice was plaintive as she looked up at Kate and went on. "Can't friends be part of our Thanksgiving family?"

Kate kissed the top of Birdie's head. "I don't see why not. That's always been true with Graham and Aunt Hattie."

"And me," Birdie said so softly that Jay could barely hear the words.

"No, baby, you're every bit family. As much family as me or Tori or Evie. We're all sisters. A family of the heart." She pulled her close and stared toward Jay, but he couldn't see her expression in the dim light. Then she was pushing the kid back again and leaning down to talk to her. "You go on to the house. Mama says it's bedtime. I'll talk to him."

"Make him come, Kate." The kid's voice was still shaky as she took a quick look over her shoulder at Jay before she ran on to the house with the dog chasing after her. Kate watched her until she went in the door, then turned to walk the rest of the way across the yard to Jay.

Jay backed up to lean against the car. The night wasn't going well. He really should have stopped to clean up before he came. Then maybe the kid would have been in bed and he could have made his excuses to Kate or Mrs. Merritt. Neither of them would have cried about him not coming. He might have hoped one of them would, but Kate was too tough for that. And now he was alone with her but smelling like a cow barn and feeling like a bum for making the kid cry.

She stopped a little away from him. He hoped it wasn't because of the smell, and then he hoped it was. Better that than just not wanting to be close enough for him to touch her.

"I wasn't aiming to make her unhappy. I told her I'd take her to the movies on Saturday." When she just kept looking at him without saying anything, he shifted a little against the car. He should have let Graham tell them tomorrow he wasn't coming. After a minute, he added, "I don't know what else to say except I'm sorry I upset her. Maybe I'd better head on up the road." But he didn't move to get in his car.

"Why aren't you coming?"

"It's a family thing for you. I'd be in the way." Jay made excuses.

"It's Mike, isn't it?"

She knew. There wasn't any reason pretending with her. "I don't want to mess up his first Thanksgiving as part of your family."

"Mike's been part of the family for a long time," Kate said. "That's not really it. Why don't you try telling the truth?"

"The truth." He let out a deep breath. What truth did she want? That just looking at her made him want to pull her into his arms and never let go, and how at the same time that feeling scared him senseless. But she meant Mike. The truth about Mike. He could tell her that. "He told me to go away, Kate. He doesn't want me around you or Birdie. He thinks I'm bad for you."

Again she was quiet for a long moment. Then she stepped nearer to him and he could see her face in the waning light. It would be completely dark soon. She pulled her sweater tighter around her as though she'd suddenly felt the chill of the night air.

"Are you? Bad for me."

In the distance a dog howled. A lonesome sound. A car passed out on the road, its lights playing over them and plainly showing Kate as she waited for his answer. "I don't know, Kate. I don't want to be."

"Then prove it and come tomorrow." There was challenge in her voice.

"That won't make Mike change his mind."

"Don't worry about Mike. Prove it to me." She reached out toward him. "Please."

He captured her hand in the air and pulled her close enough to kiss, but instead he just looked down at her. "All right. I'll come, but I don't know if that will prove anything."

"Maybe that you're not a coward," she said softly.

He frowned. "Nobody's ever called me a coward."

"Are you trying to say you're not afraid of what you're feeling right now?" She tightened her hand on his and stared up at him. "I am. And nobody's ever called me a coward either."

"I like you, Kate Merritt."

"Is that the best you can say?"

He stared down into her eyes, but he couldn't change his words. Not yet. Instead he said, "Maybe I am a coward."

"Maybe you are," she agreed, but her lips were turning up into a smile. "Maybe we both are."

Then she was tiptoeing up to kiss him. A bare brush of the lips that sent ripples of heat through him and made him want to grab her. But she pulled her hand away from him and stepped back. He sensed she didn't want him to reach for her, so he forced his hands to stay by his side.

She smiled fully then and touched his cheek. "Be of good courage, and he shall strengthen your heart. Both our hearts."

"That's Scripture," he said, too surprised by her quoting Scripture to grab her hand before she pulled it away. Mike quoted Scripture at him. His aunt and uncle had quoted Scripture at him. But no girl had ever pulled out Bible verses when she was standing alone with him in the near darkness.

"Some of it," she admitted. "It's a good verse for when you're not sure what to think. The first part of it says to wait upon the Lord."

"I've never had a girl quote Scripture to me."

"You've never had a girl like me."

"That's for sure," he said. "How about we elope?"

She laughed, the sound sending almost as much of a thrill through him as her lips touching his had moments before. "Somebody would need a bath before that could happen." She turned away from him and headed back toward her house.

"Birdie warned you that I was malodorous."

"I think her word was stinky," she called back over her shoulder without slowing her pace.

"So it was." He hesitated a moment. "Tell her I'm sorry I made her cry."

"You can tell her yourself tomorrow. At one." She stopped to look back at him when she got to the porch. "Plenty of time for that bath."

"Then we can elope?"

She didn't answer him. Only laughed again as she ran up the steps and into the house. He stared at the closed door for a long minute, the very air filled with her presence. He had to make himself get in his car to head back up the road. He was still grinning like a lovesick idiot, and he didn't even try to talk himself out of it. Some things felt too good to chase away.

The moon, fading toward a quarter, was slipping up over the horizon as he headed around the blacksmith shop for the steps leading up to Graham's room, but the shadows were deep in behind the building. He stopped at the pump and filled the bucket there. The night was cool, but not bad for November. While Graham had obviously lost all sense of smell after so many years of sharing space with Poe, Jay didn't want the dog to growl at him. He stripped off his jacket and shirt and splashed the water over him to get rid of the cow barn smell.

"Hello, Jay. I've been waiting for you."

❦ 21 ❦

Jay whirled around, cracking his elbow on the pump handle and knocking over the bucket, sloshing water on his shoes. He couldn't see the girl clearly in the deep shadows next to the building, but he didn't need to see her face to know who it was.

"Alice, what are you doing here?" He grabbed

his shirt off the ground and jammed his wet arms into the sleeves.

"You know the answer to that." Her voice sounded strange, raspy.

She had to be imitating some actress she'd seen making a move on a man in a movie. But it wasn't a movie he wanted any part in. She stepped away from the side of the blacksmith shop and moved slowly toward him, swinging her hips so outlandishly that he worried she might dislocate something. Her brain was obviously already dislocated. She stopped in a shaft of moonlight edging down between the buildings and struck a pose as though she'd found a spotlight. She didn't have on a jacket and her blouse had too many buttons undone for modesty.

Jay didn't know whether to laugh or run. "You better go on home, Alice. Your mother will be worried about you."

She moved toward him again. "My mother thinks I'm spending the night with a friend." She was close enough now that he could see her eyes glittering. "Am I?"

For a couple of seconds he considered sending her running and screaming by grabbing her and planting a kiss on her. But then he decided he was the one who needed to be running scared from her. He eased back a few steps. "I don't know, Alice. You'd better go ask your friend."

"I just did." She smiled, and suddenly she didn't

look like a high school kid. She had obviously studied that movie actress too well.

She reached to touch his chest, but he blocked her hand with his. After moving back another step, he pushed the buttons of his shirt through the buttonholes. He didn't want to get caught half dressed in the dark with Alice Wilcher.

"Look, Alice." He didn't try to soften his words. "Nothing is going to happen between us. Not now or ever. You need to head on home. And when you get there, you better write in your diary that you promise never to sneak up on a man in the dark so you'll remember this was not a good idea."

"Don't treat me like a child." All trace of her smile vanished as her bottom lip came out in a pout. "I'm almost as old as Kate Merritt with a lot more to offer a man." She turned sideways and ran her hands down over her full figure.

He took a deep breath to pull up some patience with the girl and then realized too late she might think his heavy breath was because of her figure instead of her foolishness. "Go home, Alice." He turned away from her and headed for the steps that led up to the room over the blacksmith shop.

"But I'm afraid of the dark." She sounded more like herself now.

"You should have thought of that before you came." He didn't look back at her.

"No, really. I'm afraid to walk home by myself.

Fern's probably out there waiting to jump out at me." She dropped all the way from her sultry woman impression to a little girl ready to cry. "She likes to scare people just for fun. You have to walk me home. If you're any kind of gentleman, you have to."

He didn't want to cave in to her, but she really was nothing but a stupid kid and probably right about Fern. He could believe she was honestly afraid. He was hesitating when a door opened up above his head and Poe came lumbering down the steps, directing a few booming bays toward them.

Graham stepped out behind the dog. "That you, Jay?"

"It is."

"Then how come Poe's acting like you're a coon?"

The dog made it to the bottom of the steps and went right past Jay toward Alice, who shrieked as she scrambled back from the dog. Old Poe could be quick when he had reason, and he bounded across the space between them and stuck his nose up against her.

She let out another shriek and froze where she was with her hands up in the air. "Get him away from me."

"Who's out there?" Graham asked.

"Alice got a little sidetracked on her way home from a friend's house," Jay said. "She was just going, but it appears she forgot she was afraid of the dark and should have gone home earlier."

"Is that a fact?" Graham clomped down the steps.

"Make your old dog stop poking his nose against me." Alice backed up with the dog keeping pace every step. "Please." Her voice was trembling for sure now.

Graham snapped his fingers and Poe went back to sit by him. "Looks to me you've got yourself in a fix, Miss Alice."

"Graham, you tell Jay he has to walk me home." Her voice got steadier as she regained some of her courage, now that Graham had called off Poe. She shifted her eyes from Graham to Jay. "Or he could take me in his car. It's the only gentlemanly thing to do."

"Could be the boy is some like me in not holding all that much store by gentlemanly things, but even if that's not so, there ain't a bit of use burning gasoline to take you down the road a half mile." Graham looked from the girl to Jay and back at her again. "Even if he wanted to, which I'm guessing from the evidence available that he don't. But you're in luck. I was just going to take Poe for a little stroll, so we'll go along with you to be sure nothing bothers you. Or nobody."

Graham started across the yard toward her, but she held out her hands to keep him back. "I don't want you walking with me anywhere. Mama says you're about as crazy as Fern."

"Your mama always did see things pretty

straight." Graham stopped in the middle of the yard and rubbed his chin like he was in deep thought. "That being so, I guess we've got ourselves a dilemma. Or more accurate, you're the one with the dilemma. The boy here and Poe and me, we're already home. And not a bit afraid of the dark."

She glared at Graham, who gave no sign of being bothered at all by her displeasure. She ignored him then as she began pleading with Jay. "You have to take me home."

"How about we all go?" Jay said. "You first and we'll tag along behind to make sure you're safe."

When she saw he was serious, she stomped her foot. "Never mind. I can find my way home." With a disgusted huff, she spun away from them to disappear around the side of the building.

Graham started after her. "We better go watch to be sure she makes it. Her mama might miss her if something were to happen to her. Not sure I could say the same."

"She's just a stupid kid."

Graham looked over at him. "Don't you be fooled. I'm not arguing that she don't rank high on the stupid scale, but I am pointing out that she's trouble. Plain and simple."

"You don't have to tell me that. But it's trouble I'm staying far away from."

Graham stopped a little past the store building. They could see Alice angrily stalking down the road in front of them. "We can see her house from here. No need expending any more effort than necessary. Right, Poe?" He laid his hand flat on the dog's broad head. "Not for the likes of her. And Fern won't be jumping out at her now. Not that close to her house."

"Does Fern wander every night?"

"Naw, she's probably tucked in at Hattie's, snoring away. Like I'm wishing I was." Alice slipped in her front door and Graham turned back toward the blacksmith shop. "But then again, you can't never tell about Fern. She might be wandering." He looked around him. "But she won't hurt nobody. Least ways, she never has. Not even when she had cause. But she does watch what's going on. Keeps people here in Rosey Corner on their toes."

"Is she going to be at the Merritts' tomorrow?"

"If Hattie has anything to do with it, she will. And she'll go for the girl. She's right attached to that little Lorena. She can probably get Fern to stay long enough to eat." Graham looked over at Jay. "How about you? You going to be there?"

"Like Fern, at least long enough to eat. Mrs. Merritt made me a brown sugar pie."

"Is that a fact?" Graham said. "Appears several of those Merritt girls is taken with you."

They were climbing the steps up to the door before Graham said more. "You aren't gonna let them down, are you? Those Merritt girls."

Those Merritt girls. In his mind, as he followed Graham through the door, he saw Kate smiling at him, saying he'd never had a girl like her. And he hadn't, but he couldn't promise things wouldn't go wrong. Things were always going wrong for him. Without looking around at Graham, he said, "I don't want to. I'm doing my best not to let anybody down here in Rosey Corner."

"Good." Graham went through the door ahead of him and pointed toward the table. "I saved you some beans. We'll eat some better on the morrow."

Jay spooned the beans out of the can and wondered if his best was going to be good enough. He wanted it to be, but it never had been before. He pulled in a deep breath. He still smelled like a cow barn.

Birdie insisted on sitting by Jay at the table the next day. Fern was on her other side. Jay hoped Kate would sit beside him, but she sat across from him next to the old woman who'd doctored his black eye and told him to call her Aunt Hattie. The other sister, Victoria, sat between him and her tall, skinny boyfriend. Graham was at one end of the table with Kate's father at the other. Mike and his bride and Mrs. Merritt filled out Kate's side of the table.

Jay avoided looking straight at Mike, even though he felt Mike eyeing him. Jay didn't need to see Mike's face to know disapproval was there. Or maybe "worry" was a better word. He couldn't be any more worried than Jay himself. Graham's words kept circling in his head. *You aren't gonna let them down, are you?* That was what made sitting there at the table with Mike hard. Mike thought he would. He knew Jay. These people here around the table didn't. They liked him, but they didn't know him. They liked who they thought he was. Even Kate.

He bowed his head with them while Mike prayed over the meal, but even after the amen, nobody reached to start passing the food. Instead Mr. Merritt looked at Jay and explained how they had a tradition of each speaking a reason for thanksgiving.

"I'll start off," he said. "I'm thankful for life and new beginnings and a new son-in-law. Among many other things."

"Nobody can mention ever'thing," Aunt Hattie said with an approving nod. "Nadine, you go next."

Mrs. Merritt reached over and grasped her husband's hand for a moment. "For Victor." Then she looked around the table. "And all of you here to share with us today. Aunt Hattie, your turn."

"My Jesus." She held her hands up in the air and looked toward the ceiling. "Praise his loving name." She dropped her hands and looked at Mike. "What you got to say, Pastor Mike?"

"That's easy. My new wife and her family." Mike reached for his bride's hand.

"My wonderful husband," Evangeline gushed back toward him.

Everybody smiled. Jay peeked toward Kate, but she looked as glad for them as everybody else. The only one not smiling was Fern, who looked ready to push back from the table and leave the food behind, but she stayed in her seat. Maybe because Birdie had her hand on her arm. Fern looked different sitting stiff and straight at the table in a print dress than she did appearing out of the moonlight shadows in overalls. More like a regular spinster aunt.

They kept on around the table. Victoria blushed and said her family but she was looking at Sammy. Sammy wasn't as shy. He came right out and claimed Victoria and being a senior so he'd graduate soon. They all knew what he was hoping would happen after that.

Graham was next. He got that look Jay had come to know meant he was going to say something out of the way. "Getting that blamed house painted. And chocolate bars. What about you, Kate?"

She stared down at her plate and ran her finger along the handle of her knife as though searching for what to say.

"Come on, Kate. Say something," Evangeline goaded her. "Or we'll have to put everything back on the stove to heat it up again."

Kate made a face at her sister before she smiled and let her eyes touch on everyone at the table. "All of you," she said. "Living in Rosey Corner with all of you."

Jay wanted to imagine her eyes lingered just a second longer on him. Then she was saying, "Fern, do you want to say something this year?"

Mrs. Merritt spoke up. "You don't have to say anything if you don't want to, Fern." Her voice was soft and kind. "We can skip over you to Lorena."

The woman narrowed her eyes as she stared across the table at Kate and then Kate's mother. "You think I don't have anything to be thankful for?"

"Now, Fern, don't be—" Graham started.

She talked over his words. "Trees. Trees growing back." She almost smiled.

Everybody let out a breath and Aunt Hattie spoke up. "Trees. A fine reason to be offerin' up thanks to the good Lord above." She looked around the table. "Guess that just leaves Lorena and the new one. Sorry, son. They tol' me your name again, but my old head don't hold on to names like it used to."

"That's all right," Jay told her. "My name's Jay."

"Like the bird." Fern surprised him by speaking up.

"Tanner," Birdie added as she peeked first at Kate and then Jay. "You'll have to go last, Tanner. It's my turn now. I'm thankful for Trouble."

Aunt Hattie frowned at the girl. "Lands' sake, chile, why in the world would you be thankful for trouble?"

Birdie laughed out loud with obvious delight as Kate explained, "The dog, Aunt Hattie. She named her dog Trouble."

"What kind of name is that?" Aunt Hattie said.

"One that unfortunately fits him," Mr. Merritt said. "We have Jay to thank for that. So Jay, you want to join in with something you're thankful for?"

When Jay hesitated, Kate's mother smiled at him. "You don't have to if you'd rather not."

"Oh, surely the boy can come up with something." Graham fixed amused eyes on him.

Jay knew what he wanted to say, but he couldn't. Not with Mike staring at him. Not right there in front of her family. So he kept his eyes away from Kate and looked at Birdie instead. "Birdie taking Trouble off my hands."

Everybody laughed the way Jay intended. Graham spoke up. "Poe could talk, he'd be saying the same thing."

"Wait. I'm not through." Jay held up his hand and looked toward Mrs. Merritt as he added, "And brown sugar pie."

"Thank goodness. Everybody's said something. We can finally eat." Mike's bride took a roll off the heaped-up plate of bread next to her and reached for the butter.

"I never knowed you to be so anxious about eatin', Evangeline." Aunt Hattie leaned forward to peer around Mike toward her. "You in the family way already? Is that what's give you such a hurry-up appetite?"

"No, Aunt Hattie, I'm not in the family way," Evangeline said, a little edge in her voice. "But we keep adding people to the table and we could talk all day about what we're thankful for while the rolls get too cold to melt butter. And you know dumplings have to be warm."

The little woman gave her a hard look. "Blessings is worth counting."

"They certainly are," Mike spoke up quickly. "And good food is one we can all count right now. We do thank you, Nadine, for blessing us with the work of your hands."

"I had plenty of help from the girls and Aunt Hattie." Mrs. Merritt smiled at Mike as she started the mashed potatoes around the table.

"Dig in, everybody," Mr. Merritt added.

Across from Jay, Aunt Hattie muttered something under her breath. Kate leaned over and whispered in the old woman's ear. Jay had no idea what she said, but whatever it was, Aunt Hattie's smile came back as she said, "You's right, Katherine Reece. Blessings is abounding. Ain't no call for frowning."

No call at all, Jay agreed as he finally let his eyes settle on Kate, the reason his heart was wanting to sing. She must have felt his eyes on her because she looked up at him. For a few seconds it was like there was no one else in the room but the two of them. But then Birdie was nudging his hand with the green bean bowl and Mike was eyeing him across the table. Jay dipped out some beans and stared down at his plate, but not before he saw Mike's frown.

Birdie wasn't frowning. She was all smiles as she passed him the plate of dressed eggs. "I fixed these all by myself."

"Then I better take two," Jay said. That made her smile even wider, and when he took a chance on glancing back across the table, Kate's smile was waiting for him too. Mike had turned his attention to his pretty wife, but even if he had been still frowning Jay's way, the smiles were outnumbering the frowns. The biggest smile was curling up inside Jay as the talk swirled around him, beckoning him again to feel at home here at least for this one day.

That's all any man had anyway. The one day. He remembered a preacher claiming that to be a Bible truth. That nobody could know about tomorrow and so he best grab hold of today. The preacher's words were intended to pull people down the aisle to make confessions of faith before it was too late, but that didn't mean it wasn't just as true for everything a man did. This day Kate was smiling at him. This day his feet were under this family's table. This day he was almost one of them. Tomorrow might change that. But now it was today.

After they'd eaten all they could hold and stuffed pie in on top of that, the girls began helping their mother clear the table. With a curt nod toward Mrs. Merritt and a pat on top of Lorena's head, Fern pushed back from the table and went straight out the back door.

"She's off to the woods." Graham pulled out his pocket watch and stared at it. "Two hours forty minutes. That could be the longest she's ever stayed at one of your dinners, Nadine. She must have liked it."

Jay thought about following her out, but he didn't want to look cowardly. The men got up from the table and headed for the sitting room, but before Jay could sit down, Mike said, "Let's go see how much that dog you gave Lorena has grown this week."

"Check on Poe too while you're out there," Graham said. "I ate too much to move for at least an hour. But you can tell him that I'll bring him some of the leavings."

Poe barely opened his eyes a slit and didn't bother raising his head off his paws when Jay delivered Graham's promise. The end of the dog's tail did come up off the porch to fall back down with a thump.

"You don't think he knows what you said, do you?" Mike asked. "I mean really."

"I think this old dog knows what Graham is going to say before Graham ever opens his mouth. That's what I think." Jay looked back at the dog, stretched out by the door. He wouldn't move until Graham came out to go home. "Now Trouble on the other hand, he hasn't figured out what anybody's saying."

They walked across the yard toward the clothesline where Birdie had tied the pup to keep him from being a pest at dinner. The pen couldn't hold him anymore. He'd figured out how to dig out of it. Now he was lunging against the rope that held him and barking for all he was worth.

"No wonder. Barking like that, he can't hear anybody," Mike said.

Jay leaned down and stroked the pup. "He's lonely out here all by himself. That's all."

"He does seem to have won over the family in spite of being trouble."

Jay had the feeling Mike wasn't only talking about the dog any longer. He ran his hand down the pup's back again. "He doesn't aim to be trouble. He'll get better with time."

"Time." Mike blew out a long breath of air. "Never enough of it."

Jay stood and the pup jumped up on his leg, but Jay ignored him as he stared at Mike. "Everything all right with you?"

"Right as rain," Mike said. "And I'm supposed

to be asking you that instead of you asking me. I'm the preacher."

"So you are." Jay looked straight at Mike. "Say what you want to say and get it over with, Mike."

"Will it make a difference?"

"No." Jay thought he might as well be honest.

"You don't even know what I was planning to say." Mike was squinting a little as if he was trying hard to see something he couldn't quite make out.

"I've heard a lot of it before."

"Not about Kate."

"No, not about Kate." The pup was still jumping up on him, and Jay gave him a last pat before moving out of reach. Mike followed him as the pup barked frantically behind them.

"She's a great girl." Mike had to raise his voice to be heard over the dog.

"You won't get any argument from me about that," Jay agreed. When they kept walking away, the pup gave up on them turning him loose and plopped down on the ground to wait for Birdie.

"You won't hurt her?" Mike said.

Jay didn't know if he was asking or telling. Either way he could make the promise, but could he keep it? "I won't want to."

"What's that supposed to mean?" Mike asked.

"That I could get a draft notice in the mail any day. That I'm not a preacher and sometimes I can't get everything to turn out the way I want it to."

"Nor can a preacher, my friend."

"Are we friends again?" Jay stopped walking and looked at him.

"As far as I'm concerned, we never stopped being friends." Mike reached over to give Jay's shoulder a squeeze. "And to prove you think the same, you need to come to church."

"You going to preach at me again?"

"Not at you. To you." When Jay didn't say anything, Mike went on. "Christmas is coming. Some of the best stories in the Bible are about Christmas."

"Maybe I'll come," Jay said. No Christmas wonder had ever lit up his head, and it wouldn't this year either. But maybe there would be other kinds of wonder. Maybe there would be Kate.

✿ 22 ✿

Winter swept into Rosey Corner the last weekend of November. The good weather had lingered so long that the first blast of cold air seemed more an insult than the natural changing of the seasons. Up at the store, people huddled around the coal stove and talked about the war.

Kate listened to what they said. She read the papers and tried to make sense of the news reports on the radio. Nothing was getting settled. The British forces made some gains in Libya against the Italians. The Russians were holding the line against the Germans with the help of bitter winter weather. The Japanese Premier Tojo was spouting threats against the Americans and British.

"It's nothing but talk. Those Japanese don't want anything to do with us," the men around the stove at the store assured one another. "It's Hitler we need to be worrying about."

A few of the men like Kate's father had gone over there in 1917 to win the war that was supposed to end all wars. They'd fought back the Germans then, holding on in the trenches across France. For men like her father, the war news had a familiar echo that dredged up bad memories. Kate thought it no wonder her father sometimes turned off the radio and chose his books over the newspapers.

The Sunday after Thanksgiving, Mike urged them to count their blessings and then to covenant to pray. "For peace. For all of us. Prayer is powerful. It can make more difference than all the tanks in the world. Pray for victory for those standing firm against tyranny." His voice was steady and strong, but Kate thought he looked worried.

Everybody was looking worried. So worried that Kate felt guilty to be feeling so good. She hated the war. Terrible stories were coming from overseas. She wanted the Nazis to be defeated. She wanted the bombing to stop, the war to be over, but at the same time, life went on in Rosey Corner.

Trouble kept chasing the cats up trees and finding muddy holes to dig and then making paw prints all over the house. Alice Wilcher kept coming into the store to poke Kate with reports of Carl's latest California adventures and news that he'd be headed to Hawaii soon. Graham kept coming by to lean on the counter and groan about how long it was before baseball season came around again. Her father kept reading every night about Phileas Fogg's trip around the world. Lorena kept racing out to meet Jay Tanner whenever he pulled into their yard. Kate's heart kept leaping up into her throat each time she saw him.

So in spite of the bad news from overseas, in spite of the chilly winds shoving them all toward the darker days of winter, her feet seemed ever ready to dance and her lips to smile. Her lips were ready to do more than smile. They'd kissed again. Brief, innocent touches of the lips when she walked out on the porch with Jay before he left at night. Sweet kisses that made her heart pound. With the slightest encouragement, she would have stepped into his arms and stayed there forever.

Instead he held her away all through the week

296

after Thanksgiving. Circling her like a wary dog unsure of his welcome. No bounding toward her with abandon like Trouble. Perhaps their dance in the moonlight hadn't lit up his heart the way it had hers. Perhaps he was simply out for a good time with any girl available. Including Alice Wilcher, who claimed to have spent time with him in the moonlight too.

Kate let her talk—Alice liked to hear the sound of her own voice—but she didn't believe her. She didn't want to believe her. Besides, Jay was at Kate's house every night, and even if he didn't race to embrace her, Kate sometimes thought he looked at her as though he wanted to.

Even more telling than that, he was there. Mike had claimed Jay wouldn't hang around long, but here he was, still in Rosey Corner. Every night he was sitting on the floor beside Lorena while Kate's father read the next chapter. Every night Kate walked out on the porch and down the steps with him when he left. Every night she lifted her face toward his, all but asking aloud for a kiss. Each time he touched his lips to hers as though too aware of the light spilling out of the house behind them.

Even when she walked with him away from the porch into the night shadows and let her hand brush his, he pretended not to notice. It seemed that now instead of her pushing Lorena between them, he was the one afraid of stepping too close. Yet, he kept coming back, even if he did act like somebody was looking over his shoulder whenever they were alone together. Then the answer came to her. Jay was feeling Mike looking over his shoulder. Kate had seen the two of them talking out in the yard on Thanksgiving. Mike had stepped between them with whatever words he'd said that day.

She could have probably found out what Mike had told Jay from Evie, but Evie wasn't the one to fix things. Kate fixed things. So on the Thursday after Thanksgiving when Jay came by the store to let them know he'd found a job at a feed store in Edgeville, she slipped off her apron without even asking her mother if it was okay for her to leave the store early. Feeling a little like Alice Wilcher, she took Jay's arm and turned him toward the door as she asked him to take her for a ride.

"Are you asking or telling?" he said, but he was smiling as he opened the car door to let her slide in.

"Telling," she said.

"That's what I thought." He shut the door and went around the car to climb in behind the wheel. Then he looked toward her. "Or were you planning to drive?"

"I can, you know," she said.

"I do know. I'm thinking there's not much you can't do if you want to."

"Oh, there are a few things."

"Like?" He pushed the starter to rattle awake the motor.

"Somersaults. Tori and Lorena can somersault like crazy and Tori can even walk on her hands. They've tried to teach me, but I'm hopeless."

"So are we going to practice somersaulting somewhere?" He put the car in gear and looked over at her with his foot on the brake. "Or are we finally eloping? I had a bath just last night and the tank is half full of gas."

Her heart leaped at the thought. They couldn't elope. Not really. But the idea was tingling awake some interesting feelings inside her. "We can't elope without doing some talking first."

"You're coming up with a lot of rules about this eloping stuff. No smelling like cow barns. Now talking." He pretended an exasperated sigh. "So then if we aren't eloping, where are we going? Chicago? New Orleans?"

She laughed. "I don't think so. Not unless we can get there and back by supper. How about we just ride down the road a ways? Take me by the farm you worked at for a while."

She grabbed that out of nowhere. She didn't care where they went. She didn't even care if they did that much talking now. It was enough that she was sitting beside him and that he seemed to be glad of that. She shut her eyes and leaned her head back against the seat and gave herself over to the feel of the tires rolling down the road as he headed the car toward Edgeville.

He broke the silence between them. "Hard day at the store?"

"Not really. Just confining. Somebody has to be there behind the counter all the time, from opening time in the morning until closing time at night. And people can be a pain."

"Rosey Corner people?" Jay glanced over at her with raised eyebrows.

"Especially Rosey Corner people. The better you know people, the harder it is to put up with them sometimes."

"Then maybe it's good I'm not from Rosey Corner." He hesitated with his eyes straight ahead before he said, "But I wouldn't mind getting to know a few Rosey Corner people better."

"Which people are those?"

She looked across at him, but he kept his eyes on the road as he answered, "You already know the answer to that."

"Sometimes I don't think I know any answers." She stared out the windshield at the road the same as he was doing. "Or even the right questions to ask."

"But you know some you want to ask me." He kept the smile on his face, but his hands tightened on the steering wheel.

"Maybe," Kate said. "You probably have things you'd like to ask me too."

"I've been asking you that ever since Mike's wedding."

She glanced over at him with a puzzled look. "What's that?"

"How about we elope?" He grinned over at her. "So far I haven't gotten anything but reasons we can't."

"When I think you're serious, then I might give you an answer."

"What makes you think I'm not serious?"

"A girl knows." She squeezed her hands together so tightly that her fingers hurt. "I'm beginning to wonder if you're ever serious about anything."

"Serious," he said. "Sounds like there could be a serious question behind that. Do I have to come up with a serious answer?"

"I guess that's up to you."

He didn't say anything then, maybe waiting for her question. She stared at her hands while the silence between them suddenly seemed louder than the noise of the engine chugging along, taking them who knew where. She did have questions, but she wasn't sure she should ask them. Why did she think she had to know all the answers? Why couldn't she just let things slide along? What was it about her that made her think she could always make things work out the way she wanted? She had plenty of experience to prove that wasn't true, but surely it would be better to know where she stood than to feel this awful uneasy wondering. Better to face the truth, whatever it turned out to be.

That's the mistake she'd made with Carl. Not being honest with him and telling him straight out they weren't a couple. She'd made sort of the same mistake with Mike. Not being honest with herself and seeing how much he loved Evie and accepting that nothing could ever change that. She had never wanted that to change. Not really.

None of that mattered now anyway. She hadn't been in love with Mike any more than she'd been in love with Carl. But how she felt about Jay Tanner was different. This feeling consumed her. It shot through every nerve in her body until just the thought of him set her skin to tingling.

She hadn't wanted to fall in love with him, but her heart hadn't cared when her brain said he was a charmer. Instead, she'd stepped into the moonlight with him and been lost to that charm. Even now with him gripping the steering wheel and staring straight ahead as though afraid to look toward her, she wanted to reach over and touch his hand. Connect with him. Let him know how she felt. But did he want to know?

A better question to answer might be, did she have the courage to tell him? She moistened her lips. She was not a coward. She'd been ready to go against everybody in Rosey Corner for Lorena.

She'd never run from Fern, even when the woman was doing her best to scare her. That wasn't to say she'd never been scared. But she'd done whatever had to be done. She could do this.

She separated her hands and spread her fingers out on her skirt. Relaxing them one by one. She was opening her mouth to just blurt something out when he put on the brakes and turned off the road through an open gap in the fence and bounced across a field to stop behind a barn.

"Is this where you worked?" Kate looked out the window. "Where's the house?"

"It's over the hill. We'll go on up there in a few minutes and you can meet Mrs. Franklin. She's a nice lady. But if you want serious answers, I need to look at you while you're asking the hard questions." He turned toward her and gripped the seat top behind Kate. "All right, I'm braced and ready. Ask away. Anything except what's my middle name. I don't tell anybody that." He started to smile, but then straightened his lips out in a flat line. "And I will be serious. I promise."

She stared down at her hands again. "I don't know what—"

He interrupted her. "First, you have to look at me. Eye to eye." She looked up and let him capture her eyes. "Now just say what you want to say, Kate." He hesitated a minute as though having to force out his next words. "If you're wanting to tell me to get lost, then tell me."

"Tell you to get lost?" She couldn't hide her surprise. "I thought maybe you wanted me to get lost."

"Never." He moved his hand off the car seat to stroke her cheek with the back of his fingers. "Why would you think that?"

"Then why haven't you kissed me—really kissed me—all week?" That was the question she most wanted to ask. "Didn't you want to?"

He looked puzzled as his hand stilled on her cheek. "Did you want me to?"

"Oh yes." She threw all caution to the wind, throwing open her heart to him. "Oh very definitely yes."

"You are so beautiful, Kate. I've never known a girl like you." When she started to say something, he put his fingers over her lips. "Wait. Let me finish. I am so very afraid of doing something wrong." He moved his fingers across her cheeks as if memorizing the feel of her skin. "So afraid I might hurt you. That I won't be good enough for you."

A little spark of anger ignited inside her. "Did Mike tell you that? Is that what you talked about out in the yard on Thanksgiving?"

"He didn't have to tell me," Jay said. "I knew already. I'm not good enough. You do deserve a man like him instead of somebody like me."

"I like somebody like you, Jay Tanner."

He smiled then. "Is that the best you can say?"

"Some things are better not said too soon."

"And some things you have to trust to the winds of chance and see what happens. Things like this." He gripped her shoulder and scooted toward her.

She met him halfway. This time there was no moonlight. There wasn't even any sunlight. The clouds were thick and gray. But the magic was there, sparkling inside her. What difference did it make that she didn't have all the answers? She didn't even know the questions to ask. But she knew what felt right, and it felt very right to have Jay's arms wrapped around her, his lips on hers, demanding and getting a response.

When she pulled back to draw in a shaky breath, he kept his eyes on her face. "The winds of chance are being kind to me." He sounded almost as breathless as she felt before he pulled her close against him.

She thought then about telling him she loved him, but something held her back. He wasn't saying the words. Maybe it was too soon. Who knew what tomorrow would bring?

"Look." He pointed toward the window. "It's snowing."

Fat snowflakes were settling softly on the windshield. The air around the car was white with them. Kate pulled away from Jay. "Maybe you should get the car out of here before we get snowed in."

"Snowed in with you sounds pretty good." Jay

tipped her face around toward his to kiss her again. But this time he didn't pull her into his arms. Instead he jerked open the car door and grabbed her hand to help her slide across the seat and behind the wheel.

"What are you doing?" She laughed as she stumbled out of the car.

"Have you ever seen such beautiful snow?" But his eyes weren't on the snow. They were on her. "I think Fern would tell us to dance, don't you? In the music of the snow."

And so she stepped into his arms to glide with him through the snowflakes falling around them. Wrapped in silence. Wrapped in love. The snow wouldn't last. The flakes disappeared as soon as they hit the ground and already the cloud that was sifting the snow down on them was drifting away. But still they danced. Embracing the moment.

Tomorrow would be soon enough to worry about tomorrow.

❦ 23 ❦

The last Sunday in November, Jay got up and ready for church. He could handle an hour of Mike's preaching. It could even happen that he'd feel something in his heart. For sure, his heart was awake and singing every time he was around Kate. Kate would be at church. Maybe the church words would sound different to him with a heart open to feeling. That's what Mike had always told him. That all he had to do was open up his heart and accept the Lord's love. If he could lay his heart open for Kate, then maybe it would be possible to feel this other love Mike was pushing at him. A greater love, he called it.

Mike felt it. He knew the exact day he'd let the Lord take over his heart. He'd told Jay the story a dozen times. Kate felt it. Her whole family felt it, even Birdie. None of them had actually told him they did. Not like Mike had over and over. But it was easy to see them all gliding along the path of faith without worrying a bit about the troublesome rocks that might trip up an unwary person.

Years ago, he told that worry to Mike, and Mike had found some verse in the Bible to read to him. Something to do with angels lifting a believing man up to keep him from dashing his foot against a stone. He'd said the Lord might send an angel to watch over Jay. When Jay laughed at the chances of that ever happening, Mike had stomped away and stayed mad for days. They were both so much younger then. Mike sure of angels and the Lord, Jay not sure of anything.

But now Kate was smiling at him. Dancing with him. Maybe loving him. She could be angel enough to hold her hand out to him and get him to take that step up on the path of faith with her. She hadn't asked him what he believed, but he sensed that was one of the questions that had been circling in her head last Thursday when she'd ridden with him to the Franklins'.

They had gone by the Franklins' house after their dance in the snow. Mrs. Franklin had hopped up and down and clapped her hands when she opened the door to see them on the porch. She plied them with cookies and tea while showing them the pictures of the grandchildren she'd gotten in the mail. Jay even caught a smile on Mr. Franklin's face as they sat around the woodstove and talked.

Or maybe Jay was so ready to smile, he imagined everybody else just as ready. Sitting in church beside Kate and Birdie, he wasn't even bothered when he kept noticing Alice Wilcher staring at him from across the church. Definitely without a smile.

Mike looked his way more than once after he wound up his sermon and the congregation stood to sing the final hymn. But Jay stayed in the pew. He might wish he could be as sure the Lord was in control as the good people around him, but wishing something didn't make it true. Nor could borrowing feelings bury anything worthwhile in his heart. For now, it would have to be enough for Mike that he was sitting in his church. That he was wondering. That he might be listening for that knock on his heart's door every preacher he'd ever heard preach claimed he could hear if he would only listen.

December came in with a bitter wind. The war news was more of the same, mostly bad. Draft notices were still going out. That's why Jay got the job at the feed store in Edgeville. One of the hands had gotten his summons and left for the Army.

Every afternoon when Jay came back to Graham's after work, he expected to see an envelope waiting for him with his name on it. It would come. His number would pop up eventually, but each day the draft notice delayed was a good day for Jay. A day when he could clean up and go to the Merritts' house and let the warmth of family love beckon him in. A night when Kate would walk with him down off the porch to tell him goodbye. Neither of them felt the cold as they embraced in the shadows.

Every night before he left, he asked her to elope. Each time she looked up at him, the contours of her face soft in the dark shadows of the night, and laughed. An enchanting laugh that wound down into his heart and settled there with joy. He knew she would never elope, but it was easier to say that than to tell her he loved her. And he did love her. He had quit even trying to argue that he shouldn't, that he wasn't good enough for her.

He wasn't. He would never be good enough for Kate, but that didn't keep him from loving her. Or her from loving him.

She didn't say the words out loud either, but her eyes told him. Her lips surrendering to his told him. In time one of them would have the courage to say the words aloud. Until then they'd let their love dance in the air between them as they remembered the moonlight and snowflakes.

When Sunday rolled around again, Jay got up to go to church the same as the Sunday before. The pews didn't feel a bit hard when he was sitting by Kate.

Graham gave him a raised-eyebrow look when he put on his suit. "Looks like somebody might be getting religion."

"Everybody tells me it's a good thing to have." Jay slicked down his hair before he looked over at Graham. "You want to go with me?"

"What is it today?" Graham studied the calendar he had tacked to the wall over the table. It had a picture of the Edgeville Bank on it. "December 7th. Could be the right Sunday for church, but I generally hold off till the second Sunday."

Jay put down the comb and checked how he looked in the little mirror he'd tacked up on the wall over his cot. Graham didn't have one. He claimed he hadn't had any need for a mirror since around 1920.

"Most people here in Rosey Corner go to

church every Sunday." Jay turned from the mirror toward Graham.

"That's a fact," Graham agreed. "Aunt Hattie's even got Fern going more times than not. Aunt Hattie can be a powerful preacher when she takes a mind to straighten somebody out."

"What about you?"

"I ain't got much interest in preaching."

"Or listening to preaching either?" Jay asked.

Graham tilted back in his straight chair until it leaned against the wall. "If you want to know something, why don't you just ask it straight out?"

"What makes you think I want to know something?"

"The way you're sniffing around the question like Poe around a hole he's afraid a snake might pop out of. Old Poe don't take kindly to snakes." Graham narrowed his eyes on Jay before he went on. "You're wanting to know if I've got any belief in this old heart of mine for the good Lord. Maybe because you're feeling some strange stirrings in your insides when Preacher Mike brings down the Word. Feelings you're some afraid of or I miss my guess."

Jay sat down on the cot and rested his elbows on his knees as he looked down at the floor. "Could be you're not missing your guess."

Graham pulled in a breath and let it out slowly. "The good Lord and me, we came to an understanding a long time ago. He said I could go sit in with his other children in the church buildings now and again and that other times I could just worship wherever I happened to be. It's my belief the Lord isn't near as picky about where that worshiping takes place as some church folks would have you think."

Jay looked up at him. "What do you mean?"

"Well, from what I read in my Bible about him while he was walking around down here, he ended up worshiping in some uncommon places himself. With that short little fellow, Zacchaeus, after he told him to come down from his tree. You remember that story, don't you? Or at a wedding changing water into wine. I'm thinking that might raise some eyebrows here among the Rosey Corner church folks these days."

"I know the Bible stories," Jay said. "I was at church every time the doors were open until I got out of school and took off on my own. My aunt and uncle were strong on religion."

"Must have lacked some in practicing what they preached." Graham sat forward and the front legs of his chair banged against the floor. Poe raised his head and gave him a woeful look for disturbing his sleep. "But it's like this, boy. Every man, woman, and child has to come to the Lord on his own. Somebody might lead you there. A preacher might give you a few prods, but nobody can believe for you. Not me. Not Preacher Mike. Not that sweet little Lorena who would believe for everybody if she could." He leveled his eyes on Jay. "Not Kate. Some things a man has to do for himself, and deciding what to believe is one of them."

"I want to believe. Because of Kate."

Graham's lips turned up in a sad little smile. "You've got to want to believe because of you."

Jay kept looking at Graham. "I'm in love with her." He was surprised at how easily he said the words.

"I know that." Graham's smile got warmer. "I do evermore know that. And I'll send up a little prayer for the both of you this morning while you're over there worshiping in the church house and I'm here worshiping next to my stove keeping my old joints warm." He pulled his watch out of his pocket and gave it a long look. "You'd better head on out if you aim to get there before they go to singing."

The woman at the piano was already banging out the first chords of the opening hymn when Jay went in the church. He started to slip into one of the back pews. There were empty places. But then Kate was looking over her shoulder at him and he marched right up the aisle to ease into the pew with her and her family. Could it really be possible that he might belong there? Or was he only dreaming? Nothing good had ever lasted for him.

Kate gave his hand a quick squeeze of welcome as she started singing "Bringing in the Sheaves."

313

He could be one of the sheaves, he thought as he began to sing the familiar words with her and the rest of the congregation. A sheaf of the harvest. A sinner come home. Maybe today would be the day he'd hear the call, but right then all he could hear was the way his heart was pounding because Kate's shoulder was rubbing against his arm.

They set a place for him at their Sunday dinner table. It was just the family today. The family and him. Mike seemed more accepting of him being there at the Merritts' table. Jay hadn't walked the aisle during the invitation, but maybe just showing up for church two Sundays in a row was enough to convince Mike he had changed. That maybe he'd left behind the heathen thinking that kept him wondering about things that a good churchgoer didn't question. Like if the Lord was all powerful, how come he let wars happen? How come he let people go hungry? How come he took away a little boy's mother when that little boy needed her so bad?

Mike had told him once that he didn't think the Lord minded questions. Jay didn't know if that was true or not, but he did know that his questions had made Mike uncomfortable. Mike hadn't come up with answers. No real answers that made sense. Instead he'd ended up telling Jay some things couldn't be figured out like an arithmetic problem with one sure answer. He'd said the thing Jay needed to remember was that he could trust the

Lord to have an answer for everything, even if sometimes the answer was beyond their limited understanding. Sounded like preacher talk to Jay, but that was only natural since Mike knew even then he was going to be a preacher.

The day was chilly, so they all settled in the sitting room after they'd made short work of the raisin roll dessert and cleared away the dishes. Even Trouble plopped down on the floor to take a Sunday afternoon nap after Birdie talked Kate and Jay into a game of pick-up sticks. Mike had put in a late night at the movie house, so he was grabbing a quick nap in the bedroom before going out visiting. Evangeline was chatting with her mother as they leafed through a couple of magazines. Mr. Merritt was in his favorite rocker over by the window, totally immersed in some fictional world.

The radio wasn't on. Jay liked it that way. The quiet sounds of family. The occasional pop of the fire. Birdie's laugh when he tried to pick up a stick and clumsily touched one of the sticks near it to lose his turn. The murmur of Victoria's and Sammy's voices from the kitchen where they were studying for a history test. The sound of pages turning. He'd always imagined there were places like this. He watched Kate as she deftly picked up her stick without moving any of the others. She looked up at him and smiled victoriously.

No wonder she didn't want to elope. Who would

want to leave this kind of place where love wrapped from one person to the next like a gentle web?

"Your turn," she said.

He stared at the pile of sticks, then reached down and grabbed as many of them as he could in his hand. That's what he wanted to do, grab everything in the room and hold it close to him. Kate and Birdie and the whole family. Even Trouble.

"Hey, that's cheating," Birdie protested even as she squealed with delight.

"You're right. I lose." He smiled at her and dropped the sticks back down. That's what he felt like he was doing. Cheating. Reaching for more than he deserved.

Mrs. Merritt looked up from her magazine. "Shh, Lorena. You'll wake up Mike."

"That's okay, Nadine. I'm awake already." Mike was in the bedroom doorway, smoothing his hair down with his hands. "The afternoon's slipping by. I need to get up to see Mrs. Penn. And I'd better go by the Nolands'." He kept his eyes away from Kate. "Mrs. Noland's sister told me this morning that the poor woman is beside herself after Carl's letter last week saying he married some girl out there in California before he shipped out for Hawaii. Did you know about that?"

Mrs. Merritt closed her magazine. "We heard something about it at the store, but since it didn't come from Carl's family, we weren't sure how true it was. They haven't been coming into the store lately."

"Afraid they'll have to look at me," Kate spoke up.

Jay wanted to say he'd like to sit in a corner of the store all day long if that meant he could feast his eyes on her.

"People can be so stupid," Evangeline said. "I wouldn't worry a minute about any of them."

Jay didn't know if Mike was opening his mouth to agree with her or to suggest a more preacher-wifely attitude when Trouble leaped up and began barking for all he was worth as somebody banged on the door.

"What in the world?" Mr. Merritt closed his book and started up out of his chair.

"I'll get it, Dad." Kate was already on her feet. She grabbed Trouble's collar and was reaching for the door when Graham pushed it open and burst into the room.

His face was pasty white and he had to lean against Kate a minute to catch his breath. Nobody said a word as they braced themselves for whatever bad news he was bringing. Finally he managed to say, "The Japanese are bombing Pearl Harbor! It's on the radio."

❦ 24 ❦

Graham's raspy breathing was loud in the stunned silence that followed his words. Words that hung in the air while time seemed to stand still. The clock didn't stop ticking away the seconds. Kate kept on breathing in air. The fire kept popping, but none of it was the same. She wanted to block out Graham's words. To go back to the easy time before he'd burst into the room. But she couldn't push him back out the door. Not wanting to hear his news didn't make it any less true.

Across the room her father sank heavily back down into his rocking chair like he'd been punched in the stomach. Her mother covered her mouth with a hand that trembled, dismay plain in her eyes. Mike and Evie were staring at each other in a raw, private way that made Kate almost ashamed to have glimpsed it. In the kitchen doorway, Tori and Sammy grasped each other's hands, their faces drained of color.

Her eyes slid to Jay on his feet staring straight at her with such intensity that it took her breath. She wanted to go to him, to feel his hand gripping hers the way Sammy was holding onto Tori, but she couldn't move. She felt apart from it all. From

Graham's words. From the worry on every face. It was like she was seeing it from afar.

Lorena ran across the room to grab Kate's hand and yank her back into the reality of the moment. With wide eyes she stared up at Kate. "What's Pearl Harbor, Kate? Why's everybody looking funny?"

Her questions seemed to set them all free.

"It's a place in Hawaii." Graham straightened up away from Kate, but he looked so shaky that she kept her hand on his arm to steady him. Then Jay was pushing a straight chair under Graham, who sank down in it with relief. "The Navy has a base there."

"Where Carl went?" Lorena looked worried. "Is he getting bombed?"

"I don't know, baby. Maybe he hadn't gotten there yet." Kate gently pushed Lorena's hair back from her face.

Jay stepped closer to wrap his arms around both Lorena and Kate in the kind of hug people shared when a loved one was sick or dying. People were dying. Bombs were falling on American soldiers. If it was true.

Mike must have felt the same doubts about whether it could really be happening the way Graham said. "Are you sure you heard right? The Japanese bombed us?" His voice sounded incredulous.

"Not bombed. Bombing. They're still at it. Ever

since just after daybreak there." Graham sounded weary as he looked over at Mike. "Turn on the radio. Hear it for yourself."

Without a word, Kate's father leaned forward to switch on the radio beside his chair. It took an interminable time to warm up, but then the broadcast seemed to be regular programming. A football game. For a moment, hope that somehow Graham was mistaken, that he had heard something wrong, flickered awake in Kate, but the hope died out even before the reporter broke into the program again. Graham wouldn't get this kind of thing mixed up.

They all turned toward the radio as though they could see the words spill out of it. Evie stood up and Mike stepped over beside her. Kate's father stayed leaned forward to keep from missing anything the reporter said. Kate held Lorena close in front of her and Jay kept his arm around them both as the news report began. The only one not staring at the radio was Graham. He already knew what the man was going to say.

"From the NBC newsroom in New York, President Roosevelt said in a statement today that the Japanese have attacked Pearl Harbor, Hawaii, from the air. I'll repeat that. President Roosevelt says the Japanese have attacked Pearl Harbor from the air. This bulletin came to you from the NBC newsroom in New York."

A new voice came on, promising more details

the minute they came in. Then an advertisement started up, but it was as if none of those words mattered anymore.

Kate's father stared straight ahead at the wall over the radio. "We're at war. Again."

Mama stood up. For a few seconds, she steadied herself against the couch arm before she moved over to touch Daddy's shoulder. He covered her hand with his and they stayed still and silent for a moment. They knew about war. They'd been through the war that was to end all wars.

Daddy looked over at Mike, then Jay. "I'm sorry."

Kate's mother didn't say anything, just tightened her hand on Daddy's shoulder and stared at the radio as the news reporter came on again, repeating the same news and then adding that reports were coming in that Army and Navy bases in Manila were also being attacked.

"Naturally this means war," the announcer said in a curiously flat voice, even though he had to know his words were reaching out and poking every listener. "Naturally America will retaliate."

He kept saying "naturally" like a bad record stuck in one spot. His voice ended and the regular programming started up again, but they didn't want to hear that. They stared at the radio, wanting to somehow force it to reveal more. Kate's father twisted the dial between the stations to try to pick up more reports.

Slowly, one by one they found places to sit. Her mother on the stool in front of her father's chair. Mike on the couch beside Evie, although he kept looking toward the door as if thinking he needed to be doing something else. Something more. Every time a new announcement came over the air, he squeezed his eyes shut and bowed his head in an attitude of prayer.

Kate thought she should be praying too. That they all should be praying. At the same time, she couldn't seem to get past the first words in her head. *Oh, dear God.* She had no idea what to pray. The whole idea of bombs falling on their ships, their soldiers, and what that would mean was too staggering.

Tori and Sammy sank down on the floor and leaned against the wall, heads close together, their history homework forgotten. They were listening to history being made. Their future being altered.

Graham scooted his chair closer to the radio and leaned toward the sound of the voices coming from it. He was still wheezing from his hurry to share the news with them. He muffled a cough to keep from missing a word that might be coming from the radio.

"I'll get you some water," Kate told him. She couldn't just stand there. She had to move, even if it did mean stepping away from Jay. She needed to be doing something, if it was nothing more than pouring Graham a glass of water. Lorena tagged along to the kitchen with her, holding onto Kate's skirt the way she used to when she first came to live with them.

Kate looked at Jay when she returned with Graham's water. He'd backed up against the wall next to the front door, looking unsure of his place among them. She wanted to go to him and pull him into the circle of the family, but what if he wasn't ready for that? His face was so serious, but then this was no time for smiling. Nobody was smiling.

When Aunt Gertie and Uncle Wyatt drove into the yard and practically right up to the porch a few minutes later, it was Jay who opened the door for them. They came in, talking in hushed tones the way people did when somebody died. Kate supposed death was happening. Bombs were exploding. Bombs killed people.

Aunt Hattie showed up a few minutes later. She didn't bother knocking, just came on in. She was alone, but none of them would have ever expected Fern to show up. Fern's way of dealing with bad things happening was to vanish into the trees. Reports of an attack on a Navy base halfway around the world wasn't going to change that.

Aunt Hattie had no more than settled down in one of the chairs than a bulletin came across the radio. The reporter was almost shouting. "We have witnessed this morning the attack of Pearl

Harbor and a severe bombing of Army planes, undoubtedly Japanese. The city of Honolulu has also been attacked and . . ."

The voice faded, and they all leaned toward the radio trying to hear through the static. Then they could hear him talking again. "This battle has been going on for nearly three hours."

Again a crackling noise blanked out the signal. Kate held her breath to keep from missing any of the words when the man's voice came through again. "It's no joke. It's a real war."

The voice was cut off and another announcer came on to explain that they'd just heard from an eyewitness straight from Hawaii. The report ended and regular programming started up again. Kate's father turned the dial, but he wasn't finding much but static.

Kate had stopped in the middle of the floor with her arm around Lorena while the bulletins were sounding, but she couldn't keep standing there as though she, like Jay, didn't know if she belonged. She had no doubt she belonged here with her family. Her eyes were drawn to Jay. She wanted him to think he belonged here too. Beside her. To believe they belonged together.

Wasn't that what love was supposed to be like? Two together, drawing strength from one another the way her mother and father were doing. Mike and Evie too. Even Tori and Sammy were leaning on one another. Lorena was clinging to her and that was good. She wanted to be strong for Lorena, but she also wanted more. She wanted Jay's arms around her again. But he hadn't been the one to pull away. She had.

She always had to be doing something. Like Martha in the Bible. Bustling around trying to fix things instead of prayerfully waiting on the Lord to reveal what was most needed the way Martha's sister, Mary, had done. But without Martha, nothing would get done. Nobody would get to eat. Or sit, because nobody would be bringing in chairs from the kitchen. Everybody would go thirsty.

Why did Kate have to make everything so difficult? Why couldn't she simply walk across the room and lean against Jay the way she wanted to? The way he wanted her to. His face told her that. Then again, why was she even thinking about such things when the voices crackling over the radio were shifting the world as they knew it? Nothing would ever be the same again. She sank down onto the arm of the couch and pulled Lorena back against her. It wasn't time to be worrying about whether she and Jay could ever be like her mother and father. That kind of feeling didn't happen overnight. It took years.

Aunt Hattie pushed herself up out of the rocking chair and looked toward Mike. "Have you been doing any praying, Reverend Mike?" She'd always been short, but now the sorrow of the news seemed to be weighing her down even more until she wasn't much taller than Lorena.

"I'm praying, Aunt Hattie. We're all praying," Mike answered.

"Could be we should join them prayers together then. Appeal to the good Lord above with every bit of faith we can summon up."

"You pray for us, Aunt Hattie," Kate's mother said.

Aunt Hattie looked from Mama to Mike. "Is that all right with you, Reverend?"

"More than all right, Aunt Hattie," he said. "I'll save my prayers for church tonight."

"Ain't never no use saving prayers." Aunt Hattie frowned. "The good Lord knows them before we ever utter them anyhow."

"And I'll trust him to put words in my mouth to beg for his mercies when I stand in the church later, but right now I need you to talk to the Lord for me. For all of us."

Mike tightened his arm around Evie, drawing her even closer to him. The way Kate wished Jay was holding her, but again that kind of love took time. So instead, she laid her cheek against the top of Lorena's head. She knew how she felt about Lorena. That was the kind of love she could understand. How she felt about Jay was too new.

Aunt Hattie raised her skinny arms with palms flat toward the ceiling as she looked up and began praying . . .

"Dear loving and gracious and understanding Lord. I's knowing you is lookin' down on us with loving kindness. And we thank you that you is right here with us during this hard time. We know your lovin' arms is reaching out to us wantin' to draw us close to you so's we can lean on your strength and not our own. We has trouble with that, dear Lord, time and time again. Not trustin' you the way we should. We's for sure gonna trust you now with this evil happening and all the evil happenings that's been overtakin' this old world. But we know you is in control and that in your good time you will make things right."

Aunt Hattie paused, but nobody said anything. They knew she wasn't through until she came out with an amen.

"We's some of us got a feelin' of fear down here. We's scared of what we's looking at the same as we were back when our boys went off to that other war when you took my Bo on to his heavenly home. Now here we are again. Trembling and shakin' afore you. Protect those boys over there in that Pearl Harbor where bombs is falling. Give them and us here too, give all your children the courage we is gonna need in the dark days ahead. Let us know that not even the deepest darkness can keep your lovin' light from shining through to us. Amen and amen."

Kate never knew anything to add to any of Aunt Hattie's prayers. The old woman knew the Lord was her friend. Doubt never sat down with her. Hadn't even when her son had been killed in that first war she'd just been praying about. She said the devil nudged doubts into a believer's head. Some soft and easy. Others sharp and pointed. And that then the old devil leaned back and laughed when people wiggled those doubt pins around, letting them work deeper down into a body's mind instead of yanking them out and pitching them to the side the way they ought to.

Kate didn't doubt. She didn't. Not anymore. Once she had. She'd wanted to turn her back completely on the Lord. But the Lord hadn't turned his back on her. He just waited out her doubts and then was right there the very same when she opened her eyes and reached for him again.

So now she breathed a soft amen and opened her eyes to look straight toward Jay standing by the door. He wasn't there. She whipped her eyes around the room. He wasn't anywhere. He must have slipped out the front door while they were all concentrating on Aunt Hattie's prayer. What had she said? That some among them had a fearful spirit. Maybe she hadn't been talking about the war. Not the war of bombs and bullets, but a spiritual war that had made her prayer words poke him too hard. So hard he'd left. Without so much as a goodbye.

"Where's Tanner?" Lorena asked.

"I guess he had to leave," Kate said. She listened for his car to start up, but it was quiet out front other than the sound of a hen cackling and the wind rattling the screen door.

"Before the amen? He can't do that. Nobody leaves before the amen." Lorena frowned as she pulled away from Kate to go peer out the window. "His car's still here."

"Jay's got some things bothering him right now," Mike said. "I guess I should go talk to him." He started to push up off the couch, but Evie put a hand on his arm to stop him.

"You'll have to do it later," she told him as she looked toward the clock on the mantel. "You don't have time now. We've got to get ready for church."

Evie's words seemed to make them all remember that things needed to get done the same as always.

"Getting cool in here," Kate's father said as he pushed up out of his rocker. He lifted open the stove door and emptied the coal from the bucket on the hearth into the fire. "Best get more in before dark, and the old cow's bawling. Time to milk."

Mama stood up too and let her eyes sweep around the room. "Why don't you all just stay here until church time? I'll put supper on the table in case anybody's hungry. Keep listening to see if more news comes on if you want." She looked over at Tori. "You and Sammy need to pick up your books. Lorena, you best go gather the eggs and feed Trouble before we go."

"But what about Tanner?" Lorena looked toward the front door.

Nobody said anything, but everybody looked at Kate. Kate hesitated, not sure what to say or do. He'd sneaked out in the middle of a prayer. He'd wanted to be away from them.

Her mother made her decision for her. "Kate can go tell him we're saving a piece of pie for him." Then she shifted her eyes to Lorena. "You go get the eggs like I told you to."

"Okay." Lorena let out a long sigh and her shoulders slumped, but she headed toward the back door. She looked over her shoulder at Kate. "But you tell Tanner he's not supposed to leave before the amen."

"I'll tell him," Kate said, surprised to feel a smile curling up her lips. A smile that was mirrored on the other faces in the room. How could they be smiling with all these bad things happening? But they were. "If he's still here."

Graham spoke up. "He'll still be here or I miss my guess. It's just that the boy don't understand about families."

"And what he doesn't know scares him," Mike said.

"True enough for all of us," Graham agreed.

"But could be things aren't so nerve-wracking when a man's got friends and a hand to hold on to."

"The Lord's hand is ever reaching down to help us," Mike said.

"You is right as rain, Reverend Mike, about that." Aunt Hattie lifted her hands up toward the ceiling again before she sank back down in the rocker.

"I'm not disagreeing. But I've known the times it took somebody else reaching out a hand to help me see the good Lord's hand ready for me." Graham peered over at Kate, practically pushing her out the door with his eyes.

Jay was leaning against the tree where he'd parked his car. Where Lorena liked flying high into the sky on the swing in the summer. Where the swing hung deserted and still, except for bouncing a bit in the wind this time of the year. Where Carl had proposed and then forced a kiss on Kate. Where she had welcomed Jay's kisses the last week. Laughter and tears.

She pulled her sweater closer around her. She should have grabbed her coat. The day had turned colder. Everything about the day was colder and not just because of the north wind.

Jay didn't look up at her, but she could tell he knew she was walking across the yard toward him. He kept his eyes on the ground even after she stopped in front of him. "I'm sorry," he said.

"I hope I didn't upset everybody slipping out the door like that."

"Nobody but Lorena. She said to tell you that you couldn't leave before the amen."

"I'll make it up to her."

"No more dogs." Kate held her hand palm out toward him. "Trouble is enough."

He looked up at her and almost smiled. "Then maybe a cat she could call Scout. Wasn't that what she said once she wanted to name a dog if she had one?"

"She used to say that."

Every trace of smile disappeared. "Then I brought her Trouble."

"She loves Trouble," Kate said. "But all she really wants you to bring her is you. She loves you." It was on the tip of her tongue to say she loved him too, but she held back the words. She didn't know why.

"But I'll just end up disappointing her. I disappoint everybody."

"You haven't disappointed us." Kate reached her hand toward him.

"Yet." He stared down at the ground, refusing her offered hand. He had to see it, but he kept his own hands in his pockets.

She tucked her hand back up under her sweater as she wrapped her arms tight around her waist and tried not to shiver. She didn't know what to say. He was putting up a wall between them and she didn't know why. "What are you afraid of?" she finally asked. She couldn't keep her teeth from chattering.

"You're cold."

"A little," she admitted.

He took off his jacket and covered the space between them in one step to drape it over her shoulders. "You should go back in the house."

The jacket carried his warmth, and even better, he didn't step away from her but kept hold of the coat lapels, pulling it tight around her. She looked up at him. "You didn't answer me."

"What am I afraid of?" His hands dropped away from the coat, but he stayed where he was and kept looking into her eyes. After a moment he said, "Everything. Only everything."

"The war?"

"I'll have to go, but that's not what I'm most afraid of."

"Then what is it that scares you so much?" The air was so cool, she could see her breath. Her words seemed to hang there with it.

"Love."

Kate frowned a little. "Why would you be afraid of love?"

"What else can hurt you so much?" He looked away from her then, toward the field on the other side of the house.

" 'There is no fear in love, for perfect love casteth out fear.' " When she saw the look on his face, she wanted to take the words back. Not because she didn't believe them. She did, but that was talking about the perfect love of the Lord. Not the kind of love that poked and prodded, sent a person heavenward one minute, to the depths the next. Besides, she didn't want him to think she was preaching at him like Aunt Hattie or Mike. It was okay when they started preaching, but not Kate. She was struggling to figure things out like everybody else.

His eyes came back to her face. "See, even that scares me. That you quote Scripture at me. It just shows how much I don't belong. How wrong I am for you."

"Then I won't do it anymore."

"But you can't pretend to be somebody you're not. You can't. I can't. And I want you to be you, Kate. More than anything in the world."

"Then love me the way I am. Love yourself the way you are. Don't stir fear into it."

"It's a good day to be afraid," he said.

She stared up into his eyes for a long moment before she held up her hand to him. "Dance with me, Jay Tanner."

He took her hand and stepped closer to her to put his arm around her. "There's no moonlight. No snow. No music."

"There's the wind." She began to move and he followed. "The music is always there if you only listen. Isn't that what Fern told us?"

❧ 25 ❧

Jay didn't need to hear music to dance with Kate. All he needed was her hand in his, her head against his shoulder. Why did it scare him so much to be in love with her? To see her with her family. Why couldn't he simply accept the blessing of their love? And let them know he loved them in return. Especially Kate. She was practically begging him to love her.

At this moment as they swayed to the music of the wind, he wasn't even sure she wouldn't get in the car with him and ride away from her beloved home if he asked her to elope. But he didn't ask her. He clamped his lips together and didn't let any of the words come out that were crowding into his heart. He must have been wrong when he told her he wasn't a coward. While he could face down any man and was ready to stand up for his country, he couldn't say three simple words. *I love you.*

He knew what Mike would tell him. And had told him many times. That he feared giving love because he'd never accepted the gift of the Lord's love. Mike's words echoed in his head.

"It is a gift, Jay. You can't earn it. You can't buy

it. You can't get it for another person. All you have to do is accept it."

"And believe it," Jay had told him once.

That upset Mike. "How can you not believe? The whole world is proof of God's love. The sunrise each morning. The stars and the moon. Flowers in the spring. But most of all, his touch on so many lives."

And now Jay had even more proof. Dancing to Kate's music. Yet he hesitated. The music always ended.

With Trouble at her heels, Birdie came running across the yard to end the music this time. "Mama says if you want to eat anything before we go to church, you'll have to come in now." She stopped short when she came around the car and saw them standing close together, paused in the dance. "You were dancing again, weren't you?"

Kate stepped away from Jay when the pup jumped up on him. Jay didn't try to hold onto her, even though he wanted to cling to her and never let go.

"Caught red-handed." Jay rubbed Trouble's ears and smiled at Birdie. "Or maybe red-footed."

"But you never have any music," Birdie said.

"You mean you didn't hear the music when you came around the car?" Jay asked. "Tell her, Kate. Tell her how loud the music was. I think she better have her ears checked."

"It was pretty loud," Kate said, then laughed a

little at the look on Birdie's face. "But I don't think there's anything wrong with her ears. The music must have clicked off right before she got here."

"Could be," Jay said.

"Must have been so loud it knocked off your coat, Tanner." Birdie picked up his coat to keep the pup from getting it.

"Guess so." Jay took it from her. Neither he nor Kate had noticed it slipping off her shoulders while they danced.

"Brrr!" Birdie hugged herself and shivered. "It's freezing out here."

Kate was shivering again too. Without thinking about it, Jay wrapped his arms around them both to warm them up. He shut his eyes a moment and thought this had to be what heaven felt like. But they were still trembling from the cold and Kate's teeth were chattering again.

"You two better go in by the fire." He stepped back from them.

Birdie kept hold of his hand. "But you've got to come in with us. Mama's saving you a piece of pie and then we're all going to church to pray about Pearl Harbor. Graham says the news keeps getting worse. A ship blew up." She looked sad. "That means people died, doesn't it?"

"Probably," Jay said.

"I wish they'd turn the radio off," Birdie said.

"That won't change what's happening," Kate said softly.

"I know." Birdie clutched Jay's hand tighter. "But you've got to come eat your pie."

Jay smiled at her. "I'm going to let you eat my pie for me tonight. All this news has ruined my appetite, and to tell the truth I need a little time to think about it. To try to figure some things out."

"Mike says a good place to do that is church," Birdie said.

"Mike knows," Jay admitted. "But sometimes a man needs to be by himself to figure things out too."

"Let him go, Lorena." Kate's voice sounded a little stiff, like she wasn't happy with him going either. "If he wants to go, we can't stop him."

"But I'm afraid he won't come back," the girl said, even as she turned loose of his hand.

Jay knelt down to look Birdie in the face. "Haven't I always come back?"

"But you might not next time."

Jay touched her cheek with his hand. "I'll always come back as long as you want me to." He stood up and looked from her to Kate. "As long as you both want me to."

"Make him promise, Kate. Like you promised me. Remember?" Birdie tugged on Kate's sweater. "A promise of the heart."

"He's already promised you, Lorena. Each person makes promises in his or her own way." Kate put her arm around Birdie and turned her toward the house.

Birdie looked over her shoulder at Jay, but Kate did not. There was a determined set to her shoulders as she moved away from him. After he got in his car and backed it around to head to the road, he waited, watching them in the rear-view mirror. Kate finally glanced back right before they went through the front door, but she didn't wave.

He didn't know why he didn't go inside with them to the warmth that awaited there. Warmth and love and pie. But he hadn't lied when he said he needed time to get used to things. He loved Kate. He wanted to pledge his love to her forever. But now he'd be going to the Army. There was no longer any doubt as to when. The Japanese bombs meant war. War meant every able-bodied man would have to step up to the mark for his country. There was no need waiting for the envelope to arrive. He'd have to join up. Do what he had to do for his country. But what would he do before then?

For a moment, his foot hovered over the brake. He could turn around. He could go back and ask Kate to elope. Or even better, ask if she would stand in front of Mike with him while he promised his love to her forever. Mike might not want to marry them, but he would. That wouldn't change him believing Kate was making a mistake.

That's what Jay had to think out. Whether Kate would be making a mistake. Whether he loved her enough to disappear from her life if that was what was best for her. He would be going to war. Men died in wars. Was it even right to ask for promises of love when that was about to happen?

He didn't really want to go back to Graham's and see the questions that would be in his eyes when he came home from church. He wouldn't ask them, but they'd be there. And maybe disappointment too. But it was too cold to sleep in the car. His feet were already feeling like chunks of ice. The heater was spitting out more cold air than warm. Plus he couldn't just run out all his gasoline with no place to fill up before he had to be at work the next day. He needed to show up for work if for no other reason than to let them know he'd be enlisting in the Army and they would have to find a new hand. The same scene would be playing out all over the country. Men making decisions to leave behind everything they knew and loved to fight for their country.

Many of them would have more to give up. Families. Homes. Jay didn't have any of that. Nothing but this old car. And Kate.

Jay sat in his car after the motor died and thought about all the people who would be gathering at the church to pray. He wondered what he'd be praying for if he were sitting in the church with them. Not peace. It was too late for that. Courage maybe. They were all going to need that. Then he knew what he needed to ask for more than anything was belief. Belief that his prayer would even matter.

"Are you listening, God?" he whispered.

The dead silence beat against his ears. Mike would tell him that of course God was listening. He was always listening.

"All right, God. Just in case Mike's right, I'm talking to you. I need some help down here figuring things out. We're all going to need some help down here."

Words bubbled up from somewhere deep in his mind. *The Lord is a very present help in trouble.* Scripture. Had Kate become such a part of him that she could be putting Bible words in his head even when she wasn't actually with him? That was foolish. No way that could happen. The words were just left over from the times he'd gone to church as a kid. It didn't mean anything. His memory had just decided to play a trick on him.

Even so, the words stayed with him. *A very present help in trouble.* Maybe it wouldn't hurt anything to let those words linger in his mind where he could pull them out now and again.

The wind cut through his suit jacket when he got out of the car. He'd been putting off buying a winter coat. Like he thought summer would last forever. Maybe that was how he was with Kate too. Thinking he could just continue forever with her the way they were. Dancing toward love but with no hurry.

He was already in bed with the cover pulled up over his head when Graham and Poe came back from church. Poe flopped down with a satisfied dog sigh on his rug. Graham's bed creaked as he sat down on it and began unlacing his shoes.

"You asleep, boy?" he asked.

Jay breathed in and out heavily and didn't answer.

Graham pulled off one of his shoes with a grunt and dropped it on the floor. He took his other shoe off, making even more noise than he had with the first one. Jay shifted a little in the cot, but kept pretending to be dead to the world.

He could almost feel Graham's eyes boring into him as he said, "You can play possum if you want. Don't change nothing. You should have come back inside with the girls. You can't run scared all your livelong days. That's all I'm saying."

Jay almost sat up then to ask Graham how come he'd never found a girl to marry if he believed that was true.

Graham threw his pants over the chair by his bed and pounded his pillow a couple of times. The old springs creaked as he shifted around for a comfortable position. Finally things got quiet, and Jay was expecting the old man's snores. But instead, almost as if he had sensed Jay's unspoken question, he began talking in the dark.

"You're wondering about me. How come I'm telling you not to be like you might be thinking I am." A long moment passed, and Jay didn't think he was going to say any more. Then he started up again. "I was in love once, but things happened, and I figured in my head that she wouldn't want to have any part in my troubles. With Fern and all. Could be I was right. Could be I was wrong. But I never gave her the chance."

Jay didn't say anything, but he turned on his back and stared up at the ceiling. Waiting. Knowing there would be more.

"You got to give Kate that chance. For the both of you."

Jay stared at the dark air above him. The night pressed down on him with the seconds ticking by. He wanted to say something, to let Graham know he'd heard him and that he did want to give Kate that chance. But just when he opened his mouth to speak up, Graham started snoring.

Far into the night, Jay listened to Graham snore and the old dog grumble in his sleep. The news bulletins kept playing over and over in his head. The imagined sounds of the airplanes dropping bombs. Ships exploding, sinking.

And over it all was the memory of Kate in his arms. The questions kept swirling around him. Right before he finally dozed off, he remembered her words, the Scripture she had quoted to him and other Bible words rising out of his memory. *No fear in perfect love. A very present help in trouble. God is love. No greater love than a man willing to lay down his life.* Jay wanted to put his hands over his ears to block it out, but the words weren't coming from the outside. They were inside his head.

He got up early and slipped out before Graham was awake. Tonight would be soon enough to talk to him about what he'd said in the dark. *Give Kate that chance.*

Jay's boss at the feed store brought in a newspaper. The headline type took up a quarter of the front page. Just after noon everything in the store stopped as the workers and farmers all huddled around the radio to listen to President Roosevelt address Congress. Once they heard his voice, nobody shifted their feet or made any kind of noise as they focused on his words coming across the air.

Yesterday, December 7th, 1941—a date which will live in infamy—the United States of America was suddenly and deliberately attacked by naval and air forces of the Empire of Japan. The United States was at peace with that nation and, at the solicitation of Japan, was still in conversation with its government and its emperor looking toward the maintenance of peace in the Pacific.

The president's voice was very grave as he told how the Japanese ambassador had broken off diplomatic negotiations, but without threat of war, even though the bombing of Pearl Harbor had already commenced.

He went on.

It will be recorded that the distance of Hawaii from Japan makes it obvious that the attack was deliberately planned many days or even weeks ago. During the intervening time, the Japanese government has deliberately sought to deceive the United States by false statements and expressions of hope for continued peace.

There was the slightest pause, a second of dead air, before the president continued in a voice obviously saddened by the weight of his message.

The attack yesterday on the Hawaiian islands has caused severe damage to American naval and military forces. I regret to tell you that very many American lives have been lost. In addition, American ships have been reported torpedoed on the high seas between San Francisco and Honolulu.

Jay shut his eyes, imagining the destruction as the president continued, naming other places the Japanese had attacked or were attacking. Manila, the Philippines, Hong Kong, and on. All across the nation, people were listening to the president, ready to follow his lead. His path, the only path for America, was plain in his next words:

No matter how long it may take us to overcome this premeditated invasion, the American people in their righteous might will win through to absolute victory. I believe that I interpret the will of the Congress and of the people when I assert that we will not only defend ourselves to the uttermost, but will make it very certain that this form of treachery shall never again endanger us.

Hostilities exist. There is no blinking at the fact that our people, our territory, and our interests are in grave danger. With confidence in our armed forces, with the unbounding determination of our people, we will gain the inevitable triumph—so help us God.

Not a half hour after the president finished his address, Congress declared war on Japan with only one dissenting vote. It's what had to happen. Even before the workday was over, Jay could feel the shift in everybody he talked to. The week before, the war was "their" war. Now it was "our" war. He could feel the shift inside himself.

He worked late unloading a truckload of corn in case the boss couldn't find anybody to help the next day. They were all suddenly living moment to moment with none of them knowing exactly what might happen on the day to come. Every time a news bulletin broke into the radio programs, everybody stopped whatever they were doing and bent their ears toward the words rattling out of the radio sets.

When the truck was unloaded at last, Mr. Lester put his arm around Jay's shoulder. "Come on, son. I'll buy you dinner and a drink before you head home."

"That's all right, sir. No need for that." Jay looked at the sky. The sun was going down. It would be dark soon. He needed to get back to Rosey Corner. He needed to look Kate in the eye and let her know he loved her. He had to give her the chance to love him back.

"But I want to," the man insisted. "If you go off and enlist tomorrow, feeding you tonight is the least I can do, seeing as how I'm too old to line up with you."

Mr. Lester could wield a shovel with the youngest of them in spite of his steel gray hair and deep wrinkles. He wasn't a hard boss, but he did expect people to do what he said, especially the men who worked for him. It would be easier to just go with the man, let him buy him the food and take a few sips of the drink he offered. He wasn't going to take no for an answer.

Jay followed him in his car out to the road-house where Jay had spent several Saturday nights when he was avoiding Mike. Once inside,

Mr. Lester slapped him on the back and handed him his pay in cash, along with a couple of extra bucks for the meal, before heading home.

"That ought to buy enough to fill you up and let you buy a round for the guys on me. I'd stay and enjoy it with you, but the wife ruffles up like a mad old hen if I don't eat what she cooks," he said.

Jay watched him shaking hands like a politician as he made his way out of the roadhouse. Being friendly didn't hurt business. Jay ordered a sandwich with the idea of eating it in the car on the way to Rosey Corner. It wasn't really that late yet. It got dark early in December, but he had time. He didn't know what he was going to say to Kate. What could he say when he was getting ready to enlist and leave Rosey Corner behind? But Graham's words in the dark kept running through his head. *You got to give Kate that chance.* The chance to accept his love.

❧ 26 ❧

Jay was picking up his sandwich to head out the door when a guy he'd met once or twice at the roadhouse came over carrying a couple of beers. Harry had obviously already downed a few.

"What's your hurry, Tanner? You just got here." He held out one of the glasses toward Jay. "Have a drink on me. Don't you know there's a war going on?"

He lurched toward the table. When Jay reached out to steady the man, some of the beer spilled on his arm. "Take it easy, Harry. Maybe you'd better sit down."

"I'm not drunk," the man said. "Not yet, but I intend to be before the night's over. Might as well have a little fun before I cash in my number. You know they done bombed us. We're gonna have to go over there and teach them a lesson or two."

"So you joining up?" Jay lowered him into the chair by the table and sat back down with him to talk a minute. Harry wasn't a bad guy. He just didn't know when to stop. Drinking or talking.

" 'Course I am. I'm a red-blooded American. Gotta toe the line for my country." With a salute, he tried to stand but was too unsteady on his feet and sank back into the chair.

"That's good, but maybe you ought to sober up first."

"Sober ain't no way to head off to war." Harry sucked in a long draw of his beer before he pointed at Jay's untouched drink. "Something the matter with your beer?"

"No, it looks fine."

"It ain't for looking. It's for drinking." He took another drink as he eyed Jay across the table.

"You done gone and got religion down there in Rosey Corner? I hear you can't even get a drink around there no more. Got this store, but you ain't gonna get nothing worth drinking at that place. Rubbing alcohol maybe, and that stuff will kill you. The woman that runs it, she don't hold with drinking. Leastways that's what I've been told. But they say her husband used to tie one on now and again."

He had to be talking about Kate's parents. That was the only store in Rosey Corner. "Are you talking about the Merritts?"

"You know them then." Harry tipped up his glass and drained the last of his beer. "Well, this was some time back. Maybe she reformed him. Women are good at trying to change a man, keep him from having the first bit of fun. That's how come I'm still free and single." He hiccupped. "If I want a girl's company, I come around here and take my pick from the girls that don't mind a little drinking instead of them Sunday school girls that think drink is gonna send you straight to hell. Where in the Bible does it say a thing about that?"

"You'd have to ask a preacher that," Jay said.

"The way you're giving that beer a wide berth, thought maybe you were thinking on becoming one." Harry laughed. "Come on, Jay boy. Join the party. We might all be dead this time next year once they ship us out there where the bullets are flying and the bombs are falling."

"True enough." Jay took a sip of the beer just to get the man to leave him alone, and he was thirsty. He swallowed another drink before he set the beer back on the table.

He had no intention of getting drunk. Not tonight. Maybe never again. He'd had his times of drinking too much when he was trying to drown some troubles, but the troubles always floated right back up the next morning along with a pounding headache. The last time was after Mike told him he wasn't good enough for Kate. He'd gone straight to the whiskey to prove Mike right.

But then he'd met Mr. Franklin and found the pup for Birdie. Blocked out Mike's words and went back to Rosey Corner. Now Kate was dancing with him to music only they could hear. He wasn't about to mess that up with liquor. He'd grab a bottle of pop on the way out to go with his sandwich.

When he pushed back his chair to stand up, Harry grabbed at him across the table, knocking over the beer. Jay jumped back, but not in time. The beer ran off the table and splashed on his legs. Now he'd have to go to Graham's and clean up before he went to see Kate. He looked toward the window. It was full dark. The minutes were sliding away from him. He should have told Mr. Lester he wasn't hungry and headed on down the road. He'd have been almost to Kate's by now.

"And I was gonna drink that too." Harry

sounded ready to cry. He wiped his hand through the spilled beer and licked his palm.

Jay pulled a couple of coins out of his pocket and threw them on the table. "Here, have one on me, Harry."

Harry started smiling again. "Always figured you for a good joe." He grabbed the coins and called after Jay. "You better stay and meet some of the girls. I talked to one from Rosey Corner awhile ago. Pretty girl. Hadn't seen her around here before. A mite young for me, but she was asking if I knew you." Harry waggled his eyebrows at Jay.

Jay hesitated. It couldn't be Kate. She wouldn't be in a place like this, not unless she was with somebody else. Somebody like him. Then he knew. Even before he heard her laugh and looked across the room to see her. Alice. Two men were smiling at her and pouring her a drink out of a whiskey bottle. It was plain she'd already had too much. Her head was wobbling to the side and her smile was loose.

It was none of his business, Jay told himself. The minutes were passing. Kate was waiting. Alice was a big girl. She'd been chasing after trouble since he'd first met her, and now she'd found it. But it wasn't his problem. He didn't even like the girl.

"You know her?" Harry asked.

"I know her. She's just a kid." A dumb kid.

"I think Smitty and Charley are planning on giving her some grown-up lessons tonight." Harry laughed and lurched off toward the bar to get another drink.

None of his business, Jay reminded himself again, and he didn't want to make it his business. He turned his back on her and the men. The girl would have to take care of herself. He would have never even known she was there if his boss hadn't insisted on buying him supper. For all he knew, she might be there every night. But Harry said he hadn't seen her before and Harry was there every night. Even if it was her very first time at a roadhouse, that didn't mean she wasn't getting what she expected. What she wanted.

Jay stopped at the counter and bought a pop and then headed to his car. He probably still had a couple of hours before it was too late to show up at Kate's house. Time enough.

He was opening his door to slide behind the wheel when he heard a muffled scream. From the lights shining out the windows, he could see one of the men pushing Alice up against the outside of the building. His business or not, he couldn't drive away and pretend he hadn't seen her. Not when she was so obviously struggling to get free.

The man was too intent on attacking Alice to hear Jay come up behind him. Jay jerked him back and knocked him down with one punch.

Then he grabbed Alice and hustled her toward the car.

"Jay." Her face lit up when she saw him. "You do care." She leaned against him. A sick mixture of liquor and strong perfume assaulted Jay's nose.

Jay pushed her away from him but kept a firm grip on her arm as he opened the passenger's side door and shoved her in the car. "I care that you're drunk and an idiot. Now keep your mouth shut or I'll throw you back to the wolves."

Jay was disgusted with her. Disgusted with himself for having to be a hero. He got behind the wheel and started up the car.

"I just wanted to have a little fun." She sounded near tears.

"Was it fun?" His voice was hard.

"No." She hiccupped. "He was hurting me."

Some of Jay's anger drained away. People messed up all the time. He, of all people, knew that. He blew out a long breath. "Bad things can happen to girls at places like this, Alice. But you're old enough to know that when you go somewhere looking for trouble, you're going to find it."

"I was looking for you."

"No, you weren't." Jay gripped the steering wheel harder. "Don't even imagine that."

She sniffled quietly for a minute before she asked, "Where are you taking me?"

"Where do you think? Your house." He kept his

eyes on the road. He didn't want to look at the girl. He didn't want to think about his ruined plans for the night. All because of her foolishness.

Her head shot up as she clutched Jay's arm. "You can't take me home. My father will kill me."

"You should have thought of that before you sneaked off. Now you'll just have to take your punishment." He pushed her hand off his arm.

"You can't take me home."

After a minute when Jay kept driving without saying anything, she went on. The tears were gone from her voice and she sounded almost sober. "I'll tell them you gave me the drinks, that you were trying to get me drunk so that you could take advantage of me."

"They won't believe you." But even as he said it, Jay knew that wasn't true. They would believe her long before they believed him. It might not matter that much what they believed, but would Kate and her family believe him over Alice?

She must have sensed his uncertainty because her own voice grew more confident. "You know Kate has a thing against drinking. Carl told me she was a real stick in the mud about having a good time, even though Mama says Kate's father used to drink like a fish."

Jay thought about Kate's father drinking, maybe being drunk the way Harry had said. It was hard for him to imagine, but it wasn't hard to imagine that Kate might not look kindly on somebody drinking. Especially somebody she was thinking about loving.

"All right." He gave in. "If you don't want to go home, where do you want to go?"

Her hand snaked back over to caress his shoulder. "We could spend the night in your car. You could keep me warm."

"That's not going to happen, Alice." He shifted away from her hand. "Guess I'll take you on home and take my chances on what people believe. It's not like I'm going to be around here much longer anyway."

She started sniffling again. "I thought you were nice."

"I'm taking you home. That's as nice as it gets." He stared out at the road and hoped she'd just be quiet. That was the trouble with staying in one place so long. You got to know people, and even when you didn't especially like them, you couldn't turn your back on them. Or, in spite of everything, keep from feeling a little sorry for them.

She didn't say anything for so long he thought maybe she'd fallen asleep, but then she spoke up in a small voice as they got close to Rosey Corner. "I don't feel good."

"I'll bet."

She looked out the window. "I can't go home like this. Really, Jay, I can't. You have to under-stand."

Without a word, Jay kept driving. He couldn't get to her house soon enough.

"If you'll take me on down the road to my grandmother's house, I promise not to say anything about being with you."

"You're not with me, Alice. I'm just taking you home."

"But please let me go to my grandmother's. I can sneak in there and nobody will be the wiser."

"You'd better be the wiser and think twice before you do anything this stupid again."

"Oh, I will, Jay, but I can't go home. I can't. Please. My grandmother's house isn't too far the other side of Rosey Corner. Please." She was sounding like a little girl again.

What difference did a few more miles make? As long as he got her out of his car. It wasn't like he'd never done anything dumb when he was her age. "Okay, tell me where."

He looked over at Kate's house as he drove by. The lights were on. It wasn't too late yet. He even thought he spotted a face peering out the window, maybe watching for him. He'd have to drop Alice off and go back to Graham's and clean up. He didn't want to show up smelling like Harry's beer. Or Alice's perfume.

He turned his lights off and coasted to a stop at the driveway Alice pointed out.

"Ohh, I'm sick." Alice dropped her head over and fumbled for the door handle.

"Don't you dare throw up!"

Jay jumped out and ran around the car to yank the door open. She was retching as she tumbled out against him. He tried to step out of the way, but he couldn't completely turn loose of her. Not without letting her fall on the ground. So he held onto her as her vomit hit his legs. Could the night get any worse?

After she heaved until there was nothing left to come up, he gave her his handkerchief. She was shaking all over as she leaned against the fender of his car and wiped off her mouth. She held the handkerchief back out toward him.

"Keep it," he told her. "You might need it again."

"I'm not going to throw up more, am I?" she almost wailed.

"Maybe." He turned her around and pointed her toward the house. He couldn't keep from feeling sorry for her. "You'll feel better after you get inside and warm up."

She went a few steps before she turned around. "Thank you, Jay."

"Just go." He watched her until she disappeared through the front door. He'd never been so relieved to see a door open and close in his life.

He picked up a handful of leaves and tried to wipe off his pants leg. He smelled like a bar at closing time. Nothing he could do about that. He threw the leaves down and got back in his car, trying to keep the offensive pants from touching the seat.

He wasn't going to make it to Kate's house. He'd go by the store in the morning and explain what happened. If her mother was there, he'd get Kate to take a walk with him. If it wasn't too cold. If a hundred things. But before the day was over tomorrow, he would tell her he loved her. He would.

He slowed as he got close to her house. The lights were still on. But he couldn't stop. He imagined Kate sitting on the couch reading or maybe listening to her father read. And if not for Alice, he could have been sitting there beside her.

The dog ran out in front of him. Trouble. Jay slammed on his brakes and jerked the car to the left. Too late he saw Birdie running after the dog.

"No," he yelled as he slammed the brake pedal all the way to the floor. The car stopped, but not soon enough. A sickening thump turned his blood to ice.

He was out of the car in a second. Birdie was lying in the pool of his lights, not moving. The dog was licking her face and whining, but Birdie wasn't moving.

"Oh dear God." The prayer rose from his deepest soul as he knelt down beside her and picked up her hand to feel for a pulse. She wasn't dead. Praise the Lord. Blood was beating through her veins, steady and strong. But she still wasn't moving.

Then Kate was running across the yard toward the road, screaming, "Lorena!"

"She's alive," Jay said as Kate dropped down beside Birdie. He wanted to put his arms around her and comfort her, but it wasn't the time to be thinking about Kate. He had to take care of Birdie. He carefully ran his hands down the little girl's arms and legs. Nothing seemed to be broken.

"Lorena, baby," Kate was saying softly as she brushed the hair back from the kid's face. "Talk to me."

"She must have hit her head," Jay said matter-of-factly. It would do no good for him to go to pieces and start ranting against whoever was in charge of the universe. "But I don't think she broke any bones."

Kate looked at him then. "What happened?" Her words were cold.

"I swerved to miss Trouble. Birdie must have been chasing him, but I didn't see her beside the road until it was too late."

Kate didn't say anything, just kept staring at him for a long moment. He couldn't read her expression in the glare of the headlights, but when he reached across Birdie to touch her hand, she jerked away from him.

The others were coming across the yard now. And still Birdie didn't move. Again he had to tell what happened. Not that his words mattered much. All that mattered was the kid opening her eyes and looking at them. But that didn't happen.

Mr. Merritt picked her up and cradled her against him as gently as possible. Before he started toward the house, he told Jay, "Go get Aunt Hattie."

He didn't want to leave. He wanted to be there when Birdie came around to tell her how sorry he was, but he did what Kate's father said. Got in his car, started it up, and shifted it in gear. He left the motor running at Aunt Hattie's house and was banging on the door when Fern spoke behind him.

"What are you doing here?" she asked.

Jay drew in a shaky breath to try to get his heart to slow down. Hadn't enough already happened without this woman scaring him out of his skin? "Birdie's hurt. Her father asked me to get Aunt Hattie."

"Did you hurt her?"

Inside the house a light came on and spilled out the front window onto Fern. Her face was fierce and her hands were in fists. Jay looked straight at her. "I was swerving to miss her dog and didn't see her running after him until it was too late. I didn't want to hurt her."

She raised her fists, and for a second, he thought she was going to hit him. He braced for the blow, but then her face changed. She looked as sad as he felt. "Is she going to die?"

"No," he said. He couldn't bear to think any other answer. "No."

Aunt Hattie jerked open the door. "Who's not going to die?"

"Lorena Birdsong," Fern said.

Aunt Hattie peered up at Fern. "I ain't never heard you say her full name before, Fern."

"I'm saying it for her since she can't. She's hurt. He hurt her with his car."

"Get my cane and my shoes." Aunt Hattie tied her housecoat around her. Then she stared up at Jay. "Have you been following after the devil and wallowing in his drink? Is that what brung all this on?"

"No, ma'am."

"You's smellin' like as how you did."

Fern dropped Aunt Hattie's shoes down in front of her and held her steady while she stuck her feet in them.

"It's a long story, Aunt Hattie, but there's no time for telling it. Not now."

"You's right 'bout that." She took her cane in one hand and grabbed his arm with the other. "Time's wasting."

Fern wouldn't get in the car. Instead she stepped up on the running board. Aunt Hattie rolled down her window so she had a way of hanging on. Jay had to drive slow, but it wasn't far. He pulled right up to the porch. Aunt Hattie was out of the car before the motor died. Jay followed her and Fern up the steps.

Kate opened the door. She let Aunt Hattie and Fern move past her into the room where Birdie was on the couch, but she stepped in front of Jay. "We don't need you here now," she said.

Her words stabbed through him, but even worse was the look on her face. Cold anger. "I tried to stop, Kate. I didn't see her in time."

She shut her eyes and rubbed her forehead as though wanting to block out his words before she said, "You might have been able to stop if you weren't drunk." Kate stepped back and started to shut the door, but Jay put his hand out to hold it open.

"I'm not drunk," he said.

27

If only she could believe him, but Kate had never been one to hide from the truth. It did no good to pretend something wasn't true that was as plain as the nose on her face. Lorena was on the couch behind them, perhaps fighting for her life. Because of him. Because he was drunk. Then for him to deny that truth made it even worse. She knew drunk. Hadn't she helped her father stagger into the house and land on the couch countless times years ago before he'd given up drinking? She knew.

"You can't lie to me." She looked straight at him, then glanced over her shoulder at Aunt Hattie bending over Lorena. Kate's mother and father were right beside her. Fern was standing stock still at the end of the couch. Tori was carrying a pan of water in from the kitchen. Nobody was paying the first bit of attention to Kate, but she still stepped out on the porch and pulled the door shut behind her. She didn't want either of her parents to hear her next words.

The harsh light of the bare bulb over the door spilled down on them. Jay didn't back up, so she was very close to him. She took shallow breaths to keep from smelling the alcohol and vomit on him. It made her sick. "I know drunk when I smell it."

Anger flashed across his face then, as his jaw tightened. "I'm not drunk," he repeated, his voice almost as cold as hers.

"Just go away." She started to turn away from him to go back inside.

He grabbed her arm and stopped her. "You don't even want to give me a chance to explain."

She tried to pull free, but he wouldn't let go. "I don't need to hear any more lies. I should have listened to Mike. He warned me."

He recoiled from her words as though she'd struck him, and for a moment she was almost sorry. Almost ready to hear him out, but then the drunk vomit smell rose up to her nose again. And something else. Perfume.

"Let me go," she said through clenched teeth.

He turned her loose, but took hold of the doorknob so she couldn't escape. "You may not want to hear the truth, but you're going to."

She backed up against the door and stood stiff. She wasn't going to listen to any of his excuses. She'd heard plenty of those from her father, but at least he'd had reason to give in to the call of the whiskey sirens. He'd been trying to drown his terrible memories of the war. Jay hadn't even gone to war yet. But he would. Soon.

Again she felt another poke to give in and listen to him. Maybe just the thought of war had pushed him to drink. Maybe she should try to understand. But then Mike's words were echoing in her head. Saying Jay didn't know how to love. Words she should have listened to, and then her heart wouldn't be breaking the way it was now. She kept her eyes on the top button of his shirt.

He let go of the doorknob and stepped back a little. "Look at me." It wasn't a demand, but a request. "Please."

She could open the door and leave him standing there. She didn't have to listen. She didn't have to look at him, but she raised her eyes up to meet his anyway. Even if he had been drunk, he looked totally sober now. Not a thing like her father used to look when he came in from drinking. He'd always bounced between so happy he was ready to sing or so sad he was crying.

When Jay hesitated, she felt the pull of the door. She needed to be inside with Lorena, not out here listening to lies. Her nose had already told her the truth. "Say what you want to say. Whatever it is." Her voice sounded harsh even to her own ears.

He reached toward her face as though he wanted more than anything to touch her, but he didn't. His hand hovered there in the air for a few seconds before he dropped it back to his side. "I love you, Kate Merritt."

Yesterday her heart would have leaped up inside her with joy to hear those words. She would have been ready to whisper the same back to him. But now everything was different. She couldn't think.

He must have seen the doubt in her eyes. "You don't believe me."

"I don't know what to believe," she whispered.

"Not what. Who." His eyes burned into hers. "Believe me."

She reached for the doorknob. "Lorena needs me."

"So do I," he said softly. "But without trust, the music stops."

"Yes. Yes, it does." She couldn't argue with that. She turned the doorknob and pushed open the door. "Goodbye, Jay."

He looked grim in the rush of light coming out the door. And very sad. "When Birdie comes around, tell her I'm sorry. That I'm very, very sorry."

"You can tell her yourself," Kate said.

"No, you'll have to tell her for me." His voice was flat, without feeling.

He turned and went down the steps to his car. She didn't watch to see if he looked back before she shut the door.

Across the room, Aunt Hattie was perched on the edge of a straight chair pulled up close to the couch, probing through Lorena's thick curls. Lorena moaned and her eyes flickered open.

"Just lay easy, child," Aunt Hattie said. "Whilst I see how big this goose egg is on the back of your head."

But Lorena was trying to sit up and look around. "Kate?"

Aunt Hattie pushed her back down on the couch. "We's all here. Your mama and daddy. Your sisters too. Even that troublesome dog is crouched here on the floor waiting for a chance to lick your face."

Kate knelt beside the couch and stroked Lorena's cheek as she blinked back tears and blocked from her mind the sound of Jay's car driving away. She wanted him gone. She'd told him to leave. There was no reason for her to feel like weeping. Lorena was awake.

"What happened? Why do you all look like you're about to cry?" Lorena stared up at her family around her. Her eyes stopped on Fern. "You're not gonna cry, are you, Fern?"

Fern leaned toward Lorena. "Tears don't change nothing."

"What happened?" Lorena asked again as she tried to sit up, then sank back on the couch with a groan. "My head hurts."

"That Jay bird man's car hit you," Fern said when nobody else spoke up. "He says you were chasing the dog."

"I was run over?" Lorena's eyes got big. "Am I going to die?"

"You're not going to die, baby. You're going to be just fine." Kate gave her a shaky smile. "Bruised up a little, but fine."

"That's right, little one. You'll be good as new in a few days," Daddy said as Mama reached over the back of the couch to lay her hand softly on Lorena's head. "You can trust us on that."

Trust. The word echoed in Kate's ears, but she couldn't think about that now. She had to think about Lorena, not the fact that she'd turned her back on Jay. It was the right thing to do. The only thing. She could never trust a drunk. Love him maybe. Not maybe. She did love him, but a lasting love was more than a flash of feelings in the moonlight. She wanted the kind of love her mother and father had that had carried them through the rough spots and let them lean on one another now. With hard-earned trust.

"Where is he?" Lorena was trying to raise her head up to look around again. "Didn't Tanner know he ran over me?"

" 'Course he did, child." Aunt Hattie eased Lorena back down on the pillow. "He came and fetched me down here to look you over. To see if you needed more doctoring."

"But where did he go?" Now Lorena looked ready to cry.

Kate could feel the rest of them waiting for her to answer. To explain what couldn't be explained. She hesitated and Fern spoke up again.

"Ask her," she told Lorena with a nod of her head toward Kate. "She's the one who shut the door."

Kate wanted to tell Fern to be quiet. That she didn't know anything. But that wasn't true. Fern knew more than most people. Sometimes she knew too much. Like this time.

"He had to leave, baby," Kate said. "But he told me to tell you that he was sorry. That he was very, very sorry. He wouldn't have hurt you for anything in the world." She added those last words for him, but she knew they were true.

"Well, of course not," Lorena said as though

Kate's words were unnecessary. "He loves me."

I love you, Kate Merritt. Kate shook away the echo of his words as Lorena went on. "It had to be an accident. I shouldn't have been running after Trouble. That's what you said happened, wasn't it, Fern?"

"He missed the dog. Hit you," Fern said in her short, clipped way. "Better to hit the dog."

"Amen to that," Kate's father said.

"I'm glad he didn't hit Trouble." Lorena reached toward the dog, and he laid his muzzle up on the couch beside her and whimpered.

"Whatever happened, happened," Mama said in her no-nonsense voice. "We can't go back and undo that. We just need to make sure you're all right and don't need to go to the hospital."

"That's right. We's needing to find out if all your toes and fingers is moving and no necessary parts has fallen off. So let me feel your bones." Aunt Hattie's smile set off an explosion of wrinkles, but then the smile vanished to be replaced by her doctoring face as she ran her hands down Lorena's sides. "Ribs all accounted for, but paining you some from the way you's grimacing. It ain't lookin' like any of them is broke or nothing. Bruised maybe."

Kate watched as she kept gently probing Lorena. Aunt Hattie knew how every inch of a person should feel, after so many years of helping babies be born and using her healing skills when no doctors were nearby. "And could be there's a little knot on the collarbone."

"Should I go get Uncle Wyatt's car to take her to the hospital?" Kate moved to stand up.

"I don't want to go to the hospital," Lorena wailed. "They give you shots there."

"A big girl like you ain't fearin' no shots, but I'm thinking there ain't no need in a hospital trip. You came out pretty lucky for being hit by an automobile." When Aunt Hattie shifted to feel Lorena's legs, Trouble put his nose right in her face. She glanced over at Tori. "Victoria, get that dog back out of my way."

"Come on, Trouble." Tori grabbed the dog by the scruff of his neck and pulled him back, his toenails dragging against the rug. He let out a mournful howl as she shoved him in the kitchen and shut the door.

"You need to change that dog's name," Aunt Hattie muttered. "Trouble. That ain't no kind of a name for nothing. Even a dog. And appears to me, he's workin' too hard to live up to it. I seen it happen many a time. Bad names can ruin a body."

She finished examining Lorena. "Ain't nothing else to comment on 'cepting the scrapes on your legs. We'd best get the road dirt out of them. Kate, hand me that rag, and Nadine, fetch me your Watkins brown salve."

After every scrape was cleaned and doctored to Aunt Hattie's satisfaction, Kate's father walked

Aunt Hattie home. Fern had already slipped out the door into the dark night as soon as Aunt Hattie had pronounced Lorena wasn't seriously hurt.

"She bears watching tonight with that lump on her head, and come morning, you better take her to the young doctor in Edgeville. I'm gettin' old. I ain't thinkin' I did, but could be I missed something," Aunt Hattie told them before she left.

Kate and Tori helped Lorena undress and get into bed while their mother emptied the pan of water and put away the salve. Trouble made a streak for the girls' bedroom as soon as the kitchen door was opened. He licked Lorena's hand and then crawled under her bed.

"Maybe Aunt Hattie's right. Maybe we should give him a new name," Tori said. "Something nicer than Trouble."

"But that's what Tanner called him," Lorena said.

"Jay won't care if you change his name." Kate concentrated on smoothing the covers down over Lorena just so. She didn't want to think about what Jay cared about or didn't care about right then.

"Do you think Aunt Hattie is right? That Trouble isn't a good name?" Lorena started to get up to look at the pup.

Kate gently pushed her back down on the pillow. "Aunt Hattie is usually right about most things. You know that. And she said you should lie down and rest that head." That's what she needed to do too. Rest her head and not think about Jay. She had to take care of Lorena.

"Aunt Hattie always knows," Tori said as she slipped on her gown. "Besides, Trouble doesn't act like he knows his name half the time anyway."

"He does too." Lorena's lips came out in a little pout.

"Might be he knows your voice, but watch what happens when I call him." Tori leaned over and called, "Here, Trouble. Come here, Trouble." When the dog didn't scramble out from under the bed to her, Tori dropped down on her hands and knees to peer back at him. "See, he just keeps staring at me like he has no idea what I want."

"He's afraid you'll put him back in the kitchen," Kate said with a wink at Lorena.

"Or maybe he doesn't like that name." Tori stood up.

"The right name is important." Kate tucked the covers in around Lorena. "Didn't you always used to say you wanted a dog named Scout?"

"Let's try that." Tori dropped down on her knees again. "Here, Scout. Come here, boy."

The pup scooted out to the edge of the bed to lick Tori's nose. She laughed as she lifted her head up to look at Lorena. "See? Maybe he's a Scout instead of Trouble."

"But what if you're wrong about Tanner not caring?" Lorena sounded near tears.

"Don't worry about it tonight, baby." Kate brushed the hair away from Lorena's face. "You need to rest. Tori can sleep with me and you can have this bed all to yourself."

Tori climbed up off the floor and leaned over to kiss Lorena's forehead. Yawning, she crawled into the other bed and snuggled down under the covers. "Good night, all. I'm exhausted. But if you need me, give me a shake." She barely had all the words out before she was asleep.

"My head hurts, Kate." Lorena shifted on her pillow.

"I know, but Aunt Hattie says it'll feel better tomorrow."

"Will I have to go to Dr. Lyens in town and get a shot?"

"I don't know. We'll ask Mama in the morning."

"Okay." Lorena grabbed Kate's hand and held it tight. "It's scary getting hit by a car."

"I thought you didn't remember what happened," Kate said.

Lorena wrinkled up her forehead and shut her eyes to think. After a minute she opened them and said, "I don't, but that doesn't keep it from being scary when I think about it."

Mama heard Lorena as she came into the room with a glass of water. "It was scary, sweetheart. It scared us all." She put her arm under Lorena's shoulders and raised her head up enough to take a few sips. "But don't you worry. One of us will be right beside you all night long to make sure you're all right."

Lorena looked at Mama, then Kate. "Did you see Tanner? Was he scared too?"

When Kate hesitated, Mama answered, "He was very scared. And upset. Very worried that you might be badly hurt."

"But Aunt Hattie says I'm not."

"Praise the Lord," Mama said. "I've been sending up thank-you prayers ever since you opened your eyes in there on the couch."

"Me too." Kate squeezed Lorena's hand.

Mama patted Lorena's cheek. "Now you need to close those eyes and get some rest. One of us will be right here beside you."

"Can I say my name first?" Lorena asked.

"Of course you can, my Lorena Birdsong." Mama leaned over to kiss Lorena's nose.

"My name is Lorena Birdsong."

Kate echoed her as she lifted Lorena's hand up to kiss the backs of her fingers. "Your name is Lorena Birdsong and you're my little sister, now and forever."

"And sometimes called Birdie." Lorena looked worried again. "Does Tanner know I'm okay? If he doesn't, he'll keep being scared and worried."

Mama looked from Lorena to Kate and back to Lorena. "Maybe he saw Aunt Hattie after she left here, but in case he didn't, Kate can go find him first thing in the morning and tell him."

"Before he goes to work." Lorena stared straight at Kate. "You have to tell him before he goes to work. Promise."

"I promise, baby. I'll go tell him before he leaves in the morning. Now shut those eyes, and Mama and I will sing you a lullaby."

After Lorena dozed off, Kate and her mother both fell silent as they watched the little girl's chest rise and fall. A hint of unease settled over them. Kate tried to tell herself it was simply because of their worry about Lorena, but she knew better. Her mother's unasked questions hung heavy in the air between them.

When Kate's father came back in the house after walking Aunt Hattie home, he came to the bedroom door but headed on to bed after Mama assured him Lorena was breathing fine. That was what Aunt Hattie had told them to watch. That and if she got sick to her stomach.

They heard him getting ready for bed, but when all was quiet again, Kate said, "I'll watch her for a while, Mama. If I get sleepy, I'll come and wake you."

"I guess that makes sense. I'll spell you in a couple of hours." Mama stood up and looked down on Lorena, reluctant to leave. "She's so precious to me." She turned her eyes to Kate. "I felt as though it was my body that had been hit when I saw her lying there on the road."

"But she's going to be all right," Kate said.

"Yes, yes she is. Thank God." Mama turned away from the bed and looked directly at Kate in the dim light. The lights were off in the bedroom but some light filtered in from the open door to the sitting room. "You should have let him come in, Kate. It was an accident. He didn't see her."

Kate didn't shy away from her eyes. "He was drunk, Mama."

"Are you sure?" her mother asked.

"I smelled it on him."

"But he works at a feed store. Some of that feed has a different odor." When Kate just kept looking at her without saying anything, she went on. "Even if he did have a drink . . ." She let her voice trail off.

"He was drunk," Kate repeated. "He smelled like drunk vomit. I know what that smells like and I know what it means."

Her mother pulled in a breath and let it out slowly. Both of them were thinking back to other nights. Nights when Kate's father had come home after a drinking binge. Finally she said, "I suppose you do." She stepped over to Kate and pulled her close in a hug. "I'm so sorry, sweetheart." She stroked her hair. "So very sorry."

Kate shut her eyes and swallowed down her tears. She refused to cry. No matter how wrong things were. She was the middle sister. She fixed things. She didn't cry.

After a minute, her mother kissed Kate's cheek

and turned her loose. In the doorway, she stopped to say, "Somebody still needs to go tell Jay Lorena's all right in the morning. You want me to ask your father to?"

"No," Kate said. "I guess I do owe him that much."

After her mother went on to her bedroom, Kate wondered if that was true or if she only wanted an excuse to see Jay one more time. *Oh dear Father in heaven,* her heart cried out. *Why did I fall in love with a drunk?* And he'd said he loved her. The words circled in her mind. *I love you, Kate Merritt.*

She grabbed the extra pillow off the bed and buried her face in it to muffle her sobs. Some things couldn't be fixed.

28

Jay parked his car in the usual spot at Graham's. After he turned off the engine, he sat there, hardly feeling the cold as he kept hearing the thump of his bumper hitting Birdie and seeing her so still on the road. If only he'd been driving a little slower. If only he hadn't taken Alice to her grandmother's. If only.

That wasn't all that was tormenting him. He

could hardly bear thinking about Kate and how she had shut him away even before she'd closed the door in his face. He wanted to hold his hands over his ears to block out the awful, final sound of that door shutting him on the outside. But it would do no good. The sound ripped through his mind, destroying every hope and dream he'd let come to life about finally knowing love.

He'd been foolish. So very foolish. He knew better. That kind of love was for guys like Mike. Not guys like Jay. He'd figured that out years ago. But then he'd come to Rosey Corner. He'd been pulled into the circle of the Merritt family and felt how love could be. Birdie had loved him with a heart-rending innocence. Kate had danced with him to what he thought was music of the heart.

Music that screeched to a stop when his brakes couldn't stop his car in time and he saw Birdie lying there in front of his lights, not moving. Her smile gone, maybe forever. Then Kate not believing him. Worse, not even willing to listen. What had he said to her? That without trust the music stopped. Without trust they had nothing. Now he had nothing.

His thoughts kept circling around, one sorrow after another. He wanted to be angry at Kate. He wanted to be so angry that he was ready to drive back to her house, bang on her door, and make her listen. But he only felt an overpowering sadness. He'd glimpsed an echo of the same sadness in Kate's eyes before she closed the door. The grief of saying goodbye forever.

He shifted in the car seat and smelled Alice's vomit mixed with the sickening sweet perfume she'd been wearing. When his stomach rolled, he got out of the car and went to the pump behind the blacksmith shop. At least he wouldn't have to worry about Alice hiding in the shadows on this night. He pumped the frigid water out and let it run over his clothes. He didn't care when ice crystals formed on his shirttail. His hands were numb, but he kept letting the water run over him, grateful that Poe didn't wake and start barking to rouse Graham.

Graham. He pushed the pump handle down one last time, glad Mr. Merritt kept it oiled so it didn't squeak. He headed back to his car. He couldn't talk to Graham. Not tonight.

He didn't have that much up in Graham's room. A change or two of clothes. The suit. Every bit of money he had was in his pocket. Most of the stuff he'd brought with him to Rosey Corner was still in the car. A few books. A pillow and some blankets for the times he had to sleep in the car. He'd wrap up in one of those blankets and go on down the road. His clothes would dry eventually or, come morning, he'd buy something. He wouldn't need much. The Army would issue him a uniform. He wouldn't need clothes. He didn't need anything.

That was what Rosey Corner had made him forget. That he didn't need anything. Or anybody.

He was trembling from the cold by the time he got one of the blankets out of the back and wrapped it around him. It didn't help much, with the wet clothes clinging to his skin. His hand shook so much he had a hard time pulling out the choke. The engine caught and the heater started spitting out lukewarm air. He turned the heater fan all the way up, but his teeth began chattering as he gripped the wheel and started to pull away.

That made him remember Kate's teeth chattering when they'd talked Sunday night. It was almost impossible to believe that was only last night. The world was crashing down around him. The country was at war. He'd have to go wherever they sent him to fight. Kate was lost to him.

He couldn't drive like this. Not with his bones feeling like they were going to shake out of his skin. He needed to find a way to warm up first. The forge in the blacksmith shop would be warm. Mr. Merritt kept the fire banked there all the time.

The shop wasn't locked. This was Rosey Corner. Doors didn't have to be locked. Jay stripped off his wet shirt and pants to hang on the end of the forge. Then he wrapped back up in the blanket and stared at the red coals. He thought about Kate's father showing him how he bent the iron.

How he had to heat it until it was white hot and then hit it with his shaping hammers. A wrong hit and the iron had to go back in the fire to be heated and shaped again.

A wrong hit. That's what had happened to him this night. Everything wrong that could go wrong. Or maybe the wrong hit had been way back in September when he hadn't headed on up to Chicago as he had intended. Instead he'd looked at Kate and let Graham talk him into staying. Now he had to go back in the fire. He supposed he would be literally going into the fire after he signed up with the Army. Maybe he'd die in the first battle. Plenty of soldiers did. Soldiers had already died. Maybe even the hayseed that he'd let sock him at Mike's wedding.

He stared at the glowing embers until his eyes blurred. He had to go to war. He'd known that ever since Kate's father had turned the radio on the day before. Mike would probably have to go too. Even the pimply faced kid who was in love with Kate's little sister might end up fighting if the war went on long enough. The president's speech had made it clear they were in for a long struggle.

But he had almost convinced himself he might be able to take Kate's love with him. He'd offered his love to her, but she'd shut the door on it. Graham had told him to give Kate a chance to love him. Jay had never been very lucky when it came to games of chance. Graham had no way of knowing that. He was simply playing matchmaker. An odd role for the old bachelor to take on.

Up above him, Jay heard Poe doing his snuffling bark in his sleep. Graham said the old dog did that when he was dreaming about chasing raccoons. Either that or complaining about the floor being too hard. Now the old dog could have his cot back.

Jay's pants were steaming a little and it was obvious he hadn't washed out all of Alice's vomit. Needed soap for that. He felt the material. Not dry, but he'd stopped shaking. He could stand to wear something a little damp, and he needed to be gone from here before Rosey Corner woke up with the sun. He was pulling on the pants when he knocked over a bucket. Above him, Graham's bed creaked. Jay froze. If the noise woke Graham, he might come to investigate.

Jay halfway wanted him to, so he could tell him goodbye. And thanks for a good autumn. Painting Mrs. Harrelson's house in the sun. The kindness and the wisdom. At the same time, he couldn't bear to look on another face this night that might register disappointment. In him. Even so, Jay should tell him thank you. He fastened his pants and looked around for something to write on. He didn't see anything, but he remembered noticing a stub of a pencil in his car just last week.

He didn't bother with putting on his damp

shirt. He just pulled the blanket tight around him and made his way back out of the shop, taking great care not to knock over anything else. He should have brought in his flashlight. He'd picked up one that had a button he could push down a few times to give him light for five minutes or so. At the car, he pumped up the light and found the pencil. He tore the back leaf out of the book he'd been reading. *The War of the Worlds* by H. G. Wells. Kate's father had loaned it to him last week. He hadn't finished it, but that didn't matter now. The light dimmed and he pumped it up again.

For a minute, he sat with the pencil poised over the paper. So much to explain. So many reasons to say thanks. But maybe it would be better to keep it simple.

Graham. Something bad happened. I hit Birdie with my car. She was hurt. Hoping not bad, but not sure. You can ask Kate about it tomorrow.

Jay stopped writing. He didn't want to write anything else, but he owed Graham more words than that. So he put the pencil tip back on the paper and wrote the rest as fast as he could.

I gave Kate the chance you told me I should, but guess it was too late. She didn't give me a chance back. Thanks for letting me borrow

Poe's bed for a spell, but it's time I moved on. Got a war to win.

That would have to do. He scribbled his name, folded the paper, and walked back to the steps before he could change his mind and stuff the note in his pocket instead of leaving it for Graham. He laid it on the bottom step with Mr. Merritt's book on top.

Poe barked a few times before he got back around to his car, and Jay had the feeling Graham was standing at the window watching him leave. He didn't look back to see. Once a decision was made, it was better to not look back.

He did slow down as he passed Kate's house. The lights were off. He didn't know if that was good or bad. He should have looked to see if the uncle's car was in his garage. They might all be at the hospital. Birdie might be fighting for her life. All because of him. He'd have never hit her if he hadn't swerved to miss the dog. The dog he'd taken to her to win some favor from Birdie, but Kate too. It had worked. Kate had danced in the moonlight with him. But then life had sucker punched him. He ought to be used to it by now.

For a crazy moment, he thought about stopping the car out on the road and sneaking up to the house to peer through a window. Just to see if they were there. To see if Birdie was all right. Her motionless body down on the road was in front of his eyes again. The dog whining and licking her face. Her eyes staying closed. Birdie was never still. Always running to meet him. Always ready to laugh at whatever he said.

His leg got stiff, and he almost lifted his foot up off the gas pedal. Almost. But he turned his eyes back to the road, mashed his foot down, and sped past. What if her bed was empty? Stopping wouldn't change anything. Maybe it would be better to not know. To let the door crash closed completely on Rosey Corner. No need trying to shove it back open a crack.

By the time he got to Louisville, he was almost warm. He pulled in behind the first clothing store he saw to wait for the morning. His bones ached with weariness, so he grabbed the pillow and the other blanket out of the backseat and tried to find a comfortable position. He shut his eyes and wished for sleep, but it did no good. The minutes dragged by, each seeming an hour long.

He began to wish he was drunk the way Kate had thought he was. So drunk that he couldn't feel anything. So drunk that he'd be sleeping even if the car seat was hard and his neck was in a crick.

He'd never let himself get that drunk. He had downed a few from time to time, but he'd never wanted to be the guy on the floor begging somebody to pour another drink in his mouth. He wanted to know what was happening. To be sober and ready for whatever might be coming down the road. But he'd been sober tonight and what good had it done him? Done Birdie? So why not reach for the oblivion of alcohol?

That was no real answer. He could almost hear Mike's preacher voice telling him that. And then telling him to look for answers with the Lord. Maybe he should. Maybe he should be reaching his hand up toward heaven. A man going to war where he was only a bullet or a piece of shrapnel away from meeting his Maker.

He shut his eyes and tried to think of a prayer, but nothing was there but Kate. Kate staring at him, telling him he was drunk. Telling him to go away. Saying goodbye. What had she told him the night before? Perfect love knows no fear. Or something like that. What about anger? Did it know anger?

At last the gray light of dawn began to creep into the car with him. Out in front of the store, traffic picked up as people headed for work. Jay got out of the car and pulled on his wrinkled shirt. His ice bath the night before had done little good. The shirt was still streaked and smelly. Anybody seeing him would probably agree with Kate and think he'd been on a drinking binge. He blew out a tired breath. He didn't care what anybody thought. At least nobody he hadn't left behind in Rosey Corner.

The sky was overcast and the air was frigid. It

seemed right that the sun was hiding. He hoped it wouldn't start snowing. He couldn't bear snowflakes falling down around him this morning. They'd pull up too many memories. Memories he was going to have to put behind him.

The storekeeper gave Jay a hard look when he arrived to open up, but when Jay explained he was looking to buy something new before he went to sign up for the Army, the man's frown faded away.

"Well, come on in and we'll get you fixed right up." The round little man led the way in through the back door of the store, where he yanked his fingers free of his gloves, shrugged off his overcoat, and took off the brown felt hat. He smoothed down his gray streaked hair before he unhooked a tape measure from a nail beside the coatrack and draped it around his neck. Its metal ends bounced against his knees as he made his way around boxes in the back room to plug in a hot plate.

"How about a little tea? If you're a coffee drinker, I must apologize since I don't keep coffee in the place." His eyes narrowed on Jay again. "Or perhaps you're wishing for something a wee bit stronger."

"I'm not a drunk," Jay said. "Even if I look like it."

"You do appear a little worse for the wear," the man said mildly. "But I wasn't accusing you of being inebriated. Only of being chilled from the cold. A splash of the spirits might warm you a bit more than the tea can do."

"Tea's fine." Jay looked down, embarrassed that he'd felt the need to deny being drunk.

"You're welcome to clean up a little in the water closet over there while the water's heating." The man nodded his head toward a narrow door across from them. "If you want, I can get you a pair of trousers and a shirt to change into. I'm thinking you might be looking for something economical. Am I right about that?" The man waited for Jay's answer.

"As economical as you have." Jay doubted the shopkeeper ever let the word "cheap" cross his lips. "I won't need them after I'm in the Army."

"An awful thing. Pearl Harbor." The man shook his head. "Nothing for it but to go to war. Again. We thought we'd taken care of those Germans when we were over there before."

"It was Japan that bombed Pearl Harbor," Jay said.

"True enough. We'll be rushing men to the Pacific to quell the Japanese threat, but we'll be fighting over there against the Germans too. Merely a matter of time." The man clicked his tongue. "But war talk isn't getting your new clothes." The shopkeeper eyeballed him again. "I don't think I need to measure. Give me a minute."

Jay felt like a new person on the outside by the time he left Mr. Traxler's store and headed his car down the street. The shopkeeper had told him where he might rent a room for a couple of days. A place with a bath. He was a lot warmer in his new coat. His old clothes were in a sack, along with a couple of pairs of socks Mr. Traxler had added to his purchases for no extra charge.

"I was over there in 1917. A soldier can't have too many socks," he told Jay. "If you do get shipped out, you keep in mind the need to take care of your feet first and foremost. A soldier needs his wits about him and his feet in good working order."

But while Jay felt better on the outside, the inside was still a mess. The Army wouldn't care. Not as long as he would sign up to fight.

A snowflake hit his windshield and then another. Fat, fluffy flakes like the ones that had fallen around him and Kate in the Franklins' field. Jay turned on his windshield wipers and swept them away.

29

Through the dark of the night, Kate sat beside Lorena's bed and listened to the girl's breathing. In and out. Easy and regular. That was what Aunt Hattie had told them to watch. But as hard as she tried to focus her mind entirely on Lorena and nothing else, Jay was there. Asking her to trust him. But how could she trust a drunk?

Even so, maybe her mother was right. Maybe she should have let him come in. He did love Lorena. She didn't think that was a lie. His words saying he loved her—*I love you, Kate Merritt*—echoed in her head. She even believed that was true as much as he knew how to love. Wasn't that what Mike had told her right at the beginning? That Jay didn't know how to love.

Then again, maybe it was Kate who didn't know how to love. The night seemed to darken around her with the thought. She pushed it away. She knew love. She was surrounded by love. Lorena in the bed in front of her. Tori breathing softly in the bed behind her. Her mother and father in their bedroom on the other side of the sitting room. Love was in every room of this house and radiated out to others in Rosey Corner. Graham. Aunt Hattie. Evie and Mike. She knew love well.

But a little voice whispered through her mind. *What about the romantic, music-in-your-heart kind of love? Do you know that?*

She did know it. She'd danced in the moonlight. And again with snow falling on her face. Even in the cold December wind with the thought of bombs falling on Pearl Harbor to destroy their peace, they'd danced. Jay's arms had felt warm and right around her. But now the dances were over. She'd slammed the door on the music. The terrible silence in her heart matched the darkness in the room. Then an echo of music came to her. Distant and very sad.

The clock began striking in the next room and Kate counted along. Twelve. The midnight hour. The end of the day. Who knew what the day ahead would bring? This time two days ago, they had no thought that now they'd be at war. She had no thought that she'd be sitting in the dark, wishing a hundred things different.

She tried to wipe thoughts of Jay out of her mind. She whispered another prayer thanking the Lord for Lorena's soft, normal breaths. She matched her own breathing to Lorena's. The night would pass, and it could have been so much worse. Lorena could have been badly hurt. Broken hearts were better than broken bodies. Even so, she was glad when the lamp switched on in the next room and her mother came into the bedroom.

"I'll sit with her for a while," Mama whispered. She gazed down at Lorena. "How's she doing?"

"She hasn't stirred. Breathing easy." Kate stood up out of the straight chair she'd pulled over by the bed. She and her mother touched shoulders as they looked down at Lorena. It had always been that way. Both of them watching over Lorena ever since Kate had found her on the church steps. "She seems fine."

"She may be sore in the morning." Mama was

silent a moment as she lightly placed her hand on the girl's chest to feel her breathing. "But I think you're right. She's fine. Thank the Lord." She closed her eyes, and Kate knew she was offering up a silent prayer before she went on. "I don't think we need to sit with her the rest of the night. If she cries out, we'll hear her."

"I'll sleep with her," Kate said. "That way I'll be close if she needs anything."

Her mother touched her fingers to her lips and then swept them across Lorena's cheek. She turned to look at Kate in the dim light filtering in from the next room. "She's going to be all right, Kate."

"I know."

Her mother moved her face closer to Kate's until they were only inches apart. "You will be all right too."

"I know," Kate repeated.

"Do you?" Her mother studied her face a few seconds before she wrapped her arms around her. She whispered close to her ear, "Don't give up on love too easily, my darling. Maybe there was a reason."

"He said I had to trust him," Kate whispered back.

"I guess you are the one who has to decide if you can." Her mother kissed her cheek and then stepped back.

"Did you?" Kate asked.

Mama pulled in a breath and let it out slowly. "You're asking if I trusted your father."

It wasn't really a question, but Kate answered anyway. "Yes."

"My heart did when it mattered most. My heart knew." She put her hand on Kate's cheek. "Yours will too."

Kate didn't say anything. All the trust had drained out of her heart at the stink of alcohol on Jay. Her fractured heart.

Her mother must have guessed what she was thinking. She sighed softly. "My sensible Kate. But sometimes the heart refuses to be sensible." The ghost of a smile touched her lips as she dropped her hand away from Kate's face. "Try to get some sleep. Morning will be here soon. Everything always looks better after the sun chases the darkness away."

Her mother slipped out of the room, clicked off the lamp next to the couch, and disappeared back into her bedroom. Kate eased into the bed beside Lorena and rested her hand on the little girl's stomach so she could feel her breathing. Trouble shifted positions under the bed, his toenails clattering against the wood floor. Maybe they should change the dog's name. Start over with him.

That's what she should do too. Start over with everything. The country was going to have to start doing everything different. They were at war.

One woman's broken heart meant nothing in the face of that.

All day long at the store, people had come in full of talk about the changes that might come. The shortages. The men gone. Nobody to do the jobs. The older men were full of dire warnings of hard times here on the home front as well as on the front lines. Some of them had been on those front lines back in 1917. The younger men talked of nothing but signing up. The women just looked at one another with fearful eyes. With all that trouble barreling toward them, what did sorrows of the heart matter?

She shut her eyes, but her jumbled thoughts gave her no rest. She ordered herself to be sensible the way her mother said she was and go to sleep. What good did it do to stare into the air above the bed until she began to imagine misshapen faces forming in the grainy darkness?

What had she told Jay? That perfect love knew no fear. Why in the world had she quoted Scripture at him? Besides, that was the Lord's perfect love. Nothing she could ever claim any more than he could. Why couldn't she have simply told him she loved him? In her imperfect way. The way he had simply told her. When he was drunk.

Lorena shifted beside her and groaned softly. Kate stroked the child's hair and whispered to her that it was all right. So many times she'd told

Lorena that. So many times her mother had told Kate that. *It's going to be all right.* But was it? How could any of them be sure it was going to be all right now?

Aunt Hattie's voice came into her head. "Nobody can know what tomorrow holds, Katherine Reece. You just has to hold onto the good Lord's hand and take it one step at a time whilst you keep on trusting in his providence."

She didn't know whether she had ever heard Aunt Hattie actually speak those exact words, but she had no doubt that was what she would say if she were there standing by the bed, preaching faith to her. Aunt Hattie had faith. The kind to move mountains. No matter what life threw at her, Aunt Hattie didn't let doubts sprout in her head. Weren't no need, Kate had heard her say. No need at all. The Lord had gotten her through plenty of bad times. Plenty of them. And there weren't nothing out of the ordinary about her, she'd say. If the good Lord was taking care of her, and he was, then for sure he'd take care of other folks too. She'd remind Kate that the good Lord had shined down extra grace on Kate and her sisters. Blessed in every way.

At first light, Kate eased out of the bed. Lorena slept on with no sign of distress, but when she did open her eyes, she'd be sure to ask about Tanner first thing. She'd be unhappy if Kate hadn't kept her promise. She barely made any noise at all getting dressed, but Tori stirred and opened her eyes.

She rose up on her elbow to ask, "Where are you going so early?"

"I promised Lorena I'd let Jay know she was all right before he went to work." Kate ran a comb through her hair.

"I thought he said he was going to enlist today."

Kate's heart grew heavy at Tori's words. "Then I guess I need to catch him before he leaves to do that."

"Sammy's talking about getting his folks to sign for him so he can join up."

"Surely they won't. At least not until he gets out of school." Kate kept her voice low.

"I don't know." Tori stared down at the covers for a minute. "But it scares me. It all scares me. Jay going. Daddy even said Mike might have to go. And Sammy too, whether he signs up now or not."

"Make him wait, Tori." Kate looked over at her. "It might be over before he gets old enough to be drafted."

"It won't be. Everybody says it won't be." Tori breathed out a long sigh. "And I'm not like you, Kate. I can't make things happen. If he wants to go next month or next week, I won't be able to stop him."

Kate tiptoed over to sit on the bed beside Tori and take her hand. "He hasn't gone yet."

Tori grasped Kate's hand tightly. "But if he does, I'm going to marry him first. Whether Mama and Daddy say I should or not."

"They won't try to stop you. They'll understand."

"Do you understand, Kate? Do you love Jay the way I love Sammy?" Tori's green eyes were dark and intense as she looked at Kate.

Tori's question surprised her. She didn't know how to answer her, but she finally said, "It's different for me. I haven't known Jay very long. Not like you know Sammy or Evie knows Mike."

"Love can happen quick," Tori insisted. "You do love him. I know because I know you."

Kate looked down at their clasped hands. "There are things you don't know."

"Maybe so." Tori gave her hand a little shake. "But I know this. I know if you do really love him the way I think you do, then you need to give him a chance to fix things."

"Some things can't be fixed," Kate murmured.

"Not if you don't try. I've never known you not to try."

Kate pulled her hand free from Tori. "You worry about Sammy and let me worry about Jay." She kept her voice low, but she couldn't keep out the hint of irritation.

"It's you I'm worrying about," Tori said with an echo of Kate's irritation. "Not Jay. You."

"I'm fine." Kate pushed a smile out on her face.

"You watch out for Lorena until I get back. I'll tell Mama I'm leaving. I hear her in the kitchen."

Kate was glad her mother was content to know Lorena was sleeping. She didn't ask questions about where she was going when Kate pulled on her coat. She knew.

The morning was gray. Cold hung in the air like invisible ice particles. The sun wouldn't be showing its face even after it did push up above the eastern horizon, with the way the clouds looked ready to drop snow down on them. She pushed the thought of snow away from her mind. It would be better not to think about days when the music had been loud.

Her heart began pounding before she got halfway to Graham's. She had no idea what she could say. Maybe he wouldn't be up. Maybe he would still be sleeping it off. That might be good. She could tell Graham that Lorena was all right and let him deliver the message to Jay.

Some of this mess was Graham's fault anyway —talking Jay into staying to help him paint Mrs. Harrelson's house. Whatever had possessed him to do that? Whatever had possessed her to fall in love with Jay?

I love you, Kate Merritt. Would those words keep echoing in her head forever?

His car wasn't in its usual place. Kate's heart began pounding even harder. She looked to where the sky was brightening a bit as the sun pushed up behind the clouds in the east. She had never imagined him leaving this early for work. Or to enlist.

What would she tell Lorena? That she was too late? That he'd just gone off to work without finding out about her? How could he do that? Even if she did tell him to leave.

Poe started barking when she went around behind her father's shop. Graham opened his door, and the dog lumbered down the steps to meet her with his tail whipping slowly back and forth. "You're out early," Graham called to her.

"I was trying to catch Jay before he went to work, but I guess I'm too late." Kate looked up at Graham in the doorway.

"You'd a had to have been some earlier than this for sure. He didn't never come inside here last night."

"At all?"

Poe gave up on her rubbing his head and went to nose some bushes.

"He was here. I heard him out at the pump sometime after I went to bed, but he didn't come up the steps. Then he must have gone in your daddy's shop 'cause I heard somebody messing around down there. Don't know why he didn't come on up here, but it ain't my job to keep tabs on the boy. I did hear his car start up sometime before morning." Graham stared down at Kate. "Something wrong?"

He was gone. He'd left in the night. Just like that. Just like she'd told him to. Go away, she'd told him, and so he had. Her heart was feeling too heavy to beat.

"You might say that," Kate answered Graham. She wouldn't cry. It was better this way.

"You want to come on up and tell me about it? It's a mite cold standing here in the door."

"I can't. I've got to get back to see about Lorena."

Graham stepped out on the little landing at the top of the stairs. He was in his sock feet. "Something wrong with the girl?" Poe must have heard the worry in his voice. He climbed the stairs to lean against Graham's legs.

"She got hit by a car last night." Kate had to swallow hard before she could go on. "Jay's car."

"She hurt bad?" Graham came down a step.

"Nothing but bruises. She was running after Trouble. Probably to keep him off the road. Jay swerved to miss the pup and hit Lorena."

"What was she doing out with that dog after dark?"

"I don't know." Kate had a sudden overpowering desire to drop down on the cold ground, put her face in her hands, and cry.

Why had Lorena gone out with the pup? She usually just opened the door to let him out or in, but last night she'd said something about going outside to see if it was snowing. Kate hadn't paid it much attention then, but now she knew. Lorena had been watching for Jay, expecting him to come. She'd been peering out the window for his lights every few minutes all evening. Kate had been listening for his car too, had even thought she'd heard his car a little while before Lorena went outside. It could be Lorena hadn't even been chasing the dog but had simply been running toward the road to get Jay to stop when he came by the house. For the first time, Kate wondered why he'd been coming from the wrong direction.

"But you say she's all right?" Graham put his hand on the old dog's head and waited for Kate's nod. "That's good to know. I'm thinking that must have about killed the boy until he found out she wasn't hurt bad. He sets a lot of store by that girl. Loves her plain and simple."

"He doesn't know."

"He doesn't know what? That he hit her?" Graham's frown was back. When Kate didn't answer right away, he went on. "You come on up here and tell me what's going on whilst I put on my shoes. My toes are about froze off. Your mama's there with Lorena, isn't she?"

"Yes, but . . ." Kate hesitated. She wasn't sure she wanted to talk to Graham. Not yet. Not with her heart feeling like a chunk of ice inside her chest.

"I ain't taking no for an answer. You come up here and tell me what's got that sorrowful look on your face if the girl's all right." Graham turned to go in as though the discussion was over.

What could she do but give in and head for the steps. She didn't know what she'd tell him, but she couldn't turn her back on him. Not Graham, her friend since before she could remember.

She didn't see the book until she started up the stairs. "Did you leave a book down here?" she called up to Graham as he started back through the door.

Graham stopped and looked down at the book. "The boy must have left it last night. I thought he came back across the yard before his car started up."

The War of the Worlds. Her father had loaned the book to Jay last week. A scrap of paper blew off the step when Kate picked up the book. She chased it down. A note for Graham. She'd never seen Jay's writing, but she knew it was from him even without looking to see if he'd signed it. She should have folded it to keep from reading it, but instead her eyes grabbed the words.

. . . ask Kate . . . gave Kate the chance you told me I should . . . didn't give me a chance back . . . time I moved on. Got a war to win.

The words blurred in front of her eyes. Gave her a chance? What did he mean? She stared at the paper as though she could make the letters rearrange into something that made more sense.

"He leave a letter for you?" Graham asked when she kept standing at the bottom of the stairs.

"It's not to me," Kate managed to say. "It's to you."

"Then I reckon you need to bring it on up here and we'll figure it out together."

Kate slowly climbed the stairs to Graham's room. Nothing he was going to say would matter. Jay was gone. *Got a war to win.*

❧ 30 ❧

Jay joined the line at the enlistment office, filled out all the papers, stripped down for them to poke and prod his body to be sure he could take whatever the Army threw at him. At one stop, an officer stared straight at his eyes and probed his mental state.

He could have told that one plenty, but nothing that would keep him out of the Army. The guy wasn't interested in the condition of his heart. All he wanted to know was could Jay follow orders in the face of enemy fire without losing his grip and maybe start shooting in the wrong direction. The Army wasn't worried about every answer being right. A man couldn't be too sane if he was volunteering to go halfway around the world to get shot at.

He passed. Was told to catch a train Saturday morning. They were giving him time to tell his family goodbye. But Jay didn't have anybody to tell goodbye. Not now. He didn't even have anybody to tell he'd joined up or where he was going. South, the recruiter said. He should have told them he could climb on the train the next morning. No need waiting. Nobody would be crying at home over him.

Except maybe Birdie. If she'd come around. He couldn't bear thinking she might not be okay. Wednesday night he thought about Mike going to Rosey Corner for prayer meeting. They wouldn't be neglecting that service now. Every church all over the country was having extra prayer meetings. Mike might have already been in Rosey Corner. They would have called him about Birdie.

Mike would hear the whole sad story. If Kate told him Jay was drunk, he wouldn't doubt her. It wouldn't matter that Jay had never been drunk around Mike. He'd believe it was possible. He was a friend, but one with wide-open eyes. He knew Jay's shortcomings. Jay could almost see his mouth tightening up to keep himself from saying he'd warned them. He might feel sorry for Jay. He might think he should talk to Jay or more likely preach at him. Bring him along the right path.

Jay thought he had been headed down that right path. Sitting on a church pew. Dancing to the music of the heart with the most enchanting girl he'd ever met. Being pulled into the good feeling of family. Feeling as though he had a real place to belong for the first time since his mother died. Loving Kate.

That's where the path faded away. His love hadn't been good enough. Mike would tell him to pray for that perfect love Kate had told him about. He had prayed. That night when he saw Birdie lying lifeless in the road in front of his car. A desperate prayer. Maybe he'd had no right to make that prayer. Maybe that's why the Lord had knocked him down with Kate turning her back on him.

But even now, unable to sleep as he stared at the ceiling above the bed in his rented room, that first prayer—the one pleading with the Lord for Birdie—kept circling around in his head. He couldn't block it out. What if Mike was getting ready to preach a funeral? The thought stabbed Jay, made sleep almost impossible.

The sun was shining when he dragged himself out of bed Thursday morning. Two more days before his life wouldn't be his to order any longer. The Army would be pulling his strings. That might be good. Maybe the training would be so tough he wouldn't have time to think about Birdie. About Rosey Corner.

After he ate, he checked the newspaper for a dealer to take his car off his hands. He wouldn't get much, not as old as it was and with all the miles on it. He climbed in the car and ran his hands around the familiar steering wheel. He didn't like thinking about selling it. The car had been his home on wheels for several years, so it seemed wrong to almost give it away to a complete stranger. Somebody who probably wouldn't appreciate it. Might even junk it. But what other choice did he have? He stared out the windshield. If only he had a place to leave it where he might imagine it being there when he got back. If he got back.

He wouldn't need much money where he was headed. The Army would be housing and dressing and feeding him. The only thing he'd need money for would be to tie one on at a roadhouse, and he didn't care if he ever saw the inside of another roadhouse. He was wishing he hadn't seen the inside of one on Monday.

He knew what he was going to do even before he started up the motor and headed east toward Rosey Corner. He'd give the car to Birdie. She couldn't drive, but Mr. Merritt could. Kate could.

Thinking about giving the kid the car helped him believe she had opened her eyes. He imagined her playing with the pup and maybe watching for him. He couldn't climb on that train Saturday without knowing that was true.

Besides, hadn't he promised her he would always come back? As long as she and Kate wanted him to. Now Kate didn't. But that didn't mean he couldn't go back at least this one time to tell Birdie goodbye. To make sure she was all right. That didn't mean he couldn't leave the car there and tell her to hang on to it for him until he came back for it. That would prove to her he'd be back again someday.

He slowed as he came to the Franklins' farm. Smoke was rising out of the chimney, and he imagined the little woman stirring up a cake for Mr. Franklin with one eye on the window watching for the mailman to stop at the mailbox. Waiting for a letter. He wasn't her son, but maybe he'd send her a postcard after he got to the training camp. He remembered the address she'd given him. Rural Route 2, Edgeville. It would be good to have somebody in the world know where he was.

He thought about turning down their lane, to tell them in person. He'd never worried about telling anybody goodbye before. He'd always just gotten in his car and driven away, but Rosey Corner had changed him. Made him wish for family. But wishing didn't make things true. He'd worked for the Franklins a few weeks, but they weren't family.

He pushed down on the gas pedal and sped past their mailbox. He could still send the card.

That would make the little woman happy without him dreaming up things that couldn't be true.

Is that what he'd done with Kate? Dreamed up the music? But she'd heard it too, so if he'd been dreaming, so had she. Trouble was, people woke up from dreams.

A mile from Rosey Corner, he turned down a side road to keep from driving straight through the little community. He didn't want to take the chance of seeing anybody he might have to talk to. At least not until he knew about Birdie.

After winding around the back roads, he came out at the church. A great place to leave the car. He parked it under a big cedar behind the church.

When he got out, he shut the door easy and ran his hand along the fender. He was going to miss the old car, but he'd be glad to think about it being in Rosey Corner even if he couldn't be. With a last pat on the hood, he turned and walked down to the school.

Everybody was still inside, so he leaned against a tree on the opposite side of the road and waited. It was cold, but he had his new coat on. Time ticked by. He must have missed recess time or maybe the cold was keeping the kids inside close to the stove. A gangly kid almost as tall as Jay came out and carried a bucket of coal back inside. He didn't notice Jay.

Jay stuck his hands in his pockets and wriggled his toes to warm them up. He thought about going back to the car, but he wasn't sure what time school let out. He didn't want to miss seeing Birdie run out the door toward home. That's all he wanted. To see her running. He pulled out his watch and stared at the hands. Already past two. A long time since breakfast.

He should have stopped somewhere and gotten something to eat. He could have even stopped at the Franklins' and eaten some of that imagined cake. It wouldn't be as good as Kate's mother's brown sugar pie. Just the thought of that brought the sadness down on him again. He was glad the cold was making his fingers ache. That might keep him from thinking about the ache in his heart.

He wouldn't starve. He'd wait. It couldn't be long now until school was out. He had time. At least until he had to board that train on Saturday. After he saw Birdie, he'd hitch a ride back to Louisville. Leave Rosey Corner behind, but with a reason to come back. Everything would be changed then. Him maybe most of all. War changed men. Everybody said that. And Kate would find somebody to love she could trust. Somebody she might say yes to if he asked her to elope.

He shut his eyes and could see all the different smiles she'd given him when he'd asked her that. *How about we elope?* The first time after the wedding, she'd been surprised but amused at his outrageous proposal. Then each time after that the amusement had softened, until last week he thought she was near to thinking yes even if she didn't say it out loud.

What would she say now if he had the nerve to go to the store and barge right up to the counter and ask if she wanted to elope? He blew out a deep sigh and his breath hung in the cold air. It was too late. Her smiles were lost to him. He said the words he'd never said to any girl before, and she had shut the door on them. He shouldn't have come back to Rosey Corner. He should have given the car to the first down-on-his-luck person he saw on the streets of Louisville and written Birdie a note. Then he could imagine her fine whether she was or not.

But he wanted to give the car to Birdie. He wanted the connection to Rosey Corner. It seemed necessary to have a place to think about coming back to, whether he belonged or not. Birdie might be big enough to drive the car herself by then. What was she now? Ten. Who knew how long the war would last? Two, three years? That seemed forever when he thought about it. But whatever it took to win the war. That's what every soldier had to give. Whatever it took. Even if that was everything.

At last the school door burst open and kids began to stream out. The ones Birdie's size were so bundled up in coats, hats, and scarves that he wasn't sure whether any of them were Birdie or not. He stepped away from the tree toward the road to get a closer look at the faces under the hats and scarves.

Then one of the girls broke away from the group. "Tanner!" she cried as she ran right across the road.

His heart jumped up in his throat when she didn't look for traffic. He could breathe again when he saw the road was clear. The next thing he knew, she was slamming up against him and grabbing him around the waist in a hug.

"I knew you'd come back. I knew it." She looked up at him with a smile that could light up the darkest cave.

"I had to see if my little bird was all right and didn't have any broken wings." He put his hand on top of her head and looked down at her. A purplish green bruise shaded her cheek.

"I'm not hurt. Well, nothing broken. Some yucky scrapes on my legs and you should see the bruise on my hip. Oh, and that goose egg is still on my head." She jerked off her knit cap. "You want to feel? Just don't push too hard." She peeled off her glove and pushed her fingers up through the back of her curly hair to show him where to feel. "See? Right here."

He gingerly touched the bump on her head. The bump that had changed everything. That wasn't really true. The meal his boss had wanted to buy him—that was what had changed everything. But it shouldn't have. Kate should have trusted him enough to listen. He shoved all that out of his mind. He wasn't in Rosey Corner to think about Kate. He had come to be sure Birdie was all right. And she was.

"That's quite a knot," he said.

"I went to the doctor Tuesday and he said my head must have hit the road and that I was lucky it swelled out instead of in. Told me I might still be seeing stars if that had happened. He was funny. But he promised me I won't always have a bumpy head. It wouldn't matter much if I did. My hair would cover it up." She shoved her hat down on her hair again and stuck her hand back in her glove. "I've got really thick hair."

"That's a good thing."

"I can't believe you're here." Birdie grabbed his hand and pulled it up against her cheek. "Your hands are like ice. You should have come inside. Miss Mary wouldn't have cared."

"It's not all that cold, and I didn't want to get you in hot water with your teacher." Jay grinned down at her and shoved his hands in his coat pockets. "I'm real glad you're okay. You weren't looking too good last time I saw you."

She looked upset. "I'm sorry you didn't know I woke up. The doctor said I had a concussion, but it wasn't anything to be worried about."

"I was worried."

"I told Kate you would be. She got up early that next morning to tell you I was okay, but you were already gone." Birdie peered up at him. "Graham said you left in the middle of the night. Why did you leave like that?"

"When it's time to leave, it's time to leave. Kate told you I was sorry, didn't she?"

"She didn't have to. I knew you didn't hit me on purpose. You love me." She smiled up at him without even a trace of shyness to be talking about love. "Not like you love Kate. But like a little sister. Do you have a real little sister?"

"I used to, but then I lost her." He blocked out Birdie saying he loved Kate. Better to not think about that right now.

"How can you lose a little sister?" She looked puzzled. "Do you mean she died?"

"No, I just had to move away from her."

"Oh, you mean like I had to stay here while my real mama and daddy went somewhere else to find food for them and my brother. I have a brother, you know. Kenton. Kenton Birdsong. When I get old enough, I'm going to go find him." She stared up at Jay. "Don't you want to find your little sister?"

"Maybe someday," Jay said casually. Wasn't any reason to tell this kid that he never thought about his sister at all. "But I found you. Birdie Birdsong. That's good enough right now."

She giggled. "Kate still can't believe I let you call me Birdie."

"Or that your daddy lets you call me Tanner."

He pulled his hand out of his pocket and touched the top of her knit cap.

She shivered. "It's cold out here. Come on." She grabbed his hand and started up the road. "You can warm up at the store."

"Can't." Jay stopped her. "I've got to get back to Louisville. I'm in the Army now and I'll have to leave for the training camp soon."

"Today?" She stopped to look up at him.

"Not today, but I still have to start back. It's a long way."

"You and Kate had a fight, didn't you?" She sighed and stared at the ground. "Because of me. Tori says so."

"Not because of you." Jay squatted down in front of her. "It didn't have anything to do with you. Kate and me, well, it just wasn't working out."

"But you love her." Birdie got a fierce look on her face. "I know you do."

Jay smiled a little. "You're right. I do. But sometimes love isn't enough."

"She loves you too," Birdie said.

"Maybe," Jay said. "But maybe not enough."

"How much is enough?"

"I don't know. I guess more than she did."

"She cried last night." Birdie stared at him without blinking. "She'd get mad if she knew I told you that. Kate never cries. But last night she did. She thought me and Tori were asleep, but I wasn't."

415

Jay tightened his lips and swallowed hard. "I can't change what happened, Birdie. I would if I could. I'd go back and live the whole night over and for certain not hit you with the car."

"But then you might have hit Trouble. I mean, Scout." She sneaked a guilty look at him. "We changed Trouble's name. Aunt Hattie said we had to. That names were important and she thought maybe Trouble was trying to live up to his name. So we're calling him Scout now. You don't care, do you?"

He smiled, relieved to be talking about something besides Kate and tears. "Scout. I like it. Does he like it?"

Birdie opened her eyes wide and bobbed her head several times. "He does. He even comes right away when we call him now."

"Well, see?" Jay smiled and stood up. "Aunt Hattie was right."

"Kate says Aunt Hattie's always right." She shifted a little uneasily on her feet before she went on. "You want to go talk to Aunt Hattie? About Kate? She's probably at home."

"Maybe Kate can go talk to her. But I told you. I've got to head on back. The Army doesn't look kindly on you missing your train."

"I don't want you to leave." She gripped his hand a little tighter. "Can't you at least come see Scout? I'll fix you a bologna sandwich. There might be pie."

He couldn't keep from laughing. "There's no pie. I can tell by the look on your face."

She grinned sheepishly. "But Mama might make one if she knew you were going to be there for supper. We could ask Graham and Aunt Hattie. Fern too. Let you tell everybody goodbye before you go to the Army."

He didn't know when he'd wanted to do anything more. Let them put their family arms around him. Let Mr. Merritt give him advice about going off to fight a war. Hear Graham tell another Rosey Corner story. See Kate again. Especially to see Kate again. But she didn't want to see him. She had closed the door on the music in their hearts.

"You want to come," Birdie said when he hesitated.

"You've got my number, Birdie Birdsong, but I can't stay. Gotta get back to Louisville. Things to do there before I leave." Things like staring at the wall. Pretending to read. Playing solitaire. He pushed a smile across his face.

Her bottom lip was quivering. He didn't know whether it was from the cold or if she was about to cry. He pinched her chin a little. "Don't you go to shedding tears on me. Else you might see me joining in and that wouldn't be a bit pretty. A grown man crying like a baby. I just came back to make sure you were all right and to leave you my car."

"Your car? Why would you do that? I can't drive." Birdie's forehead puckered as she tried to puzzle that out.

"You know some people who can, and I didn't want to leave it in Louisville. I was sitting there wondering what to do with it, who might keep it for me until I get back from beating the Japs and the Germans, and I thought of you. You'll do that for me, won't you? Talk your daddy into keeping it in your yard until I come back for it? He can drive it if he wants to. Kate too. She can take you to the movies."

Birdie's frown disappeared. She looked around. "Where is it?"

"Somewhere in Rosey Corner. You don't think you get something for nothing. You'll have to look for it. You and Kate."

"That's silly. You can't hide a car. It's too big."

"Yeah? You see it anywhere?" He laughed as she looked around again. "So I think I just did, but you'll find it. Now, I'd better be hitting the road and catching me a ride. Not too easy to hitch rides after dark."

He lightly punched her shoulder and started away. But she grabbed his hand and then hugged him again. "You will come back, won't you, Tanner?"

"I'll have to come back for my car. See, that's another reason I'm letting you keep it for me. So that you know I'll come back."

"But people are saying the war might last a long time."

"Could be. But you won't forget me no matter how long it lasts, will you, kid?" He lightly cuffed her chin. "You keep in mind it's my car. You can polish it up for me now and again. Keep it shiny." He pulled away from her.

"I will, Tanner. I promise."

"I'm really glad you're all right, but you pay attention to roads now. Take care of my little sister."

She blinked back tears and gave him a shaky smile as she let go of his hand. "I'll write you."

"That'd be great, kid." He headed back toward the church. He could cut across the yards and find his way back to the road without going by the store. He couldn't go by the store. He wouldn't be able to trust himself to keep walking. Even if he did remind himself that Kate wanted him to.

As if Birdie was reading his mind, she called after him. "You want me to tell Kate anything?"

He looked back at her with a grin. "Sure thing, Birdie. Tell her if she ever wants to elope, look me up." Then he took off in a jog. The Army was waiting.

Once back on the main road, it wasn't five minutes before a farmer he recognized from the feed store stopped to give him a lift to Edgeville. He'd find somebody heading back to Louisville from there.

✤ 31 ✤

Kate was pumping gas for Mrs. Perkins when Lorena raced up and grabbed her arm. "Come quick."

"Watch out, Lorena. You'll make me spill the gasoline."

"But—"

Kate stopped her with a look. "You know I have to take care of the customer first."

Mrs. Perkins rolled down her window and stuck her head out. "If you get any of that on my car, I'll expect you to clean it off. Every drop of it. Mr. Perkins keeps this car looking like new, and I'll never hear the last of it if I bring it home with gasoline streaks running down the side."

"Yes, ma'am." Kate used her extra-polite, agree-with-the-customer voice before she turned back toward Lorena and made a face as she worked the pump.

Lorena didn't even grin as she bounced on her toes and looked ready to explode with whatever news she had. Obviously exciting news. Maybe she'd made a hundred on her math test.

Kate finished pumping the gas. Mrs. Perkins handed some bills out the window, and Kate pulled the woman's change out of her pocket.

Lorena grabbed it out of Kate's hand and pushed it toward Mrs. Perkins. "Here you go. Thanks and come again."

"What about my windshield? Aren't you going to clean it?"

"Not today." Lorena blocked Kate from the car. "We'll wash it twice next time. There's a war on, you know. Got to do what needs doing most first."

"Well, I never." With an angry huff, Mrs. Perkins cranked up her window and took off like somebody was giving her car a shove.

"Good thing we're the only gas pump for miles or we'd never see her here again." Kate frowned at Lorena. "What is the matter with you?"

"He's here. I just saw him." She was jumping up and down in her excitement.

"Saw who?" Kate asked. But she knew. Her heart heard his name without Lorena saying it, and she looked past her toward the road. But all she saw was Mrs. Perkins heading out of Rosey Corner.

"Tanner. He came to make sure I was all right."

"Then where is he?" The empty road mocked her.

"He said he had to go back to Louisville. That he was in the Army now." Lorena grabbed Kate's arm again and pulled her toward the road. "But if we hurry, maybe we can catch him."

Kate went a couple of steps before she stopped.

"We can't catch him if he's already left. Besides, he knew where he could find me if he wanted to see me."

"Oh, he wanted to, but he thought you wouldn't want to see him."

"He said that?"

"Not exactly. But he loves you. He told me he did, and I know you love him. So come on. We're wasting time." Lorena jerked on her arm.

Kate pulled free and placed her hands squarely on Lorena's shoulders. She bent down to stare straight into her face. "You're not making sense, Lorena. If he's gone, he's gone. We can't chase after a car." How could he have passed without her seeing him? Maybe the better question, the one she didn't have an answer for, was what would she have done if she had seen him?

"But he's not in his car. He's walking. He gave the car to me to keep for him until after the war."

"He did what?"

"He gave me his car. Well, us anyway. It's somewhere in Rosey Corner, but he didn't say where. Maybe at the house, but I saw which way he went back toward the road. If we run, we might catch him." Lorena's eyes were begging. "You want to catch him, don't you?"

He was drunk. Maybe he had a reason. I love you, Kate Merritt. Without trust, the music stops. Her head was spinning with all the things that had been driving her to distraction all week.

"Please," Lorena said. "He wants to elope with you."

"What?" Kate wasn't sure she'd heard Lorena right.

"He told me to tell you that if you ever wanted to elope, to look him up."

Kate couldn't keep from laughing then. "He knows I'm never going to elope."

"But you do want to see him. To tell him goodbye before he goes to the Army."

She did. Heaven help her, she did. Drunk or sober. With a reason or not. "Okay. Which way?" She grabbed Lorena's hand and took off down the road with her.

It felt good to be running. Letting everything blow away from her. She'd been hoping for a sign, something that would tell her what to do. The hope had been circling in her mind like a prayer. She'd felt guilty praying about Jay when she ought to be concentrating every bit of her prayer energy on the dark days of the war hurtling toward them. Hundreds, even thousands of soldiers had died. Carl might be one of them. His family hadn't heard the first thing from him since Pearl Harbor. Alice Wilcher said Mrs. Noland was frantic. That was where she should be focusing her prayers. Not on her need for love.

Then Aunt Hattie's voice was whispering in her ear as Kate ran. *It's forever an amazement to me how folks is always tryin' to limit the good*

Lord's mighty power. Thinkin' they can only ask for one piddlin' thing like as how they has to pick and choose. You keep in mind, Katherine Reece, the good Lord, he owns it all. Ain't never no prayer too big nor too little for him to set his ear to hearing. That don't mean you'll get the answer you want. The good Lord, he gives and he takes away. But he don't never do no forsaking."

How many times had she heard that from Aunt Hattie? Or something similar. If anybody knew about proper praying, it was Aunt Hattie. Kate's father said Aunt Hattie could pray up a rainstorm in the middle of the desert. If only Kate had time to stop at Grandfather Merritt's house and talk to her as they ran past it. To ask her to pray the music back for Kate and Jay.

That's your prayer. And this time Kate wasn't sure if it was Aunt Hattie's voice or Mama's voice or maybe her own voice.

They ran past Aunt Gertie's house and then Alice Wilcher's. The houses gave way to fields with cows clustered around the barns waiting for their feed. They rounded a curve to where the road stretched out straight in front of them for a long way. A gray, empty stretch of road. No man walked along ahead of them. A couple of cars passed by. One sounded its horn. Probably someone they knew, but Kate didn't even look to see. A truck lumbered past. She slowed to a walk. She was breathing hard. The elation of the run, of thinking she might see Jay, drained away.

Lorena kept going for a few more minutes. Then she stopped to wait for Kate. She leaned over with her hands on her knees to catch her breath. In between pants, she managed to beg, "Can't we go just a little farther? At least over the next hill."

"No use." Fern stepped away from a tree beside the road. They'd both been so intent on looking ahead for Jay they hadn't noticed her there. "If you're chasing the Jay bird man, he's gone."

"Are you sure, Fern?" Lorena had finally caught her breath, but now her bottom lip was quivering.

"Sure as night coming." The bulky man's coat Fern wore over her overalls was buttoned all the way up to her chin. A navy knit cap was pulled down low over her forehead. "That Garvice Jefferson stopped. He got in his truck."

"How long ago?" Kate asked.

"Long enough to be gone." Fern's voice was blunt, her words true.

"Fern's right. We can't catch up with Mr. Jefferson's truck, and Mama might worry if we don't head back." Kate put her arm around Lorena's shoulders and turned her back toward the store. She couldn't bear the sight of the empty road. Fern fell in beside them.

Fern was right. He was gone. Maybe this was her sign. That the music wasn't meant to start up again. The Lord gives and the Lord takes away. Aunt Hattie's words were echoing in her head again. But had the Lord taken away Jay or had she pushed him away? Now she might never see him again.

As though Lorena were reading her mind, she said, "He'll come back for his car. He'll come back to see us."

"Sure he will." Kate swallowed down the tears that wanted to come and tightened her arm around Lorena. "When he can. After the war." Months, even years from now. Maybe never. But she wouldn't tell that to Lorena.

"I told him I'd write." Lorena's face brightened at the thought.

"I know he'll like that."

Then her face fell. "He didn't tell me where he was going, so I won't know where to send any letters."

"He wants a letter, he'll write you," Fern said.

"Sure, he will." Kate pushed belief into her voice that she didn't feel. Jay wouldn't write.

"He said you could take me to the movies in the car. That you could drive it since I'm not big enough yet." Lorena seemed to be searching for something, anything to try to feel better.

"Well, that will be good. Won't it, Fern?" Kate didn't know why she felt the need to include Fern in the conversation. Fern didn't care. She could stay right beside a person all day long and never utter more than a dozen words and none of them over one syllable.

"Got no use for cars," Fern said flatly.

"Movies are a good use, Fern. You could go with us sometime." Lorena looked over at the woman. "You can get popcorn to eat while you watch the movies. Tanner always bought us popcorn." Her mouth turned down again.

"Let's go find the car," Kate said. "If it's really here."

Lorena looked up at her with a puzzled frown. "Why would he say it was if it wasn't?"

Fern gave Kate a hard look overtop of Lorena's head. "You think he lied."

Kate couldn't tell if it was a question or not, but before she could think of what to say, Lorena jerked away from her and glared at both of them. "He wouldn't lie to me."

Fern answered before Kate could. "Everybody lies, Lorena Birdsong."

Hearing Fern say her whole name seemed to steal the words out of Lorena's mouth.

"Even you, Fern?" Kate asked. "I can't imagine you lying."

"Don't now. Learned better." Fern stared at Lorena a moment and then narrowed her eyes on Kate. "You can learn better too."

"We haven't been lying to anyone," Kate said.

"Maybe not the girl."

Lorena spoke up to defend Kate. "Kate doesn't lie."

"Everybody lies," Fern repeated. "The lies to

yourself are the worst kind." Then she turned on her heel and headed toward the fence beside the road to climb over a stile.

They watched her cross the field away from Rosey Corner to who knew where.

"Sometimes I can't figure out what Fern's talking about," Lorena said.

"You're not the only one." And sometimes that was true, but not this time. This time she did know. Fern had seen right through Kate. She knew. But whether Kate was lying to herself or not about loving him, Jay was gone either way.

She pushed a smile out on her face. "But come on. We've got a car to find."

Kate's first thought was that Jay might have left the car in his old parking spot beside the blacksmith shop, but Mr. Harlow's truck was there. He was in the shop with her father. As Kate and Lorena headed away, the ring of Daddy's hammer shaping a piece of metal followed them.

That had always been a good sound to Kate. A sound that meant her father was at work and all was right with the world. But now nothing was right anywhere.

Next they tried the house to see if he'd parked the car in his usual spot under the tree, but the yard was empty. So very empty. A chill wind picked up some of the fallen leaves and sent them spinning through the air.

Scout raced toward them, his tail going a mile a minute. Kate rubbed his ears and asked, "You happen to see a car, boy?"

"Scout can find it for us," Lorena said. "That's what scouts do, don't they? Find things like the best trail or where to set up camp. Or track down things."

"I don't know if he's really a tracking dog," Kate said.

"Everybody said he lived up to his name when we called him Trouble. Maybe he will now that he's Scout. And you were right about Tanner. He thought Scout was a good name."

The dog jumped up in the air as if he understood what she was saying.

"See, Scout knows Tanner's name too. Tanner." Lorena spoke louder and the dog's tail whipped through the air. She pointed toward the road with one hand while she leaned down to speak close to the dog's ears. "Go find Tanner's car."

Kate couldn't keep from laughing when all Scout did was lick Lorena's face. The laugh surprised her. A minute ago she'd thought she was too worried and sad to laugh, but there it was—a laugh bubbling up out of her. The Lord's way of telling her that even in the midst of troubles, life kept happening.

She touched the dog's head and told Lorena, "I think we'd better do the tracking ourselves. A car's a big thing. There's no place for it to hide in

Rosey Corner. Where were you when you talked to Jay?"

"He was waiting across the road when school let out."

"Then that's where we start."

They found the car tucked up close to a cedar tree at the back of the church. Scout ran to it with Lorena right behind him the way they'd always run to meet Jay when he pulled in the yard. The way the dog must have run to the road with Lorena chasing him the night Jay had hit her. The night he was drunk. Why had he told her he wasn't drunk? Maybe she would have given him a chance to explain if he hadn't lied.

What had he put in the letter to Graham? That he'd given her a chance, but she hadn't given him one. She hadn't asked Graham what that meant on Tuesday morning. She'd merely folded the letter and handed it to him. Then even though he'd wanted her to explain what was going on, she'd only told him the bare bones of what happened and left before the tears could spill down her cheeks. She didn't cry. At least not where anybody could see her.

Lorena pulled open the driver's door. No one was in the car. Of course no one was in it. Fern had seen Jay get in Garvice's truck. Fern had seen him go.

"Do you think Tanner would care if we let Scout

ride in the backseat?" Lorena asked over her shoulder.

Kate moistened her lips and blinked hard. "Not as long as his paws aren't muddy. And it's way too cold today for mud."

Lorena held up the seat and the dog hopped right in as though he remembered riding to their house in this car. "Do you think you can start it?" She scooted past the gear stick and settled in the passenger's side, waiting for Kate to get in.

The seat wasn't still warm from Jay sitting in it. It couldn't be. Yet she was totally aware that he had sat in the seat only a few hours before. That his hands had been on the steering wheel she was gripping. The car even smelled like him.

And the music started in her heart. More than anything in the world she wished she could dance to that music with Jay.

❧ 32 ❧

It wasn't as cold in Alabama as it had been in Kentucky when Jay had boarded the train the middle of December. That part was good. All the farm work had kept him in shape, so the running and marching and training weren't as hard for him as some of the other recruits. That was good. He didn't have to make any decisions. Just follow orders. That too was good.

March here. Run there. Line up for this. Fall in for that. Eat what was plopped on his tray. Say "yes sir." Become a machine. A killing machine. Above all, don't think.

Don't think. That was what he needed to remember. Not to think about what he'd left behind in Rosey Corner. Not to think about the other guys stretching out on their bunks at night reading the letters from home. Not to see the packages of cookies and socks the other men got in the mail. He didn't need any of that. He'd always been on his own. His months in Rosey Corner had done nothing to change that.

Night after night, he lay in his bunk and told himself that, but he couldn't convince his heart it was true. His heart wouldn't let him lock out Kate and Birdie and Graham. He couldn't even keep them from sneaking into his thoughts while he was marching in the rain or sunshine. Instead he wrote letters in his head to Mike and Graham. He thought about what he might write to Birdie and what she'd write back to him. And he thought about getting a letter from Kate.

If only he hadn't been so worried about a door slamming in his face again. If only he had marched right to Merritt's Dry Goods Store and leaned on the counter until Kate talked to him. If only. But instead he had sneaked around Rosey

Corner like some kind of criminal who needed to leave the scene of the crime as fast as possible.

He didn't know why he had taken Birdie the car. Oh, he'd come up with reasons. The car wasn't going to bring him all that much money if he sold it. He was attached to the heap and wanted it to be somewhere for him when he came back. If he came back. He owed Birdie something after hitting her on the road.

But hours of marching gave a man too much time to think. It was hard to keep lying to himself while he was slogging through mud with a cold rain slashing him in the face and a sergeant yelling in his ear that if he thought this was bad, he'd better learn to be a hundred times tougher before he went overseas.

The truth was, he'd gone back to Rosey Corner with his car for one reason and one reason only— in hopes that Kate Merritt would stumble across his path. And then he'd done everything possible to keep that from happening. He could have lingered. He could have not looked for the first ride down the road. He could have stopped and talked to Fern when he spotted her staring at him. But he hadn't.

March. Don't think. Forget Rosey Corner.

Christmas came. Nothing to celebrate in his corner of the world. Mike would tell him different. Mike would tell him that the reason for celebrating Christmas was the same every year no matter what else was happening. He wondered about Mike. Whether he'd been drafted. Whether the Army would be able to make him into a killing machine. A man who preached love. Now he might have to carry a gun instead of a Bible.

The Army had chaplains. And plenty of lay preachers in the ranks, if Jay's division was any indication. Men with Bibles in their hands morning and night. Men who kept telling the others, the ones like Jay, that they needed to get right with God before they boarded a transport ship for their first battle.

Perry Stoddard latched on to Jay as his personal missionary project. Perry wasn't much more than a kid. Claimed to be twenty, but he didn't look eighteen. Whatever his age, he was ready to step up to save America the same as the rest of them. He was slim to the point of skinny and lacked some being as tall as Jay. Perry said that would be a plus in the tank divisions. He figured he would fit real well down in the gunner's position.

They hadn't been assigned to units yet. Training first to toughen them up for war. To make them soldiers instead of merely recruits. Perry was tougher than he looked. He could keep up with Jay on most of the training courses and was generally ahead of him when it was crawling under and climbing over.

"Lean's the way to go," Perry told Jay with a laugh. "Don't have to dig as big a foxhole and makes me a lot smaller target for the enemy."

"Tanks are plenty big," Jay said.

"They are." Perry's eyes lit up. "That's how come I want to be in one. Then I'll be plenty big too. For the first time ever."

They were in the barracks waiting for the lights-out order. Perry, who had the bunk next to Jay, was sharing a box of cookies he'd gotten in the mail earlier that day. He was always getting mail. Around them, the men were settling in for the night. Some of them were shooting the breeze with the men close to them, the way Jay and Perry were doing. Others were already sacked out, their heads under their pillows to block out the noise and the light. A few were reading, and here and there a man was propped up against the wall, writing a letter.

"Your mama bake the cookies for you?" Jay asked. They were heavy on cinnamon and tasted a lot like some Mrs. Franklin had made while Jay was working on their farm. Maybe he should write to her and see if she would send him some cookies. She'd be surprised if he wrote her, but he didn't have any trouble believing a letter from him in her mailbox would make her smile.

"Yeah, I always tell her to send double when she sends something to eat so I can share with you and the other guys." He fingered the letter that had come with the box. "Mama, she didn't want me to sign up. She thought I should wait awhile, see what happened. Like she thought it was all gonna be over quick as anything. But it's not. I've got a little brother chomping at the bit to join up too. He'll be old enough to enlist come June."

"That'll be hard on your folks, having both of you in the Army."

"Well, we won't be the only brothers in the Army." Perry looked up at Jay. "It's funny how I feel plenty old enough to be here, but I don't like thinking about my little brother going over there to get shot at."

Perry took a bite of the cookie and chewed awhile before he asked, "You got family, Tanner?" When Jay didn't answer right away, he rushed on. "I guess I shouldn't pry, but you never get no mail."

"That's okay," Jay said, smiling at the boy. "Answering a few questions is a fair price to pay for some of your cookies. I parted ways with family a long time ago after my mother died. I might be able to find my old man if I took a notion, but I doubt he could find me. I don't guess anybody knows where I am."

Perry looked like he wasn't sure he could believe Jay. "Nobody?"

"Nobody."

"But that's awful."

"Oh, it's not so bad." Jay reached for another cookie. "Not as long as I have a bunk buddy like you I can bum cookies off of."

"But everybody needs family. Somebody to worry over you being gone and pray about you when you go off over there." Perry looked almost sad, and then color crept up into his cheeks, as if he was afraid he might have said the wrong thing. "I mean, it seems like that to me."

"I've got this little sister praying about me," Jay said to keep the kid from feeling sorry for him. Birdie wasn't really his little sister, but thinking about her maybe remembering him in her bed-time prayers gave his own heart a little lift. Could be Kate would be sitting right beside her when she prayed. Could be Kate might whisper a prayer for him too.

He pushed the thought away. If prayers did any good, a lot of things would be different. The Germans would have stayed in Germany and not tried to take over the world. The Japanese wouldn't have bombed Pearl Harbor. He wouldn't be sitting there in an Army barracks feeling like the loneliest man in the world.

But Perry looked cheered at once. "Well, see, you do have family. Whether she knows where you are or not, she's asking the Lord to watch over you. And the Lord knows where each and every one of us is. All the time. He'll take care of us."

"Yeah, kid, maybe he will." Jay wasn't about to say anything to rob Perry of his belief. In that tank, if he ever got in it, he'd need all he could get. An odd yearning feeling crawled through Jay. It might be good to have something to put in that empty spot inside him. To have the feeling that somebody was watching over him, loving him in spite of his shortcomings.

Kate hadn't been able to do it. He used to think Mike did, but then he hadn't wanted Jay around Rosey Corner. Right now, Birdie did, but that was simply because she was so young. She didn't know him all that well. But the Lord Perry believed in, the one Mike said was his personal friend, if he really existed, he was supposed to know everything about everybody and love them anyway. Why was it so easy for others to believe and so hard for him? Maybe his aunt had been right and his heart was too hard for anybody to love.

"I better write Mama and tell her I liked the cookies so she'll send us some more." Perry opened up the box where he kept all his letters. He pulled out some paper and a pencil and held them toward Jay. "Here. Why don't you write your little sister? Maybe she's got big enough to bake some cookies herself."

When Jay hesitated, Perry pushed the pencil and paper toward him. "Go ahead. Take it. I've got plenty. Mama makes sure I don't run out of writing material. She says she can't stand it if she doesn't hear from me every week. In fact, if you don't want to write to your little sister, you can write to Mama. Or my little sister. Sally would like having a feller like you to write to. Mama says she's getting boy crazy, and if she don't watch her, she'll be getting married before she's seventeen."

Jay laughed and took the paper and pencil. "Guess I'd better stick to writing my little sister then. Don't want to encourage that."

After writing the date, Jay stared at the blank page as though he expected words to appear without him putting the pencil lead on the paper.

Perry didn't notice as he scribbled away on his letter. "You ain't already married, are you, Tanner?"

"Nope." He hoped his short answer would stop the kid's questions, but it didn't.

"You got a girl?"

"Nope." The truth of that sliced through him. Maybe he should write to Kate. Beg her to forgive him for being drunk even if he wasn't. He wondered what Alice Wilcher had told anybody about that night. He hoped the silly girl had learned her lesson. He wished there had been somebody else there that night to keep her out of trouble. But maybe it turned out for the best. Maybe it wasn't supposed to work out between him and Kate. If he couldn't believe in the Lord and answered prayers, maybe he could simply believe in fate. Fate had thrown them together. Fate had torn them apart.

"How about you, Perry?" Jay said to keep the kid from asking more questions. "You got a girl at home?"

The color rose in Perry's cheeks again. "There is this one girl, but she doesn't know I'm alive."

"Well, maybe you'd better take this back and write and tell her that you are." Jay held the paper out toward him. "Could be that's all she's waiting for. To know you're breathing."

Perry waved his hand away. "Keep it. I told you I got plenty. I can write Rosa if I take a notion, but that's for your little sister."

Jay scooted back on his bunk and leaned against the wall. He thought about writing *Dear Birdie*. He thought about it a long minute. Even went so far as to write *Dear*, but then he hesitated. He held the pencil poised over the paper, but he didn't touch the lead down as he thought about what he might write. *Dear Birdie, How are you? Is Scout okay? Hope he's keeping out of trouble now that he's got a new name. How about you? Are you keeping the car all shined up? Has your mama made any of those brown sugar pies? Wish I had a whole one to eat all by myself right now. How's Kate doing? Tell her I wasn't drunk. That I don't plan to ever get drunk again even here in the Army where getting drunk is pretty popular.*

He mentally scrubbed out those last lines. He couldn't write that to Birdie. If he wanted to say that, he should be writing *Dear Kate* first. He thought about simply folding the blank paper and laying it aside, but Perry kept peeking over at him to see if he was writing.

The kid was harmless. He meant well. He just couldn't understand somebody without family. He had grandmothers and grandfathers and aunts and uncles and too many cousins to count. The whole kit and caboodle probably got together every Sunday after church. Enough family to suffocate a person. Jay didn't have to worry about that. He had breathing room. Plenty of breathing room.

"You'd better hurry and get something written before Sarge yells lights out," Perry said.

He shouldn't have let Perry think he was a friend. But what else did a man have in the Army but his buddies? Jay held in a sigh, put the pencil point down on the paper, and told himself to think about all the cookies the kid would be sharing with him from his mama and all those aunts and grandmothers. Cookies. That was it. He'd make Mrs. Franklin happy when she made one of her mailbox treks. He'd write to Birdie. He would. Just not yet.

Dear Mrs. Franklin, he wrote. It was easy to scrawl a few words across the paper for her. He didn't have to write the first thing about Kate. Instead he could write words that didn't mean a whole lot. And while he wasn't really writing to the person he wanted to write to, it felt good to be writing to somebody.

33

Christmas came, but the cloud of war hanging over it stole a lot of its merry. The same as any other year, children at church put on a program about the birth of Jesus. Lorena wore a white robe made from an old sheet and balanced a tinsel halo on her head. She always wanted to be an angel, and this year she got to be the one who announced the good news to the shepherds.

"Behold I bring you good tidings of great joy!" Where some children got stage fright and mumbled when they saw people in the pews, Lorena loved performing. Her voice rang out strong. She had good news to tell.

Bombs falling all over the world didn't change the truth of that joyful news of a babe wrapped in swaddling clothes and lying in a manger. After the play, they all sang carols and then ended the service by praying fervently for the young men going off to war.

On Christmas Day, their table was still loaded down with good food in spite of some grocery items being in short supply. Kate didn't hear anybody complain about the shortages at the store. Doing without became a badge of patriotism. If they had to give up some things they'd once thought necessary, then they'd find other ways. Hadn't they just come through the Depression? They knew how to do without. Besides, those kinds of things were a lot easier to give up than their sons and husbands and brothers. And preachers.

Mike cut his sermon short on the third Sunday in January to break the news to his church that he was enlisting. "It's my duty to step up and do my part for my country." He looked grim as he gripped the sides of the pulpit. A grimness that was reflected back to him from the pews.

With tears making trails through the powder on her cheeks, Evie gripped Kate's hand on one side and their mother's hand on the other. All over the church, others were crying with her, but not Kate. Kate was drained of tears. She'd spilled them all in the deep of the night for Jay. Now listening to Mike say he too was joining the Army, her sorrow went beyond tears. How could they expect a preacher to become a soldier?

As if he heard her unspoken question, he went on. "The Army needs chaplains. I'll go through the same training as any soldier, but then I'll be assigned to a unit to help with the spiritual needs of the fighting men. I'll be marching with them, fighting with them if I have to, as we push back the enemy." His jaw tightened and his voice rose a bit as though he were pounding home the point of a sermon. "Our cause is just. The Lord will be with us."

He stared down at the pulpit a long moment. At last he looked up and went on in a softer voice. "Your job, your sacred duty here at Rosey Corner Baptist Church, is to lift me up in your prayers so that I will be empowered to comfort and encourage the men on the front lines. I'll be writing back to you every week to let you know how much your prayers are needed. I might not be able to tell you details of where I am or who I'm with, but I know you will gather to faithfully pray for the men I'll be shepherding through this man-made hell on earth. The Lord will know the needs and he will hear and bless your prayers."

He paused and looked around the church. "Some of you have already been touched personally by the hardship of war." His eyes touched on Carl Noland's parents in the second row from the front. "I want you to continue to lift up one another to the mercies of the Lord and to remember to pray fervently for the healing of one of our own. The last letter from Carl's wife says she expects him to be brought back to a hospital in California very soon where he will continue to get treatment for the severe wounds he suffered at Pearl Harbor. He needs your prayers. So do all the wounded and their families and the families of those men who gave their lives in that battle and the battles since. Never stop believing in the power of prayer."

Mrs. Noland began to sob and Mr. Noland put his arm around her. Evie squeezed Kate's hand even tighter, but at least she wasn't dissolving into a puddle of tears. She was being braver than Kate would have ever thought possible. Crying silent tears. She even managed to curl up the corners of her mouth in a sorrowful smile when Mike settled his eyes on her.

He didn't try to veil his obvious love as he went on. "And I do covet your prayers for my wife as she faces our separation with courage, as so many others are doing all across our great nation. We will conquer the tyrants tearing our world apart. We will win, but as President Roosevelt continues to remind us, it could be a long fight."

He turned his eyes back to his congregation as his voice strengthened. "Long or short, at whatever cost, we must stay steadfast in our resolve to defeat the evil threatening us. With your prayers and the prayers of all Americans, we will be victorious and bring peace back to our country and the world."

He stared out at them, demanding their commitment to the Lord and to their country. "Let us pray together for victory."

He bent his head and the church was silent except for a few muffled sobs. Somehow the sound of tears only made the silence that much more profound.

Evie didn't bend her head, but kept her eyes locked on Mike as though gathering in the sight of him as much as possible while she still could. Kate understood what she was feeling. But at least she was sending Mike off to war with love. At least she hadn't slammed the door on that love the way Kate had.

Every morning when Kate got up, she thought maybe she would begin to forget. That the ache in her heart would be less. Time was supposed to heal all wounds. Everybody said that. Not to her. She didn't talk about the pain in her heart. She pretended to be fine. She smiled as much as anybody else. The human spirit demanded smiles even in the darkest of times.

But her mother knew. Lorena knew. Even Evie knew. And of course, Graham knew. They looked at her with sympathetic eyes, but they didn't talk about it. What good would that do? Even if she did want to write Jay to see if they could find a new beginning, she couldn't. She had no idea where he was. He didn't write. Not even to Lorena.

Every day Lorena raced for the mailbox as soon as she got home. Even after weeks went by without a word from Jay, she didn't give up hope of one day finding a letter from him there. If Kate was with her when she looked in the box, she'd stare up at her with a defiant set to her chin and say, "He will write. When he can. I know he will."

And so the coldest days of winter passed. Mike left and Evie found another Army wife to share her apartment. Reverend Winston, an older preacher Mike had met in Frankfort, came to fill the pulpit at the church until Mike returned. He lacked Mike's fire and humor, but they had church. They sent up concentrated prayers. For Mike. For Carl, who, the news came in, had lost his left leg at Pearl Harbor. He was rehabilitating in California with the help of the woman he married out there.

"I saw a picture of her," Alice Wilcher said one day in late March when she came in the store. "The woman, I can't remember her name. It's Juanita or Solina or something like that. Anyway, whatever her name is, she said Carl asked her to send her picture to his mother. Mrs. Noland showed it to me because she knew I used to write to Carl when he first joined up."

Kate mumbled something to let Alice know she was listening as she filled a rack with packets of garden seed that had just come in. Radishes, cucumbers, melons. She and Alice were alone in the store. Mama had left early to see about Tori, who was in bed with a bad cough. Lorena had been by the store after school, but she'd gone home to gather the eggs and feed the chickens before dark. It was a chilly, gray day with clouds blowing past that didn't seem to know whether to rain or spit snow. Kate had been hoping Graham would stop by, but he and Poe must be staying in by the stove. Nobody was coming out.

Nobody but Alice, who needed no encouragement to keep talking. Alice laughed a little. "She's always saying how she wished Carl had fallen for me. Poor woman. I never had the first bit of romantic interest in Carl, but no use letting her know that. She likes to tell me how much better I would have been for him. A Rosey Corner girl and not some foreign-looking girl out in California."

"Is she foreign looking?" Kate asked, not because she cared, but because it was something to say. Alice was different now when she came in the store. She still liked to gossip, but the war had changed her. The war had changed everybody. Helped them focus on what was important instead of what wasn't.

"Hard to tell much about what she looked like, except she did have real dark-looking hair down around her shoulders."

"Sounds pretty." Kate didn't want to talk about Carl. She didn't really want to talk about anybody. She just wanted to know what to do next. To have a purpose. To do something to make a difference.

"Well, she must not be Japanese or they'd be rounding her up to ship off to those internment camps with all the others out there on the coast. You read about that in the papers, didn't you?"

Alice leaned on the counter. "How many did they say?"

"A hundred thousand."

"I can't even imagine that many people. How many of us are there here in Rosey Corner? A hundred maybe."

"I don't know." Kate rearranged some of the packets of seeds. Carrots, squash, marigolds. The onion sets, corn, and bean seeds were in buckets in front of the rack with a measuring cup and paper sacks for people to buy however much they needed. She put her hand down in the pole beans and felt their silky smoothness. She let the beans slide off her hand and reached to straighten some cans of peaches on the shelf behind the rack.

Somebody had come in the store last week talking about how they'd heard canned food might be rationed soon. Because of the metal. Already manufacture of new cars had been banned with those factories now being readied to turn out tanks and airplanes and guns. Women were lining up for jobs at some of those northern factories. Maybe that was what she should do. Get a job building planes or making parachutes. There was a parachute factory right up the road in Lexington.

"We ought to know that," Alice said. "At least somebody should."

Kate shrugged a little. "Aunt Hattie might know, or maybe Graham."

Alice looked down and fiddled with her pocketbook catch. "Graham ever hear from Jay Tanner?"

Kate held in a sigh. The last thing she wanted to do was talk about Jay to Alice Wilcher. "Not that he's told me."

"He'd tell you." Alice pulled a handkerchief out of her pocketbook to dab at her nose. Not a lady's handkerchief, but a man's. She glanced around as though to make sure they were alone in the store. "What happened with you and Jay? I thought you were a couple. Then he just up and left."

"He joined the Army."

"Lots of men are joining the Army, but they get married or engaged first. Just think about Carl. When you threw him over, he went straight out to California and found a wife. And then there's Victoria. She claims she and Sammy are getting married the minute school's out."

"Sammy is bound and determined to enlist." Kate's throat tightened at the thought of him going to the war. That was even worse than Mike leaving. Sammy was just a kid. Barely eighteen. She could hardly bear to think about it.

She did think about pretending she needed to go to the toilet in hopes Alice would go on home, but her mother had left Kate in charge of the store. Alice was a customer, even if she hadn't laid the first thing on the counter to buy.

"That's what Victoria told me. Funny how her

and Sammy have known forever they want to get married. Doesn't happen like that for everybody, does it?"

"No, I guess not."

"Carl wanted you to marry him."

"He thought he did." Kate pulled an old towel out from under the counter and began dusting empty spots on the shelves.

"What about Jay Tanner? Did he ever ask you to marry him?" Alice kept her eyes on the handkerchief as she folded it back into a square, matching the sides and corners precisely.

When Kate's lips turned up, she was so surprised to be smiling that she answered without proper thought. "He used to ask me to elope almost every time we were together. I guess that might count."

"But you didn't." Alice peeked up at her and then went back to work on her handkerchief.

"Obviously, since here I am." Kate put down her cleaning rag and stared out the window instead of looking at Alice. "Maybe I should have." What in the world was wrong with her? Saying something like that to Alice Wilcher. Everybody in Rosey Corner would know Kate was pining after Jay Tanner now. Alice wasn't a secret keeper.

"I would have," Alice said. "If he'd asked me, I'd have been in his car in nothing flat."

Kate looked back at Alice. She couldn't quite read the look on the girl's face. Worried maybe, or sad. "You were too young for him, Alice."

"That's what he kept telling me." Alice sighed, then after a few seconds, she started talking again in a hesitant voice. "You know how people in Rosey Corner love to gossip?"

"You can't believe everything you hear," Kate said. "Or repeat everything you hear."

"Well, just between us . . ." Alice studied the handkerchief in her hands as she pushed out her next words in a rush. "I heard you got mad at Jay because you thought he was drinking the night he hit Lorena."

Kate went stiff. "Whatever differences Jay and I had are nobody's business but our own."

"I suppose so." Alice flashed her eyes up to Kate's face and then back to the handkerchief. "But what if you were wrong? And he wasn't drinking. What then?"

"You weren't there, Alice. I don't know why we're even talking about this." Kate wanted to shove the girl toward the door, get her out of the store and away from her sight.

Alice blinked her eyes a couple of times and pulled in a deep breath. "You're right. I wasn't there." She very carefully placed the folded handkerchief back in her pocketbook.

Kate mashed down her irritation with the girl. Having a curvy figure didn't necessarily mean a girl was mature in other ways. She wasn't much older than Tori. Maybe she didn't know any better than to poke and prod and meddle. "Did you need any groceries, Alice?"

Alice snapped her pocketbook closed and pushed away from the counter. "A box of crackers. Mama made soup. And some peanut butter. Mama says to put it on our tab."

"All right." Kate got the crackers and peanut butter off the shelves and sacked them up. "Soup sounds good on a day like today."

She hoped Alice would pick up the sack and leave without saying anything else about her and Jay. Heaven only knew what the gossips would be saying tomorrow after Alice told them Kate wished she'd eloped with him. Sometimes it didn't do to speak the truth out loud. If it was the truth. If only she knew the truth.

Alice stopped with her hand on the door to go out. She looked back toward Kate. "It was nice Jay bringing you the car to use while he was gone."

"He didn't bring it to me. He brought it to Lorena." Kate wanted to tell her to just go on out the door. They could talk forever and nothing would be changed. She'd still be here at the store and Jay would still be in the Army. Somewhere. Maybe even in Africa by now or in the Pacific where the war was not going well.

"Lorena can't drive." Alice started to pull open the door, but again she stopped. She turned full around and rushed out her next words as though she needed to say them fast before she lost her nerve. "I know you're smart, Kate. Smarter than I ever hope to be, but you aren't always right. You can be wrong. And that's all I'm going to say."

Then she was out the door, slamming it behind her.

Kate stared at the door and muttered, "Goodbye, Alice. Don't hurry back." She had no idea what Alice was trying to tell her. Or even if she was trying to tell her something or only doing her best to be irritating.

The clock on the wall behind the counter ticked off the seconds. More than an hour before closing time. But at least a few people usually stopped by on the way home from work, and sure enough, the bell at the gas pump clanged as a car drove up. Kate grabbed her coat and hurried out into the cold air, glad to have something to get her mind away from Jay Tanner and what she'd told Alice Wilcher about eloping with him. Alice was right. Sometimes Kate was wrong. She didn't really wish she'd eloped with him. Stand up in the church and marry him, maybe. But not elope. The only reason he had ever asked her that was because he knew she wouldn't.

At last Kate saw the last customer out the door and flipped over the OPEN sign to CLOSED. After she checked the washroom to make sure it was in good shape, she put her coat back on, turned off the lights, and stepped out into the chilly air. She never drove Jay's car to the store. It was such a short walk from the house that it seemed a waste of gasoline to drive.

The thick clouds were making night come early. Icy rain hit her in the face and Kate pulled the hood of her coat up over her head. It would feel good to get home and see what her mother had fixed for supper. Maybe soup, like Alice's mother. She looked over toward her father's blacksmith shop, dark and closed up, but a lamp glowed in the window of Graham's room above it. She slowed as she passed. She hadn't talked to Graham for a couple of days, and it always made her feel better to talk to Graham. Maybe he'd even heard from Jay.

She shook her head and kept walking. She was getting as bad as Lorena, wishing for a letter. Wishing for what couldn't be. But they might have gotten a letter from Mike. He was almost through with basic training, and then according to where he was assigned next, Evie might go join him until he shipped out. He was also hoping for a few days' leave so he could come home and be the one to perform the marriage ceremony for Tori and Sammy.

Kate counted back the weeks since Pearl Harbor. Jay would be through with his basic training. He could already be on a troopship on the way to war. He could already be in the middle of the fighting. He could be dead.

She couldn't keep thinking that. Else she was going to lose her mind. She was so deep in her thoughts that she didn't see Fern until she stepped up on the road beside her. "Fern, what are you doing out in weather like this?"

Fern peered at her from under the man's felt hat she had pushed down on her head. "Don't mind rain. Snow. Just weather."

"You might catch something the way Tori has."

"Might." Fern pulled a bottle out of her coat. "Hattie said give you this for the sick girl. A tonic. So I was waiting for you."

"You could have brought it to the store." Kate took the bottle and slipped it down in her coat pocket.

"Thought about it, but that other girl was there. Her talk hurts my ears."

"Yeah." Kate could agree with that. "Well, thanks, and thank Aunt Hattie for us too." She started on toward the house and was surprised when Fern kept walking along beside her. After a few steps, Kate said, "You want to come to the house? Get some supper to carry back to you and Aunt Hattie?"

"Hattie's got beans. Cooked with a ham hock."

Kate didn't try to think of anything else to say. If Fern wanted to walk with her, Fern would walk with her. And if she wanted to say something, she'd take her time saying it. Throwing words at her wouldn't hurry up the woman.

They were nearly to the edge of the yard when Fern said, "Did that Jay bird man write to the little girl?"

"Not yet."

"Think he will?"

"No." Kate felt like Fern, answering with as few words as possible. What was it about today that had everybody talking about Jay?

"Want him to?" When Kate hesitated, Fern added, "No use lying to yourself. Told you that already."

Kate looked over at the older woman, bundled against the weather. Scarred by storms in her past, but changed in the last few years by the way she cared about Lorena. "I don't need to answer. You already know."

The woman nodded. "Good to quit lying. Hattie says to tell you." She shut her mouth tight and looked at Kate and stopped walking.

Kate stopped too. Across the yard, the house waited with warmth and food, but she couldn't walk off without hearing what Fern had to say. What Aunt Hattie had told her to say.

"Jay bird man wasn't drunk."

"Why would Aunt Hattie want you to tell me that?" Kate stared at her in the dim light. "She knows I know drunk."

"Drunk on him. Not in him."

"What makes you say that?"

"Saw him. Rode on the fender of that car he

give you." Fern poked Kate's chest with her finger. "Hattie worries about you. Thinks you're getting skinny."

"Tell her I'm fine."

"Not fine. Lovesick. I know. I saw you dancing." Fern blew out a loud breath of air. "Lovesick can make you crazy like me." She made the sound that passed for her laugh. "No second chance for me, but Hattie says you can have one."

"What does she think I can do? I don't even know where he is."

"You fixed things when the girl needed things fixed. You can fix this." Fern poked her again before she turned on her heel and stalked away.

She didn't turn her head, but Kate heard her anyway. "Don't want to be like me."

Kate watched her until she was out of sight. *Drunk on him. Not in him.* Could that have been true the same as it was once true for her father? When the whiskey had spilled on him after he quit drinking. Her mother had believed him. Why hadn't Kate at least tried to believe Jay?

34

They finished up basic. Perry went off to learn how to drive tanks, taking his never-ending supply of cookies with him and his Bible. He'd never given up talking to Jay about the Lord, but it was easy talk. Not preaching like Mike. Jay had always felt like he was failing when he couldn't step up the aisle the way Mike wanted him to. But when Perry talked about the Lord, it was more like he was simply trying to get two friends together, just knowing they'd like one another if they'd only start talking.

Perry's mother had sent Jay a pocket-size copy of the New Testament with the Psalms and Proverbs. Jay hadn't ever written to her the way Perry said he could, but he supposed Perry telling her about how he liked her cookies had been enough to pull him into her family circle. Some women were like that. Always ready to mother anybody within hug's reach, even when that hug had to be by mail.

That made him think about Kate's mother. She hadn't been a hugger the way he had a feeling Perry's whole family would be. But she'd always accepted him. He wondered what Kate had told her about him being drunk. It didn't matter that he hadn't been. Kate thought he was and that's what she would have told her mother. If what he'd heard at the roadhouse was true, Mrs. Merritt knew about dealing with a drunk. But she had never slammed the door on her husband's love. Or maybe she had. Maybe they'd ironed out things after Mr. Merritt gave up the drink. It wasn't always possible to know what had happened in other people's lives. Even when they told you about it, it wasn't the same as living through it.

He was sorry to see Perry go, and not only because of the cookies. Mrs. Franklin had stepped up to the plate for him there. He got mail nearly every week from her, telling him about what Mr. Franklin was doing on the farm and about those grandchildren she was relieved weren't old enough to go off to war. It wasn't a chore to write her back. But he did feel guilty when he posted the letters. At the same time he could almost see the sweet old lady smiling when she saw his letters in her mailbox, he could picture Birdie peering in the Merritts' empty mailbox. He intended to write Birdie. He did. Just as soon as a knife stopped stabbing through him every time he thought about Rosey Corner.

Jay was more than glad the Army hadn't decided he'd fit in a tank like Perry. Instead, an officer had come to talk to them, trolling for volunteers for a new unit open only to the strongest and the best. Jay was strong. He was tougher than the average man. Around him he could see other men thinking the same thing as they sat up a little straighter and listened a little closer. But then the officer had let them know they'd be jumping out of airplanes with parachutes. Some of the men smothered laughs as they sank back into their chairs, but not Jay. At the end of the man's speech, he got in the very short line and signed up.

The next week he boarded a train to Fort Benning, Georgia. The officer had been right. The new training made basic seem like a picnic. But Jay took what they dished out and got tougher. They ran to everything. Walking was for other soldiers. Not a paratrooper. To be a paratrooper took something extra. Something Jay wanted to prove he had as they climbed aboard an airplane for their first real jump.

It wasn't that none of them were afraid. A man stepping out of a plane into the air for the first time would have to be more than a little crazy not to feel some nerves. For sure, Jay's mouth went dry, his heart started beating too fast, and his hands were sweating as he grabbed the outside of the airplane door and pulled himself out into the empty air. Free-falling for one terrifying but amazing moment before the static line jerked out the parachute. Then he was floating high above the earth with dozens of parachutes dotting the sky around him. Before this, they'd jumped off towers. They'd learned how to land. But nothing in that training had prepared Jay for the heady feeling of being between heaven and earth.

Then that earth was rushing toward him. The field was flat, a good landing spot for first jumpers. He rolled on impact and absorbed the pain of banging into the ground. He was up at once, folding his parachute and running toward the sound of Sergeant Kerr counting the men off as they got to the truck.

"How was it, Tanner?" the sergeant asked. He was a couple of inches shorter than Jay and the skin on his face looked like dried leather. He hailed from Arizona where he said the sun never stopped shining.

"Fine, sir. Better than advertised."

Sarge almost smiled. "Ready to go again?"

"Yes sir," Jay said.

"Won't be as much fun if you land in a tree next time." Sergeant Kerr made a sound that might have been a laugh.

"I'll try not to let that happen, sir."

That night he sat on his bunk and wished he knew Perry's address so he could write him about the jump. He wanted to tell somebody. He fingered the little Bible from Perry's mother. For the last few seconds before he pushed himself out of the airplane, he'd had the weirdest urge to say some kind of prayer. That could have been because the man behind him was muttering the Twenty-Third Psalm under his breath. Jay had almost whispered the words along with him.

He opened the little Bible and flipped through Psalms. He had forgotten there were so many. One hundred fifty of them. He leafed through the tissue-thin pages until his eyes caught on a verse in the middle of one of the pages. Verse eight in the hundred and thirty-ninth psalm. *If I ascend up into heaven, thou art there: if I make my bed in hell, behold, thou art there.* Funny that his eye would catch on that. It could be a paratrooper's verse for sure. Flying up in the heavens to make a jump and then training to be dropped behind enemy lines into the hell of battle.

Thou art there. It wasn't that he didn't believe God was there. He just had never believed he was there for him, but maybe a man going to war might consider changing what he believed.

Jay shut the Bible and shoved it under his pillow. He should have told Perry to give the Bible to somebody else. From somewhere in the deep recesses of his mind, a Bible story surfaced that he'd heard some preacher use in a sermon long ago. A prophet, Jay couldn't remember his name, had told this widow woman to let him live in her spare room. And then her son died. She went out to the field where the prophet was working or doing something and told him straight out that she wished he'd never come around her. She was sure that the prophet being in her house had caused the Lord to notice her sins and punish her by taking her only son. In the Bible story, the prophet had fixed things. He'd prayed over the son and the boy had started breathing again.

But Jay didn't have any prophets around to fix things when the Lord took notice of his sins. Look what had happened when he'd been sitting in a church pew, ready to believe the sermons Mike was preaching. The Lord had closed that door fast. A little voice whispered in his head that it wasn't the Lord who shut that door. It had been Kate. And what about Birdie running out of the school? Breathing and smiling.

Thinking about Birdie made him smile too. Made him want to tell her about jumping out of an airplane. She'd think that was something. How many months had it been? Five. Almost half a year. She'd probably given up checking the mailbox for a letter from him. His smile got bigger, and before he could change his mind, he pulled out a piece of paper. He wanted to tell somebody how it felt to jump out into the air. To just turn loose and trust the training. Trust the parachute. Trust.

Dear Birdie,
    I'll bet you're surprised to get this. I haven't forgotten you or Rosey Corner, but I've been busy letting the Army turn me into a soldier.

Guess what I did today? I'd make you really guess if I was there to hear what you might guess, but since I'm not, I'll just tell you. You wouldn't ever guess anyway. I jumped out of an airplane. Don't worry. I had a parachute and I didn't land in a tree. My sergeant said that might happen next time. If it does, I'll just climb down like a monkey.

How's Scout doing? Living up to his new name, I hope. Scout sounds brave and smart. That might be a stretch for the old Trouble. Ha. Ha.

You keeping my car all polished up? You haven't let Kate run it into any fence posts or anything, I hope.

He stopped and chewed on the end of his pencil for a minute. He wanted to write something to Kate. He wanted to write down the words, *I love you*. He'd said them and she'd shut the door on him, but maybe if he wrote them, she'd be readier to see them. *I love you, Kate Merritt.*

He couldn't write that. For all he knew, Kate had a new fellow by now. A new fellow she could trust. He sighed and started writing again. The letter was to Birdie, not Kate.

Tell Kate hello for me. Did you tell her what I told you to when I brought the car? About eloping? I bet that made her laugh. I hope everybody else is doing all right and that Graham and Poe are still out there chasing their old friend, Mr. Raccoon. I sure would like a piece of your mama's brown sugar pie about now. Tell you what. You eat two pieces next time she makes that pie. One for you and one for me.

Well, I got to go. I just wanted to tell you about stepping out into the air and trusting the parachute. A fine thing. Trust. Remember, I'm trusting you to take care of my old heap. It sure will be nice to see you and Rosey Corner again once we win this war.

Your buddy,
Tanner

He stared down at his words a minute. Maybe he shouldn't have put that about trust. It might make Kate remember him saying that the music stopped without trust.

He could mark it out. Start all over. Or tear up the letter and forget about writing altogether. He hesitated, but then he folded the paper and shoved it into an envelope. He wasn't sure about the address, but Rosey Corner wasn't so big that the mailman wouldn't be able to find a kid named Birdsong. He printed her name on the envelope. *Lorena "Birdie" Birdsong.* Then he wrote his own name and address in the corner. He'd put it in the mail first thing in the morning. She'd write to him. Letters from her and cookies from Mrs. Franklin. If he didn't watch out, the other guys would decide he hadn't been telling the truth when he said he didn't have any family.

The late afternoon sunshine was warm on Kate's shoulders as she headed home from the store. A beautiful May day full of sunshine with birds singing and the fragrance of lilacs in the air. Nothing like the battlefields must be. Kate read the accounts in the papers, saw the pictures of ships blowing apart, soldiers marching into battle, while here in Rosey Corner spring had come the same as any other year.

But not really the same. Sunshine or not, the war shadow was over them all.

Just a couple of weeks ago, President Roosevelt had asked everyone in America to help win the war by sacrificing. He said they'd pay in hard work, sorrow, and blood. The sorrow was already happening.

The Japanese were winning in the Philippines. Bataan had fallen after months of hard fighting. Over thirty thousand American and Filipino soldiers killed or captured.

Kate tried to imagine that many men, but she couldn't. And now they were all either dead or prisoners. Perhaps men she knew. Not Mike, thank the Lord. He was in Arizona, getting training, so she knew he was still safe. Evie was out there with him, but in her last letter, she said he expected to get orders soon. Evie was being stronger than Kate would have ever thought possible. She'd squared her shoulders and put on a brave face for Mike and the world.

She hadn't been quite so brave when Kate was helping her pack for Arizona. She'd sunk down on her bed and let the tears flow unchecked. Kate dropped down beside her, put her arms around her, and wanted to cry too. But she didn't. Instead she whispered things like "it'll be all right" and other words that people always said when things were definitely not all right but they wanted them to be.

"I'm so afraid," Evie managed to say between sobs. "So very afraid. What if Mike . . ." She couldn't voice her thought. Instead she covered her mouth with her hand and stared at Kate with wide eyes.

Kate gave her a little shake. "Mike is going to be fine."

The despair didn't leave Evie's eyes. "How can you know that? Men are dying over there every day. Somebody's husband probably just died while we've been sitting here talking."

"Mike's going to be a chaplain. You don't think they put the chaplains on the front lines, do you? They'll want them helping the wounded and the new recruits." Kate didn't know if that was true, but it sounded reasonable. "You know Mike. He'll go over there and have the soldiers all laughing and talking about the Bible in nothing flat. And then once the war's over, he'll be right back with you. Preaching to all of us again."

"Do you really think so?" Her voice was that of a child needing assurance that there weren't really any boogiemen hiding out behind the bushes.

"I do. I really do," Kate said. She couldn't bear to think anything else. "What's Mike tell you?"

"To pray." Evie sounded almost irritated. "You know Mike. Always thinking prayer will fix everything. We have a tiff about him leaving his shoes in the middle of the floor and he has us praying about it." Then she was sniffling again. "I wish I could trip over his shoes in the middle of the floor tonight."

"Prayer's good. We'll pray him through. Mama and us, Aunt Hattie and all the church people." Kate pushed a smile out on her face. "Besides, by this time next week, you'll be fussing about tripping over those shoes in the rooms he's found for you close to the base."

"I wish I was strong like Mike," Evie said. "Like you are too, Kate. You don't let things get you down. Bad things happen, you just get stronger and figure out a way to fix them."

Kate wanted to tell Evie how wrong that was, how she wasn't strong at all, and how instead of figuring out a way to fix things between her and

469

Jay, she had totally messed them up. Beyond fixing. But instead she simply tightened her arm around Evie and didn't say a thing. She could be strong for Evie, even if she couldn't fix the reason for her tears. The war. That was the reason for a lot of tears. And the reason for a lot of prayers, Kate reminded herself.

Evie sat up a little straighter and swiped the tears off her cheeks with her palms. "I know you had a falling out with Jay, but don't you think you should try to make up?" She didn't wait for Kate to answer her, but rushed on. "I can tell you still love him. You've been going around looking like you lost your last friend for weeks. Months even. Don't you think you should do something about it besides just sit in his car and cry?"

"What makes you think I do that?" Kate pulled away from Evie.

"A little birdie told me."

Hearing the word "birdie" was like a punch in the stomach. Kate stood up and began folding one of Evie's dresses very precisely as she said, "Well, she shouldn't have. I'm fine."

Evie jumped up, her own tears forgotten. She grabbed Kate's shoulder and spun her around to look in her face. "You're not fine. You're not even close to fine. You're keeping it all bottled up inside and hardly eating enough to keep a bird alive. You've even got Aunt Hattie saying prayers for you."

"Aunt Hattie has always said prayers for me. For all of us. It's what she does."

"And what you do is figure out what needs doing and then do it. You've always done that. Helped Daddy when he was having his troubles." Evie never spoke about their father's drinking problems. Never. Not even when they were happening. "You helped Lorena when that nasty Mrs. Baxter was being so mean to her. You've probably even tried to help crazy old Fern."

Kate looked right at Evie. "So? I don't see what you're trying to tell me."

Evie leaned closer until her face was only inches from Kate's. "I'm trying to say that now you need to help my sister, Kate Merritt. Stop being so hardheaded and do something."

Kate didn't back away from Evie. "I can't do anything. I don't know where he is."

"Then find out!" Evie said, as though that would be the easiest thing in the world to do.

"He doesn't want me to find out."

"How do you know that?"

"If he did, he'd write. If not to me, then to Lorena." She sank back down on the bed. Evie sat down beside her. "He hasn't written to Mike, has he?"

"You know I'd tell you if he had. I don't think he's forgiven Mike for telling you to stay away from him."

"Mike was just trying to protect me."

471

"I know. Be your big brother after we got married. But he should have known better. Love can't be ordered. It comes, and when it does, it gets its claws in you and won't let go."

"I'll get over him," Kate said. "People get over broken hearts all the time."

"But why do you think you should get over him? He loves you too. I saw the way he looked at you. You don't want to get over that kind of love. You want to grab it and hold it tight."

"That's what Fern told me."

"Fern?" Evie frowned. "I don't know why in the world you'd listen to anything she said, but you do need to listen to me. Don't throw away love."

"Mama said that," Kate said.

Evie put her hand up to her forehead. "So what did Lorena say?"

"That Tanner told her to tell me if I ever felt like eloping, to come find him."

"And do you feel like eloping?"

"It's an idea, but doesn't that take a guy with a ladder and an upstairs window?" A bubble of laughter rose up in Kate and popped out.

"You're absolutely nuts. It's Rosey Corner. It drives everybody nuts." Evie fell back on the bed, laughing.

Days had gone by since Evie had told her she was nuts. Kate was ready to agree with her. She felt a little crazy because she was beginning to believe that if Jay were right there in front of her

472

asking her to elope, she would. Without a minute's hesitation.

If only she knew where he was. If only she knew he was safe. She stopped walking and looked up at the sky, as though hoping to find answers in the fluffy white clouds.

"Kate! Kate!" Lorena shouted as she ran up the road toward her with Scout on her heels. She was waving a letter in the air over her head. From the joy exploding off her face, Kate had no doubt who it was from. And suddenly she felt like dancing.

35

Jay liked getting Mrs. Franklin's cookies and notes, but until he wrote to Birdie, he'd never come looking for mail with his throat tight and his hands sweaty with anxious anticipation. Birdie would write. He had no doubt about that, and when she wrote, she'd say something about Kate. That was what was making his heart do a stutter step inside him whenever they passed out the mail.

Every morning when he got up, he tried to figure out how long it took letters to wind their way up to Kentucky and then back down to

Georgia. Days? Weeks? He'd think about how many days had passed since he'd posted the letter to Birdie. He'd think about her reading what he'd written and showing it to Kate. He tried to always imagine them both smiling while they read about him jumping out of airplanes. Then he'd think about Birdie writing and maybe Kate writing too. He hoped she'd think it was her patriotic duty. But she'd never written the hayseed who'd gone off to the Navy. At least, he didn't think so.

It might have been good if she had. Things had gone pretty sour for their soldiers in that part of the war. The hayseed kid might even now be a prisoner of the Japanese Army. Or dead.

That was it. Death was looking over all their shoulders. They might not have much time to make things right. He might not have enough time. The rumor was going around that they were going to be sent overseas to a new camp to practice jumps in an area more like the war zones. Not that any of the enlisted men really knew. It was all just whispers in the wind that might be true or might be nothing but empty air.

Whether this rumor turned out to be true or not didn't matter. It would happen sooner, he thought, than later, and he didn't want to be on a ship going overseas with the letter here and him there. A letter that might have sweet words. *Dear Tanner. Kate told me to tell you she loves you.*

That was the letter he saw in his dreams. When

several days passed with nothing except a box of homemade fudge from Mrs. Franklin, Jay got worried that something might have happened to Birdie. That another time she'd forgotten to check the road and had run in front of a car. Or that she'd gotten sick or that . . . He made himself stop. The kid would write. Probably already had written.

The letter came on a Tuesday. They were going out to do a jump that night. They'd done a couple of night jumps. A whole different feel, coming down through the dark sky, having no idea what was rushing up toward him on the ground. Once he'd clipped that tree the sergeant had warned him about, but he hadn't gotten hung up in it. He liked the day jumps better, but it wasn't hard to figure that if a man was going to drop in behind enemy lines, it would be better to do it in the dark. A paratrooper floating down through the air under a big billowing marker would make an easy target for enemy sharpshooters.

So he didn't have much time before he had to report back to duty. When he unfolded the notebook paper, he had to smile at the sight of Birdie's little-girl handwriting.

Hello, Tanner,

How are you? I'm fine. We were excited to get your letter. I showed it to Kate first and she thought it was great that you wrote me. I even let Scout sniff it and his tail almost wagged off. Kate said he must have known it was from you.

We were all surprised to hear that you'd been jumping out of airplanes. That sounds like fun. Kate thought so too. Evie would have shivered and said you must have lost your mind if she'd been here. But she's in Arizona where Mike is in the Army. Everybody is talking about being in the Army. Even Sammy. That makes Tori sad. And us too. They're getting married before he goes. Kate is going to be her maid of honor like she was for Evie. Kate says she guesses I'm next, but I tell her I don't think so. Boys are all yucky. Not you or Mike, but boys my age.

Mama says to tell you she'll send brown sugar cookies, but she doesn't think a pie would make it in the mail. Might give you food poisoning or something. So I'll just keep eating your extra slice. Daddy says to let him know if you want any books to read and he'll send them to you. Graham says that next time you come to Rosey Corner you better not leave without saying something to him. Poe's not doing too good right now. Graham has to help him up and down the steps. Kate says she doesn't know what Graham will do when Poe can't make it anymore, but Mama says Graham is pretty tough and he'll be all right.

Kate says I shouldn't try to tell you everything in one letter. But don't worry. I'll write again soon. Daddy says soldiers need letters from home.

Your friend forever,
Birdie XO XO

P.S. I forgot to tell you what Aunt Hattie said. She said to tell you that the best friend a soldier can have is Jesus and that she's praying you've took hold of his hand. Me and Aunt Hattie want everybody to know about Jesus. Especially people in our family like you. You came to Thanksgiving dinner so you're the same as family. And don't try to say you're not, because you are. Kate says so too. And that's that!!!

He read over the letter again, letting his eyes dwell on the mention of Kate. She thought it was great that he'd written Birdie. She thought he was the same as family because he'd eaten with them on Thanksgiving. That was about all. Not much. Not enough. Maybe after the jump tonight, he'd write Birdie again. He could write Kate too. He could write *I still hear the music and remember the dances, my beautiful Kate. Do you?*

First the jump. He stuffed Birdie's letter in his pocket. It wasn't a love letter, but it was a letter from Rosey Corner. From home. That's what Birdie said at the end. That soldiers needed letters from home and that he was family. He wanted to pull the letter out and read those words again, but Sarge was yelling. No time for anything but going.

They queued up the same as they did every jump. The routine was becoming automatic. Jay checked the back equipment of the man in front of him. Artie Persons. Behind him Harold Whitt checked Jay's and then they waited for the signal to begin leaping out into the darkness. Harold started whispering the Twenty-third Psalm the way he did before every jump.

"The Lord is my Shepherd. I shall not want. He maketh me to lie down in green pastures; he leadeth me beside the still waters. He restoreth my soul."

An echo of the words whispered through Jay's head. It was a comforting sound, the familiar words of the psalm. Harold claimed to need to say it in order to jump. He said he needed to think about the Lord holding his hand as he slung himself out into the air. Being beside him through the shadow of death. Watching out for him. That was the only way he could jump.

Jay thought about Harold whispering the words of the psalm over and over. He couldn't hear him now. The rush of the wind was too great. Then the sergeant tapped him to let him know his turn

478

was up, and Jay grasped the edges of the door and stepped out into the black sky. Darkness wrapped around him like a velvet glove as he fell. Then the parachute popped open and the straps tightened and jerked him upright. Harold's voice reciting the psalm was still sounding in his head even though Harold was above him and to the right.

Birdie said Aunt Hattie was praying for him. That they all were. Maybe that meant Kate was too. But what had Mike told him a thousand times? A person had to say the prayer himself.

"Dear God." The rush of air grabbed the words out of his mouth and scattered them into the dark night. Soon he might be jumping behind enemy lines. He wanted to feel the Lord beside him as he started through that valley of the shadow of death. He wanted to believe like Mike and Perry and Harold did. The way Aunt Hattie said he needed to. But what was the prayer Mike said he was supposed to say? He couldn't remember as he floated down through the sky.

He bent his head a little to look at the ground. The night shrouded everything. Here and there were darker patches. Trees. To the south, unless he'd lost his directional sense, was the glint of water. Wouldn't want to land in that and end up sinking under the weight of all the equipment he carried. His pack. His gun. Ammunition. But where to land? Not much in the way of wind drafts this night, but maybe enough to pull him off course. The clouds were thick and no moon pushed light through. He couldn't see what was coming up toward him. All he had was hope for a safe landing.

Mike had once told him that hope was something like faith, but that without faith, hope was empty of meaning. Empty, that's what Jay had felt for a long time, and then Kate and Rosey Corner had changed him. He didn't want to be empty. He wanted something to hold on to while he drifted through the darkness of possible death.

"Please, Lord. I want to believe," he whispered as the air slipped past him, feeling faster as the shadows on the ground came closer.

He reached his hand out into the dark air and had the strangest sensation that he touched something. Not something, someone. What was that verse he'd found in the Bible Perry had given him? The one that sounded like it could be a paratrooper's verse. *Thou art there.* In the heavens. In hell. Wherever he was, the Lord was promising to be there.

Maybe faith was like a parachute in life, the thing that kept a man from smashing into the hard places that came to everyone, something to cushion the fall when things went wrong. Maybe faith meant giving himself over to the air around him and trusting that the Lord's love was going to be there. *Thou art there.*

Bits of another verse came to mind. Something about nothing separating a person from God's love. He'd heard Mike preach on that back in Rosey Corner on one of the Sundays Jay had parked on a pew beside Kate. He wasn't sure exactly how it went, but a few of the words scratched awake in his mind.

Nothing, not death nor life, not tribulation, not things happening right now or things that were going to happen would get in the way of God loving a man who put his faith in him. Mike had read the verses in his preacher's voice. Not angels either, but why angels would want to get in the way of God's love, Jay hadn't understood. Then there were the principalities. That word had stuck because Birdie had liked the way it sounded and let it slide off her tongue over and over as they walked back to the house for Sunday dinner. Maybe he should try to find that verse in Perry's Bible.

Then again, what had he, Jay Tanner, ever done to be worthy of love? Nothing. Absolutely nothing. But in spite of knowing that, he felt the love awakening in his heart in answer to his prayer. He couldn't explain it, but arms of love were cradling him as he fell, accepting him the way he was. He suddenly felt lighter than air, like he might drift back up instead of keep falling. A good feeling. A joyous feeling. He looked up at the parachute floating above him, holding him up. A parachute of faith.

481

A man could tell when the ground was ready to grab him. The air felt different. His nose picked up different smells and told him to prepare for impact. He held his arms tight against him and pointed his toes with his legs together. He didn't know what he was about to hit. All was dark, but every jumper knew the ground didn't soften up for anyone. He rolled on impact, did everything like he'd been trained to do. It was his bad fortune that he landed where a rock jutted up out of the ground and caught his foot. He tried to jerk his foot free, but it stayed caught as the force of the fall slung him forward. The snap of bone was loud in Jay's ears and pain seared through his leg. Red flashed in front of his eyes as he grabbed at the dirt and rocks to stop his tumble. His foot pulled free, but the damage was done.

Jay sat up and ran his hand down his lower left leg. There was an ominous bump right above his ankle. But maybe it wasn't broken. After all, hadn't the Lord been floating down through the air with him? Surely right after he reached for the Lord, he wouldn't land in a pile of rocks and crack a bone. That wasn't the way this stuff was supposed to work. Prayer was supposed to protect him, not slam him down. Then the words of the psalm Harold had been reciting came into his head. *Yea though I walk through the valley of the shadow of death*. That didn't say he wasn't going to have to walk through the valley. Or land on rocks if that's where he happened to come down.

He thought of that widow woman in the Bible again. The one who'd thought the prophet had brought trouble down on her and her son. For a few seconds he felt like lying back on the ground and having a good laugh. He could almost see the Lord smiling in the darkness with him, enjoying the joke. Was that all it was? Nothing but a joke? But then he was probing the feeling in his heart and the bad landing hadn't made it leak out. His leg hurt, but he liked the idea of the Lord sitting there in the dark with him, letting him know that the worst things could happen to a person whether his heart was filled up with faith or not.

He heard the trucks coming and Sarge counting them off. Around him the other men were gathering up their parachutes and running toward the pickup place. Jay tried to stand up, do what he was trained to do. Gather his parachute and run toward the truck. His foot wouldn't work. Pain shot through him, but he managed to get upright. No way was he going to be able to run anywhere without a crutch. He stood on one foot and pulled the parachute toward him. Every time his balance wavered and he had to touch down his left foot, it screamed at him.

"Drop any good sticks in this rocky hole, Lord?" he said under his breath.

Artie Persons, the man who jumped in front

of him, ran by him. "You all right, Tanner?"

"Landed on a rock. Maybe broke my leg." Jay tried not to let the pain sound in his voice. "Wish I'd landed in that tree Sarge keeps warning me about."

Artie turned and ran back to Jay. "Mighta broke your neck then. Better settle for the leg." He grabbed up the rest of Jay's chute and shoved it at him. "You hold onto that and lean on me. Or I can just tell the medics where you are if you can't make it."

"I can make it." Jay grasped the chute with one arm and clasped the other arm around Artie's shoulders. "Thanks."

"That's what buddies are for. Good practice for the war zone. Wouldn't want to desert a comrade there either."

"You might have to," Jay said.

"Could be. But I don't think so."

They started toward the sound of Sarge barking out orders for the men to pick it up, run faster. Sarge was going to give him heck for landing on a rock. A man ought to see a rock glinting in the dark and twist away from it.

With the noise at the trucks getting closer, Jay opened his mouth and surprised them both by asking, "You believe in God, Artie?"

" 'Course I believe in God, Tanner. I'm from Alabama. Ain't nothing to do there but church. Anyway, what kind of heathen don't believe in

God?" Artie twisted his head to look over at Jay without slowing their pace. "You ain't no heathen, are you?"

Jay smiled in spite of the pain shooting up his leg. "Not that much of one. I'm from Rosey Corner, Kentucky. Plenty of churchgoing there too."

"Far enough south to know what's what. That's for sure," Artie said.

Then Sarge was in front of them, yelling about how slow they were moving and coming out with a few choice words when Jay admitted to his bad landing. "If I've told you boys once, I've told you a hundred times, you gotta roll when you hit. What was you doing, Tanner? Dreaming about some girl?"

"No sir. Trying to stay away from the trees, sir." Jay was feeling sick to his stomach and dizzy from the pain. He pulled his arm away from Artie's shoulders and stood on one foot in front of the sergeant. He managed to bite back the yelp that wanted to come out as pain stabbed from his ankle all the way to his shoulder.

"He must be hurt bad, Sarge. He was talking religion," Artie said.

"Religion?" Sarge peered at Jay. "You drunk, Tanner?"

"No sir," Jay said. "I don't drink, Sergeant, sir. Not anymore. Drinking breaks hearts, sir."

"What'd you say?" But it wasn't a question he

wanted answered as he leaned closer to Jay. "If you aren't drunk, you must be crazy."

"Yes sir. Now that I can admit to, sir."

That's the last thing he remembered before waking up with a medic beside him as they bounced along toward a hospital.

"Easy, soldier." The medic put his hand on Jay's shoulder. "Banged up your leg a little, but don't you worry. You'll be good as new in a few weeks. Then you'll be right back out there."

Jay looked up at him in the dim light from a lantern hanging over their heads. "Do you believe in God?" That must be his favorite new question. Maybe Sarge was right. Maybe he was crazy.

The man didn't answer his question. Instead he said, "You aren't about to die or anything, soldier."

"Thank you." Jay shut his eyes to absorb the bounces of the truck. But he wasn't sure who he was thanking. The medic or the Lord. Maybe both in his crazy way.

❧ 36 ❧

She'd known what she was going to do from the moment she saw the address on Jay's letter. Georgia. That wasn't across the ocean. She had a car. His car. If Evie could go to Arizona, Kate could go to Georgia.

Now and again the uncomfortable thought nudged her that Jay hadn't written to her. He'd written to Lorena. But he had asked about her. That meant he still loved her, didn't it? She desperately wanted to believe it did. She thought about writing him and asking straight out if she'd ruined their chances the night he'd hit Lorena with his car. Lorena didn't hold that against him. She knew without a worried thought that Jay would never hurt her if he could avoid it. She didn't know he'd been drinking.

Kate was beginning to not know that too. She'd been absolutely certain that night. She'd smelled the drunken vomit on him, but everybody else was acting as if her nose had betrayed her. Maybe it had. Fern said it had. And Fern didn't lie. Kate's mother told her to not give up on love. Evie and Tori said the same. Lorena looked at her with sad brown eyes, trying to understand.

487

Kate thought even Scout looked at her with accusing eyes sometimes.

Everybody loved Jay. And heaven help her, so did she. So much that it was like a constant burn inside her. She had to see him again. She couldn't let him go off to war without telling him she was sorry. Without telling him she loved him. She wanted to offer him her love without conditions. That was surely trust, wasn't it? She wanted to beg him to hear the music with her again.

Every time she got behind the wheel of his car, she thought about driving it away from Rosey Corner. She studied the maps she found in his glove box. She traced off the roads with her finger and tried to imagine being that far from Rosey Corner. Alone on the road. It gave her shivers, but she was the middle sister. Nobody had ever babied her. She could do whatever had to be done. And she had to see Jay before they sent him overseas. She had to.

But she couldn't leave before Tori and Sammy got married. A matter of days. Surely a few more days wouldn't matter, but nearly every night she had the same dream where Jay was standing at the rail of a ship. Down on the dock she kept jumping up and down, screaming his name. He never gave any sign of hearing her, and then the ship would begin moving away.

When the ship disappeared, she always jerked awake. With her heart pounding in her ears, she would stare at the dark air pressing down on her and listen to Tori and Lorena breathing softly in their sleep. A familiar sound of family. She'd think about Evie out with Mike in Arizona. But mostly she thought about Jay. She pulled his smile that always looked a hair away from a laugh out of the darkness. She wrapped her arms around herself and remembered the feel of his arms as they danced to the music of their hearts. Oh, to dance in the moonlight with him again. She imagined him jumping out of airplanes and wasn't surprised. That was Jay. Embracing the moment. Why hadn't she done the same?

The night before Tori's wedding, the dream shook Kate awake yet again. But this time Sammy and Tori were on the ship, disappearing with Jay. Tori wouldn't be on the ship. Kate knew that. She'd be here at home fighting off her own nightmares after Sammy was sent to the war zones.

Kate sat up in the bed and watched her sister in the silvery moonlight that was slipping in through the window. She was so very young. Only sixteen. She'd always been skinny and had a way of catching every cold that came around. But Tori was tougher than she looked. She was teaching Kate a few things about going after what she wanted. She hadn't spent months worrying about what she should do. At least not after Pearl Harbor changed all their lives.

But it was different for Tori. She and Sammy had long been on the path of love. The war had merely hurried things along for them. He planned to enlist the day after his nineteenth birthday on July 5th. A little over a month after their wedding day. A month Tori was ready to treasure.

How many months had it been since Jay left? Since she'd pushed him away. Five months they might have spent together. Five months she'd never get back. But how could she promise her life to a man who drank? She loved her father. She hadn't stopped loving him while he was drinking. Her mother hadn't either, but there were times when Kate thought she wanted to. Times when the drinking was more than her mother could handle.

The thoughts spun around in Kate's head until she couldn't stand it. She eased out of bed and tiptoed out of the bedroom. Scout scooted out from under Lorena's bed and followed her across the sitting room, his toenails clicking on the wooden floor at the edges of the rug. The screen door squeaked when she opened it, but she was careful not to let it slam shut after she and Scout went out on the porch.

With June only a couple of weeks away, the night air carried the fresh scent of summer. Kate pulled in a breath and held it, letting it seep through her. The trees were still dripping from a late afternoon shower, and off in the distance, a rumble gave notice more rain might be coming. A little thunder didn't bother Kate. There'd been plenty of times in years past when they'd prayed for the sound of thunder and rain on the roof.

Kate pulled the housecoat she'd grabbed off the bed tight around her and sat down on the swing. The chains rattled against the hooks in the porch ceiling and then were quiet. Scout went out to sniff around the yard. When he came back to settle at her feet, water drops were clinging to his back. She never even thought of his old name anymore. No trouble now. She reached down and stroked his head, glad for his company.

How many problems had she mulled over on this very swing? She was sitting right here when she told her mother she didn't believe there was a God. Kate cringed when she thought of how mixed up she'd been then. She'd been so sure that a just God, a loving God wouldn't have let Grandfather Merritt take Lorena away from them, but Grandfather Merritt had taken Lorena and given her to the Baxters. At least for a while. A too long while. Even now, nearly six years later, the pain of knowing Lorena needed her then and being helpless to change things made Kate's heart hurt.

She'd been so young. Only fourteen. She'd thought she could figure out all the answers then. She was Lorena's angel sister. The sister with the answers. But she'd found out some things didn't have easy answers. She still knew that, but she no longer doubted God.

A dark stain of evil was spreading over the world, but God hadn't deserted them. He was hearing their prayers in the trenches, in the fox-holes, in the airplanes. He was ready to hear Kate's prayer as she pushed against the wooden porch floor with her bare toes to rock the swing gently back and forth. But what to pray? She stumbled through her mind searching for the right prayers. The ones that mattered.

For peace, of course. For Mike and Jay and every soldier lining up to do battle against the enemies out to destroy their world. For Tori and Sammy as on the morrow they would speak their wedding vows and cling to one another a brief while before the war yanked them apart. For Lorena, so full of trust. For herself. Why was she always so ready to pray for everybody else and so reluctant to pray for herself?

When the screen door opened, Kate expected her mother to be the one stepping out on the porch, but instead it was her father. He'd pulled on his pants and shirt but hadn't bothered with shoes. Scout's tail thumped against the porch as he raised his head up to welcome him.

"I'm sorry I woke you, Daddy." Kate scooted over to make room for him.

"Your mother thought it would be Victoria who would be sleepless tonight." He reached over and laid his calloused hand over hers. "But instead here's midnight Kate."

"Is it midnight?"

"No, midnight's long gone. It's the underbelly of the morning. Two a.m." With a laugh, he squeezed her hand and stared out toward the night sky. "It's pleasant out here this time of night. Quiet. At least other than the tree frogs and katydids. But they add to the quiet. I missed this when I went to war. The good sounds of night. Nothing was ever quiet for long over there. The earth was crawling with noise and people."

"Do you still have the nightmares?" Kate asked.

"Sometimes. Some things a man can't forget. The boys going over will come back with their own nightmares. Those who come back."

When a tremble went through Kate at the grimness of his words, he wrapped his arm around her and pulled her over next to him. "Sorry, baby, I didn't mean to make you feel bad, but you've never been one to duck away from the truth. War's worse than anything you can imagine. It demands and takes all a man has to give. And then it gouges out a little more." His arm felt suddenly a little stiff around her.

"Why do there have to be wars, Daddy?" Kate felt like a little child asking for answers to questions that had no answers.

"That's a question somebody wiser than me will have to answer. Throughout history there

493

have always been wars and rumors of wars." He blew out a long breath of air. "When I went over there, they told us we were fighting the war to end all wars, and here not thirty years later it's all happening again. Only worse."

"Do you think we'll win?"

"President Roosevelt says we will." Silence wrapped around them for a moment before he went on. "I think we have to. You read the newspapers. Men like Hitler have to be stopped. Whatever it takes."

"It scares me to think about it," Kate said. "The war. At the same time it all seems so far from here. From Rosey Corner."

"Thank the Lord for that." Her father tightened his arm around her. "I'm glad I don't have to worry about my girls being safe here at home."

"Some women will be joining up in the new Women's Army Corps."

"Are you thinking about doing that?" Her father's voice sounded a little tight. "Is that what's got you out here on the worry swing in the wee hours of the morning?"

"I don't know." Kate sighed, but she did know. "No, I wasn't thinking about that."

Her father waited for her to say more, but when she didn't, he said, "So it must be matters of the heart. What happened between you and Jay?"

She hesitated, not sure what to say. She couldn't talk about Jay drinking. Not to her father. The thunder was staying in the distance, but from the woods a whippoorwill called. A lonesome sound. At last she said, "I didn't trust him enough."

"Trust is important between a man and a woman."

"That's what he said. He said without trust we didn't have anything." Her voice trembled a little as she said the words, but she swallowed down her tears. She wasn't the kind of person who cried over everything. Not like Evie.

"Your mother says you thought he was drinking the night Lorena got hurt."

"I didn't think it. I knew it."

"But . . . ," her father said. "There's more, isn't there?"

"He said he wasn't."

"But you didn't believe him."

Kate shook her head a little. She didn't trust her voice.

"And now you wish you had."

"I don't know what I wish."

The sounds of the night wrapped around them again. At last her father broke the silence between them. "I've never really told you how sorry I am for what I put you through when I was drinking. I shouldn't have ever let alcohol get hold of me. You were just a kid. You shouldn't have had to take care of a drunken father."

For a few seconds everything froze inside Kate. This was a door to the past they never opened.

She moistened her lips and wasn't sure what to say. "Mama couldn't."

"I'm not blaming her. I'm blaming me."

"It's okay, Daddy. It doesn't matter now."

"It wasn't okay and it will always matter. But what has happened in the past can't be changed. We can only step out on tomorrow and try to do better."

Kate twisted around to look up at him in the near darkness. "And you did."

"But not before I hurt people."

"You didn't hurt me," Kate said quickly. Shadows hid the expression on his face as he stared out into the night, but he sounded so sad.

"I think my drinking may still be hurting you." He turned his eyes back to her.

Kate's heart was doing a nervous dance inside her chest. She didn't want to talk about her father drinking. It hadn't made any difference in how she loved him. Not then and not now, but some things were better left buried. Forgotten the way the Bible said sins were after the Lord forgave them. As far as the east is from the west. Cast into the deepest ocean. That's the way she wanted her father's drinking problem to be.

"What happened between me and Jay didn't have anything to do with you."

"Are you sure about that?" Her father's voice was gentle, but his eyes were probing her.

She looked down at her hands. "You didn't make Jay go out and get drunk."

"No, you're right about that. Each man is responsible for his own actions." He pushed his foot against the floor and rocked the swing back and forth, being careful not to disturb Scout. "Each girl too."

"I know. You and Mama have been telling me that for years."

"So we have." He kept the swing moving slightly, a comfortable rhythm as he rubbed his hand up and down her upper arm.

Kate thought maybe they'd tiptoed past all the bad talk and she was thinking about going inside when he began talking again in a wondering tone of voice. "Funny thing that we never noticed him drinking any other time. You said yourself that Graham was surprised when you told him Jay was drunk. He lived with Graham for several months. You'd have thought he'd have noticed if the boy drank like I used to. Everybody in Rosey Corner back then knew I had a drinking problem. Wasn't a secret from anybody."

"Only because of the war," Kate said. "Aunt Hattie said you learned to drink in France."

"Aunt Hattie might have been right about that, but I could have left it in France. I didn't have to carry it home with me."

"Jay hasn't been to France."

"But he was thinking about maybe having to

go." He stroked her hair. "That doesn't really matter now. What matters now is this. Do you love him?"

Kate hesitated, but she saw no need in avoiding an answer with so much truth already in the air between them. "I do." She touched her hand to her chest. "I feel like there's a hole inside me that might never go away if I don't see him again."

"So why don't you write him and tell him that?"

"I could write him." She smoothed out the wrinkles in her housecoat. "But I need more than words on a paper. I have his car."

Her father didn't sound surprised. "Your mother was afraid you might be thinking about doing something crazy."

"Georgia's not so awfully far away. People drive that far all the time."

"Not young women. Alone. Young women who've never driven anywhere farther than Edgeville." He sounded very sure. "Not young women who bear my last name."

Kate had been expecting her mother and father to be against her making the trip across three states. It didn't matter. She was twenty years old. She could do what she wanted. Even if the thought of it did make her heart keep doing its nervous flutter. "I'm going." She pushed all the firmness she could into her voice.

He surprised her by laughing. "Of course you are. Nobody has ever talked Katherine Reece

Merritt out of doing anything she makes up her mind to do, now have they?"

"Then you're all right with me driving to Georgia?" She could hardly believe her ears as she twisted around to look at him again.

He was smiling. "I've always wanted to go south. For a visit."

"But—" she started, but he held up a hand to stop her.

"Don't worry. I'll go sightseeing or something if the two of you decide two's company and three's a crowd."

"Oh, Daddy." A blush warmed her cheeks as she gave his arm a shove, but she felt like laughing too. It wouldn't be nearly as scary with her father riding with her. Even if he didn't know a thing about cars, he obviously knew a few things about love.

"So pack up what you'll need in the morning and gas up the car. We'll leave right after Victoria and Sammy tie the knot." Suddenly he sounded a little sad again. "I'm losing all my girls."

"You can never lose us, Daddy." Kate gave him a hug. "We'll always be your girls. Especially Tori. She was your baby for too many years before Lorena came to live with us."

"She's not much more than a baby now. Way too young for marrying, but these are not normal times." He blew out a breath. "And when I think about it, she's not much younger than

499

your mother was when we got married. That too because of war. A few weeks of heaven that kept me going when I stepped into the hell of war. Sammy and Victoria deserve the same chance for happiness. We couldn't deny them that."

He kissed her forehead. "I want you to have that chance too, baby. Love is worth chasing." When he stood up, the swing bounced and Scout scrambled to his feet.

Kate caught her father's hand. "What if he's found another girl? Or he could be gone already."

"Lots of what-ifs and maybes. I mean, the crazy guy is jumping out of airplanes. Anything could happen." He squeezed her hand again. "But if any of those worrisome maybes have happened, we'll stare them down together. Then we'll get back in the car and come on home to do whatever we can here to win this war. Just be ready tomorrow."

Kate and Sammy's little brother, Eugene, stood up with Tori and Sammy in front of the preacher at one o'clock on Saturday. Mike couldn't get leave and so there was a gap in their family circle as they celebrated with Tori. Kate could imagine Evie sitting lonesome in the rooms Mike had rented for her, staring out her east window, if she had one, and wishing with all her might she could be in Rosey Corner with them. She'd talked to Kate and Tori on the phone at the store that morning and told Kate to give Tori double hugs for both of them.

Tori looked so young but so beautiful in the simple cream-colored dress Mama had made for her. Her straight black hair fell like silk down her back and her green eyes shone with expectant love. She hadn't wanted a big affair like Evie's. She'd even turned down the idea of cake at Aunt Hattie's house. She just wanted to say the marrying words in front of their friends and families at the church and be off with Sammy to a weekend at Cumberland Falls without wasting a minute of her time as Mrs. Sammy Harper before the war parted them.

After the ceremony, everybody hugged and shed a few tears and hugged again. Then they waved the newlyweds off from the church. A half hour later, Kate stowed a box of food and a jug of water in the backseat of Jay's car, and everybody went through another round of hugs.

Lorena clung to her for a long minute. "You will come back, won't you, Kate?"

"I'll always come back, sweetheart." Kate leaned down to look directly into Lorena's face. "You know that. I'm your forever sister."

Lorena sniffed a little. "You're my angel sister. And don't say you aren't." Her face turned fierce.

"Oh, sweetheart." After grabbing her close in a hug, Kate pushed Lorena back to kiss her nose. Then she touched Lorena's dress over her heart.

"You remember, no matter what, I'm right there with you whether you can see me or not."

"I know."

"You take care of Mama and Scout until I get back."

"I will," Lorena promised.

They left the two of them standing on the porch, looking as lonesome as she had imagined Evie earlier. Kate's father leaned out the passenger-side window and waved until they couldn't see the house any longer. Kate kept her eyes on the road. A smile soaked through her when she saw Aunt Hattie on the side of the road walking toward their house. The little black woman always knew when she was needed.

Graham was out in front of the blacksmith shop waiting to wave at them as they passed by. Beside him, Poe raised his head and barked once at the car. Then on the south side of Rosey Corner, Fern was standing by the road. She didn't wave at them, but Kate thought she saw a smile slip across the woman's face.

❧ 37 ❧

It was a bad break. In more ways than one. The doctors had to operate on Jay's ankle and lower leg to put it all back together.

"What about jumping again?" That was Jay's first question for the doctor after the anesthesia wore off.

"According to how high you want to jump." The doctor smiled at his own joke without looking up from the chart he was holding.

If Jay hadn't been so doped up, he'd have popped the man right in the nose. But then again, it was never a good idea to antagonize the person holding the scalpel or the hypodermic needle. He took a breath and tried to marshal his thoughts. "Out of airplanes. I jump out of airplanes."

"You paratroopers are all nuts." The doctor put down the chart and stuck his stethoscope in his ears to listen to Jay's chest. After a minute he sat back, pulled the ear pieces loose, and tucked the end of the stethoscope in the chest pocket of his scrubs. "Healthy nuts, by and large, at least until you land on a rock or in a tree."

"The luck of the drop," Jay said.

"I'm afraid you drew the short straw this time,

503

soldier. I'm not saying you'll never jump out of airplanes again, but I am saying you aren't going to be doing any jumping at all for several weeks. Bones take awhile to heal." The doctor laughed at the look on Jay's face. "Don't worry. You won't miss the war. Uncle Sam will still want you as long as you can march and carry a gun. I am sure you'll be able to do that soon enough."

That had been almost a week ago. A week in the hospital learning to use crutches while his buddies were jumping out of airplanes. At night. Then practice was over. Orders came through for their unit. The whole bunch of them loaded on a train and headed north to climb aboard a troopship. Leaving Jay behind. It seemed he couldn't even do Army right.

The doctor said Jay could have leave to go home while his ankle and leg were healing, but Jay didn't have anywhere to go. No home but Rosey Corner and that was only in his dreams. Dreams he thought about trying to make real by imagining over and over picking up the phone and calling Merritt's Dry Goods Store. He could almost hear Kate's voice in his ear saying hello, but that wouldn't let him see her. The dream got better when he considered hobbling down to the train station to buy a ticket for Rosey Corner. He couldn't actually do that. The train didn't stop in Rosey Corner, but it did stop in Edgeville. He could walk to Rosey Corner from Edgeville—

even with crutches. Heck, he could run from there.

A chaplain came to pray over Jay's ankle. Jay didn't mind. It was good to hear an expert pray. While he'd heard dozens, more like hundreds, of prayers in his years of going to church with his aunt and uncle and then at Rosey Corner too, that was before they meant anything to him. Jay hadn't exactly figured out what had happened to him when he made that last jump, but he did know whatever it was, it stuck. In spite of the broken ankle.

Before, whenever he'd been ready to step up closer to believing in the Lord and something bad happened, he'd thought it proved all that religion stuff didn't mean anything. A person prayed, that person expected something good to happen. He didn't expect to get punched in the gut and go down in a heap. He'd always thought what a joke that was and simply turned his back on the feeling he might need something the church had to offer.

Maybe that had been his mistake. Thinking the church had the answers when he should have been going straight to the source the whole time. Straight to the Bible. *Thou art there.* High or low. And he had been there. Jay had felt a presence as he drifted through the night. The Lord had landed on the ground with him, shaking his head and smiling along with Jay at the irony of life. Here Jay was actually believing for the first time ever and there hadn't been anything but a rock to land on. Or maybe the Lord was smiling because it took jumping out of airplanes to blow open the doors of Jay's heart.

Chaplain Wilson said there wasn't anything wrong with questions. "That doesn't mean you'll get an answer you understand. God's ways are not man's ways. Sometimes things can't be understood with the head, but only known in the heart. That's what faith is."

The man put his hand flat over his heart. He looked even older than Sarge, with a balding head and deep wrinkles around light blue eyes that watched Jay with easy kindness. He told Jay he'd fought in the World War. Said he heard the call to preach in the trenches over there and had been at it one way or another ever since. After Pearl Harbor, he got back in uniform as a chaplain. Nothing Jay said seemed to upset him, so Jay didn't see any reason not to be honest.

"I've never had much faith in anything," Jay said. "At least not till this year."

"What happened this year?" The chaplain leaned a little closer to Jay's bed as though he didn't want to miss a word of whatever he was going to say.

"You mean besides feeling somebody floating down through the air with me?" Jay raised his eyebrows at the man. That was certainly a happening.

"I'm thinking something must have softened your heart so that the Lord could finally get your attention." One corner of the man's mouth turned up. "Something even more than jumping out of an airplane."

"Could be." Jay shifted his position in the bed to try to ease the pain in his leg. He remembered how easy it was to run down the road with Birdie and Kate after the wedding. Funny how Kate had grabbed his eyes that day and not let go. He'd known even then that he'd never met any other girl quite like her.

"You want to tell me about it?" Chaplain Wilson asked.

Jay blew out a long breath. "I guess it was really last year. My buddy, who happens to be a preacher too, by the way." He looked over at the chaplain. "Anyway, he got married last September."

"And?" Chaplain Wilson frowned a little, trying to make sense of what Jay was telling him.

"And his bride had a sister."

"I see." The chaplain leaned back in his chair with a smile. "A very pretty sister, I take it."

"An angel of a sister." Jay let his eyes drift to the window as Kate's face floated up in his memory. Another thing he hadn't been able to do right. Love.

"So what happened?"

"So what happened is that I didn't head on to Chicago the way I intended after my buddy got hitched. Instead I stayed in Rosey Corner. I could have stayed there forever, I think."

"But you didn't."

"Wars mess things up. People mess things up." Jay stared down at the cast on his leg. "I mess things up. I always mess things up."

The chaplain looked down at Jay's cast too. "Rocks can pop up in the worst places."

"They can for a fact." Jay tapped the hard plaster of his cast.

"But sometimes rocks can be shoved out of our paths to clear the way." Chaplain Wilson leaned forward again to look straight at Jay with kind eyes.

"Some of the rocks in my path are more like boulders." Jay didn't shy away from his eyes. "Way too big to budge."

The chaplain smiled slightly. "No rock's too big for the Rock of Ages." He touched Jay's arm. "Together, we'll pray that he'll make gravel out of the rocks in your path to happiness."

"Should a man even expect happiness with a war going on?" Jay asked.

The chaplain paused a moment, considering Jay's question. "I think so. Doesn't mean you'll necessarily find it. But war's bad enough by itself without us giving up all hope of happiness." The chaplain stood up. "We serve a God of hope. For what is our hope, or joy, or crown of rejoicing? That's in Paul's letter to the Thessalonians and every believer knows the answer. Not what, but who. The Lord, a friend closer than a brother and ever with us."

"If I ascend up into heaven, thou art there: if I make my bed in hell, behold, thou art there."

"Scripture." Chaplain Wilson looked a little surprised. "Psalm. I know that one. 'If I take the wings of the morning, and dwell in the uttermost parts of the sea; even there shall thy hand lead me, and thy right hand shall hold me.' You hang on to that, son, and you'll be fine."

He started away, but then turned back to say, "I'll pray for you and your girl."

Jay watched him move on to another soldier in another bed. If only he could claim Kate as his girl. Was that something it was all right to pray? For Kate to be his girl? He wanted to believe there was a chance for them to dance in the moonlight again.

Kate's father didn't like to drive, but Kate loved it. At the beginning when she'd driven out of Rosey Corner and then on straight through Edgeville and kept going, her hands were sweaty on the steering wheel. Everything from there on was new territory. Places she'd never been. The whole world spread out in front of her alongside the strip of road she was following south.

She was thankful for her father in the passenger's seat. They didn't talk much about where they were going or why. Daddy studied the map and fretted some about Mama and Lorena at home. They talked about Tori and Sammy and Evie and Mike. And Kate kept driving.

Before they got out of Kentucky, they had a flat tire, but Kate's father had brought along a patching kit and air pump. On Sunday morning, they picked up a newspaper after spending the night just over the border in Tennessee. Her father took the wheel some then, and whoever wasn't driving read the news aloud if the scenery alongside the road didn't grab their eyes. That didn't happen often as they passed through towns and by farms and trees. Some of it looked the same as Rosey Corner, but a lot of it didn't. Even the rocks alongside the road looked different.

Kate made a wrong turn in Knoxville, but after winding around with an eye to the south, they found their road again. The car overheated in the Tennessee mountains and they had to stop a couple of times to let the engine cool. Her father said at least the mountain air was refreshing. Every time the gas gauge showed half empty, they started watching for a place to fill up. When all the food they brought with them was gone, they stopped at a country store something like their own store back home to get sandwiches and drinks.

In Georgia, the dirt went from brown to almost red, as though the hotter sun had burnt it. Her father laughed at her amazement that dirt could look so different, but she thought he was sharing some of the same surprise.

As they got closer to Fort Benning, Kate became quiet. Through all the miles before, it had been a kind of adventure, like Phileas Fogg going around the world, but now the end was in sight. Before the sun went down, she might see Jay. Her chest began to feel tight and her heart did a few stutter beats. She'd thought she had it all planned out. What she would say. What she hoped he would say back to her. But now she moistened her lips as she drove and wondered if she'd be able to say anything.

Her father reached over and touched her shoulder. "You okay, baby?"

Kate glanced over at him. "What if he—"

Her father held his hand up to stop her words. "No what-ifs right now. Right now we just have to worry about finding him. We'll worry about those what-ifs if they happen."

"But what if they do? Maybe I should have never come." She felt a little queasy.

"No second-guessing now. Not after we've driven all this way." He patted her shoulder. "Besides, I don't think you've got any worries. I saw the way the boy looked at you. A look straight from his heart. That kind of feeling doesn't melt away. Trust me."

"Thanks, Dad." Kate managed to smile over at

him, but her heart kept trying to jump up in her throat. Maybe she should have prayed this whole thing through a little better before she drove across three states chasing after Jay. Maybe she should have written Evie to see what she thought. Maybe a thousand things. But then the Bible verse she'd told Jay slipped into her mind. *There is no fear in love; but perfect love casteth out fear.*

She couldn't claim perfection, but she could claim love. And she could claim prayer. First, she could pray that she would find Jay, then that he would be glad to see her, and last that whatever first words came out of her mouth would make sense.

At the visitors' entrance they were directed to the headquarters. Kate's father leaned forward in the car seat and kept peering out the window as if he couldn't see enough. Being on the base was bringing back memories of his training years ago. Some good memories, he said. More hard ones. When he got out of the car, he stood a little straighter, as if the soldier in him was waking up.

An officer directed them to a desk inside a large building where a young man wearing thick glasses was shuffling through a stack of papers. Without putting down his papers, he asked, "Visitors? Yes, miss. This is the right desk. What's the name and do you know the unit?"

"Jay Tanner." Kate moistened her lips. "Paratroopers. 505th Unit."

The man looked directly up at Kate and then shifted his eyes to Kate's father as he put down the papers and stood up. "Sir, did your soldier know you were coming to visit him?"

"No, we were hoping to surprise him," Kate's father said. "But we got a letter from here not long ago." The two men locked eyes.

"Letters can be in transit for a while, sir, as I'm sure you know." The man slipped his eyes over to Kate, then back to her father. "I regret to inform you that the paratrooper unit completed their training here and received orders last week." He glanced over at a clock on the wall. "By now they should be on a troopship headed overseas. Exact destination classified."

Kate stared toward the man, but she wasn't seeing him or his desk anymore. She was back in her nightmare of the weeks past, standing on the dock watching Jay's ship disappear.

The soldier's voice sounded far away and a little panicked. "Your daughter's not going to faint, is she, sir?"

Kate wanted to tell the man she wasn't the kind of girl who got light-headed over things no matter how bad they were. She could handle whatever had to be handled, but at the same time, she had the awful feeling that if she opened her mouth, nothing would come out but a sob.

"No, no." Her father slipped his arm around her waist. "She'll be fine if we can find a place to rest a minute while we decide what to do next. We've been on the road all day and we're both tired. And naturally disappointed to hear your news."

"I am sorry." His voice lowered with sympathy. "Tell you what, sir. The chaplain's office is right down the hall and I think he's in right now. Why don't you go talk to him? He knew the men in the 505th." The man came around his desk to lead the way down a hall to another office.

Kate concentrated on the man's shoes clicking off the steps on the tiled floor as she pulled in a couple of deep breaths and pushed away the image from her nightmare. A nightmare that had come too true. Jay was gone with absolutely nothing she could do about it. She'd simply have to wait for him to write Lorena again. When he did, she'd write him back and pray that the letter would find him wherever he was sent in the war zone. She would picture him reading the letter and smiling. She'd know he would write back to her. She'd believe he'd forgive her and would someday come back to Rosey Corner. If that happened, she'd be there waiting. However long the war lasted.

❦ 38 ❦

The young soldier introduced them to Chaplain Wilson, briefly explained about them coming to see one of the men in the 505th, and then hurried back to his desk, obviously glad to be shed of them.

The chaplain looked to be about her father's age, with kindness imbedded in the wrinkles on his face. He shook her father's hand and touched Kate's arm with sympathy. "So, how far have the two of you come?"

"From Kentucky," Kate's father answered. "I guess we should have called to see if the unit was still here, but we didn't think ahead."

"As it turned out for you, that would have been wise, but it's too late to worry about that now." He smiled at them. "Come sit down and maybe I can tell you something about the man you came to see. Those boys who jump out of airplanes are a different breed, but it's soldiers like them who are going to win this war for us."

Kate perched on the wooden chair and waited for whatever he was going to tell them. It wouldn't change anything, but she'd have to listen. Then they'd have to climb back in Jay's car and make the sad drive back to Rosey Corner.

"The orders came in rather quickly. Maybe your young man didn't have time to send you the news that he was shipping out. Or you could have been already on the road." The chaplain settled his eyes on Kate.

Kate found her voice. "He didn't know we were coming."

"Oh," the chaplain said. "I see." And he did sound as if he understood way more than Kate said. "And who was it you came to see? Several men in the unit were from Kentucky."

"Jay Tanner," Kate said. "Did you know him?"

Looking at her as though he wasn't sure he'd heard her right, the chaplain leaned toward Kate. He stared straight into her face. "Let me ask you something, Miss Merritt. Have you been praying for this young man?"

When he let out a laugh before she could say a word, Kate edged back in her chair. She peeked over at her father, who looked as surprised by the man's laughter as she was.

"Don't worry." The chaplain's smile reached clear across his face. "I haven't lost my mind, but the two of you may find it hard to believe what I have to tell you. Because it is certainly true that our Lord can work in mysterious ways his wonders to perform." He stood up. "Come on. Let's head over to the infirmary while I explain."

The chaplain was right. She could hardly

believe her ears as he told them about Jay's bad landing and broken ankle that had kept him from leaving with his unit. By the time they reached the infirmary, she was almost floating on air. Jay's bed was empty, but a nurse said they'd probably find him under some shade trees outside.

When they came around the corner of the building, they spotted Jay on a bench in the shade with his back toward them, his eyes on the pages of a paperback book.

Her father touched her arm to stop her. After a quick glance at the chaplain, he said, "Why don't Chaplain Wilson and I wait here? Give you a little privacy."

"Great idea, Mr. Merritt." The chaplain smiled at Kate. "I like your young man."

"Everybody likes Jay." Kate's voice was little more than a whisper. It was like she was afraid to speak loud enough for Jay to notice.

Her father tightened his hand on her arm briefly. Then he and Chaplain Wilson turned and went back around the building.

She wanted to run to Jay, but instead her steps were hesitant as she crossed the space between them. Her heart was beating a mile a minute. What if he slammed the door in her face this time?

He was so deep in the story he was reading, he didn't notice her walking up behind him. She had to try twice before she could find her voice.

"Mr. Tanner," she said, moving around in front of him.

He looked up from his book and stared at her as though he couldn't believe his eyes.

"Kate?"

Her lips trembled as she smiled and said, "How about we elope?" It wasn't what she'd practiced saying on the drive down, but it seemed right when she looked into his eyes.

"Elope?" Jay echoed her last word as he let his book fall to the ground. Kate couldn't really be there right in front of him, close enough to touch. He had to have gone to sleep while reading and now he was dreaming. But never, even in his dreams, had she appeared before him talking about eloping.

She didn't say anything then, but she was really there. So beautiful that it took his breath. He managed to push out some words. "That's my line, isn't it?"

"I know. I borrowed it." She clasped her hands in front of her as her smile wavered a little. "Do you wish I hadn't?"

Jay grabbed one of his crutches to clamber to his feet. If she was really there and not a hallucination brought on by that pain pill they'd given him earlier, he didn't intend to mess up his chance for love again. "Just worried a little that I won't be able to climb the ladder up to your window."

"I'm right here. No ladder needed." She moistened her lips and reached toward him but let her hand hang in the air without touching him.

He wanted to grab her hand. He wanted to grab her and hold on forever, but something more than the cast on his leg and the awkward crutch seemed to be holding them apart. He searched for the right words to make the space between them disappear.

Before he found them, she said, "And no door between."

In his mind, he saw her closing the door on him when he had opened up his heart to her. Not trusting him. Could he trust her now not to do it again? "I wasn't the one who shut the door." His voice sounded harsh even to his own ears, but he couldn't take his words back.

Every trace of smile disappeared from her face as she dropped her hand back to her side. "No, you weren't. I was. But I want to push it back open. So I can say I'm sorry."

"I wasn't drunk, Kate. Scared, but not drunk." He looked straight into her eyes. "I'm scared now."

"So am I." Her words were barely a whisper of breath. "Scared, I mean."

That surprised him. "I didn't think Kate Merritt was ever afraid of anything."

"Oh, but she is. She's scared senseless right

now that you might not forgive her." She moistened her lips. "Not her, me. I'm afraid you won't forgive me. That I might have driven all this way and now you might want to shut the door on me." Her hand came up in the air between them once more.

This time he leaned on his crutch and captured her hand. Pure joy shot through him at her touch. He pulled her gently toward him and she didn't resist. "Listen."

A smile appeared in her eyes and spread across her face. "For what?"

"The Fern lady's music."

"It's not Fern's music. It's ours and I've never stopped hearing it." She stepped into his free arm.

He held her close and hated the crutch that kept him from wrapping both arms around her. Then again, without the cast on his foot, he'd be on a ship out on the ocean. Maybe that rock he'd landed on hadn't been so bad after all. It was giving him a second chance at love. A second chance at home.

He balanced on his good leg and the crutch and pulled her closer. Her head rested in the hollow of his shoulder, and she fit against him perfectly, the very way he'd remembered and imagined these last few months—like a piece of himself he hadn't realized was missing until he met her. Without moving their feet, they swayed back and forth.

After a moment, he whispered into her hair, "Can I have this dance forever, Kate Merritt?"

"Forever and a day." She raised her head to look at him. "I love you, Jay Tanner, with all my heart."

"So how about we elope?"

"I like that idea." Her eyes were bright with the most beautiful smile he'd ever seen. "But can a soldier elope? I mean, without getting in trouble."

"I've heard Georgia's a great place for eloping." He grinned down at her. "I know this chaplain at Fort Benning, Georgia."

"I don't think he'll be too hard to find," Kate said. "He's waiting around the corner with my father."

"Your father?" Jay frowned down at her and then laughed. "That might make this eloping idea a little harder."

"You mean girls don't take their fathers along when they elope?" Now she was laughing too.

"Not usually. I like your dad, but three on a honeymoon is a little crowded."

"Don't worry. Daddy says he's been wanting to ride a train again." The smile slipped off her face. "But can you even take a honeymoon?"

"I'm not much use to the Army right now. They said I could have some leave time while my leg heals." Jay stared down at her and forced out the next words. "But I will have to report back. I'll have to go to war."

She looked worried, but then her lips straightened out in a resolute line. "But not today."

"Or tomorrow," he said.

"Will you still be jumping out of airplanes?"

"Maybe. I hope so."

"What's it like?" She got a wondering look on her face. "To simply thrust yourself out into the sky to fall through the air."

"It grabs your breath and squeezes your heart tight inside your chest." He stared down into her beautiful eyes. "Actually, it feels a lot like loving you. Scary, but at the same time, a jump I'd do anything to take. No matter the landing."

He kissed her then. A kiss that might never have happened except for a rock. If he could find that field where he'd made that last jump, he'd dig up that rock and keep it forever. But then what did he need with any kind of lucky piece? He had Kate. And the Lord.

When he lifted his lips from hers, she leaned close to him and murmured, "Is Georgia a good place for a honeymoon?"

"No, I don't think so." He kissed the top of her head. His leg was aching, but he paid it little notice. "I know this little town. A place called Rosey Corner. You think you'd like to honeymoon there?"

"I think some of the people there will be so happy to see you they'll have a parade right through the middle of town."

"As long as it's a moonlight parade."

"Why's that?" she asked.

"You can't beat moonlight music." He laughed and dropped his crutch to wrap both arms around her. It wasn't a good idea as he toppled back down on the bench with Kate falling on top of him. Another rocky landing that turned out fine.

Acknowledgments

Writing a book and then seeing it into print is a long process and one that involves many people. First an author's family must give the writer time and space to go into an imaginary world and live there for hours each day. I thank my family for their support and love as I returned to Rosey Corner.

My first visit to Rosey Corner in *Angel Sister* was inspired by my mother's stories of growing up in a small community here in Kentucky. The echo of her life and the lives of her sisters is not quite as strong in this story, but the little town of Rosey Corner still owes its creation to them. I'm indebted to these four women for their examples of strength and love and for their stories and laughter.

I thank my wonderful editor, Lonnie Hull DuPont, who encourages me to tell my stories and then helps me make them better. Barb Barnes makes sure the words sing with as much clarity and beauty as possible. I thank the whole team at Baker Books who work on each of my books to make them the best they can be, from the beautiful covers and the right titles to every word inside.

My agent, Wendy Lawton, is a continuing source of encouragement and caring, and I appreciate all she does to walk me through the business side of book publishing while at the same time helping me focus on writing the best story I can.

I'm ever thankful for the gift of words the Lord has given me. He is the source of all words and all love.

Finally, I thank you, my readers. It has been a joy to share my stories with you and to hear your comments and stories in return.

About the Author

Ann H. Gabhart, a small town girl herself, still lives on a farm just over the hill from where she grew up in central Kentucky. She loves books, playing with her grandkids, and walking with her dogs. She and her husband are blessed with three grown children and their spouses, along with nine grandchildren. Ann is the author of more than twenty novels for adults and young adults. Her Shaker novel, *The Outsider*, was a Christian Book Awards finalist in the fiction category. *Angel Sister*, Ann's first Rosey Corner book, was a nominee for inspirational novel of 2011 by *RT Book Reviews* magazine.

Visit Ann's website at www.annhgabhart.com.

Center Point Large Print
600 Brooks Road / PO Box 1
Thorndike ME 04986-0001 USA

(207) 568-3717

US & Canada:
1 800 929-9108
www.centerpointlargeprint.com